Broken

MEGAN HART

Broken

Spice

Spice

BROKEN

ISBN-13: 978-0-373-60515-6
ISBN-10:   0-373-60515-3

www.Spice-Books.com

Printed in U.S.A.

To Natalie Damschroder for the after-midnight parking lot adventures, the honest critique and the squeeing. Thank you for helping me make this book the best it could be.

To Lauren Dane for the afternoon IM madness and constant support. Thank you also for helping me kick this book in the butt.

To my family, for helping me become the person I am.

To my children for their loving support and pride. "My mom writes books" still makes me smile – even though you're not allowed to read them until you're over eighteen!

To Jude Law…well, duh. Because.

To my Internet and real-life friends who listen to me blather on about my writing and actually buy my books. A million thanks!

To Joshua Radin, whose song "What If You" was the backdrop for the scene on the stairs. Thanks for giving me the perfect song as inspiration. I listened to it a hundred times and could listen a hundred more.

To Stevie Falk for letting me borrow her house and her profession, and for answering all my questions.

To my agent, Mary Louise Schwartz, my editor Susan Pezzack, the cover artists and staff at Harlequin who worked to get this book on the shelves – thank you for your hard work and dedication. I can write it, but you're the ones who put it out there for the world to see.

And finally, to my husband, who listened to me talk about this book for months and months, offered insight, kept me going, hooked me up with medical information and told me how great I was. (And still does.) Thank you for helping me reach my dreams.

Acknowledgments

This book couldn't have been written without the knowledge and help of the following:

Jake Fischer, who offered insight into living with SCI

Elaine McMichael and Karen Heffleger, who answered my questions and helped me get the details right

And Michael F. Lupinacci, M.D., who helped me put all the pieces into place and in the right order.

Chapter 01

January

This month my name is Mary and, apparently, I'm as contrary as the nursery rhyme. First I said I wanted to fuck, but now I'm refusing to come out of the bathroom. What I don't know is that Joe doesn't like cock teases, nor does he suffer wasting time. He's already done the wooing, bought the drinks, made the compliments. If I don't put out in the next five minutes, he'll put his coat on and go.

I don't know this because I only met him three hours ago in a bar downtown. His name seemed as if it were a cosmic joke, but out of all the men I met tonight, Joe's the only one who bothered trying to have a conversation with me. That's why I picked him. That, and the fact that's he's hot and well-dressed, with a charming quirk of a smile that tries to look sincere but mostly doesn't.

"Mary, Mary quite contrary. How does your garden grow?"

His voice presses against me through the bathroom

door. I've heard that rhyme a thousand times. Been called Proud Mary. Bloody Mary. Mary Poppins. My parents gave me the name thinking it had no diminutive, but people will always find a way to tease, if they want.

The doorknob is cool under my fingers and turns easily. I open the door to show Joe I'm ready for him. That the wait was worth it. I've stripped down to a set of lacy white panties and a matching bra, and I fight to keep from crossing my arms to shield myself from his scrutiny.

His eyes widen a bit. His tongue snakes out to slide along a mouth I haven't even kissed yet. I want to kiss it. He looks as if he'll taste good.

"Damn." The word's a compliment, not a curse, and I manage a slightly more confident smile.

I turn, slowly, so he can see me from all sides. When I come around again to face him, Joe reaches for my hand and tugs me one step, two, until, like magnets, our bodies attach to one another.

He's unbuttoned his shirt and the hair on his chest scratches my soft flesh. I shiver. My nipples peak against the lace and heat coils in my belly. Joe's fingers splay on my hips. I'm all of a sudden too shy to look into his eyes.

He pulls me to the bed—the nice, big king-size he requested from the clerk at the front desk with that same quirky smile that first attracted me. "I'm a bad boy," that smile says. "But I'm so good you won't care." It had worked on me and the clerk, too, who'd taken the extra time to find us a room with a bed big enough for an orgy.

There's no orgy, though, just me and Joe and the sound of the heating unit blowing the curtains. The hot air coming out of it smells stale, but what did I expect? Frankincense and myrrh?

"C'mon." Joe's getting impatient, tugging me onto the bed.

He kisses me, finally, my throat and the curves of my breasts. A shoulder. I arch a little under the feeling of his mouth on my skin, and though my lips part, he doesn't kiss them.

His hands smooth up my sides and over my belly. When one goes between my legs, I'm startled. He doesn't notice, or maybe he doesn't care. He strokes me a few times and I melt into his experienced touch like sugar in a hot pan, all crumbling, scattered grains melting and smoothing into one liquid ooze.

This is all happening faster than I'd imagined it would, but I can't seem to find the words to tell him to slow down. His fingers find the small, lace-covered bump at the front of my panties and begin a pattern of slow circles. I decide fast isn't such a bad thing.

"You like that?"

I nod. He smiles and reaches to flick open the front clasp of my bra. My breasts surge out and I moan in the back of my throat. I want his mouth on me, his tongue swiping across my tight pink nipples. I want him to suck on them, one and then the other, while his hand moves between my legs. I'm already wet from his caress. I can feel it when I shift.

He pauses to shrug out of his shirt and I admire his chest. He has a body clothes are made to hang on, but naked, his shoulders are broader than they seemed before, his belly flat and tight with muscles but not rippled with them. His arms look strong, the cords in his forearms standing out as he tugs his belt buckle, unbuttons and unzips his pants. The hair on his chest, arms and belly is a little darker than that on his head, where his hair is the color of a lion's mane. I wonder if he colors himself blond or if all men's bodies show such disparity.

He pushes his trousers over his thighs and takes off his boxer briefs. I can't look. I turn my head away, my breath lodging in my throat and my heart beating pitter-pat under my left breast. The bed dips as he kneels beside me. His hand returns to its shelter between my thighs and strokes me again. I lift my hips, an uncertain cry leaking from my unkissed lips.

"Take these off," he whispers, giving me no time to comply before he hooks his fingers into the strings at the side and pulls them off himself.

I'm bared to him. My carefully waxed and trimmed bush of candy floss pubic hair. The hard button of my clitoris. My tender flesh, soft with arousal, wet from his touch.

He parts my thighs, spreading me, and I moan. Joe seems to like this, because his breathing gets heavier, faster, the way mine is. He runs an inquisitive finger along my folds and then up to my clit again and, oh, the sensation is indescribable. He rolls my own moisture over the tight bump and my hips jerk.

I feel an unaccustomed weight in my pussy, an emptiness, an ache. More heat blooms in my belly and breasts, that secret cavern between my legs. He rubs my clit and liquid trickles down the curve of my ass, tickling.

He takes one of my nipples in his mouth and it feels so good I whimper. I put a hand to the back of his head, feeling his soft blond locks on the backs of my fingers. He suckles, and my fingers tighten. He mutters something but doesn't stop sucking my nipple or rubbing my clit, and my breath comes faster and faster until I'm light-headed.

I've been with boys before. Making out. Petting. I've given furtive hand-jobs in the back seat of a car, stroking and jerking and wondering what all the fuss is about. I've been with boys before, but not yet a man, someone who doesn't plead or fumble. Joe doesn't even ask, he just does. There's something so perfect about that, just what I was looking for, and I have no more time to be shy.

Not even when his mouth slides down my body and centers between my legs. I go stiff at once in my surprise, but my small protest becomes a moan when Joe's tongue flicks along my clitoris.

Oh, holy mother of God.

I've imagined this, using my hands or the pulsing jet of a hand-held shower to make myself come. Nothing has prepared me for the reality. His tongue is soft and warm, gentler than his fingers. It's like water against me, softly lapping like waves against the shore. I arch into the sensation. He licks me. I shudder. He licks me again, and I'm helpless to do anything but spread my legs for him and give him my body.

Tension coils in my belly, and my nipples have grown as hard and tight as pebbles. Tiny moans leak from my throat. Joe pauses to blow against me, his hot breath making me writhe.

I've never had an orgasm with another person. I'm not sure I can. I've been close a couple times and it always slipped away from me at the last minute.

He stops again, and I'm sure I'm going to lose it. My thighs vibrate. The muscles in my belly tense and release. It will take only the barest pressure to make me go over, just the right touch, but he's not giving it to me.

He's doing something I can't see. Something crumples. The bed moves as he shifts. His body covers me, chest hairs tantalizing my nipples wet from his saliva. His thighs and belly press against mine.

I have time to think of one more name I've been called, one that is appropriate but nevertheless tiresome, before Joe grunts and moves.

"Holy hell!" he cries, astonished when I shriek. "You're a virgin?"

I'm embarrassed by the entirely involuntary scream, and I stutter, "Y-yes."

"Well…shit."

He's not climbing off me, though I wouldn't blame him if he did. The pain has faded, replaced by a sensation of fullness, of being stretched. It's not unpleasant. It's not exactly comparable to the stories of bliss my girlfriends have been telling, but it's not as awful as the tales the nuns told of unbearable agony, either. I've always wondered how a nun would know.

"I'm sorry," I say. "I hoped you wouldn't notice."

A smile tilts one corner of his mouth as he pushes up on his hands to look into my face. "The scream gave it away."

"I was surprised."

Something tender creeps into his eyes and he leans in to kiss my cheek. "You should've told me. I'd have been gentler."

Now comes the truth of why I'm here. "I really just wanted to get it over with."

He looks perplexed. "Why?"

"I'm twenty-three. It's time. All my friends have done it. I'm tired of being a virgin. I just wanted to...do it."

He's still inside of me and it doesn't hurt, but I'm becoming uncomfortable. This isn't going the way I'd planned. None of it has except for the part where I find a guy in a bar to take me someplace and get him to divest me of my maidenhood.

He gives a gentle, exploratory thrust. I tense, waiting for pain that doesn't come. Joe bends to trace the curve of my ear with his tongue.

"You shouldn't have to just get it over with," he whispers, voice deep. "Not the first time."

He slides a hand under my hair, which has spread out on the pillow. He kisses my earlobe, then my neck. His teeth press into the sensitive skin of my shoulder.

He pushes inside me and slides out, inch by inch. He does it again. The next time he moves inside me, I gasp and curve to meet him.

He smiles. "Good?"

It *is* good, but he doesn't seem to care when I don't say so. He moves a little faster and pushes himself back up on his hands. The tendons in his arms stand out. I can look down between us, to the point where our bodies have joined. His dark curls tangle with my lighter hair. He pulls out and I see the base of his erection, the ring of latex sheathing him, glistening. He pushes in and I watch, fascinated, as he disappears inside my body.

Sex isn't like I'd imagined, but I can't say whether it's better or worse. It brings a flush of red out on my chest, and it must spread to my throat because I feel the same heat there. I watch him move in and out of me, and I think, *connected. We are connected.*

His face has gone solemn in concentration, eyes squinting, mouth creased. Sweat forms along his hairline. I smell him, a crisp bite of soap mixed with something musky and rich, like earth turned over in the garden after a heavy rain. Something like blood. I think it's lust. I slide my hands up along his chest, feeling his muscles bunch and move, touching the twin tight nipples so different than mine. I pinch one, experimentally, and he groans, so I do it again.

His thrusts are a little less smooth and a tremor runs through his body. He stops and looks down at me. I look back.

Without a word, he rolls us both until I end up on top, legs straddling his waist. I've put a hand on his chest for balance, and his fingers grip my hips. He shifts us both with practiced ease, and a moment later I gasp aloud as this new position allows him to sink deeper inside me.

"Lean forward and put your hands on my shoulders."

I do what he says. When he begins to move again, I'm glad I did. Oh, shit, this is good. Oh, fuck. He fills me all the way, in and out. My clit bumps his stomach with every thrust, and the weight, the heat, the ache is back, though the emptiness has been replaced by the delicious fullness of him stretching me.

He slides a hand between us, his thumb cocked to press against me, and this extra pressure sends exquisite bolts of pleasure shooting through me like lightning.

"Come on," he whispers. "I want you to come."

This time, I really think I might.

He fucks me faster. Every thrust rocks my clit against his thumb. I'm being stroked inside and out. My thighs shake. My breath comes in hitches and gasps. I'm burning and frozen at the same time.

He grunts and thrusts harder. Our bodies smack together, my ass against his thighs, belly to belly. My fingers have dug into his shoulders, the palms of my hands pressed hard to his collarbone. The pulse in his neck beats fast and hard.

I can't stop myself from crying out. It feels too good. I no longer feel my arms, legs, back. I've become coiled in tension, everything growing tighter, like a key winding a spring, and I know it won't be long before it happens, before I spring free.

But not yet. Right now he pushes me to sit up straight. My breasts bounce as his thrusts lift me up and down. There's no more push-push pressure on my clit, but he replaces it with direct stimulation with his finger, which circles in time to his thrusts. This is even better, almost unbearably better, so good I don't think I can stand it, so good it almost hurts.

I cry out, "Joe! Oh, God, Joe!" And understand now

that the dialogue in romance novels isn't so unrealistic, after all. I want to shout out more, words of love and gratitude. It would be easy enough to fall in love right now, with pleasure coursing through my veins headier than any wine has ever made me. I shout his name again, then I stop trying to speak and end up making sounds.

My clit is wet from my juices and his finger slips and slides against me. He's thrusting, I'm rocking, we're jerking and pumping but somehow managing to keep the pace together.

I'm not quite sure how, but I feel him getting thicker inside me. He closes his eyes, his brow furrows in concentration, and I wish he'd open them to look at me when I come. I want that sense of connection again, but he doesn't give it to me. I have to be satisfied with looking down between us, to the place his body joins with mine.

Electric sparks tingle in my thighs and down to my curling toes. I quiver. My center burns with spreading outward warmth while the pleasure goes up, up, up, and I'm stretched thin with it. So thin, until at last, I break.

I can't make a sound this time, knocked so breathless with ecstasy I can't even cry out. My head tips back so far my hair tickles my back. I explode outward and become scattered pieces connected by nothing more than breath. When I inhale, I merge back together. A second time I burst apart and reform, more quickly and without as much drama.

I breathe in, slow and deep. I look down at Joe, who's opened his eyes finally, but if I hoped to see something in his gaze I'm disappointed. He's gone far away inside his own climax. He gasps, thrusting once more so hard he pushes my whole body upward. His cock pulses and he makes a series of small, stuttering groans that trail away as he falls back onto the pillow, spent.

When I can breathe normally again, I get off him. He slides out of me, and I feel an unaccustomed sense of loss. The emptiness has returned, but different than before. The place between my legs aches, too, but the way my body feels after I've given it a good workout, used muscles hard they way they're meant to be used. It's not a bad feeling at all.

I give myself a mental going over, testing limbs and organs, testing for disruption in the way my body functions. I thought having sex would somehow make me feel as if I sat differently inside myself, but right now all I feel is flushed and drowsy.

I lie down beside him, my head pillowed on his shoulder, and allow myself the familiarity of a hand on his chest. He might be asleep, I can't be sure. His chest rises and falls steadily. I peek downward, emboldened by my new status as a well-fucked woman, and look over his penis. It rests, still wrapped in the condom, against his thigh. It looks as spent as I feel, and I want to giggle but I hold it in.

"That was better than just getting it over with," I say.

I tip my head up to see his reaction. Though his eyes are still shut, he smiles.

"I'm glad."

I wish he'd say more. With passion fading, I feel the need for some reassurance. That I did all right, for my first time. I wish he'd at least look at me.

I don't expect a declaration of love, or anything, but...something...more. I just gave him my virginity, after all. Even if I'd intended just to get rid of it, it was still a gift. Wasn't it?

Maybe Joe doesn't think so. Maybe he's counting the minutes until he can get dressed and head out. Maybe I should leave before he can.

I get up and swing my legs over the side of the bed. The carpet feels matted under my feet. Dirty. I don't want to think of who else has walked on it, or for that matter, how many couples have fucked on the bed I'm sitting on. My skin crawls suddenly and I shudder. I pick up my bra, then look for my panties. The white lace has vanished against the white tangle of the sheets, and I paw through the hills and mountains of fabric we made with our fucking.

Joe opens a sleepy eye and rolls on his side to watch me. I find my panties and snatch them up triumphantly. I want to wash, rid myself of the stickiness. There's no blood, at least, and I send up a prayer to the real Virgin Mary, though, of course, she'd hardly have approved of this night's adventure.

I go to the bathroom, grab a washcloth, and run it under hot water. Joe enters behind me, and I keep my gaze focused on the water running in the sink. He strips off the condom and tosses it in the trash, then lifts the lid on the toilet and urinates, a long, hard stream. I'm mortified. He reaches into the shower and turns it on. Steam wreathes the air.

"Want to join me?"

"No!" My answer blurts out louder than I'd meant it to.

I step into my panties and hook my bra, then grab my blouse and skirt from the hook on the back of the door. I put my clothes on faster than I'd taken them off, even though my fingers are shaking and I have to redo the buttons.

He's staring. He's naked. I smooth my hair and catch sight of my face in the mirror, blurred by steam. Eyes a dark smear, mouth a red slash. I've become faceless, which is good because I don't need to see myself right now.

I can't read his expression. I'm not sure I want to. A few minutes ago I was desperate for connection. Now I can't wait to get away.

"What's the matter?" he asks.

"Nothing. I have to go."

"Are you sure?"

I'm torn between gratitude that he's being so calm, and despair he's not more solicitous. "I'm sure."

"All right," he says and turns to step into the shower. "Drive carefully."

My breath squeaks out of me and I snatch up my purse from the bathroom counter. He looks at me over a shoulder marked by my fingers. His brow raises.

"You sure you're all right?"

"Yes!" I shout, though I'm not. My voice has gone high and wavery, as if I'm holding back tears. I clutch my purse to my chest. "Thanks for the favor!"

He turns all the way around, hands on his hips, and I wish he'd at least wrap a towel around his waist.

"Look, I'm not sure what the problem is—"

"Of course you don't!" I won't insult myself by explaining, either.

"Mary." Joe's voice is calm. "Did I misunderstand you back at the Slaughtered Lamb when you put your hand on my ass and whispered, 'I've got at condom with your name on it?'"

That had been my friend Bett's idea. Not mine. It had worked, yes, but—

"Hey." He pulls a towel from the rack and covers himself before stepping toward me. He reaches to push my hair over my shoulder. "I thought it was what you wanted. It's what you said you wanted."

I can't argue with that. I'd like to put the blame on him, make it his fault, but the truth is clear. The burden of my virginity had been lifted from me in a pretty spectacular fashion. I was only being a fool if I expected more.

"I did." My voice still sounds thick, as if I might cry. But I know I won't.

"You knew what you wanted and you went out and got it," Joe said. "What's so wrong about that?"

"Nothing!"

"Sure I can't convince you to join me?" Joe backs toward the shower as he drops the towel. His grin is quite tempting, but I shake my head. "Okay. You're sure you're okay?"

"I'm fine." I think it's only half a lie. "I have to go."

"Drive carefully," he says again.

When the shower curtain rattles closed, I almost change

my mind. Instead, I finish dressing and flee the hotel room, leaving behind the stranger who made me into a woman.

"That's a nice story," I said. "I like the part about how you made her a woman."

Joe reached for his paper cup of soda and took a long drink, as though talking had made him thirsty. "Didn't I?"

"What I find interesting is the idea that a woman has to have sex to become a woman."

He shrugged and tore open the paper wrapped around his sandwich. He always waits until after he's told me the month's tale before he eats, then falls to with gusto as though the telling has given him an appetite. He has turkey on wheat, the usual, but this time with tomatoes. I watch him pick them off, one by one. Joe hates tomatoes.

"Doesn't it?"

I say nothing, content to sit and watch him eat. I needed time for my body to ease back to the real world, for my heartbeat to slow and my breath to follow. I pulled my sweater around me, feigning a chill, to hide the fact my nipples had gone stiff. Later, at home, I would recall his story, the small details of it, and I'd touch myself until I came. For now, I played the cool observer, the same as I did every month when we met on this bench in the atrium or the one outside in the garden.

"I don't know what her problem was." Joe chewed and swallowed. A pearl of mayonnaise clung to the corner of his mouth, and I pushed a napkin toward him.

"She'd just lost her virginity to a stranger. Maybe she felt awkward."

Of course, I had no idea what Mary felt, any more than I knew what any of Joe's women thought or felt. My imagination filled in the details of their coupling, taking what he told me and painting a picture from the feminine point of view.

"She was on me like butter on a biscuit. How was I supposed to know she was a virgin? She didn't act like one."

"How's a virgin supposed to act?"

He shrugged again. "I don't know. But she acted like she knew exactly what she wanted. So why was she so upset when she got it?"

I didn't answer for a moment, thinking. "Maybe she was disappointed."

He gave me the grin, the bad boy smile. "Sadie, I did *not* disappoint her."

"Oh, that's right. You made her a woman."

Joe frowned. "You didn't answer my question."

"No. Losing my virginity didn't make me a woman. Did it make you a man?"

His one-eyed squint shouldn't have been as enchanting as it was. "I lost my virginity to Marcia Adams, my mother's best friend. It made me a man pretty fast. I wouldn't have survived it, otherwise."

This is a story I'd never heard and my face must have shown it. Joe laughed, one eye still squinted, face tipped up toward the atrium's glass ceiling.

"Are you going to tell me about it?"

He looked, for one strange moment, shy. I hadn't

thought him capable of it. He shifted on the bench, and I was sure he was for once not going to tell me.

"I was seventeen. She asked me to take care of her garden. Money for college. She told me I could use her pool every day, when I was done mowing the lawn."

"Sounds like you did more than mow her lawn."

He rubbed a hand along the back of his neck. "Yeah."

"And you really think that's what made you a man?"

I watched him curiously. He turned to look at me, his face solemn and nodded slowly.

"Yeah. I think it showed me what to expect, anyway."

"I'm not sure that's the same thing."

"Well, if losing your virginity didn't make you a woman," he said, "what did?"

I said nothing to that, a topic into which I didn't wish to delve. After a moment, he shrugged. "Mary acted like I was handing her a twenty and kicking her out."

"Maybe she assumed you were the sort of guy who picks up women in bars and sleeps with them, then expects them to leave."

"I'd have let her shower first!" He cried, indignant. "Jeez, I'm not a total asshole."

Yet he didn't deny he was, indeed, the sort of man who picks up women in bars and sleeps with them, perfectly satisfied with one night.

I didn't respond, just sipped my drink. Joe set his sandwich down. The sun shining through the glass overhead cut through the giant Boston ferns hanging above us and striped shadows in his dark blond hair. His frown pulled his full mouth into thinness.

"Say it."

I pretended not to know what he meant.

"Say it," he repeated. "You want to. I can see it in your eyes."

"Say what?" I relented. "That you *are* the sort of man who does that?"

"Keep going." He sat back against the bench, his arms crossed.

I smiled. "That you're a cheater? A rogue? That you don't know the meaning of fidelity? That you go through women like wind through lace?"

"Don't forget that I'm a silver-tongued devil who'll say anything necessary to get into a woman's pants. That my Holy Grail is pussy. That I've split more peaches than a porn star."

I laughed. "Split more peaches? That's a new one."

Joe wasn't laughing. "Go on and say it, Sadie. I'm a manwhore. You think I'm a slut."

I studied him before I answered. "Joe…"

He wrapped up his food and stood, then tossed it in the pail next to me. He moved like a marionette dancing under the hand of an uncertain puppeteer, all jerks and twitches. He was angry. Really angry, and I stood, too.

"Joe, stop."

He turned to me. His suit today was black, his shirt bright blue, his tie black with tiny blue dots scattered on the fabric. He put his hands on his hips, ruining the cut of his suit, which probably cost as much as my car payment.

More shadows speckled his blue-green eyes, his high cheekbones, the slope of his nose. No sign of a smile. His glare wrinkled the corners of his eyes, and it wasn't fair they only made him better looking instead of haggard.

"I know you think it, so you might as well say it."

"But, Joe," I said gently. "It's true."

"It won't always be true!" His words rang out, echoing.

The plants seemed to recoil, startled at this shout interrupting their usual peace.

I shouldn't have scoffed, but his anger had made me angry, too. "Oh, please."

Joe stalked toward me. I didn't move away. He stood only a few inches taller but he seemed bigger in his anger. I refused to flinch even when he leaned in so close he could have kissed me, if he'd wanted. This was my role, disinterested observer, as his was playful rogue. I acted as though I wasn't intimidated, though the truth was, being so close I could count his eyelashes, smell him, feel the heat of his breath on my face, I was. Underneath, I always was. Intimidated and turned on.

"It's true," he insisted through gritted teeth.

"I've heard that before. But every month you come back here and tell me a new story about some new woman. Or more than one. So you'll have to forgive me if the idea of you suddenly becoming Mr. Faithful sounds a little funny."

He jerked away from me, his finger pointing. "And every month, you listen."

I lifted my chin. "Is it my fault you have stories to tell?"

He made a disgusted noise and gestured with his hands

as if he was throwing something away. Maybe me. I wasn't sure.

"I don't have to prove myself to you."

"No," I agreed. "So why are you trying so hard?"

We'd never argued. Arguments were for people more intimate than I'd ever have admitted we were. Now my heart thumped and heat rose in my cheeks. My stomach churned and a sharp sting in my palms made me realize I'd clenched my fists. So much for the cool demeanor. I relaxed them with conscious effort, and the motion drew Joe's gaze. He looked at my hands, then back at my face.

"What about you? What are you trying to prove?"

"Me?" The question surprised me. "I don't know what you mean."

"Why do you listen?"

Now it was my turn to gather up my garbage and toss it in the trash. I gave him my back, intensely aware I didn't have to see him to know he was looking at me.

"Not so nice when it's turned around on you, is it?" I could hear his smirk.

I looked at him again. "I've been listening to your stories for more than a year now, Joe. I guess it's just become a bad habit."

His body didn't flinch, but his eyes did. "Bad habits should be broken, though, right?"

He turned on his heel and stalked away. Panic flared in me. He was messing up the parts we'd been playing for the past two years. What did that mean? That he wouldn't be back? Or just that he wouldn't have another story?

"Joe!"

He didn't turn, and I had too much pride to call after him again. I waited until he'd disappeared beneath the hanging greens and I was alone in the quiet before I sat on the bench again, my mutilated fists in my lap.

The flowers reproached me, but since they had no voice, I didn't have to listen.

Chapter 02

I met Adam at a party my freshman year of college. Not at a frat house, this party was at "lit house," a three-story Victorian monstrosity that had been home to half the English department, grads and undergrads, for as long as anyone could remember. It was its own frat house, in a way, though the graffiti on the basement walls featured quotes from Wilde, Shakespeare and Burns, and the limericks were clever in addition to being filthy. I was there by invitation of my roommate Donna, an English major.

I wasn't much a fan of beer, but I carried a cup anyway. Donna had abandoned me to hook up with a cute guy from one of her classes. I moved among the crowd in search of the bathroom, listening to drunken discussions about iambic pentameter and poetic imagery along the way.

In the kitchen, looking for the toilet I'd been assured was "just through there," I found Adam. He lounged on top of the kitchen counter, his incredibly long legs encased in faded blue corduroy pants, immense feet shod in the shabbiest brown oxfords I'd ever seen. He wore a T-shirt emblazoned with the name of a famous punk rock band. He had an earring glittering in one lobe and long hair. He had a cigarette in one hand and a green short-neck bottle of Straub beer in the other.

"Bathroom?" When I nodded, he pointed to the small door just beyond the door to the cellar. "The door doesn't lock. But I'll watch out for you."

He flashed me a grin of perfect white teeth, the upper front tooth slightly crooked. I was smitten. I used the bathroom and came out to find him in discourse about the writing of Anaïs Nin and how it compared to present-day erotica. I didn't leave the kitchen for the rest of the night.

It was the first time I ever got drunk.

Later, stumbling home, Donna asked me who he was.

"I don't know," I said with beer-bleary lips. "But I'm going to marry him."

Two weeks later, as I left my room to go to class, I saw him leaving a message on the door of Rachael Levine, my resident assistant. Rachael was fond of lecturing the rest of us on the dangers of drinking too much and having indiscriminate sex. She didn't seem much good at applying the same lectures to herself, though, even at twenty-two still hitting the frat parties and making a point of leaving her ample supply of condoms out in her room for anyone to see. She also liked bragging about her "brilliant" boyfriend.

His name was Adam Danning.

He turned and flashed me the smile that had so intoxicated me. "Hey. I know you."

Between one heartbeat and the next, my entire life changed.

"You're Sadie."

He knew my name.

How did I talk to him? Tall, handsome Adam. Brilliant lecturer on the differences between erotica and pornography. Drinker of Straub beer and smoker of Marlboro. Boyfriend of Rachael.

As it turned out, I didn't have to talk much. He walked me to class and spoke about his work in the English department. About the University. About a movie he'd seen the night before. He made it easy to be silent, and I drank his words with more enthusiasm than I'd consumed the beer.

"Lit house party this weekend," he said as we parted ways at the top of the hill, he to work and I to my introduction to psychology class. "Will you be there?"

Oh, yes. I'd be there.

Six weeks into my first semester, we were eating lunch together three or four times a week and walking to class more often than that. We talked about everything. Politics, movies, art, books, sex, drugs and rock and roll. He recited poetry to me. Adam introduced me to the power of words.

He never talked about Rachael, though she spoke of him, often, to anyone who'd listen and anyone who didn't. Though Adam and I made no secret of the time we spent together, she didn't seem to consider me a threat. She went out of her way, in fact, to take me under her wing. She gave me advice, unsolicited, and kept back rolls of toilet paper for me during rush week when the fraternity pledges were ordered to steal it from the dorms and all the stalls went empty. She treated me like an amusing, perhaps slightly retarded, younger sister. She didn't view me as a threat, probably because I'd carried my "smart" façade along with me from high school. If I'd been "the pretty one," she might have worried more.

Adam quickly became the mirror in which I saw reflected the woman I wanted to become. He didn't tell me what to do or think, nothing as crass as that. He just made it easy to like what he liked. Adam led me to discover places in myself I'd never known. I didn't know what I wanted to study; he was already beginning his graduate work in English literature. He was a devout agnostic and I still went to Sunday mass. He liked the Sex Pistols and I listened to Top 40 radio. There were five years between us, which at the time seemed like an eternity. He was more mature than the boys in my dorm. He had his own apartment, a car, a job. Adam thought and fought with passion burning bright. He was vibrant and alive in a way I envied, admired and coveted. He smoked. He drank. He rode a motorcycle fast on dark roads and had insane hobbies like bungee jumping.

He was brilliant and wild, my Lord Byron, whom Lady Caroline Lamb had called "mad, bad and dangerous to know."

While playing the part of the brainiac, my sexual experience had been limited to one high school boyfriend who'd been a fan of receiving but not giving oral sex. I'd held onto my virginity more by circumstance than determination. Most of my friends had already taken the plunge into "womanhood," few with stories compelling enough to make me want to consider it myself. I'd dated a few boys but never tumbled head over heels into the crazy tempestuousness of adolescence so many of my friends had undergone. It might have been better if I had. A sort of training. As it was, I'd never felt the depths of emotion that sent me soaring and plummeting within minutes of each other.

Until I met Adam.

I told nobody of this internal roller coaster. Not Donna, who'd become my best friend. Not my sister Katie, who, two years younger than I, had her high school dramas to keep her busy. I kept the secret of my love inside and turned it over and over constantly, seeking a way to either break it up or figure it out. Like a Rubik's Cube, or one of those pictures with the hidden images not everyone can see. I'd never been so confused, despairing, desperate and so elated and infused with joy.

I was in love with Adam Danning, and I had no idea of how he felt about me.

I should've been ashamed of asking Rachael to give me some of the condoms she was so proud of displaying when I knew I meant to use them to seduce her boyfriend. But when you're mad, bad and dangerously in love, many things seem excusable that normally wouldn't.

My first semester had passed unbearably fast. Faced with a month of distance in which Adam would be spending his time with Rachael, I could wait no longer. The day before I was supposed to go home, I armed myself with brand-new panties and the handful of condoms, and I went to Adam's apartment under the pretense of dropping off the gift I'd bought for him.

He opened the door, shirtless, hair wet from a shower. My throat clutched. Every nerve thrummed. My heart beat in my wrists, the hollow of my throat. Between my legs.

"You got me a present?" He seemed pleased and took the package, which I'd been careful to wrap in non-denominational paper. "Sadie, wow. What is it?"

"Open it."

Standing in his living room, my knees shaking and my palms sweating, I felt I'd reached a precipice. I wasn't one for leaping, but I was ready to jump, no parachute necessary and no bungee cord, either. I was going to leap, and I was going to fly.

Adam hefted the volume in both his hands, his grin all the thanks I needed. *"e.e. cummings, the Complete Poems."*

"You don't have it, do you?"

He shook his head and leafed through the pages with the reverence every true book lover has when touching a new volume for the first time.

I'd marked one page with a ribbon of scarlet silk, and as I watched his fingers turning page after page on the way to revealing it, I forgot to breathe. I waited, each moment like drops of honey dripped from a spoon, every one its own universe but tied to all the rest by the thin strands of time.

He stopped when he found the ribbon, and his eyes scanned the words on the page, top to bottom, before he looked up to me. I remembered to breathe, sipping oxygen like wine. My pulse pounded in my ears, similar to the rush and crush of waves.

"Any illimitable star," he said, and I knew at once I hadn't made a mistake.

Adam put the book aside. We stared at each other without words but needing none. He held out a hand, and I took it. Our fingers linked, his hand warm and mine cold.

He pulled me onto his lap, straddling him. His shoulders beneath my palms were warm, his skin smooth. My groin snugged up against his bare stomach, and his hands fit naturally on my hips, as if they'd always meant to be there.

We kissed for a long time, sitting that way. His hands moved up and down my body. His erection nudged my rear until we shifted and it pressed up between us. I explored the lines and curves of his body every place I could reach without leaving his mouth or his lap. I traced the lines of his ribs, the bulges of his biceps. I circled the twin round spots of his nipples and counted the bumps of his spine with my fingertips.

By the time we moved toward the bedroom, I was wetter than I'd ever been. My nipples were taut and aching. Sensation crackled along my nerves like Independence Day sparklers, and everything had gone slow and languid, petroleum jelly smeared on the camera lens. Soft and out of focus.

Adam pushed aside the covers on his rumpled bed to lay me down on sheets that smelled of him, his mouth never leaving mine. We stretched out, my legs opening to cradle him against my body. His lips left mine to find the sensitive places on my jaw and throat, then lower as he unbuttoned my blouse to reveal my breasts in my new black lace bra.

He unwrapped me like a package, with slow fingers and low murmurs of appreciation. His hands passed over my skin as he unhooked, unbuttoned, unzipped. When I was naked, he bent to kiss my mouth again and his body aligned with mine, a puzzle with only two pieces. Adam and me. Fitting.

He traced my body with his lips and tongue. I tensed when he nuzzled the curve of my belly, then my thighs. He parted my curls with a fingertip and kissed my clit. When he licked it, I arched into ecstasy at once, giving myself up to his touch. Adam made love to me with his mouth, slowly, until I couldn't do anything but ride the waves of pleasure and try to remember to breathe.

Adam didn't fumble with the condom or struggle to figure out how to enter me. He used a hand to guide himself inside, dipping the head of his penis first to smooth the way for the rest. I was so wet he was able to fill me with one thrust.

We both cried out. He bent over me, his face buried in the curve of my shoulder. His teeth grazed me, and I answered with the scrape of my nails on his back. We didn't move at first. Pleasure had immobilized us. The immensity of what we were doing became real. Only for a moment, and then he eased out with a smooth shift of his hips. Back in, all the way, and I lifted my hips to meet him.

Inexperience should have made me clumsy, but arousal choreographed us. In and out, bodies shifting. Give and take.

It didn't last long enough for me to come again, a feat of which I didn't know myself capable at the time. Adam cried my name when he came. His last thrust hurt me more than the first had and I cried out, too.

After, I lay curled in the circle of his arms and slept until it was time for me to get up and leave for home. It took my body three days to recover, until I could no longer feel the effects of him inside me, and by that time Adam had called me twice a day and made arrangements to come see me at my parents' house. I never asked him what he told Rachael. I didn't really care.

We were inseparable after that. We got married the June after I earned my masters in psychology. A year later, while I was working on my post-doctoral experience so I could sit for the licensing exam, the binding on Adam's left ski broke as a result of a manufacturer's defect. He skied headfirst into a tree, suffered a C5-level spinal cord injury that put him in a coma for three weeks and left him without sensation or voluntary movement from the shoulders down. He was only thirty-six.

Losing my virginity hadn't made me a woman, but almost losing my husband had. He could have died. There are days I weep with gratitude that he didn't.

And then, there are days I wish he had.

At home that night, I let myself in the front door with my key. I smelled something good, savory. Probably soup. Mrs. Lapp likes to make soup in the winter.

"Mrs. D?"

She always asks, though who else would be coming in at dinner time? "It's me."

She bustled out of the kitchen, wiping her hands on her apron. Her tidy gray bun had gone a little askew and wisps of hair had come down around her flushed face. Dolly Lapp cooks and cleans like a dream come true, but she's more than a housekeeper. She's a mother, nurse, friend and my life would be impossible without her.

I hung my coat on the hook and set my briefcase in its accustomed spot by the front door. Everything had to stay in its place in my house. There could be no room for clutter, nothing to snag or catch on wheels and block the way.

"I made soup. Come in and have a seat. I was getting worried. You're so much later than usual."

"Traffic was bad." I lied with nary a flinch. Traffic had been fine. The fight with Joe had so unsettled me I'd gone driving, around and around, unable to face the idea of coming home. "But you're right, it's late. I should go check on Adam."

Mrs. Lapp nodded her apple-doll head. "He's in bed already, I helped him in about an hour ago. Soup's in the Crock-Pot, Mrs. D, and I'll just get going. Samuel's been here since half past five. I set him up in the kitchen with a mug of coffee and the newspaper, but you know how he gets rutchy, setting too long."

Guilt at my selfishness pricked me. "You go on ahead. I'm sorry you had to wait."

She fluttered her hands. "Pshaw. Not to worry. Just remember to turn it to low when you're done, so's it don't boil down, and I'll put it away in the morning. Oh, and your sister called. I wrote down her message by the phone."

She really took excellent care of us. I smiled. "Thanks, Mrs. Lapp."

She nodded and headed back the hall toward the kitchen and her impatient husband. Belly empty and growling, I postponed my dinner for another few minutes. I climbed the narrow stairs, a hand on the carved and polished railing Mrs. Lapp kept so clean.

At the top of the stairs, I stopped to listen. To my right was the short part of the hall, with the bathroom, the guest room, the elevator and the stairs to the third floor. To my left, the long part of the hall, with two more rooms, the entrance to the back stairs and the master bedroom and bath. From upstairs I heard the faint sound of the television and then the creak of footfalls. Dennis. A moment later he peered over the railing.

I liked Dennis. At six-foot-two-inches and 230 pounds, he looked like a linebacker, but he was equally sensitive as he was strong. Though he'd only been with us for two years, I could no more do without him than I could with Mrs. Lapp.

"Hi, Sadie. You're home late."

"Traffic," I told him, too.

"I'll be going out in about twenty minutes. I'll check on him before I go," he told me and disappeared into his room again. I heard him talking, then making some calls.

Everything has its price, and the cost of having Dennis and Mrs. Lapp was my privacy. No matter how often I wistfully remembered being able to walk around in my underwear and eat peanut butter straight from the jar, that life was a part of the past. My mother-in-law euphemistically called them "help." I called them necessity. The three of us worked together like synchronized machinery to keep this household functioning. Without them, I'd have been lost.

I paused in Adam's doorway to put on the right face. A pleased half-smile with just the right touch of weariness to indicate the battles of the highway. A fond gaze.

Adam was already in bed, but he turned his head to look at me when I came through the doorway. He'd been reading something on his laptop. "Close program," he ordered the computer. He could operate most everything in his room via the voice-operated command system. "You're late tonight."

"I feel so loved. You're the third person tonight to tell me so." I kept the reply light, joking, slipping so easily into the role of wife.

I pushed the computer table out of the way and bent to brush his lips with my evening kiss. His mouth felt cold beneath mine, and I closed my eyes, willing it to warm.

"Long day?" Adam asked when I'd pulled away. "You look bushed."

Even before I could answer, my stomach gurgled, and I put my hand overtop to quiet it. "Mrs. Lapp made soup. I'll go have some. I wanted to say hi, first."

He smiled again, still looking so much like the man I'd fallen in love with it made my guts hurt. "Hi."

"Hi." I reached to push his hair off his forehead. His mouth had been cold but his forehead and cheeks were flushed. "You feel warm."

"Ah, you caught me reading." He wiggled his eyebrows. For a man without the use of anything below his shoulders, Adam never had a problem making his expressions clear.

I looked at his laptop. "You're reading smut again?"

"Please." He affected a haughty tone. "It's literature."

"For class or for fun?" I stroked my hand across his forehead again, pretending a caress but really checking for fever.

"Class."

Adam's poetry had once won national awards. Now he taught online English courses for Penn State University. As far as I knew, he no longer wrote poems.

"Prison Poets?" I straightened a hand that had fallen askew, legs that had bent a bit during the course of the day. I tucked blankets in all around him with swift, practiced movements, making him a mummy.

"The Marquis de Sade versus Oscar Wilde." Adam's eyes followed my course around the bed.

"Sounds positively kinky."

I leaned across him to tuck the blankets on his other side. He breathed in deep and his lips grazed my throat. Heat and memories flooded me.

"You smell so good." Adam's voice was hoarser than usual.

I froze. He tilted his head to brush his lips against my skin, and breathed in again. He nuzzled me. My nipples tightened and knees got weak as instant arousal, eager as a puppy, bounded through me at that one, simple caress.

His tongue flickered out. "You taste good, too."

I turned my face to his and kissed him, our mouths

parting. His tongue stroked mine and another bolt of pure liquid pleasure washed over me. I put a hand on his shoulder to steady myself. The flannel of his pajama shirt was soft, the bones beneath padded enough by the fabric not to hurt my palm.

I wanted to kiss him forever, to melt into him. The kiss broke and left both of us breathing hard. I leaned in again, my mouth seeking his and finding it closed to me. Shut out, I pulled away.

"Hey, how about we watch a movie tonight?" My hand lingered on his cheek. "Give yourself a break."

"Can't." He smiled, rueful. "I'm already behind on this stuff from being sick."

Even a simple head cold knocked him harder than it would have for me. I understood. Even so, my heart still hammered in my chest and my thighs trembled with desire. Joe's stories did that, but so did Adam's kisses, as they always had. I leaned close to breathe into his ear and run a hand over his chest.

"I could make it worth your while."

"Sadie," Adam said after a moment. "I really need to get this done."

We looked into each other's eyes for a moment infinite with silence. I had no illusions that my husband did not know every part of me, every thought, every single stir of emotion. The accident that had taken the use of his body hadn't damaged his mind. He'd always known me better than anyone ever had.

So why did it so often feel like he'd forgotten?

I pulled away, putting the mask back on. This was not

the first time he'd lacked interest in physical intimacy. It wouldn't, I was sure, be the last. I could've asked him why he'd rather read about sex than have it, and in the past, in our life before, I would have. But that was long ago and far away, and those sorts of questions often hung between us, never spoken. We both bore scars, and not all of them were visible. There was enough damage to contemplate without creating more.

"You'd better go eat," Adam said. "Your stomach is growling."

I nodded. "Do you need anything?"

"No. I'm good for now. I'll finish this up and go to sleep."

The entire room had been adapted to his use. He was perfectly capable of putting himself to sleep without me or Dennis to help him, though he'd still need help with the regular turning that helped prevent pressure sores. Tonight was Friday, and that meant it was my job to wake every two hours and check on him, since Dennis was off-duty for the weekend.

I kissed him again, without the heat from before. "Call if you need me."

His attention had already gone back to his work, shutting me out. "'Night, babe."

"G'night." I pulled the door half-closed behind me and stopped to lean against the wall with one arm crossed over my stomach and the other elbow resting on top of it to support the hand covering my face. I was trying hard not to shake, but not quite succeeding.

"Sadie? I'm heading out now."

At Dennis' concerned tone, I straightened up and

shifted my features again into neutrality. "Thanks, Dennis. Have a good time."

He studied me and looked as though he were about to comment, but instead just grinned. "Yeah. It's open mic night at the Blue Swan."

I laughed, the sound barely hollow. "Ah. And what are you planning on reading?"

"Me? Nothing. I'm there for moral support. Scott and Mark are going to sing."

Envy attacked me from behind, biting the back of my neck and jabbing its stinger into my spine like an electric shock. I wanted to go out with friends, have some drinks. I wanted to—

"Have fun," I told him, and he nodded.

"I will. See ya Monday."

He headed down the stairs two at a time, quiet despite his size, and I waited until I heard the front door slam before I went down the stairs after him.

I lingered over a single bowl of soup and a mug of hot tea. I washed the bowl and mug carefully by hand instead of using the dishwasher. I fed the fish and set the timer on the coffee maker. I checked the locks on the doors, all three downstairs and the one in the basement.

When at last I climbed the stairs again, the hour had grown late enough that it almost made me wonder if I should bother to go to bed at all. After all, I'd only have to wake again in a couple of hours. I'd regret it if I didn't, but though every muscle ached and my head throbbed, my mind was too restless for sleep.

I peeked in on Adam. His lights were out and his breathing slow and steady. The faint green glow from the night-light gave his face an alien cast. I didn't need light to see what I was doing. Adam barely woke as I turned him. We didn't speak. We never did if we could help it, as if somehow silence made all of this a dream. I finished everything I had to do and made sure he was all right before I crept away.

Though I slept in his room on the weekends when Dennis was off-duty, we no longer shared a bedroom. The room that had been ours now needed every inch for the equipment and supplies that kept Adam functioning. I'd made that room a haven for us in the early days of our marriage, when the rest of the house had been a hodge-podge shambles of late '70s décor and early '80s substandard renovation. I'd loved that bedroom and our art deco furniture, salvaged from thrift stores and auctions. I'd loved the bathroom, with its claw-foot tub and Victorian toilet with the pull chain. Now gutted to accommodate a wheelchair-capable shower and toilet, it was a room of function, not luxury.

The room I used was just on the other side of the back stairs. It was much smaller than the master, but I'd cut an arched doorway through the wall into the room next to it, creating a sitting room/study that gave me all the space I needed, and that room connected to the bathroom also accessible to the hall. I only had to share when we had houseguests, since Dennis had his own bathroom on the third floor.

I made certain the intercom was working and set, in case Adam woke and needed me, then set about stripping out of my work clothes. The mirror tried catching my attention, but I ignored it. I no longer knew the woman who lived in there.

I ran a bath and added essence of lavender, then dimmed the lights. I settled into the water and let it enfold me. Hold me. It cradled me, and I slid deeper, up to my chin, while my hair spread out around me like seaweed.

I found sanctuary in the dark and quiet, in the one place where I didn't have to be strong, optimistic, happy, or anything else anyone thought I should be. Where I couldn't and didn't have to pretend I didn't know the truth.

My husband didn't love me anymore, and I didn't know how to make him.

I met Joe two years before, two random strangers sharing a bench in the atrium of a local business complex for lunch. Frigid January weather had made our secluded bench a real treasure, and we'd shared it with the glee of kids who'd stumbled onto a candy shop giving away free samples.

We'd made polite conversation, nothing serious, nothing deep. We checked each other out in the surreptitious way men and women do when they have no intention of flirting but want to see if it might be worth the effort. I noticed his smile first, the expensive suit some time later. He made me laugh almost right away during a time when I thought I'd forgotten how.

Remembering Joe's smile, I slid my hands over my body in the hot water. The bath oil made my skin slick. Smooth. My palms skidded over my belly and thighs. I sank lower, my ears covered, listening to the secret underwater shush shush of my heart beating.

With one thing or another, I didn't make it back to the atrium until an entire month had passed. It was something like a magic number—thirty days—and when I flipped my calendar something reminded me about the man on the bench and my feet led me back there as if I had no choice but to see if he were there again. I'd ignored the way my heart jumped into my throat when I saw him striding toward me beneath the hanging ferns. The sun had lit his hair into shining gold. His smile was even brighter than that. That was the first time he grumbled about tomatoes on his sandwich. We spent an hour and half on that bench talking. I didn't ask him if he had to get back to work. I was late for my first afternoon appointment. And something unspoken had passed between us. An agreement.

In March, I made sure to wear lipstick. In April, we moved outside to the park, where a hanging willow muted the echo of our laughter and made it something secret. In May we shared a thermos of lemonade, in June he brought me a muffin and I'd lent him a book we'd talked about the month before.

By July, the conversation was no longer polite.

The first time he told me a story, I'd sat, riveted to the bench, my sandwich eaten but untasted. Joe was an exquisite raconteur. He left out not even the smallest detail of sensation. He'd enthralled me, bound me with his words.

Joe, in his words, loved women. Their curves, their scents, their moods. He loved long hair, big asses, sturdy thighs, concave bellies, tiny, cherry-tipped tits, blue and green and brown eyes. He loved women, and he loved fucking. And every first Friday of the month, when we met for lunch, he had a new story to tell me. He was Scheherazade, saving not his own life, but mine.

I cupped my breasts, their weight made light in the water's embrace. I stroked them, passing a palm over my nipples before pinching them both between forefinger and thumb. A sigh leaked out of me as they burned and tightened. I tugged and felt an answering pull in my clit, my cunt, my ass. I moved the firm flesh back and forth, jerking them like twin erections.

My thighs fell open as my hips pushed against the water. Eddies left behind by the motion swirled heat against my clit and I rocked harder, but the pressure was too light to do more than tease.

Still tugging on my left nipple, I slid my right hand between my legs. My clit already poked out of its hood, hard, ready for my touch. I bit my lip, the gentle stroke-stroke enough to make my hips jut forward again. I pinched my clit like I pinched my nipple, moving in time, alternating. The water supported and lifted me. My shoulder blades bumped the bottom of the tub as I pushed my pelvis against my fingers.

My clit swelled. My cunt opened, aching to be filled, and I left my nipple to slide three fingers inside. It wasn't enough. It wasn't what I wanted—a thick, hard cock fucking me. I dreamed of it, being filled, dreamed of taking an erection down the back of my throat while another filled my vagina, another in my ass, while hands stroked and pulled my body all over. I dreamed of being consumed by men who made me come over and over again with their tongues and fingers and pricks, until I exploded and disappeared.

You didn't need a doctorate in psychology to analyze that.

I might dream of faceless men who consumed me with their sex, but when I fantasized, it was about Joe. I didn't need to analyze that, either.

My skin had gone pink from the hot water and arousal. I looked down over the curve of my breasts and belly to where my hands moved between my legs. I wanted more than my own hands there. I wanted Joe's mouth on me. I wanted to feel him lick the soft, wet slit of my cunt, feel that smile on my clit. I wanted him to fuck me with his mouth until I came.

I slowed my hands, fingers sliding in and out of my pussy without friction. I pinched my clit again. It had gone dark red, pushing up from my trimmed-short pubic curls. I stroked it up and down and my pelvis jumped again. A spasm shuddered through me.

I wanted to scream myself hoarse with this pleasure. I wanted to moan and whimper. I bit my lip, hard, to keep back a cry, mindful that I was not alone, not ever alone.

I moved my hands away and rocked my hips, moving the water over my clit. Fuck, it was good, almost but not quite like a tongue. I let it lick at me for a while until I shuddered and banged my elbows against the side of the tub.

I could bring myself off in another second. I'd been on

the verge all day, first in anticipation of my lunchtime meeting, then with Joe's story, then with Adam's unexpected kiss. I'd been slick from need all day, my clit aching. Another second, one more touch and I'd go over.

I waited, breathing hard, heart pounding. The water began to cool. I wanted to come and I wanted to stay poised here forever, with every nerve on fire and every muscle tense. I wanted to feel alive just a while longer.

I waved a hand in the water over my body, not touching my skin but letting the water do it for me. The ripples felt good, and I imagined Joe's hands. His long, strong fingers and clean, neat fingernails. I'd memorized his hands— every wrinkle of every knuckle, every vein. The exact spot on his wrists where the hair on his arms began.

Thinking of Joe's hair, I fought back another moan. My hands slipped down to stroke myself again. I wanted to bury my face in his chest hair, to rub the coarse curls of his arms against my eyelids. I wanted to feel his hair on my belly when we fucked, cock in cunt.

I couldn't stand it any longer. I had to come. I thought I might die if I didn't let myself finish, right then.

I thought I was dying when I did.

Everything stopped.

Then all at once, it started again. My heart, beating. My breath, held in my lungs, rushed out. Water splashed as my body quaked. My clit had filled to the point of bursting and now it emptied in small, perfect spasms of ecstasy. My anus puckered as my cunt rippled, bearing down on nothing.

Unable to hold it back, I gasped. My back arched and water sloshed over my face. I closed my mouth, fast, so I didn't choke myself. Some got in my eyes, stinging, but the pleasure was so intense I didn't care.

When I was done and returned to myself, I put a hand on the edge of the tub to haul myself upright. I was cold and shivered, my nipples peaked now not from arousal but from chill.

Nausea twisted my gut in the aftermath. I was light-headed when I got out, and had to stand, head down, for a moment or two before I felt steady enough to grab up my towel from the hook on the wall.

I moved too fast and the room spun. I got on my hands and knees, my hair sodden and stringy over my shoulders and down my back. I shivered, teeth chattering, and then I wept.

The towel I clutched smelled of lavender and I pressed my face against it to stifle my sobs as I'd bit my lip to hold back my sounds of pleasure. I dissolved on the bathroom floor, giving in to magnificent and overpowering grief.

I loved my husband but wanted to fuck another man. I wanted it so much it tore me apart and knitted me together over and over. I lived for the stories Joe told that let me imagine myself as the women he took to bed. I had called him names, but I was wrong. It wasn't Joe, it was me.

I was the cheater.

Chapter 03

February

This month, if I have a name, it's lost in the pounding beat blaring from the speakers in the club. I'm wearing a short, tight skirt and a shirt made up of two scarves tied behind my neck. No bra, and my tits push against the silky fabric like twin melons. They barely bounce when I dance, and I'm proud of them. They're worth the college tuition they cost to buy.

Guys have been approaching me all night. I let them buy me drink after drink, but I dance alone or with a girl-friend, shaking our asses in time to the pounding rhythm. My skirt rides up over tanned, taut thighs, and tawny hair glistens in the blue strobe lights. I'm hips and tits and hair. I'm smooth, fluid motion. I'm sex for the sake of sex.

There's a guy watching me from across the dance floor. There are lots of guys watching me, but this one is differ-ent. He's alone, not part of a pack. Just standing there, watching. His long-sleeved, black sweater hugs his shoulders and chest and fades into the black of his trousers, making him a shadow.

I put on a little more effort for him, a wiggle of my hips and ass and tits. I crook my finger. *Come hither, stranger.*

He detaches himself from the dark and moves forward, cutting through the crowd. I lose sight of him and frown, my dance losing a little of its steam until a moment later when the crowd parts and he's standing in front of me.

He smiles. I smile. I raise my hands over my head and wiggle, turning, writhing. He likes it.

And damn, he's a good dancer, too. He molds along my body. One hand goes to my hip. With the other, he curls my fingers around the back of his neck. The back of my head rests against his chest, because even in my four-inch heels he's still about five inches taller.

We move in time, ignoring the other dancers who sort of bounce up and down, as if on pogo sticks. We move more like water. His hand on my hip drifts down to brush along the hem of my skirt and the bare skin of my thigh.

My nipples get hard. He's subtle but I know what he wants. I want it, too. It's not like I'm here to find Mr. Right. More like Mr. Right Now.

The song changes and some people on the dance floor leave. Others join. I turn and tilt my head to smile at him. Fuck, he's got pretty teeth.

We can't talk, really. The music's too loud. We communicate with a look, a touch. He's good at that, too. He actually looks at my face.

If we're not going to dance, we need to get off the floor. Besides, I'm hot and thirsty. I gesture toward the bar and he nods, so I grab his hand and tug him along to the bar where he buys me a margarita and he orders a bottle of water.

I don't think he's drunk, which is really interesting, considering it's Saturday night and the entire bar is halfway to wasted, including me. I lift my margarita, and he toasts it with his bottled water. We smile and sip. It's quieter here by the barest margin, but still not enough for real conversation.

"You wanna go someplace?" I have to shout the question twice before he answers.

He leans in to say directly into my ear, "where do you want to go?"

That's how we end up at my place. I feel okay with him driving me home since he hasn't been drinking, and it saves me cab fare, anyway. I live on the third floor of a converted brownstone, and the margaritas have made the stairs too steep for me. Laughing, I stop to take off my shoes. His eyes follow the motion of my fingers unbuckling the ankle strap. His eyes look dark until he raises them to my face, and then I see they're not dark at all, it's just that the pupils have gone wide and black.

At the top of the stairs I unlock my door and push inside, then turn and grab him by the front of his black leather jacket. I back him up against the door, closing it, and press my body to his, still cold from being outside. He smells like winter air and leather and smoke, and I pull him down to kiss me, but he turns at the last second so my mouth lands on his cheek.

His hands have found their way to my tits without a problem. His hands are cold, too, and they slide up over the silk scarves and my tight nipples. I push his jacket off his shoulders and toss it on the floor. He bends to pick it up and hang it over the back of a chair.

"Oh, you're fussy," I say, as if that's cute.

He doesn't deny it. He even smirks a little. Maybe he's proud of it. I take off my jacket and make a show of hanging it up on the coatrack, using exaggerated movements he watches without changing his expression.

"What's your name?" This I toss over my shoulder as I head to my kitchen and yank open my freezer to pull out a bottle of lemon vodka.

"Joe."

I set out the bottle, a shot glass, the sugar bowl. I grab a lemon from the basket on the counter and slice it into quarters.

"Joe, you want a lemon shooter?"

When I turn for his answer, I see he's followed me into the kitchen.

"Sure."

I pour a shot, wet the back of my hand with the lemon and sprinkle it with sugar. "Bottoms up." Down goes the shot, lick the sugar, bite the lemon.

He does one, too. I like the noise he makes when he sucks the lemon. It's a little half-growl. I wonder if he'd make that same noise if I sucked hard on his cock. And suddenly I want to find out.

I move closer to him and grab his belt. I'm not as drunk as I was an hour ago but I'm still pretty buzzed. Holding his belt helps keep me steady. I'm glad I took off my tottery heels.

"C'mere," I tell him. "Be nice to me."

His hands come up to hold my hips. I don't bother with trying to kiss him. I undo his belt with a couple quick jerks that move his whole body. He's already hard, and I stroke him through his pants. Up and down. I look up at his face. He's still smirking, but I recognize the bright gleam in his eyes. He wants to fuck. Well, don't they all?

As soon as I undo his button and zipper, I push his pants and briefs down over his thighs. He's got a nice dick. I take it in my hand and stroke it couple of times, hard, and he puts a hand over mine to hold it in place against him.

It's my turn to smirk. "Too rough?"

"You don't want to break it."

He thinks he's clever, and I have to admit, he's cute enough to get away with it. Besides, I'm not exactly thinking clearly at this point. I stroke again, moving both our hands along his erection, but softer.

"That better?"

"Your mouth would be better."

My heart skip. "Yeah?"

He looks down at his cock, and at our hands, then back to my face. "Yeah."

It's because he's looking at my face when he says it that I get on my knees. The tile is cold and hard but I don't really notice. Maybe tomorrow I will, when I'm sober and my knees are black and blue, but right now I'm focused on taking him in my mouth.

My inhibitions are loose and so's my throat. I can take him all the way in, a skill I'm proud of. I close my lips around the base of his prick and suck, working my mouth on him a couple seconds before sliding off to add some suction to the head. He pushes forward, into my mouth. I put a hand on his cock to control it. I don't want to gag. Drunk as I am, I might just puke all over him.

My hand also lets me stroke and suck him at the same time, so he gets twice the pleasure. In another minute, he makes that growly noise and I smile. I suck him a little bit more, getting into the rhythm the same way I did at the club. It's just a different kind of dance.

He puts a hand in my hair and his fingers tangle, pulling. I wince and suck him a little harder. He's thrusting hard, now. I let my mouth pop off and look at his cock. It's wet from my saliva. I pump my fist up and down along it, looking up to watch his face. He's not looking at me now. His eyes are closed.

A second later, he opens them. "Get up."

I'm a little clumsy from alcohol and being on the floor for so long, but he helps me with his hands under my elbows. I laugh when he pulls me upright, but the laugh becomes a squeak of surprise when he turns me so fast my head spins. He pushes my hands flat against the table.

I'm bent over at the waist, surprised at how fast he moved. He pushes my skirt up to my hips. Cool air caresses my ass, bared by my thong panties. He runs a finger along the string at the small of my back, then pulls it out of my ass crack and takes my panties off before I can say a word. He pushes my feet apart with one of his and I bend further over the table, my hands skidding along the slick surface. I knock into the shot glass, which rolls off onto the floor but doesn't break.

I'd protest but he's already stroking my clit. My pussy's as surprised as I am, but way faster at acclimating. I'm already wet, I know, because he pushes a finger inside me and then brings it up to my clit again and every motion gets smoother, coated in my slickness.

I make a noise, too. His cock nudges my ass and I spread my legs wider on my own. I lay along the table, pushing my ass into the air so he can reach my cunt. When he puts two fingers inside me, I cry out. He's doing this thing to me that feels so good I shake, something with two fingers inside me and his other hand fingering my clit. He puts a third finger inside, stretching me as he pinches my clit. The sensation's so startling, I jump and moan.

"Where've you been all my life?"

He doesn't answer, but I don't care because he's finger fucking me so good. My hips rock and I push my cunt against his hand, wanting to take all of him inside me.

"Fuck me!" It's a command and an invitation. I grope for my purse, slung over the back of the kitchen chair. I pull out the rubber and pass it back to him.

"Just a minute."

I moan a protest but in a second he's started up that twin fingering thing again and I'm jittering and jumping under his touch as if he's hooked me up to a socket in the wall.

I'm so wet he fits a fourth finger inside me. He jerks my clit, up and down, rolling it every so often in a way that makes me fucking mindless.

I think I'm begging him at this point, even though I don't really want him to stop doing what he's doing with his hands. All at once I go from "ooh" to "hell yeah!" And there's no way I could stop myself from coming even if I wanted to. My fingers clutch the table and I shout.

My pussy closes around his fingers. My clit spasms. He stops moving for a moment while my body shakes around him. I lay my cheek on the table and close my eyes. It's good, so good. I'm spent, breathless.

He takes his hands away. I don't move. I'm boneless. He puts one hand on my hip. His cock nudges my cunt. He pushes inside me slowly, and I make a sleepy noise. He fills me all the way. I push up on my hands a little to take the pressure off my boobs.

He sets a slow steady pace, and I'm happy to take it because I already came and I really don't care what he does to finish himself off. My clit's buzzing a little, but I'm not really ready for another orgasm.

"Yeah, baby, fuck me harder." This seems like a good thing to say.

He keeps the same steady pace. I push up higher, and he unhooks the clip holding my shirt closed behind my neck. The scarves fall open. He reaches around to grab my tit, tweaking the nipple upright. That feels good, too. My clitty's buzzing harder, oh, fuck, and I'm so wet he slides in and out of me as easy as anything. I moan and push my ass against him.

Maybe this is what he was waiting for, because he moves faster. Our bodies make a slapping sound. His thrusts move me and the table, which skids on the tile floor. I moan louder when he twists my nipple, but what I really need is a finger on my clit to get me off again.

Sudden wetness on my back startles me. He's stroked the lemon wedge across my shoulder blade. He takes the sugar. Grains tickle my back. The next moment his tongue follows it and he licks me clean.

Wow. I'm really getting closer now. He's fucking me so hard and fast I have to clutch the table edge to keep from moving. He's making small, sexy grunts that are driving me crazy with lust.

I'm getting closer but I need a little more. Just a little more something. Then, he gives it to me. His fingers trace the cleft of my ass, probing. His thumb presses against me back there, right on my pucker. My moan catches in my throat and I jump. My hips buck forward. Fuck, fuck, oh fuck, that's not what I was expecting, but damn, it's so good…

In another second I'm coming for the second time. My breath stutters out. I try to gasp in another but my orgasm has stolen my breath and the best I can do is sip at the air.

He thrusts into me once more and cries out, voice hoarse. We pant together after that, coming down. My legs tremble and my belly hurts from where it's rubbed on the table edge, but don't really care too much because I'm so utterly, totally sated.

He pulls out. By the time I turn around and tug my skirt back down over my thighs, he's already tossed the rubber in the trash and pulled up his pants. He washes his hands at the sink while I watch.

I'm bleary and tired and still mostly drunk, but I give him a big, smug smile. "Wow."

He looks at me over his shoulder. Like an afterthought. He smiles. "Yeah, thanks."

I move closer to him, lazy and cuddly the way really good sex makes me feel. I reach for him, and he lets me hug him but even though I tilt my face up to his, he doesn't kiss me.

"Hey," I say, soft and purring. "Be nice to me."

He bends and kisses my cheek, then gently but firmly pushes me from him and leaves the kitchen. I stare after him, pissed off. I follow him.

"Hey!"

He's put on his coat. He turns, hand on the doorknob.

"You're leaving?" I put my hands on my hips, indignant. "Just like that?"

Joe nods once, so solemn I feel like I can't really rage at him. I mean…it was a hookup, yeah, I get it. But it was really, really great sex, the kind that's worth breakfast, at least.

"But…"

He shakes his head, stopping me. Then he opens the door and leaves. Only when it's closed behind him do I realize he never bothered to ask my name.

Joe twirled a straw paper in his fingers, knotting it. He didn't look at me. He hadn't looked at me since he sat down.

"Why didn't you ask her name?" I hadn't eaten anything. I hadn't even opened my lunch bag. Though I was only a few inches away from Joe on the bench, it might as well have been miles.

He turned, slowly. Our eyes met. I drew in a breath and held it. The look he gave me was a challenge of some sort.

"Because it didn't matter."

Maybe her name didn't matter, but his reason for not asking did. His story comforted me. This was the Joe I knew, the teller of tales and splitter of peaches. Not the man who last month had threatened to upset the balance of our relationship by wanting to change.

"About last month," I said finally. "I'm sorry."

He shrugged. "You were right."

I nodded, as if he'd made a longer explanation. Not even when we first met had our silence been so uncomfortable. I had to look away, at last, afraid my face showed too much of what I couldn't say.

"I wasn't even planning on going home with her," he said after a minute. "Or with anyone."

"So…why did you?" I couldn't help the fascination.

"C'mon, Sadie. You know how it is."

"No, actually. I don't."

Joe let a puff of air seep from his lips, not quite a whistle. "You've never?"

"No. Never." I shook my head to further emphasize my point.

"You've never been with someone only once." His tone sounded disbelieving or envious, I wasn't sure which.

"I've only been with one man." The admission wasn't shameful, just…the truth. It seemed to shock Joe, who probably couldn't comprehend my experience any more than I could his.

"Only one."

"Yes."

He shook his head a bit. "Good for you."

I laughed a little. "You're avoiding the question. If you weren't planning on going home with someone, why did you?"

"Because I could. Because she asked. Because…I always do."

I made a small noise, shaking my head as I unwrapped my lunch. Joe looked over at me as he unscrewed the cap on his bottle of soda. He took a long, slow drink. I imagined him tasting like lemon and vodka and kept my eyes carefully on my sandwich.

"Haven't you ever done something just because it's easier to do it than not?"

I didn't have to think long before answering. "Of course."

"Tell me."

"It's not as exciting as your story, Joe."

He smiled, leaning forward. "No? That's too bad. Tell me, anyway."

I was used to giving people what they wanted. Joe was used to getting it. I told him.

"When I was growing up, my sister and I fell into these…stereotypes, I guess you could say. I was the smart one. She was the pretty one. We kept it up through college, and I guess even now. It's stupid, but you know how families are."

"Try being the disappointing one."

I leaned back on the bench to study him. He was impeccably dressed, as always. Today his shirt was blue, his favorite color. It made his eyes seem greener than usual. He was the epitome of a clean-cut businessman. Whatever he did, he did it too well to be a disappointment.

I laughed. "Oh, you aren't. You can't be. Look at you, Mr. Successful."

He shrugged, smiling. "My parents aren't impressed with fancy suits and expensive ties."

I knew he had a sister who was married with children and a brother who'd died. This was the first time I'd heard him talk about his parents.

"As far as ties go, it's a very nice one," I told him. "Even if they don't like it, I do."

He gave me a one-eyed, squinting grin that made me laugh. "Yeah? You're impressed by this tie?"

"Keep in mind my knowledge of men's haute couture is pretty limited."

He stroked the fabric. "I like this one, too."

The silence between us wasn't awkward this time.

"Sometimes," Joe said after a bit, "it's just easier to keep being what everyone expects you to be. Even if that's what you're not, anymore."

I nodded, agreeing, and he got up to toss his trash into the pail. "I wasn't sure you'd be back, after what I said."

"I couldn't stay away. I thought about it all month. Just not showing up."

"So...why did you?"

A slow, hot smile spread across his mouth. "Because I always do."

I was trying to decide between two mugs of the same shade but different shapes, my concentration entirely focused on my choices, when the distinct sensation of a foreign gaze on the back of my neck prickled my skin. I glanced up, but the man across the aisle appeared as engrossed in his shopping as I was. A look to either side showed us as the only two customers in housewares. Convinced I was imagining it, I bent back to my decision.

Again, I sensed someone staring. This time, instead of looking up, I let my eyes shift from side to side. Nothing. A gradual turn of my head revealed my fellow mug aficionado had moved a bit closer. He picked up a flowered coffee mug, turning it to and fro, then set it back on the shelf.

I turned back to the selection in front of me, but couldn't concentrate. I wanted something new for my bathroom. It wasn't brain surgery. I needed to pick one, just one, and yet my every sense now strained toward the man standing behind me. I grabbed up one of the mugs, finally, and stuck it in my cart. I looked over my shoulder.

He was looking at me.

"Excuse me," he began.

Time slowed as I turned, expectant of something benign. A question. "What's the time?" or "Do you work here?"

"Are you available for dating?"

My face must have shown my shock. "What?"

Details registered. He had long hair, more than a bit unkempt. He wore a shapeless fatigue jacket and matching, slightly ragged pants. Oh, lord. He was probably part of some outpatient program at the V.A. Hospital.

"Well, I didn't see a wedding ring..."

I looked automatically to my left hand, where I was,

indeed, wearing my wedding ring. I was so stunned by this, the first outright proposition I'd had in as long as I could remember, that I couldn't even speak. I could only stare.

He moved closer, looking hopeful. "So? Are you?"

"I'm…no, I'm not."

The man took off running down the aisle. I looked after him, the absurdity of the situation giving the entire experience a surreal flavor. I paid for my purchases, fumbling with my change and laughing too hard at the cashier's unfunny jokes.

I'd carried myself as a married woman for such a long time, I'd considered myself under the radar of outright flirtation. Either men didn't notice me, or I didn't notice them noticing. After the ineloquent come-on, though, I kept my eyes open a little wider. Was the man in the next car checking me out? Was the guy holding the elevator door for me doing it to be polite or was he giving me a once-over when I reached to push the button for my floor? Even if they weren't, the possibility that they might be preparing to accost me with the offer of a night on the town kept me smiling.

Adam didn't find it so amusing. "What did he say to you?"

I paused in showing off the new mug. "I told you. He asked me if I was available for dating."

"He asked you on a date? In the middle of the store?"

"Well, to be honest, I think he was a little off, Adam." I put the mug back in the bag.

Adam maneuvered his chair away from the computer desk so we were face-to-face. "What did you say?"

"I said I wasn't." Even now, the memory made me laugh. "And really, if you'd seen him—"

"What about him?"

I described the man, exaggerating a little to make the story better, but not too much. "I think he was probably on outpatient leave from a mental program. He had that look. Poor guy, his therapist probably told him to go out and take a chance, ask a woman out, and I shot him down. I probably set him back months in his progress."

Adam didn't laugh. "Right."

"Adam," I said with a sigh. "It wasn't a big deal."

"Some guy comes on to my wife and it's not a big deal?" Agitated, he swung the chair around. It was big and heavy, and though he could operate it with agile grace, it still needed room to move. He nudged the edge of the desk and let out a curse when his papers fell down.

I bent to gather them up. A few lines of text caught my eye, phrasing from his lectures. I put them back in the folder.

"Honey, he wasn't even cute!"

The look he gave me was long familiar, sardonic, verging on mean. "What does that mean? If he had been cute, you'd have taken him up on it?"

A snappish response teetered on my tongue but managed to cling to the inside of my mouth without spitting itself out. "Don't be silly," I said instead.

Adam grunted. His version of pacing was to rock the chair back and forth in small arcs. The room wasn't big enough for him to move more than that, the chair too bulky to allow for the tight turns he'd need to crisscross the space.

"Adam, it was a funny story. I thought you'd like it. I'm sorry I told you."

His eyes flashed. "What does that mean, Sadie? You won't tell me about it again?"

"I'm sure it won't happen again," I replied with a sigh. "C'mon. It was just a fluke."

He grunted again and stopped the pacing. "Were you wearing that outfit?"

I looked down at my clothes. "I was, yes."

He'd always been a master of expression, with words or without. His snort made his feelings very clear. "Well, no wonder he hit on you."

That made me laugh out loud. "Oh, really? Because this outfit is so sexy?"

My work clothes were the farthest thing from sexy I could ever imagine, most of the time. Then again, so was I. The Beatles might have written about Sexy Sadie, but that wasn't me.

"I don't like men hitting on you, that's all." Adam sounded less fierce, more what Mrs. Lapp called *grexy*.

I went to him and kissed his cheek. "You have nothing to worry about."

He wasn't so easily appeased. "Weren't you wearing your wedding ring?"

That was it. I crossed my arms over my chest. "Yes. I was! You act as if I was out trolling for business! Stop it!"

Maybe I shouldn't have told him the story, which had been amusing and a bit of an ego boost to me. Adam was moody on the best of days. It wasn't difficult to figure out why, but once he'd had a much better sense of humor. It was hard to remember he wasn't the same man I'd seduced with a red ribbon stuck in a book of poetry.

He stopped talking. He went back to his computer and ignored me. I took my mug and left the room.

If he'd been cute, would I have taken him up on the offer? Gone out with a stranger I met while buying a mug? Maybe gone home with him, to his bed, or to a hotel room, to a car, to a back alley where he'd push me against a wall and merge his flesh with mine in anonymous passion?

According to Joe, things like that happened all the time, to him. But Joe never came on to me. I only listened to him talk about it, month after month, and wondered what it would be like to be asked and answer, "yes."

Chapter 04

"*V*alentine's Day is the pimple on the ass of the year."

My patient's blunt statement made me laugh. I know her well enough to understand she was using humor to cover up insecurity, but that didn't matter. What she said was funny, anyway.

"Why do you say that, Elle?" I poured us both another cup of tea.

"It's a martyr's holiday." She added sugar and cream to her cup.

Sometimes, patients are ashamed of me, or rather, their need to see me. Sometimes they embrace me so fully it compromises our working relationship. Elle, whom I found to be bright, funny and compassionate, had managed to strike the perfect medium. We were friendly but not quite friends—with friends the sharing of trouble goes both ways and with us it was necessarily one-sided. Still, our sessions had taken on the tone of two girlfriends chatting, rather than of a doctor counseling a patient. It showed me she was comfortable with me. It had taken her a long time.

I added lemon to my cup. "Ah, yes. Poor St. Valentine. But it's not that anymore."

She sipped and gave me a familiar raised eyebrow. "Sure it is. The search for the perfect gift? The despair if you don't get just the right thing? The depression of not having someone to buy for, or having someone to buy for but not the person you want."

"I'm sensing some anxiety over Valentine's Day." How easily I put on the doctor's cap. Girlfriends or not, Elle was there to talk, and I to listen. She didn't always take my advice but then, not all of it was good.

The way she tapped her fingers on the arm of her chair meant what I'd said was true, but I didn't push. Some of my colleagues favor a more antagonistic approach, call my methods the "soft and fuzzy" school of psychology. Sometimes it works and sometimes it doesn't. I can only do my best.

"I do love him." She spoke low, but not hesitant. "It's not that I don't."

A year before she wouldn't have admitted that much. I offered a smile. "So then, what is it? You're afraid to buy him something?"

"It's so much pressure." Elle shrugged and spun her spoon around in the cup. "And I think…I think he's going to make this a big one."

"More than flowers and candy, you mean."

She nodded, her face shadowed. "Yeah. I think so."

"We've talked about this." I sipped my tea, watching her. "How relationships grow. It's part of change."

She laughed, ruefully. "I know. Dr. Danning, I know that."

I knew she did. Elle had been with her boyfriend for over a year. She danced around the idea of marrying him and having children, of making what she called a real life. She had other issues, bigger ones, but it all came back to that in the end. Marriage and children, whether she could take what he offered her or not, whether the past had any right to influence her future any longer. She'd come a long way in the year she'd been seeing me, but sometimes it's the sunshine that frightens us more than the big black shadows.

"It's just hard." She sounded ashamed. "It shouldn't be. He makes it so easy. But it's hard, anyway. Even when I fight with him, he just comes back with something so perfect I can't chase him away."

"Do you really want to?"

She sighed. "No. But do you know how hard it is to be with someone who's perfect?"

"Nobody's perfect, Elle."

She gave me a look. "Some are more perfect than others, Dr. Danning."

I laughed a bit. "Yes, that's true."

She stirred her cup as if she could dissolve her troubles the way she dissolved the sugar in the tea. "I keep thinking…"

"Yes?" I asked, when waiting for her to continue failed to prompt her into speaking.

"What if he's the last man I'll ever sleep with for the rest of my life?"

I fussed with my own tea to create distance from a question that hit too close to home. "Would that be so awful?"

Elle put her cup on the edge of my desk and rubbed the arms of her chair, her face angled away from mine. "No?"

"You don't sound so sure."

The look she gave me was pure, vintage Elle Kavanagh, stubborn and self-effacing with a hint of snark. "I anticipate the rest of my life being a very long time."

"From your mouth to God's ears," I told her, and we both laughed.

"I don't want to cheat on Dan. But I'm afraid I might. Just because."

"Those things don't happen by accident."

She seemed chastened by my sterner than usual tone. "I know."

I studied her before saying, "The offer still stands, if you want it."

She looked up. "See both of us. I know."

"Dan's a wonderful man and he's been good for you. You know putting the onus of your happiness on someone else isn't healthy. But neither is refusing to allow someone to help you gain it."

"I know, I know, I know!" She groaned, tipping back her head. She grimaced. "Bleah! I know! Stupid fucking Valentine's Day!"

"Maybe you're getting yourself too worked up. What are you doing for him?"

She straightened in her chair. "Heart-shaped meatloaf. With asparagus. And some sex."

I meant to answer right away, but sudden immobility stifled my words. I filled my cup with tea. I didn't want to cover the fact I couldn't speak. The teapot rattled against the cup and I had to force my hands to steady.

I envied her. Fiercely. Suddenly. Horribly. I envied Elle for her meatloaf and plans for lovemaking to celebrate a holiday she hated. I envied her fear that she had something to lose.

"Dr. Danning?"

I put on the doctor mask. I owed her that. We might laugh and drink tea, and I might be privy to her deepest, darkest secrets, but we were not friends.

"It sounds lovely. I'm sure he'll enjoy it."

She nodded, slowly. "Yes. I think so."

"And whatever happens after, Elle, remember that he's doing it because he loves you. And it's all right for you to love him back."

It wasn't the first time she'd cried in front of me, but this time her tears made my own throat close in sympathy. Or perhaps I wanted to weep for myself, and not with compassion for her. Either way, when I handed her the box of tissues, I took one for myself, too.

"When does it stop?" she asked, as though I had all the answers.

"I don't know, Elle. I wish I did."

It wasn't the first time I didn't give her the answer she was looking for, but it was the first time I felt I'd failed her.

When did it stop? That was the question of the day. When did the fear go away, when would I stop longing, when would I cease wanting something that was wrong?

It was easy for me to sit in my doctor's chair and counsel Elle not to cheat on her lover, but what right did I have to be so smug? I could give my patients advice but couldn't take it from myself. If I'd been in front of me, I'd have counseled myself to understand that my feelings were normal and natural. That my marriage had undergone tremendous strain and changes because of Adam's disability. That wanting and missing sex was natural and normal, and the desire to be held, to make love…yes, even to fuck, that was normal, too.

I was normal.

But I also would have counseled myself to stop seeing Joe. That the emotional infidelity was as real as if I'd gone to bed with him, and perhaps worse because merely sating a physical need was one thing but the inevitability of what was happening was something else, entirely.

Just because Joe and I never touched didn't mean we weren't having an affair.

I knew it. I didn't want to stop it. Frankly, I couldn't stop it. The first Friday of every month, our lunches, his stories and the relief they gave me were a bright and shining thing in the otherwise gray palette of my existence.

It was wrong, and I didn't want to let it go.

The ringing of my cell phone distracted me from my navel-gazing. I took the call at once, fearful as always it would be from one of Adam's caregivers, telling me there was a problem.

"Sades, it's me."

My sister Katie. She sounded tired. She usually did, now.

"How are you?"

"Fine. Did you get my messages?"

For one shameful moment, I actually thought of blaming Mrs. Lapp on my lack of response, but in the end good morals won out over self-preservation. "Yeah, I did. I'm sorry, I've just been busy."

"Tell me about it. I know what you mean."

I couldn't. She didn't. It was just something she said, not a literal invitation. I made a noncommittal noise.

"What's up, Katie?"

"Oh, the usual. Haven't heard from you in a while, that's all. Thought I'd check in."

That meant she needed to talk. "What's going on?"

Her muffled sigh made me frown. "Oh, the usual. Lily's been driving me crazy and Evan's no better. He's been out of town traveling and just doesn't seem to get that staying home all day with a cranky toddler is not the best way to get me in a good mood. And I'm still feeling sick almost all the time. First trimester sucks."

I made my voice as soothing as I could. "I can imagine."

"I really need a night out." Katie sounded close to tears. "Can you come to the movies with me?"

"I wish I could, but—"

Going to the movies meant juggling Adam's care schedule. It meant staying out late when I had to be up at four in the morning the next day so I had time to get ready myself before helping to get him started on his daily routine. It meant having to put on the happy face for my sister, who had problems of her own and didn't need mine.

"Oh, Sadie, c'mon."

"Katie, I can't. Okay? I just can't."

Her sigh punched my eardrum. "How's Adam?"

"He's fine."

"You have big plans for V-Day?"

I cleared my throat. "Same old thing."

"Are you guys coming over for Dad's birthday?"

"I'll be there." I'd already arranged for Dennis to be available on Saturday for a few hours.

"Just you? Not Adam, too?"

Sisters always know just how to push. "If he wants to, Katie, but I don't know how he'll feel."

She didn't call me on the lie. I already knew Adam wouldn't want to go to my parents' house. He didn't ever want to go anywhere anymore, even though he could.

"I could come over there and watch a movie, if you can't go out. I just need to get out of the house, Sadie, you can't even imagine."

When I didn't reply, she stopped, maybe embarrassed. "Hey, if you can't, that's okay."

A good big sister would have been there for Katie. I wanted to be the good big sister I'd always tried to be, but in the end the thought of it was simply too daunting.

"Maybe next week, okay?"

"Sure. Fine. Whatever. I'll talk to you later."

I wanted to be there for Katie, the way I always had. I wanted to listen to her troubles and offer advice. Make a difference. Do the right thing. I wanted to help her the way I helped my patients, but when it came right down to it, I couldn't. I was afraid.

Not that I couldn't help her, because I was pretty sure she just needed a compassionate ear. I was afraid listening to my sister's woes would prompt me to reveal my own, and I couldn't risk it. Putting a voice to my feelings, saying aloud the thoughts that gnawed daily at my conscience, would make them real in a way I was certain I didn't want them to be.

I'd spent the past four years wearing a brave face, convincing myself by convincing everyone around me that I was fine. That we were fine, Adam and I, as fine was we could be. If I didn't have that façade, I wasn't sure what I would have.

Joe was right. It's easier to keep being what you are, even if the only person who expects you to be it is yourself.

Adam and I didn't share a heart-shaped meatloaf. Mrs. Lapp cooked a pot roast and potatoes in butter and parsley, which I ate in his room with him at a table lit by candlelight. I cut his food into tiny pieces and fed it to him, bite by bite.

"Happy Valentine's Day." His smile was as bright and charming as he could make it. The smile I'd fallen in love with.

I toasted him with champagne in a glass that had been a wedding gift. We talked about our day. About Dennis, who'd left earlier for a big Valentine's Day party at the Rainbow.

"I told him not to bother coming home early." Adam wiggled his eyebrows. "Told him I had big plans."

"Oh, really." I settled back in my chair. Champagne had made me giddy. Lighter. "You think so, huh?"

"Oh, I know so." He looked toward the wardrobe in the corner.

I'd found it at a flea market, covered in dust and cobwebs, the handles broken and the door off its hinges. I'd fixed the door, polished the wood and replaced the broken handles with authentic ones I'd bought from an online auction. It was my favorite piece from our bedroom suite and had once contained my frilly lingerie and pajamas. Now medical supplies filled the drawers.

"Look in there." He jerked his chin, the extent of his ability to gesture.

I got up and crossed to it, giving him a backward glance. "Adam? What did you do?"

"Just look and see."

I opened the door. A box wrapped in red foil waited for me. I lifted it out, my heart thumping as fast as it had the first time he'd handed me such a gift. It was large but not heavy, and a giggle bubbled out of my throat.

"What is it?"

"Open it."

I hesitated, looking toward him. He looked hopeful and a bit mischievous. I'd seen that combination in him before. He'd been on one knee at the time, a much smaller box in his hand.

All at once, I was afraid to open the package, afraid to see what my husband had bought for me. I caressed the smooth wrapping. It felt cool under my fingertips, and slippery.

"Open it, Sadie."

I took the box back to my chair and fussed with the

table, pushing it out of the way so I could sit and hold the box upon my lap. It weighed far heavier on my legs than it had in my hands.

"C'mon."

I couldn't put aside his eagerness any longer. I slid a fingernail beneath the taped edge and the paper fell away. The box under it was plain and white, without markings. I lifted the lid.

"Oh, Adam."

He laughed. "Do you like it?"

I lifted the sheer red fabric and held it to my chest. I wanted to cry but didn't. I forced a dry tone.

"Who'd you buy this for, you or me?"

"Are you kidding? They don't make those in my size." He grinned and raised the bed a bit higher with the remote control. "Stand up. Put it on."

I stood. The baby-doll nightie had thin straps and a pair of matching thong panties. It wasn't something I'd have chosen for myself, but I could see the appeal.

"Where did you get this?" A vision of Adam sending Dennis on the errand heated my cheeks.

"I ordered it online. Dennis wrapped it for me, but don't worry, he didn't see what was in the box. I was worried it might not be what I ordered but I knew you wouldn't want him to check it out."

"Is it what you ordered?" I held it up, turning it from side to side.

"Oh, hell yes."

We hadn't made love in a long time. Nearly a year, as a matter of fact, the last time prompted by Valentine's Day.

It had ended badly, with both of us in tears. I wondered, now, what had prompted this effort and knew it was the man in the store I'd told Adam about.

"Put it on." Adam's voice was hoarse with a familiar longing, and I couldn't deny him.

I'd been naked in front of him thousands of times. In the dark, in the light. He'd seen me change a tampon, use the toilet. Held my hair when I puked. And still, I hesitated to strip out of my clothes in front of him now.

"I'll go into the bathroom." I offered it hesitantly, uncertain, and to my relief he nodded.

"Yes. Do that."

In the bathroom I avoided my reflection as I took off my clothes and laid them neatly on the chair. I held up the lingerie to my bare skin and shivered with sudden, fierce longing. When had I last worn something like this? Garments made to arouse? I favored the practicality of cotton panties and bras, serviceable underwear meant to cover, not entice.

I felt like a virgin again. I slipped the panties, no more than a triangle of lace held together by two straps, up my legs. The thong slipped between my buttocks, an odd but sensual sensation I wasn't sure I liked. The lace covered my pubic hair while the straps crossed my hips, where the bones most definitely didn't jut forth as they had on our wedding night.

"Sadie?"

"I'll be right there!"

I pulled the gown over my head and adjusted the fit. It barely covered my breasts and split in the front to swing open as I moved. The hem hit me mid-thigh but provided no real coverage. The entire outfit had been designed to reveal and enhance, not conceal.

When I looked at last into the mirror, I saw my cheeks had flushed and my eyes sparkled. My nipples had gone tight beneath the nylon, and already the lace between my legs was rub-rubbing in a way that made me shiver.

It's a rare woman who can view herself in an outfit like that and not find flaws, but I wasn't unhappy with what I saw. I was no longer a bride, true, but time hadn't been cruel, either. No children had stretched my stomach and breasts, and diet and exercise had kept me in shape. There was no reason for me not to show my husband my body, displayed in the finery of his gift. Yet it took me a full minute to gather the courage to turn the door handle and step out.

Candlelight is forgiving, but if I'd had any doubts about how Adam would see me they vanished the moment I stepped through the door. His eyes gleamed, and his low whistle of appreciation sent a warm flutter through me. I moved closer to the bed, foolishly shy, and twirled slowly so the material flared out from my hips and thighs.

"You're fucking gorgeous," Adam said.

My heart skipped at his words, so affecting. It had been a long time since he'd written poems praising the arch of my eyebrows and fullness of my lips. "You like it?"

"What do you think?"

In the past, his erection would have let me know how much. Now I had to be satisfied with the curve of his mouth and tone of his voice. I was ashamed to find them poor substitutes, and forced myself not to think about it.

"Come here."

I moved closer to the bed. Déjà vu hit with me with force and I stumbled and had to steady myself. For one moment I'd imagined him reaching for me with such clarity I'd felt his hands on me. Breasts, belly, cunt. I'd felt his kiss on my bare skin, his tongue on my clit.

"Kiss me." Adam's voice was rough. His eyes roamed over my body, touching me in all the places he'd once stroked and licked and nibbled. He looked at the sheer triangle between my thighs, and his eyes gleamed. He licked his mouth.

Always, in our life before, Adam knew what he wanted and how to get it, was never afraid to ask for things I'd have been unable to voice aloud. Adam had liked dirty talk, bedroom games, adventure, all things in which I'd been content to follow but never lead.

I kissed him. Our breath mingled. He stroked my tongue with his, making me gasp. I wanted his hands on me but had to be content with putting mine on him. His shoulder blades jutted forth and I moved my hands to cup his biceps, so still.

Our faces so close, I could almost forget the rest of him had changed. I could pretend it was like the past, when he could lift me with one arm to toss me, laughing, onto our bed where he'd cover me with his body and pull orgasms out of me like pearls on a string, one after the other.

"I want you so much," Adam said.

"You have me."

Something flickered in his dark blue eyes, and I

wondered if he was thinking about the man who'd propositioned me in the store. "Touch yourself for me?"

I had to swallow hard at that request. Masturbation was such a private thing, a solo pleasure. For me, a necessity. Release. It kept me faithful, at least in body.

"Sadie? Will you?"

I nodded and stepped back. My hands went up to cup my breasts. Adam's gaze went there, avid. Bright color had flushed his cheeks. I let my thumbs rub across my nipples, making them hard again.

"I love your breasts."

This was how it had to be, with us. He would make love to me with his words while I acted out his commands, bringing myself the pleasure he couldn't.

"Take them out of the nightgown."

I did, easily enough, for it was made for easy access. I licked my fingertips and pinched my nipples, wetting them. Adam groaned. I did it again, until they glistened and darkened with arousal.

"Yeah, just like that. Stroke them. I love to lick your tits, just like that."

My breath caught at his words. He used to whisper them to me before taking my nipple between his lips and suckling. The memory made my nipples throb, and I rolled them with my fingers until I had to moan, myself.

"I want to taste you, Sadie. Let me see your pussy."

I sat in the chair, my legs spread so wide the panties could no longer cover me. I pushed the scrap of lace to the side, showing him my clit, my cunt, my thighs. His words became his hands and tongue, my hands his cock.

He told me how he wanted to lick me, to suck my clit between his lips and eat me until I screamed. I groaned, spreading myself open to his sight. I licked my fingers and circled my clit, rubbing fast until my hips jerked upward. I pushed a finger inside me, then another, feeling my wetness. The heat. I closed my eyes and lost myself in Adam's voice, in the story he wove of our passion.

"You're so tight and hot," he told me, and he was right.

My cunt closed around my fingers. My hips lifted again. I withdrew and used my slickness on my clit, making the motions smooth. I found a pace I liked, mimicking the way he'd have used his tongue.

"You're so beautiful," he told me, over and over, until I wanted to scream at him to shut up. To stop talking and fuck me. To come with me so hard there would be no breath for speeches.

I came, but alone, and at the last minute it wasn't Adam's face I saw between my legs, but Joe's. I cried out, the noise of passion not so different from despair, and was ashamed the pleasure ripping through me was made no less because of my guilt.

I kissed him when I could breathe again, and we smiled at one another. I nuzzled his neck, the way I used to, and peppered kisses all over his face. Our embrace was no less because only I could make it.

I love you.

Words that used to slip from my lips without thought now stuck in my throat. At times like this, when he was being soft and warm, I could almost believe this was all working the way it should. That tomorrow would be better than yesterday and we'd move past this pit stretching deeper and wider between us every day.

I'd always wondered why people who'd throw away an appliance that had ceased to function would hang on to a marriage that no longer worked. Next to my husband, the only man I'd ever loved, ever made love with, ever slept beside, I thought I knew.

Hope.

Chapter 05

March

This month my name is Brandy, and I giggle a lot. This annoys Joe, but he pretends it doesn't because he wants to get laid. I also snap my gum while we're talking, unaware this makes him want to scream. You wouldn't know it by the way he smiles. All teeth.

I met Joe a while ago in the coffee shop where I work. He comes in a few times a week for coffee and muffins for his office. The other girls and I giggle about him all the time, because he's so cute. A businessman. I have a thing for businessmen, all buttoned up in their suits and ties. I like to think about what they look like under all those clothes.

He asks me out, not for coffee, thank god, though you'd be surprised how many assholes do. What, I work in a coffee shop, you think I don't like to do anything else?

No, Joe asks me out someplace real nice, a real fancy place with tablecloths and flowers and, like, waiters who describe the specials with all these fancy words like they're reading a play.

I borrowed a dress from Cyndi, the girl I work with. She's way jealous Joe asked me out, but that's cool because she's got a boyfriend anyway so she can't really go out with Joe even if he did ask, which he didn't because he asked me, instead. Brandy.

"Like the song?" He asks when the waiter's gone with our orders.

"Huh?" I never heard of a song called Brandy, though I do know it's a kind of booze.

"Never mind." Joe doesn't seem to talk much, which is cool, because I talk enough for both of us.

I tell him all about the classes I'm taking, and he seems really interested that I'm studying communications. I want to be an anchorperson on the news someday, but, like, it's totally cool if I have to be the weather girl first because everyone has to start somewhere. Joe nods at this, like he totally gets it, and I'm glad because my last date just tuned me out and tried to get into my pants right away, if you can believe it. Like I'd just put out, just like that. I work in a coffee shop. I'm not a prostitute.

Joe listens to me all through dinner, which is awesome, real linguine and clam sauce. I ask him if he wants some but he just shakes his head and says he doesn't eat shellfish. That's fine, because he doesn't mind if I nibble at his dinner. I mean, maybe I should have asked before sneaking a bite, but then he says don't worry, go ahead and finish it if I want, he's done.

Well, hey, I'm not about to pass that up. I don't make

much working in the coffee shop and college is a real bitch to pay for. Linguine beats the hell out of ramen noodles.

"It's nice to see a girl who eats." Joe settles back with his glass of wine, watching me, and I pause.

I figure he's making fun of me, maybe, because I know I could lose a few pounds. I straighten my back to make sure there aren't any rolls showing over my belt and I push my boobs forward. When the waiter asks if we want any dessert, I'm dying to dive into a piece of chocolate lava cake, but I say no, thanks.

"You're sure?" Joe lifts one perfect, golden eyebrow, and my whole body feels gooey and warm. He's so cute. "We could share a piece."

Sharing's okay, so I tell him that's great. His grin is like looking at sunshine. I melt a little more. God, he's hot. And sweet. And a really, really good listener. He's the nicest guy I've been out with in, like, forever.

The waiter brings our chocolate cake and two forks, but Joe pushes the plate more toward me. I love that he's a gentleman, letting me take the first bite. All of the bites, actually.

He watches me eat. His eyes follow the fork from the plate to my mouth and stay there. I lick my lips, afraid I've smeared them with chocolate. My heart's beating a little faster with all the attention he's paying me, and I'm not sure what to think of it. He's looking at my lips as if he might want to eat them instead of the cake. My thighs quiver at the thought.

I wouldn't mind if Joe wanted to lick away the chocolate from my lips. That'd be super hot. It's been a long time since a guy kissed me, nearly a month. I made out with someone from my Comm Media class down at the Hardware Bar, but that's all. He wanted more, and, like, I'm cool with the whole friend with benefits thing. It's just that you've got to be friends first, and I barely knew him.

By now I've finished all the cake and Joe's only licked up the whipped cream. He eats the strawberry, too. It's my turn to watch his mouth work. I watch the way his tongue licks the cream off the berry's pointed end and I imagine he's licking me, instead. This time, my clit pulses and I shiver.

"Are you ready to go?"

I'm not. I'd really like to sit here with Joe for a few more hours. I don't want our date to be over, not when I'm having such a good time.

It's not like I can say that, right? I nod. "If you want."

I still hope he'll say, "let's have another drink, Brandy, 'cuz I'm having so much fun I don't want to leave." But, of course, a smooth guy like Joe doesn't say stuff like that. He might look as yummy as a movie star, but this isn't the movies.

He helps me with my jacket and when his hands stroke my shoulders, I want to throw myself into his arms and attack his mouth, right there. I hold off, though, because this is a real classy place, and besides, I don't want Joe to think I'm easy.

He listens to me talk some more on the drive back to my place. I've never been with a guy who listens like Joe does, and I know he's really paying attention because every so often he makes a little noise and nods his head. I give him directions to my apartment building. When we pull up in front, I look up to see if the lights are on in the front room. It's dark, which means my roommate isn't home yet. I really, really, really don't want this night to end. It's been so perfect, from the way he held the door for me to the way he picked up the tab without a second thought.

So I invite Joe inside.

For a second I'm sure he's going to say no. His face has that look guys get when they're trying hard to think of an excuse to turn you down. But then he smiles at me again, until I'm like, a puddle of goo on the front seat of his car.

"Sure," Joe says. "That sounds nice."

Will he think it's nice when I jump on top of him and shag him silly? That's what I wonder when I lead him inside and show him where to hang up his coat. I hang mine, too, and I'm turning to ask him if he wants something to drink when the sight of him dries up every single word I meant to say.

He's taken off his suit jacket. His shirt is pink. Damn, that is hott with two freaking t's. Dark pink oxford shirt with a deep maroon tie. His pants and jacket are charcoal grey with the hottest pin stripes I hadn't noticed in the restaurant's dim lighting. He's watching me gape like the biggest dork ever as he tugs his tie loose from his throat and unbuttons the top button of his shirt, and so I recover real fast and pretend I had something in my throat to clear it.

"Want something to drink?" I squeak and my cheeks like, catch totally on fire. Joe doesn't seem to really notice, or maybe he's such a gentleman he pretends he doesn't.

Either way, his smile fills me up like someone pumped me full of helium. I want to float up to the ceiling from that smile.

"Just water."

I've seen him drink coffee, sometimes tea, a glass of wine with dinner. Now, water. I don't have any bottled water and I'm a little ashamed, but he says tap water's fine, and can he have some ice?

I have ice. I have some limes and lemons, too. They've been in the fridge for, like, ever, and they're actually my roommate Susie's but she won't care if I use them. I slice them into quarters and Joe takes a slice of each for his glass. I do, too. It tastes good, but then I get a full-on taste of lemon and it makes my mouth twist.

Joe laughs. "Sour?"

I realize he's moved pretty close to me. He smells as good as he looks, which I've already noticed is pretty damn delicious. In fact, he smells better. It's not Drakkar or Polo but something else, I'm not really sure what. So I ask him.

Joe laughs again and puts his glass on the counter. He leans against it, one foot crossed over the other. Even his shoes are pretty and I realize I've never asked him what he does. I don't really know anything about him, even though I've told him plenty about me.

"Soap and water."

"You don't wear cologne?"

Joe shakes his head and passes a hand over his face. "Irritates my skin."

He's got my hand in his before I can think about it, and

he passes it down his cheek. His skin is warm and smooth, but I can feel a hint of bristle waiting to come out. His hair's the color of the butterscotch cake we sell at the coffee shop. His eyebrows, too, which are bushy but perfectly shaped at the same time. The bristles on his chin faintly scratch my palm.

"That would be bad," I say. "Irritated skin, I mean."

I want him to kiss me. I want it so bad I'm already tipping my face up toward his. He's not that tall, maybe not quite six feet, and I don't have to get on tip-toe to reach his mouth.

He lets me kiss him. I say lets me because he doesn't move away, but he doesn't pull me closer, either. I'm used to guys diving down the back of my throat with their tongues right away, but this kiss is sweet. Our mouths don't even open.

I pull away, giddy at the taste of his lips and fear I've just made an ass out of myself again. Joe's smile gives me confidence. He doesn't look mad or anything.

"Brandy," Joe says. "You're a very nice girl."

I groan and roll my eyes. "But…?"

"But nothing." He shrugs.

"But you don't want to kiss me?" I have to ask, even though I'm sure the answer will disappoint me.

It doesn't. "There are lots of places to kiss you."

Whoa. Hot. Hot, hot, hot. I'm suddenly so hot I have to fan my face with my hand. A flurry of giggles burst out of me like bubbles. Joe smiles and puts his hands on my hips.

"Why don't you take me into your bedroom?"

I'm more than willing to do that, all thoughts of him thinking I'm easy flying right out of my head. Joe doesn't make me feel as if I'm being easy when he takes my hand and pushes open the door to my tiny bedroom. Joe makes me forget I've vowed to be more than a random drunken hookup or a friend with benefits.

I'm really glad I cleaned up in here before I brought Joe home. I got the small bedroom because Susie's the one who signed the lease first. The bed takes up most of the space, with just a few inches to walk around it, but Joe's there to do the horizontal boogaloo, not the cha-cha. We don't need anything but the bed.

We stand at the foot of it. His hands go to my hips again. I put my hands on the front of his shirt, which feels smooth under my fingertips. I pull on his tie, undo the knot, slip it free. I undo the next few buttons of his shirt while he stands there. I don't look up at his face. I concentrate on his body. I pull his shirt from his waistband, finish unbuttoning it, fold it open.

I run my hands over his chest. The hair there's a little darker than butterscotch, more like…caramel. Suddenly, I'm shivering, and I lean forward to kiss his chest. The hairs tickle my cheeks and I close my eyes to breathe in his scent. Soap and water never smelled so good.

When I look up at him a second later, he's smiling. I love that smile, how it spreads across his face and wrinkles the corners of his eyes. It makes his top lip disappear and when it gets bigger, I catch a glimpse of straight, white teeth.

I help him off with his shirt. He stands, wearing only his pants. I want to lick him all over, gobble him up as if he's a cinnamon roll. That's what he reminds me of. A piece of golden pastry. He looks delicious and I give in to the temptation. I lean forward and lick his chest. His heart beats under my tongue. I want to make it beat faster. I want to make him sweat and moan. I want to make him jerk and cry out. I want to make Joe come.

Joe pushes my shoulder gently until I stand up straight, and then we're sinking slowly onto my bed. He's kissing my throat while his hands slide up from my hips to my chest. My head hits the pile of stuffed animals and pillows and I reach up to toss them aside so we have more room.

I'm a bigger girl, but Joe made me feel like he's all over me. In a good way. Like a guy should be all over a girl, be bigger than her. He covers me with his body as his hands and mouth roam.

I expect him to take my clothes off right away, to get right down to business, totally like guys my age. Joe doesn't seem in a hurry. He kisses my throat and shoulder as he rubs my boobs through my shirt. He unbuttons my shirt slowly, one button at a time, moving his mouth lower and lower as he does.

He kisses the tops of my breasts, then hooks his finger into the catch at the back of my bra and tugs it. I hold my breath when it opens and he peels away the lace. I really want him to like my body.

When he sucks my nipple, I can't stop the little moan. He's so good. He knows how to flick his tongue over it, then suck so sweet and soft. Some guys latch on as though they're trying to breastfeed, but not Joe. He mouths my nipples, one then the other, moving on and off until I can't stay still beneath him and have to squirm.

He pauses long enough to help me out of my shirt and bra, then pushes me gently back against the pillows. He looks me over again the way he'd watched me eat the cake.

Everything inside me is hot and liquid from the way he's been sucking on my nipples. I feel shivery all over, too, when he touches me. The feelings echo between my legs. I'm wet, my panties damp and rubbing my swollen clit.

Joe puts a hand to his belt. I get up on my elbows to watch him unbuckle it. When he opens the button of his pants, I catch myself licking my lips. I look up, and he's watching me.

"You sure about this, Brandy?"

Whoa. He's asking me? No guy bothers to ask, not once we've gotten this far.

"Yeah, Joe, I'm sure."

I'm more than sure. I'm aching for it. Susie told me how she gets when her boyfriend goes away, how she gets so horny her pussy feels like it's crying. I've never really understood what that means. I mean, I know what it's like to be horny, but I've never really felt my body crave cock like it did when Joe pushed his pants down over his hips.

He gets naked real easy, too, and why not? He has nothing to be ashamed of. His body's just as nice bare as it is dressed. He's lean, but muscled. Thick hair covers his legs, makes a nest for his cock, spreads up his belly to surround his nipples. More hair covers his forearms. I've never liked hair on a man before, but then…well, I'd only ever really been with guys before. Joe's a man. All man.

Intimidated, I hesitate with my hands on the elastic waist of my skirt. It's fine for him to strip out of his clothes; he looks like something out of a fashion magazine. Me, on the other hand…

"C'mon, Brandy," Joe urges, his voice low. "Don't be shy."

Hell, fine, okay. I push down my skirt and lay back, hella glad I put on my good panties for this date. They're pretty and lacey and cover most of the bulges without looking like granny panties.

Joe kneels by my shins and slides his hands up my thighs. His hands have long fingers without calluses. His nails, blunt and square, scratch lightly at my skin. My thighs, when my legs are closed, have no space between them, but his thumbs part me like a knife slicing cream cheese. He opens me slowly, carefully, leaving me no room to resist.

His hands smooth over my legs, catching me just behind the knees and bending them a little. His smile reassures me. My heart pounds so fast I feel it in my eardrums, in the base of my throat and my wrists. Especially between my legs.

He lifted my foot and turned his head to kiss my ankle. His mouth leaves a wet spot. My hips lift in response, but he doesn't look away from my leg. Ankle, shin, knee. By the time he gets to my thigh he's on his hand and knees. His mouth moves higher and his body stretches out on the bed. By the time he gets to my pussy he's laying between my legs and I'm holding my breath.

He props himself on his forearm and uses a finger to

rub the front of my panties. Up and down, over the bump of my clit and down lower. The lace is wet, it has to be. It presses my pussy, the thin band of fabric narrowing as I shift. I can't look down at him now. I have to throw my head back, close my eyes. Joe traces a finger along the material between my legs. He strokes my skin, then hooks his finger under the edge of my panties and pulls them down. I moan again. He's looking at me down there, at my pussy. I might fight with my weight and worry about my ass and thighs and belly, but my pussy is always what it is.

I tense, waiting, breathless. Joe's tongue flicks along my belly. I think of how he'd licked the cream off the strawberry and my thighs open wider, inviting him.

He doesn't lick me, though. He uses his fingertip, wet from his mouth, and at first I'm disappointed. A few seconds later, though—and it's so good, better than anything I've ever had before—I'm moaning and jerking, like, in five minutes.

Sometimes when I play with myself I can come real fast, but it's usually so much harder with guys. They don't ever really seem to know what they're doing. They're too fast, too slow, too hard, too soft. I mean, they try real hard and stuff, but mostly they don't want to take the time to really figure out how to get me off. Guys watch too many pornos where all the dude has to do is give a couple rubs and the girl's ready to come. In real life it takes a lot more than that.

Joe's not having any trouble. His hands move up and down my thighs, tickling my pussy lips and even back toward my ass. I don't have time to be thinking about anything but how good he's making me feel. I want to come so bad I can't think of anything else, and I think it can't get any better until he puts his fingers inside me.

I totally can't stand it. My body shakes. I toss my head back and forth and arch my back, crying out his name. I don't care who hears me, not even if Susie has come home. I can't be quiet.

The pressure in my pussy builds up and up. My toes curl, digging into the bed, and I push myself against his hand. I think he puts a third finger in me. I'm coming. Everything pulls in tight like a fist closing. Then I explode.

It takes me a minute to catch my breath. I look down. Joe's rolled onto his side, one hand on my thigh. His eyes are closed. I can't tell what he's thinking.

"Joe?" I sound hesitant, but it's just I'm not really sure I can talk.

He cracks open an eye and tilts his head to look at me. "Yeah?"

"Wow." I lick my mouth, not sure what to say.

That smile again. Super yummo. I was afraid I'd be embarrassed after that, but I'm not. I can't be anything but, like, totally just…whoa.

"Good?" He asks me. His hand rubs my thigh, up and down.

"Yeah, really good." I push up on my hands. "I want…I want to make you feel good."

His smile lifts more on one side than the other. "Good."

He moves without hurrying, getting on his knees. His cock isn't hard, and that worries me. Maybe I'm not turning him on. I mean, I've never been naked with a guy who wasn't hard. I've never really even seen a soft dick before, not up close. Not that Joe's cock is soft, really, it's sort of in between.

I sit up. Does he want me to suck him a little bit? I wouldn't mind. Joe strokes himself and I watch, fascinated, as his dick gets longer and stiffer. His thighs and butt are lighter than the rest of him, but his prick is a cool pinkish color that gets darker as he strokes it.

He asks me why I'm staring, and I have to tell him the truth. I haven't really seen a lot of dicks up close. His mouth twists again when I say this, one side going up and the other going down, like he's not sure if he wants to laugh at me or not.

"I mean, I've totally seen a few," I say, backtracking hastily. "Just…"

"Not up close. I get it." Joe's hand moves up and down along his cock and that sight is getting me turned on again. He's so easy with himself, it's not embarrassing at all.

None of it is, actually, which is totally cool, because usually I'm, like, nervous being naked because I'm not small and skinny. But with Joe, I don't feel like the bulges matter as much. Maybe because he's not staring, he's just…looking.

"I haven't been with a ton of guys," I tell him. I know it's nothing to be ashamed of. I mean, it's actually something to boast about, you know, because lots of girls my age are total skanks and just, like fuck any guy who wants them.

"That's all right." He says it like it doesn't matter to him, one way or the other.

He keeps stroking his dick, and I can't tear my gaze away. His forearms are so fucking sexy, I can't stand it. Every time he twists his wrists the cords stand out in his forearms and I want to lick them the same way I wanted to lick his chest earlier.

Joe moves to sit with his back against the wall, since my bed's on a Hollywood frame and I have no headboard. He opens his legs and pumps his dick in his fist. Now it's really hard. I can see his veins. It's a lot bigger, too, and I'm kind of scared to think that could fit inside me. But I want it to fit inside me.

"Come here, Brandy."

I move a little closer to him. Joe takes his hand away from his dick. It stands up, bobbing a little, and I bite my lips against a smile.

"Here's your chance to have a look."

I look up at his face, fast, trying to see if he's making fun. He is smiling, but in a nice way. He leans back and puts his hands on his thighs.

He's all mine. Whoa. Hotness. I move closer on the bed and there's really nothing to be shy about. In the porn movies, dicks are always these huge, purple, disgusting things. Joe's isn't like that. It matches the rest of him. Looking at it, I want to touch it and taste it. I want to see if I can make him feel good, too.

He puts his hand on the top of my head when I move closer and put him in my mouth. I go too far at first and choke a little. He doesn't push into me right away, which is totally great. I suck him a little. The skin on his dick feels thin and it moves up and down when I do. Underneath it's hard, but not like metal or anything. It's got a little bend to it, too, which I discover when he makes a noise.

"Sorry." My cheeks are hot, but Joe only shakes his head.

"Like you're sucking a popsicle," he tells me. "Up and down, with a little extra at the tip."

I never had a guy give me pointers before, and I'm worried that I suck…at sucking. So the next time I go down on him, I concentrate on pretending his dick's a popsicle. Cherry, 'cuz that's my favorite. He doesn't taste like a cherry popsicle, he's more like spicy and tangy. It's still good, though.

I must be doing all right because Joe starts to pump his hips into my mouth a little. I choke again and pull off. I move like I'm going to get on top of him, thinking it would be better to just let him fuck me, but Joe stops me.

He looks into my eyes. "Brandy. Put your hand around the bottom of my cock and use that to guide it in and out of your mouth. That way, if I thrust too hard, you can keep me from gagging you. And it feels good for me, too."

This feels like a lesson all of a sudden but he says it in such a way I can't really do anything but nod. I do what he says and wrap my fingers around his dick before I slide it into my mouth. He's right, it does give me more control over it. Even when he lifts his hips, I can keep him from pushing in too far.

Hey, being able to keep him from sticking his dick in too far makes me actually like sucking it. I'm not afraid he's going to gag me. And listening to him moan is a real turn-on.

"Use your other hand on my balls."

I never had a guy talk to me like that, and I want to giggle. I do giggle, but I do what he says. They're soft and warm, covered in hair. I hold them like eggs. He likes it, I can tell, because his dick pulses in my mouth and his breathing gets faster.

Joe gathers my hair at the base of my neck to keep it out of my face. It's totally nice of him to do that. I suck him harder and faster, and when I start to use my hand at the same time he really lets out a groan.

The hand not holding back my hair ends up between my legs, and I move a little so it's easier for him to reach my pussy. Facing away from him, I can also take him deeper inside my mouth, and I'm not afraid to do it now that I know how.

I'm on my knees, a hand on his dick and one on his balls, using my mouth to suck him off. Joe's got his hand on the back of my neck and the other stroking my clit again. He pinches and rolls it, and my hips jerk. I have to rock against his hand, hard, it's like my body's taken over. I suck him faster and hump his hand. I'm moving all over the place, this feels so good. Everything's wet. My pussy's dripping, his dick and my hand slide in my spit. I try real hard to remember his dick's supposed to be a popsicle, but with his thumb rubbing my clit I really can't think of anything but that.

We're both moving. I try to match him but my body's shaking. I'm coming again. Whoa, I never had two orgasms before. I suck down, hard and Joe lets out a groan. He pulls my hair hard enough to pull my mouth mostly off his dick, and when he does that, he comes. His dick gets huge in my mouth and I can feel it squirting. I'm stunned as his jizz fills my mouth, and I swallow it before I really know what I'm doing. I pop my lips off his dick with a sound. My pussy's still humping against his hand and another wave of orgasm rolls over me, smaller, but still awesome.

Whoa. Joe just jacked off in my mouth and I didn't puke. He made me come three times. My pussy's leaked all over my legs and his crotch is wet with my spit and the last drops of come that missed my mouth. I think I'm in love.

"Wow." I roll off him and onto my back, my arms and legs loose and floppy. His knees are next to my face, but my hair's covering them.

I think I might fall asleep like that, I'm so busted. Joe doesn't move either for a couple minutes. When he does, it's to push my leg off his chest.

I sit up. "You are so not like any guy I've ever been with."

His eyes are closed, and he doesn't open them to answer. "Is that good?"

"It's great!" A giggle bursts out of me and I curl up next to him. I just want to touch him all over. I want to attach myself to him. "You're so not a dude."

He cracks open an eye and tilts his head to look down at me. "I'm not a...dude?"

I shake my head. "You're not a boy, I mean."

He shifts a little out from under me. "I guess I'm not."

I sigh happily and put my head back on his shoulder. I can't get close enough to him. I throw an arm over his chest and he makes a small sound, like "oof!"

"I'm real glad you asked me out tonight, Joe."

He sort of goes "uh huh," and we're quiet for a few minutes. I'm getting a little cold, but I don't want to get up just yet. I'm full of what I've heard Susie call "afterglow," which I never understood until now.

"Man, this is what really great sex feels like."

Joe shifts a bit again. "Glad I could oblige."

I push up on my elbow to put my head in my hand and look at him. I chew my lower lip for a second until I figure it can't hurt to ask. "Was I okay?"

"Yes, Brandy," Joe says, his eyes closed again. "You were okay."

"Just…okay?"

He doesn't open his eyes, but he does smile. "You were good."

That makes me feel all warm and fuzzy. I've had a couple guys tell me I'm good before, but coming from Joe it seems more of a compliment. Even though he was giving me tips and stuff, he still thought I was good.

"You must've been with lots of women."

He's quiet for a second. "Depends on what you think is a lot."

"More than I've been with guys, I mean."

This makes him look at me. "I'm older than you, Brandy."

Yeah, I knew that. "How old are you?"

Not that I care, really. I rub my fingers through his chest hair until he puts his hand over mine to stop it. Joe rubs his forehead a little, as if he's getting a headache.

"I'm going to be thirty-five."

"Whoa!" I hadn't meant to sound so surprised, but it slips out. "I thought you were, like, twenty-seven or so."

"I'm not."

I sit up. "Whoa."

Joe sits up, too, and there's a space between us that wasn't there a minute ago. "Why 'whoa?'"

I shrug. "You're, like, twelve years older than I am, that's all."

I don't know why he looks so annoyed by that. It's not like I ever pretended I was older or something. I mean, what did he expect? I work in a coffee shop and go to college, how old did he think I could be?

"Is that a problem?" I ask as he swings his legs over the side of the bed.

"No, don't worry about it."

I don't need a degree in advanced rocket science to figure out he's leaving. "So…how come you're leaving?"

He looks over his shoulder at me. "I have to work in the morning, Brandy."

"Oh." I don't want my voice to sound small and hurt, but it comes out that way. "But…you'll call me, right?"

The second it's out of my mouth I wish I hadn't said it. I can tell by the way he hesitates that he's going to say no, or say yes but be lying. I'd rather he didn't lie.

"I don't think so."

That's not a yes or a no, and I'm not sure what to think. "Is it because I'm fat?"

Joe whirls, face shocked. "Brandy, no! You're not fat."

He reaches out to push my hair off over my shoulders, and I believe he means it.

"Is it because you think I'm a slut?"

Joe sighs, real heavy, and rubs his forehead again. "I don't think you're a slut."

I frown. "Are you sure?"

"Yes. I'm sure." He turns his body to face me. "You're not fat, and you're not a slut. You're a nice girl and we had a good time tonight. Going to bed with me doesn't make you a slut, okay? I hate it when girls think that."

"You do?" The way he says it makes me think he's been with lots and lots of girls. Jealousy's bubbles aren't nearly as nice as giggles.

"Yeah, I do. There's nothing wrong with two people having a good time together in bed, as long as they're both careful and they both want to do it."

He sounds like he's trying to convince himself instead of me. We stare at each other for a minute. I don't know what to think. A little while ago I was sure he was going to be my next boyfriend, but now I'm not sure I ever want to see him again. Joe seems complicated. Maybe it's because he's old.

"Well then," I ask him, "what is it?"

"You're young," says Joe, as if that makes sense, even though it doesn't.

"Huh?"

He sighs again and gets up to start putting on his clothes. "You're young, Brandy. Really young."

"I'm…I'm young?" I think I should be pissed off.

"Really young."

I get the feeling he doesn't just mean my age. "Well, you're old!"

He's got his clothes on now, though nothing's buttoned or zipped, and he's got his tie clutched in one hand like it's a snake he's trying to choke. Joe runs a hand through his hair. I've never seen him look so rumpled.

"No hard feelings?" He asks.

"No. I guess not."

What else can I say? I can diet and exercise to shrink my ass and I can keep my legs closed, but I can't make myself any older than I am.

Joe leans over to kiss my forehead. "See you, Brandy."

He lets himself out of my bedroom, and a few moments later I hear the front door slam. I go to my window and watch him drive away. The next time I see him at the coffee shop, I make Cyndi wait on him and I pretend I don't see him.

Joe looked pensive. We ate and drank in mutual silence for a few minutes. I didn't have anything to say about what he'd told me.

"It was like getting a blow job from a puppy," he said finally. "All slobber and gobbling and wriggling around."

I burst into laughter, though I felt bad for poor Brandy. "Oh, Joe."

He gave me a sly smile. "It's true. She was…"

"Young," I finished for him. "She sounded young."

He toyed with his drink. "Yeah. She was."

"Maybe you shouldn't go out with girls in college," I ventured. "If it bothers you."

He looked up at me, one brow raised. "It doesn't. At least, it didn't."

It wasn't quite warm enough to eat outside, but in the atrium, the sun beating down through the glass was brutal. Everything seemed moist and sticky, but also some-how…waiting. The plants seemed to know spring was coming. Maybe they waited for it the way children wait for Christmas. I took a long drink from my bottle of water, but sweat still pearled in my hairline and trickled down the knobs of my spine to tickle the crack in my buttocks.

I don't know what to think. I'm never really sure half the things Joe tells me are true. I certainly know my own imagination provides details I can't know, things he can't know, either. Our lunches are absolutely about fulfilling fantasies, and if Joe's lying to me about the women he fucks, I'm not sure I want to know.

There's a lot about Joe I do know. He doesn't like to share food or drink, or kiss on the mouth. He lost his virginity to his mother's best friend. He has expensive taste. I know where he went to high school. We shield ourselves with stories of the past because revealing the present would be too intimate.

I know everything and nothing about him all at the same time.

"But it bothers you now?"

I looked at him. He studied his hands. The cuffs of his shirt, a dark pink, like the petals of a Stargazer Lily, peeked out from the edges of his dark suit.

"Yeah."

"Why?

"Hey, even ice cream tastes bad after a while if that's all you eat."

"Oh, Joe." For a couple hours, every month, he made it easy for me to be a woman who could laugh. "Don't tell me you're becoming more discriminating in your old age."

Joe tipped his face to the bright sunlight streaming through the windows. I admired his profile when he wasn't looking at me. He'd had a haircut, and he looked shorn. His ears protruded endearingly. The nape of his neck looked vulnerable. I caught a glimpse of silver in the gold of his hair, which seemed darker in its shorter state.

"D'you think I'm old?" He asked me.

"If you are, I'm ancient."

He looked at me with one eye squinted shut against the brightness. "Oh, you're a real grandma."

His story had revealed his age to me, something I hadn't known before. One more piece of Joe for me to ponder over. I wished he'd been older, or younger, but we were almost exactly the same age.

"When's your birthday?" he asked suddenly.

I didn't want to tell him. It betrayed our unspoken agreement not to discuss the now, only the then. But a birthday was then, wasn't it? Even if it was also now? I'd been born in the then, in the past we could talk about.

"April nineteenth. I'll be thirty-five, too."

Joe snorted. "So you are older than me."

I laughed at that, too. "Thanks."

"My birthday is April twenty-fourth."

We both stared. Heat rose in my cheeks. Along my throat. Even into my fingers, which busied themselves with crumpling my trash.

"So…" I said slowly. "What do you suppose that means?"

"It means," Joe said, leaning infinitesimally closer, "you're not young."

The clatter of heels on the slate floor sent us apart like rubber bands stretched to snapping. The couple rounding the corner was laughing and didn't stop when they saw us, but the moment had passed.

Joe got up and threw away his trash, then held out his hands for garbage. I let him take it. He put it in the can while I fussed with an imaginary problem in my purse.

I heard more laughter, and when I looked up, he'd already gone.

*M*ost people I knew relished the weekends and dreaded Monday's return to work. I was just the opposite. My weekends were harder than anything I ever had to do during the week. On days when other people looked forward to sleeping in, I woke, bleary-eyed from regularly interrupted sleep to take care of Adam. I couldn't go anywhere or do anything without making arrangements for someone to be there to care for him—and, much like parents of young children who most often felt that the effort of arranging for childcare made the pleasure of going out to dinner and a movie not worth taking, I just grew accustomed to staying home. It wasn't solely the inconvenience, it was the expense. With our combined salaries and the carefully invested money from the settlement granted by the ski boot company, our lives were much easier, financially, than many others of spinal cord injury patients. We were lucky. But even with all that, finding someone to stay with Adam on weekends was more effort and money than I generally cared to spend.

Another Friday night and I was already yawning when Dennis rapped on the door. He waited until Adam called out for him to enter. That politeness, the willingness to grant Adam the courtesy of waiting until he was ready, was but one of the qualities that endeared Dennis to me.

"I'm heading out, guys, but I'll be around tomorrow when you're ready to go, Sadie."

"Thanks." I smiled at him. "You look very dapper."

He did, in a clean white shirt and dark trousers. His arm muscles bulged under the fabric. His shoes gleamed, and I knew he'd spit-polished them.

"Hot date tonight?" Adam's chair is chin-operated, and now he turned it to face Dennis.

It was funny to see such a large man blushing. "Yeah. Sort of. You ready for bed?"

"Sadie?"

I'd been covering my yawn with the back of my hand, and I smiled a little guiltily. "I think we're just going to watch a few movies, Dennis, so sure, if you could help me…"

"Be happy to." Dennis is always happy to help.

Together we maneuvered Adam from his chair into bed and Dennis did a last check of all the vital and important facets of Adam's existence. I appreciated his concern. I could do everything he'd just done, but by doing it for me, Dennis allowed me to be Adam's wife, not his nurse. It was a small gesture, one I doubt anyone outside of the situation would have noticed.

"You didn't answer my question." Adam reigned from his place in the special bed that adjusted to nearly any position and allowed his body to be moved easily to prevent sores. "Hot date, or not? Sort of isn't an answer, man."

Dennis gave me a look, but I could only shrug and laugh. "You'd better tell him. He won't let up until you do."

"Yeah, I have a hot date." Dennis made a show of arranging Adam's blankets. "With Henry."

"Henry? The guy from the gym?"

"No, that's Alan. Henry's the one from the coffee shop."

"Would you listen to this guy?" Adam's laugh drew my attention. "Don Juan."

Dennis shook his head. "Not true, man. Not true."

They laughed some more. I'm sure they didn't mean to exclude me. I watched their conversation without a clue about who they were discussing. It was silly to be jealous of my husband's caregiver, especially when I didn't envy the tasks he performed with such ease. I envied that at any moment, at his whim, he could leave. I imagined it would have been simple for me, too, to put on a cheery face and work at making Adam happy if it was just a job to me, instead of the rest of my life. Except that was being unfair to Dennis, who never made us feel as though caring for Adam was just a job.

"Have a good time, Dennis," was my advice.

"Be careful," came from Adam.

"I'll be back tomorrow," Dennis said and gave Adam a casual flip of the bird when he hooted something lewd. "Yeah, yeah, man. Whatever."

Then he was gone, leaving us to our rather bland Friday

night. I changed into sweats and a T-shirt while Adam indulged in some mindless TV. I tidied up the room, putting away his computer desk and moving the wheelchair out of the way so I wouldn't stub my toes on it if I needed to go to the bathroom in the night. On the weekends I slept on the oversized recliner Dennis used at night. We'd talked about getting a cot but somehow never had.

"I hope Dennis has a good time tonight," I said after a while.

"He will. I've been telling him to ask the guy out."

I settled into the recliner. "I didn't even know he was interested in anyone."

Some celebrity gossip show had stolen Adam's attention. "Yeah. He is."

"Oh."

It took him a second, but he looked at me. "Oh?"

I shrugged, pretending interest in my ever-present knitting bag. I never worked more than a few rows, but I always had it. I looked up to see Adam staring. "What?"

"We talk about it, sometimes," he said, almost defensively. "Is that a problem?"

"Of course not. I just didn't know, that's all."

His face creased. "Sometimes I can't sleep. Dennis is there."

When you're not.

He didn't say it, but that's what I heard. I put my eyes back on my sad excuse for a scarf. The droning of the television buzzed in my ears.

I never forgot that, while I went out into the world and

talked to people almost every day, even something as mundane as going to the grocery story was an adventure of epic proportions for Adam. Telephone and email conversations were not the same as face-to-face interaction. For a man who'd thrived on social contact, his isolation was harsh and not made better with knowing it was largely self-induced. Adam had decided the effort of getting ready, and the discomfort he most often felt when out of his environment, wasn't worth the effort. He got angry when I tried convincing him otherwise, so I'd stopped trying.

It's easy to learn who your real friends are after an accident like Adam's. There were those who visited, and those who didn't. Who was I to begrudge him a friendship with Dennis?

"Debbie sent me some pictures of the girls." Adam pointed with his gaze toward the desk where the mail lay in scattered piles. "She's thinking of coming out for a visit."

"Sounds great." I forced more enthusiasm than I felt. Adam's sister and her kids were a handful and not the best houseguests. Not only did a visit mean I'd lose what little privacy I had already, but I'd be expected to entertain them, too.

"Maybe next month?"

He sounded so hopeful I couldn't bear to tell him no. After all, it was his sister and nieces. Since we couldn't visit them, they had to come here. I understood it. I just didn't feel like dealing with all the hassle of preparing for and cleaning up after them. Mrs. Lapp took most of the burden off me in that respect, but while they were here I'd be expected to entertain and occupy them. Adam's sister was high maintenance, her kids as much so. It would have been nice if she'd come to spell me in Adam's care, give me a bit of a break, but she didn't. She'd sit with him for an hour while her kids ran rampant in my house, but she wouldn't stay with him for an evening while I went to the movies.

"She said maybe my mom would come with her."

There was no way I could feign enthusiasm for that, and Adam knew it. I said nothing. Adam's mother had no compunctions about advising me on everything from the temperature of his shower to how small to cut his meat, but she didn't lift a finger to actually help out when she's here. Once, exhausted from a night of interrupted sleep and a small medical crisis, I'd confronted Alice Danning about her constant "advice."

Affronted, she'd drawn herself up with a sniff. "I guess I know what's best for him, Sadie. I am his mother, after all. If you had children, you'd understand. A mother never stops knowing what her children need."

I wasn't so sure that was true. You'd think a woman who wiped his ass when he was an infant wouldn't have big, scary issues with doing it now when his need is just as great, but I never dared argue the point with her. After all, I didn't have children, and it didn't look like I ever would.

Would things have been different had we been parents? If I'd learned to nurture a child before having to learn to take care of my husband, would I have taken to it more easily? Maybe children would have kept me focused on our family, given me a reason not to resent the way my marriage, which had once been my greatest pleasure, had become my greatest burden. Childish hugs and kisses and the sweetness of a baby's smile might have filled my need for the physical touch and affection I no longer had. Or maybe having children would have been just more of an additional burden, would have stretched me so thin I broke, taken more than I had to give.

I'd never know what difference children might have made. Adam and I had assumed we had all the time in the world to procreate. We had careers and our infatuation with each other didn't allow much room for anyone else. Children had been a someday dream, an adventure on which we had plenty of time to embark.

There was no real reason why we couldn't entertain the notion of trying to have a baby now. Men with spinal cord injuries of Adam's level made babies all the time. True, it might require more effort, some help and we'd probably need to involve expense and embarrassing procedures to make it happen, but that wasn't the reason why I never discussed it with Adam. Nor was it my age, which was rapidly approaching the upper end of the safe pregnancy spectrum.

The much simpler reason behind my absolute lack of desire to become a mother was selfish. I didn't want the responsibility. Caring for Adam took up nearly all the time in my life I didn't spend at work. I had nothing to give a baby.

"I haven't seen them in a while," Adam said somewhat defensively. "Is it a problem, Sadie?"

"Of course it isn't. What movies came today?" I

changed the subject deftly, already heading to the table to check out what our internet movie rental company had sent.

Adam was in charge of keeping our queue. He spent more time on the Internet than I did. Not only that, but he cared more.

He rattled off the names of several blockbuster hits, some big-budget action pictures with lots of guns and explosions. I didn't really care. I'd end up falling asleep halfway through the first one, as I always did.

"Sounds great," I told him.

He laughed. "Think you'll stay awake?"

"Probably not."

We laughed together, this time, and his gaze caressed me. He tilted his head for a kiss, which I gladly gave him. Our mouths, slightly parted, brushed before I pulled away. I kissed his forehead.

"I'm going to take a shower," I told him. "And bring us some ice cream. Then we'll watch the big bangs, okay?"

"I'm tired of ice cream."

"You know," I said, after a pause. "So am I."

"Maybe Mrs. Lapp made some pie."

"I'll see."

"Good," Adam said, as if pie solved the problems of the world.

If only it could.

"I'm worried about your sister."

At my mother's whispered words, my eyes automatically searched the room for Katie. I found her laughing in the corner, bending to feed Lily a bite of chocolate cake. Her husband, Evan, lounged in a chair next to them. He was laughing, too.

I looked at my mother, whose mouth had pursed in concern. "Why?"

"She looks tired."

"She probably is."

My mother made a tutting sound and shook her head. I took another look, seeking to find what had so disturbed her. Katie had always been the fashion plate, but gone were the designer suits and flawless makeup. Now, her belly swelling in her fourth month, she wore a loose cotton top daubed liberally with chocolate and faded cotton pants. Her hair, naturally a few shades lighter than mine, was tucked up in a messy knot. Yes, there were faint circles under her eyes and her cheeks were slightly hollowed, but that came from lack of sleep and morning sickness. She wore a necklace made of macaroni and yarn with as much aplomb as she'd before worn pearls.

"She looks fine to me, Mom."

"Maybe you should talk to her."

How many times had I heard that over the years? When Katie had a fight with a friend, or lost a role in the school play, I talked to her. When her college boyfriend had broken her heart, I talked to her. When her boss at the bank passed her over for a promotion because he was schtupping her competitor, I talked to her.

"Oh, Mom." I sounded more annoyed than I'd meant to, and she didn't miss it.

"You're her sister, Sadie. She'll talk to you about what's bothering her."

Katie's laughter drifted over to us. I watched her swat at Evan's hand, which had crept out to give her a surreptitious squeeze. Lily danced in front of her parents, and they both gave her looks of such adoration it made me smile.

"What makes you think anything's bothering her?"

"I can tell."

My mother fussed with platters of deli meats and cheese that we spread out on the counter. They'd all been pretty well picked over, the turkey tumbled with the roast beef and impolitely nudging the ham. My mother, fork in hand like a dagger, stabbed the slices and rearranged them into neatly segregated rows.

I was no more willing to argue with my mother's statements about a mother's ability to judge what her children needed than I was with Adam's mother. I wouldn't have won against either one of them, in any case. Besides, what she was asking was nothing new.

"Then you talk to her."

My clipped reply made her look up again, fork poised in the air. There's nothing quite like pissing off your mother to churn your stomach. Mine, however, had been in an uproar for so long it didn't seem to make much difference that my comment had made my mother's mouth thin in that telltale way. It wasn't only mothers who know their children; daughters know our mothers, too.

"I think your sister could use your help," my mother said stiffly. "With Evan traveling so much and the baby on the way, I think she's got too much on her plate—"

It was more of the same old story, the one my mother'd been telling since Katie was born. 'Take care of your sister.' It didn't matter how old we were or what was going on in our lives, I was the older sister. The responsible one, the smart one… I was never the one who needed taken care of. Watching my sister with her husband and child, I couldn't stand to listen to my mother any longer.

"Mom, I can't, okay?" I must have been sharp, because she flinched. "Get off my case about it. I can't."

"Fine." She bent back to her task. "Though I have to say I'm very disappointed in you. I think she could use someone to talk to. She needs you. I'm worried about her…."

"She's always the one you worry about." The words, like acid, burned my throat. I sipped my drink to wash away the bitter taste of sibling rivalry, but it wouldn't go.

"What's that supposed to mean?" My mother turned, still wielding her fork.

"Nothing. It means nothing."

I excused myself and sought solace in the den, abandoned at the moment in favor of the places serving food and drink. The small room had once been part of the garage, but my dad had converted it as his domain when I was in high school. The far wall had been built with floor-to-ceiling bookshelves filled with photo albums and paperback novels. I recognized the faux white leather cover of my wedding album, and I yanked it from its place on the shelf.

We'd had a simple ceremony. Struggling on Adam's meager salary and with my bills for school, we hadn't had the money or the desire to throw a lavish, traditional wedding. I'd bought my dress from a local thrift store and waitressed to pay for the wedding pictures. We both looked gorgeous.

We looked happy.

Married five years after me, Katie'd planned a vastly different affair. Bridesmaids, formal wear, a cocktail reception and a candlelight service. Both she and Evan had high paying, successful jobs and similar skills in the art of consumption. They'd spared no expense, either from their own pockets or their parents. Even their honeymoon had been lavish and exotic, a two week stay in Greece. Adam and I had gone to Niagara Falls for the weekend and went back to work and school the Tuesday after the wedding.

We'd made different choices, my sister and I. I didn't envy her the grand, expensive ceremony, or the five thousand dollar wedding dress; those were things that had been unimportant to me. Yet now, as I pulled her far thicker wedding album and laid it next to mine, resentment bubbled up. Not because she'd had her hair and nails done for professional portraits and looked like a princess while my photos weren't as pretty. And not because she and Evan had served steak and lobster at their reception while Adam and I had been happy with chicken and fish.

She'd always had more. More of my parents' attention, more friends, more parties, more clothes. More sense of style, more money, more adventures. More of everything but grief.

I didn't hate my sister, but my mother's admonishment, not the first and far from the last, had tipped me over an edge upon which I'd been teetering for a long time without knowing it.

I felt like shit about it, too.

I put the albums away. I needed to find my dad, wish him happy birthday and get home. Dennis was great and apparently Adam's new best buddy, but he still cost time-and-a-half to work weekends, and I wanted to be able to buy a new car before the end of the year.

The books on the shelf had shifted and wouldn't allow me to replace what I'd removed. Irritated, I shoved them aside to make room for the wedding albums, and in doing so scraped my knuckles. The cut was shallow but bled, and I sucked them with a muttered curse.

"You all right?" said Katie, her belly leading the way as she appeared in the doorway. "Sades?"

"Fine." I blinked back tears of fury while anger rose in my throat and threatened to choke me. "Just fucking dandy."

My sister had perfected the art of the pause. "Okay…"

I couldn't look at her. Couldn't see her flushed cheeks or the bulge of the baby inside her. A baby I wasn't having. A joy I didn't want and wouldn't ever have. I pushed my hair off my face and straightened my shoulders.

"I've got to go home."

"Hey," she said. "What's wrong? Was mom giving you a hard time?"

"No."

"Jeez, sorry, it looked like she was, that's all. Sadie, what's wrong with you?"

It was just the question my mother had wanted me to

ask Katie. I looked at her. She gave me a half smile, quizzical. She had no fucking clue.

"Mom wanted me to talk to you. She's worried about you. Again."

Katie rolled her eyes. Normally it would have made me feel better, and we might have shared a laugh at my mother's overconcern. Today it only set my teeth further on edge. She had all the concern in the world, and didn't need it.

"Yeah, she's been on me," she said. "Thinks I'm not taking care of myself, or something. Hey, she takes Lily for me, though. Gives me have some downtime."

Caring for a grandchild was different than caring for a disabled son-in-law, there was no question of that. Knowing didn't ease the surge of resentment flooding me. It was irrational, and I could do nothing about it.

"Hey, maybe she'll watch Lily and we can grab a movie next week?"

"Katie, I told you, I can't."

"Oh." She sighed. "Because of Adam."

"Yes, because of Adam!" I snapped. "I can't just leave him alone, Katie!"

"I thought you had someone—"

I cut her off. "Mrs. Lapp leaves at five-thirty and Dennis doesn't come on duty until nine. It costs me money if they stay with him any other time, okay? It's expensive, and I'm sorry if I don't lead the grand lifestyle you're used to, but that's the way it is."

Without giving her time to reply, I shouldered past her. "I have to go."

"What bug crawled up your ass?" she cried. "God, Sadie, I just thought maybe you could use a break."

There were two people in my life who'd been able to drive me into a state of white-hot fury. Adam and Katie. The two people I loved most.

"You don't understand," I snapped.

"Maybe if you told me about it, I would!"

"You never ask!" Our shouts grew progressively louder.

"You never want to talk about it!" Katie's fists clenched. "You never talk about him to any of us! We ask you how he's doing and you give us one word answers, he never comes around anymore and when we go over there he stays upstairs. Lily barely knows him!"

"I never talk about him because none of you like hearing about it! It's uncomfortable and you'd rather not have all the details! It's easier for you to just pretend it doesn't exist. It's easier for you if I just keep it all to myself!" The cry echoed in the room. Guilt, transparent, flashed over her face and I knew I was right. I also knew I was being unfair.

"Sadie, I'm sorry."

"Don't worry about it," I told her, wanting to soften and unable in my misery to manage. "It's easier for me, too."

I left and she didn't call after me. My mother caught me on the way out.

"Sadie Frances, what on earth is going on?"

I stopped, defeated. "I'm sorry, Mom, but I've got to go."

"Did you talk to Katie?" My mom looked past me toward the den.

"She's fine. You don't have to worry about her."

"Of course I do. She's my daughter."

"Well," I answered stiffly. "I'm your daughter, too."

"Oh, Sadie." My mom reached to pat my shoulder. "I never have to worry about you. I know you can take care of yourself. Don't you know that?"

Smart one. Pretty one. The roles we play come back to bite us in the ass. "Yeah, Mom. Okay."

I wanted to be what she thought I was. What I'd always been. I'd told Katie the truth. It was easier for all of us, in the end, to maintain the status quo. Besides, it was a party. I put a smile on my face, gave my mom a hug and wished my dad a happy birthday. At home, I stood outside Adam's door for ten minutes, listening to him and Dennis laughing and trying not to hate the world and everything in it.

Elle was silent today, not unusual for her, but not a step forward, either. She fidgeted in her chair, her fingers knotting in her lap. Today she'd gone back to wearing black and white. Definitely a step backward.

"It's Dan's mother," she said finally. Then nothing else.

She rarely spoke of Dan's family. "What about her?"

"She's nice."

Expecting a complaint, I had to think of how to reply. Knowing Elle had a penchant for talking around a subject before she got to the heart of it, I asked, "Do you mean nice as in really nice? Or are you being kind?"

She looked up, her smile guilty. "You know me too well, Dr. Danning."

"I think that's the point, isn't it?" I teased gently, not a tactic for all my patients but one that worked with her.

"Yeah. I guess so." She sighed, her shoulders tensing for

a moment before she made an observable effort to relax them. "No, I mean she's really nice. Super nice. She's like…everything a mom should be. Mom Deluxe. She's Mom Squared."

"Unlike your mother."

This earned a laugh from her that she covered with one hand, a guilty gesture, as if she didn't want to find humor in what I'd said.

"Yes, unlike my own mother."

"Elle, unless everything you've ever told me about your mother has been a lie, I think I am safe in saying she could have used a bit of motherhood training."

She laughed again, the hand away from her lips this time. "Oh, I won't argue with that." She paused. "Do you think I've been lying?"

"No. I don't."

"Good." Her brow creased. "Because I haven't."

"Good."

She gave me another look. "Dan's mother has taken me shopping. She's offered me her secret recipe for brisket. She's…um…oh, shit, Dr. Danning, she likes me."

I let that hang between us for a moment or two.

"And why shouldn't she?"

She made a wordless noise.

"Elle. Believe me, a lot of women would be glad to have their boyfriend's mother like them."

She let her head fall back to stare at the ceiling for a moment.

"Dan doesn't have any sisters. His mother is thrilled to finally have a daughter. Her words."

I could guess at the problem, but she needed to be the one to tell me. I waited for her to speak. She rubbed her forehead and shifted in her chair again before finally sighing as though it came all the way from her toes.

"I don't know how to do it."

Again, I waited.

"I don't know how to be a daughter." The words blurted from her lips and she took a deep breath like she'd been starved for air.

"Do you think she's got high expectations?"

"Yes!"

Her vehemence startled me. Her fingers tapped the arm of the chair. Watching her consciously smooth the lines of tension in her body was like watching a ball of yarn unravel. One small section at time, she relaxed.

"Why do you think so?"

"She's always wanted a daughter. Now, all of a sudden, she thinks she's got one. Don't you think she's going to expect long, mother-daughter chats and giggling over shoes?"

"I don't know Dan's mother."

"Well, I do," Elle said. "And she likes shoes."

"Don't you think she likes other things, too? Would it be hard to find something you both enjoy and can connect on?"

"No, I guess not. I'm just not good at that sort of thing."

She made a funny face and reached for her purse. She pulled out a bundle of fabric. I waited. She made the face again.

"It's…a sweatshirt."

"From Dan's mother?"

She nodded.

"Are you going to let me see it?"

Elle's sigh came from the toes of her classy black pumps. Fabric unfolded and kept unfolding, until she held up a garment easily large enough to fit two of her. She stood to show me the front of it.

"Oh, my." I bit my lower lip, not wanting to offend with laughter.

"Kittens," Elle said in a slightly strangled tone. "Playing with…yarn."

I had to put my hand over my mouth, and even that didn't stop the chortle.

"Go ahead and laugh," she advised. "God knows Dan did."

I gave in and laughed as she tucked the voluminous tribute to cuteness away. "Did he?"

"He says I don't have to wear it."

"But you feel you should, because it's a gift."

"Well, I sure as hell can't make brisket!" She looked sour. "At least not without the fire department coming. He laughed about that, too."

Her mouth tipped up into a smile. "Too bad the sweat-shirt didn't burn instead."

"Maybe next time."

She sighed again, looking at the clock. "Our time's up."

"I've got a few more minutes," I told her. "Listen. Do you like her?"

"Yes." She squirmed a little, laughter gone. "That's why I'm so bothered."

Pleased she'd admitted to it, I smiled. "Because you don't want to let her down?"

"I don't want to let her down, Dan, me…my mother…" Her voice trailed off, low.

Now we were getting to the crux of it. "Your mother?"

She nodded, slowly. "Yeah. I might be a shitty daughter but I'm hers. And…"

"You feel disloyal."

Again, she nodded. "Yes. I do. Because I really like Dan's mom."

"Elle," I told her gently. "It's okay to like her. You don't have to feel bad about that."

"I'm afraid I've spent too long being a bad daughter. I know how to do that. I don't know how to be something else."

"Is that an excuse for not trying?"

She made another wordless noise, this one half a groan and half a sigh. "No. It's just easier to keep doing the same thing. Play the same part, that's all."

Her words made me blink, hitting close to home as some of our previous conversations had. "There's nothing that says you can't change."

"Not even if it changes everything else?"

I shook my head. "Not even then."

Elle got up and reached a hand for me to shake. "I know you're right, Dr. Danning."

I squeezed her fingers. "I know you know I'm right. You have to know you're right, too. Good luck with the kittens."

She snorted delicately. "Thanks. I'll let you know how it goes."

When she left, I picked up the phone to call my sister to apologize. Then I put the handset back in the cradle, uncertain of what I meant to say.

Chapter 07

April

This month, my name is Honey Adams. No, really it is. My daddy says the second he saw me all bundled up in my sweet pink blanket there in the nursery, he just knew I was going to be as sweet as honey. And he's right.

My sister's name is Angel because that's what Daddy said she is. It's her baby being baptized. My darling little nephew, Noah. He looks so cute in his little white baptismal gown with everyone oohing and ahhing over him.

Daddy's so proud of his new grandson he's paid for a party almost as lavish as the reception he gave for Angel's wedding to John. There's a huge buffet table, an open bar, even a DJ to help us all celebrate. Angel looks tired and John's a little annoyed, but I figure they should just put smiles on their faces and be glad someone else is picking up the tab. They'd never be able to afford a party like this, not on what John makes. That's what I heard Daddy say.

I can't wait until it's my turn. I'll be a gorgeous bride,

and when I start having babies, I just know they'll be even more adorable than little Noah. I'll be the best mother ever, and I won't ever complain and cry like Angel does. I won't turn into what Daddy calls a "puddin" either.

Daddy's carrying Noah around as if he were a trophy. Mom's over by the bar, supervising the caterer. I've got on the cutest new pink skirt, but there isn't anyone to talk to here. I'm bored, and when I spot Joey from across the room, suddenly I'm all smiles.

"Jooooey!"

My daddy and Joey's daddy are old hunting buddies, and I guess I've known Joey since I was born. There's seven years difference between us, which used to matter a whole lot when we were kids but doesn't so much, now. At least it shouldn't.

He looks up from his conversation with some redhead I don't know. He's got a drink in his hand. He looks really good, but then, he always does. I've had a crush on Joey since the summer between fourth and fifth grade, when he used to come over to our house almost every day to swim in the pool. He used to jackknife off the diving board and come up with the water slicking his hair back, and everything about him was golden.

He smiles when he sees me, and I can't help throwing the redhead a triumphant glance as he says goodbye to her and crosses the room to get to me.

"Honey. Long time no see."

I give him a coy glance. "And whose fault is that?"

"All mine, I guess." He lifts his glass and sips, and it's

impossible to miss the looking-over he's giving me. "You look good."

Of course I do. Thousands of dollars worth of orthodontia, plastic surgery and several years of an eating disorder have changed the chubby girl with an overbite and glasses. I flip my hair over one shoulder and give him a smile I know is blinding white and perfect.

"Thanks. You do, too."

Getting together with Joey would guarantee daddy would stop calling me his "other daughter." He'd throw me a wedding twice as fancy as Angel's, I know he would. Daddy doesn't like John, but Joey's like the son he never had.

We chat for a while, idle small talk about our jobs and lives. I know what he does and where he lives. Joey's mom and mine are best friends, and you can believe I hear all the gossip. He's got a great job and house and a smoking hot car, and he doesn't have a girlfriend. I know that for a fact, because his mother's starting to get a little worried, even though I've heard my mom tell his there's no way he's gay, and she shouldn't worry so much.

I tell him about my job, which is so boring I can barely stand to talk about it. Joey's nodding in all the right places and making little noises like he's listening, but his gaze keeps going to my chest. It's quite a bit larger than it used to be and I like showing it off. My nipples tighten a bit under his gaze. He notices.

"So, Joey." I keep my voice a little breathy, just like I've practiced in private until I can get it just right. I lean forward to take his wrist and bring his drink up to my mouth. "What are we drinking?"

I take a sip from his glass. He's got whiskey—nasty, nasty stuff. I swallow it down, but I don't let go of his wrist.

"I'm drinking Jameson. And it looks like you are, too." Joey takes my other hand and puts it under the glass so he can let go while I'm left holding it.

I'm a little confused. "Huh?"

"Why don't you keep that one. I'll get myself another."

He nods a little and backs up a step, then turns on his heel and heads toward the bar. I'm left blinking, holding his glass, and shit, shit, shit, this isn't how it's supposed to go.

"Well, how about a freshener?" I catch up to him and flash him another smile.

"Sure, Honey." Joey waves to the bartender and asks for another whiskey.

"Actually, I'd like a white zinfandel."

I hand the guy Joey's old glass and he hands us two new drinks. I sip mine right away, but Joey holds on to his and doesn't drink from it. The redhead's watching us without even bothering to hide it.

People in the corner are laughing, and we both turn to look. It's Joey's dad Frank and my dad. Frank's shaking Daddy's hand and clapping him on the back. They're passing cigars, too. Joey watches them for a moment before he turns his back, and because I want to keep his attention, I turn away, too.

"Some party." Joey lifts his glass.

He's right, but I don't really want to talk about the party, which is Angel's, not mine. "Your dad's having a good time."

"Doesn't he always, at parties?" Joey's got a smile I

heard my mom say could spread a nun's knees, but right now it looks more like a smirk.

"Everyone likes a party, don't they? Especially when someone else is paying for it?" I sip my wine and look around the room, crammed full of people. "Oooh, look! There's Mindy Heverling!"

I smile and wave to her. She went to school with Joey, Angel and Joey's brother Eddie. Mindy turns with a half-smile to wave at me, but in a second her face changes and she turns back around. Why's she cutting me cold? Angel's the one who used to steal her boyfriends, not me. Well, screw her. I look back at Joey, but now he's looking at Mindy, and I realize she wasn't cutting me cold at all. She was ignoring him.

"Didn't Mindy used to go out with Eddie?"

"Yes."

He's still staring at her. I feel a little bad, bringing it up. Eddie died when Joey was in high school. Nobody talks about it much. In fact, I don't want to talk about it, so I take his elbow and make my move.

"It's hot in here. Want to take a walk with me?"

I know Daddy booked this place because it had a ballroom big enough to hold all of his friends, but the gardens are nice, too. Lots of color-coordinated tulips and daffodils, a Greek-looking patio and two cement fish ponds with carp the size of my arm…and a maze. It's not a very complicated maze but all I really want is to get to the center of it with Joey.

After that, it's not long before my tongue's in his ear and his hand's up my skirt.

"Honey," Joey says when I reach for his belt buckle. "Aren't you a bad girl?"

"Do you like bad girls?" His thighs are hard under my ass and my knees are pressing against the metal bench as I straddle him. I work the zipper on his trousers and slide a hand inside.

I'm looking at his face when I say it, and I'm expecting to see the look guys get when they're about to get some action. Joey's expression surprises me, makes me pause. He looks serious and considering, not at all like I want him to look, which is glassy eyed with lust.

"Not really."

I falter, my hand closing around his thing. It's hard enough, anyway, so even if he's saying he doesn't like bad girls, he's still turned on. At least, I hope he is.

"N…no?"

Joey shifts a little and puts his hands on my hips to hold me from sliding off his lap. "Not really. No. I like girls who are good."

Oh, he's teasing me, playing with words. He's always been good at that. A brain. Even in high school, he was always top of the class.

"I can be good, Joey."

He winces a little and I loosen my grip, figuring I was holding too tight. His thing throbs in my fingers. Maybe he's worried about being caught, but we'd hear anyone coming through the maze in plenty of time to button up, if we have to.

"I bet you can."

His thumb slides into position against my tootsie. I bite

my lower lip and lean in to kiss him. He turns his head so my lips land on the corner of his. I settle for nibbling his jaw and neck. His skin is warm and clean, and a little shiver tickles my spine.

This is Joey, but he's also a stranger.

The thought makes me bite down a little, and he winces. He slides a finger beneath the lacy edge of my panties and inside me. I take his thing out all the way and start stroking him harder.

"Honey…slow down…" His voice is hoarse. His fingers are moving faster against me, no matter what he's telling me to do.

"Nuh-uh." I shake my head. "I want this."

"I can see that." His finger moves in and out of me while his thumb keeps pressing on my bump.

"Ooh, Joey," I moan, pushing myself onto his hand. "Tootsie likes that."

He makes a little noise, a kind of snuffling snort. He's got his face turned even more away. He's smiling.

"…does she?"

"Mmm, hmmm. Oh…Oh! Oh, God…Joey!"

I've been with other guys, it's not that I'm a virgin or anything. But this is Joey, so I'm determined to make it so good he'll be back for more.

"Fuck my tootsie…oh, oh…OH!"

I never shout when I have a real orgasm, but guys like it when girls make a lot of noise and wriggle around a lot. I want Joey to like me. A lot.

"Yes, yes!" I writhe around on his hand and finally fall forward to put my face on his shoulder. I've still got his thing in my hand. It's not as hard as it was a couple minutes ago. I look up.

"Want me to put your thing in my mouth?"

At first he says nothing. He takes his fingers out of me. This position is starting to hurt my knees.

"Did you like that?"

I lick my lips. "Mmm, yeah, that was great, baby. Want me to suck you, now? Or use my hand?"

"Suck my what?" His eyes are heavy-lidded and his expression inscrutable. He's playing with words again.

"Your thing. Your you-know."

"My cock? You want to suck my cock, Honey?"

"Yes!" I nod. I don't really want to suck his cock…I mean, I will because this is Joey, the guy I've had a super-mega crush on forever, and it's what guys like. But sucking cock is sort of icky.

"Honey, somehow I don't think your father would approve you sucking my cock out here in the middle of the maze."

I glare. "I don't do everything my father approves of."

He's getting soft, so I move to get down and take him in my mouth. Joey stops me by grabbing my elbow to keep me on his lap.

"Why are you doing this?"

"C'mon, Joey, it's not like we don't know each other. Remember when you were in grad school and you came over to my parents' house for Christmas dinner?"

His thing…his cock…is getting harder again. His head tips back against the bench. His eyes are closed. His thighs tense and relax under my ass.

"Yeah."

"And there was mistletoe?"

"Jesus, Honey…" He licks his lips and they part as he half-gasps. "That was a long time ago. You were just a kid."

"You still kissed me." I lean forward to whisper in his ear. I lick his lobe, then nibble it. His thing jerks in my fingers. "And I decided right then I'd marry you."

At that, his eyes fly open. This time, I'm off his lap and almost on my ass on the ground before I catch my balance. He takes my hand out of his pants.

"Whoa, whoa, wait a minute." He runs a hand through his hair and does this whole weird squirmy thing where he tucks himself back in his pants and runs his hands over the rest of him like he's making sure his clothes aren't wrinkled. "Who said anything about getting married?"

I straighten my own clothes and turn to face him on the bench. "Maybe not right away, but–"

"But nothing. But never."

That stings, and I frown. I cross my arms. "You were happy enough to put your hand up my skirt."

Joey looks stunned. "Holy shit, Honey. Fucking hell."

"What?" I cry, offended. "Is it such a crazy idea? We'd be great together!"

"How do you figure that?" Joey asks. "You don't even know me!"

"What you do mean, I don't know you? I've known you forever! Mom and Daddy know your parents, they'd love to see us hooked up. You've got a great job and could easily support me and we'd make beautiful babies…"

"What fucking decade are you living in?" Joey's voice is even, but bemused. "You can't be serious."

"Why not? What's wrong with wanting to get married?"

"Usually you marry someone you love, who loves you."

"But I do love you! What, you like redheads better?" I lean toward him, my tone snide. "You'd rather hook up with that nobody than me? How about Mindy Heverling? You know, there was a rumor about you and her—"

I reach for his crotch again, but he moves away before I can touch him.

"Don't."

I give him the look that usually gets me whatever I want. "Joey. Of course we can date for a while, first. This was just a little taste of what I can give you."

He shakes his head. "I don't think so."

"Why not?" I stand and put my hands on my hips. "I'm not good enough for you? I'm good enough to suck you off but not good enough to date?"

Joey stands, his hands up. "Honey, cut it out. This isn't flattering."

"Oh, is that it?" Tears burn in my eyes and I swipe them away. "You're turning me down?"

"Yeah."

"Do you know how many guys would love to take me out?"

"A lot, I'm sure. Why don't you go back inside and find one? I think the party's still going on—"

I slap him, hard enough to turn his head. "How dare you!"

The imprint of my fingers is first white, then slowly fill

in red as I watch. I'm breathing hard. My nipples are hard. Heat has spread up my throat to my cheeks. Finally, I'm turned on.

So, I slap his other cheek just as hard. Joey puts a hand to the marks as he slowly turns his face to look at me.

"You're lucky I'm a gentleman," he says evenly. "Or I'd knock you on your ass for that."

I sneer, getting up in his face. "I'd like to see you try."

My thighs are trembling. My tootsie's gone all hot and soft and I think about his fingers inside me. If he did that again now, I'd be wet for him.

I lift my hand to hit him again, but this time he catches my wrist. His grip is tight and it hurts just enough to make me gasp. Is he going to hit me? Oh, is he going to push me?

Joey lets me go. I stumble back, just a little and look up at him. Disgust has twisted his face, and I realize I've gone too far. I reach for his hand, but he's backing away.

"Joey, wait, wait. I'm sorry. I wanted to move too fast, I know. We could take things slower…"

"Honey, I don't want to go out with you. I don't want to hurt your feelings, but I don't want to date you, be your boyfriend or marry you."

"Well, why not?" I cry suddenly, feeling more naked than when he had his hand in my panties. "What's wrong with me?"

"Nothing is wrong with you." Joey puts his hands in his pockets. "But you really don't even know me."

"I know everything I need to know!" I step toward him, and he steps back. It's a dance I don't like.

"No," Joey says. "You don't."

Then he leaves me in the middle of the maze and I have to find my way back to the party alone. When I get back, he's gone. So is the redhead.

"Did you leave with the other girl?"

"No. That would have been a good ending to the story, though, wouldn't it?"

Joe's grin was unabashed and I had to return it.

"Are you on Daddy's shit-list, now?"

He shrugged, tipping his head up toward the warm spring sunshine. It shot threads of yellow across his face. It was our first lunch outside of the atrium since last October, and the fresh air and flowers gave everything a festive air.

"I doubt she told him. What would she have said?"

"True. You'd better hope she didn't tell him you touched her tootsie, though, or else it sounds like Daddy might show up at your door with a shotgun."

Joe cracked open an eye to look at me. We both started laughing, which escalated into a flurry of guffaws. Sunshine and giggles. It felt great.

"Tootsie," I said again, just because it sounded so ridiculous.

"Lot of good touching it did." Joe's laughter is like a stream chuckling over rocks, swift and strong, dipping down every so often. "She didn't even get off."

"You're sure?"

"Sadie," Joe said. "I might not always be able to tell when a woman *does*, but I sure as hell know when she *doesn't*."

We laughed harder. My sides started to hurt. I had to wipe away a tear. I caught his eye and we both sobered a bit.

"She sounds like maybe she still thought of herself as that chubby girl with braces, even though she's done a lot to move away from that image."

"Is that your professional opinion, Doctor?"

We rarely discuss our careers. I didn't, in fact, even know what he did for a living. His words sobered me further, brought me back to the reality instead of letting me stay in the fantasy. I cleared my throat and cut my gaze from his.

"I can't possibly analyze someone I don't even know."

Joe stopped laughing, too. He wadded up a napkin and threw it toward the garbage can. "I liked her when she was that chubby girl with braces. She was a good kid."

"So why not go out with her? It sounds like it would make your families happy."

Joe gave me a look. "Daddy might be thrilled, Sadie, but I could assure you Mommy would throw a shit fit."

"Ah." I hadn't thought about that.

"Besides, I could never go out with a woman who calls her pussy a tootsie."

That set us off again. I felt bad for laughing at poor Honey, who sounded like she had real issues, not the least an Electra complex. Leave it to Joe to get jerked off in a garden at a baptismal party.

"Everywhere you go," I said when the laughter again had died down. "How do you do it?"

He was quiet for a moment or two. "I'm a good-looking guy. It opens doors."

I'd been staring at his profile, fascinated by the way the sun cast shadows on his skin. He looked up and caught me and I looked away.

"You don't always have to say yes, Joe."

"Sadie," Joe murmured. "I don't always say yes. I only tell you about the ones I say yes to."

Which was enough. I laughed again, but it sounded fake after the true guffaws we'd shared. I wrapped up my trash, disappointed as always that the hour had passed and I had no more excuse to linger.

"They're like sharks. Circling. Cute, single guy, good job, nice car. It's all they know about me." His tone was light but his expression serious.

"Maybe that's because it's all you show them."

"Maybe it's all they want to see."

I stood to put my garbage in the can. I brushed some crumbs off my hands. "Maybe you need a mesh suit. Or a shark cage. Or maybe you just need to stop tossing out so much chum."

Joe smiled. "Then what would we have to talk about at lunch?"

I didn't have an answer for that, and it was easy to see he knew it. "So, what was the rumor about you and Mindy Heverling?"

Joe scuffed the gravel with the toe of his shoe. "Mindy was my brother's girl."

There was a story there, one he wasn't telling. One I had no right, perhaps, to hear. "And?"

He ran a hand through his hair and shifted on the bench, all part of the ritual I'd grown used to seeing when

I dug too deep. Most of the time it was enough to get me to back off and change the subject. These times weren't about analysis, after all, not about pushing buttons.

"Never mind," I said. "You don't have to tell me."

"Eddie was a year younger than me. He was the smart one, I guess you could say." Joe laughed.

"And you were the pretty one?"

I liked the fact he knew when I was teasing, and he took it. "You got it."

"So, what happened?" I thought I could guess.

Joe leaned forward, elbows on his knees, hands linked. The gravel seemed suddenly to have captured his interest quite thoroughly. "She got pregnant."

"Oh?" I hadn't expected that answer.

He turned his face toward me. "Yeah."

It took me a second to understand. "Oh. Oh!"

Joe nodded. "More like, 'oh, fuck.'"

"What happened?"

"She had an abortion. I had to borrow the money from my dad to pay for it. He told me I was a disappointing bastard, and he was right. Eddie never knew about it. By then he was sick. He had leukemia. Anyway, he…died."

"I'm sorry."

"It was a long time ago."

"Joe," I said softly and waited until he looked at me. "I'm still sorry."

I might have reached for him, but we didn't touch. We never touched. He nodded slightly.

"Thanks." He got up, the story told, our time spent. "Oh, I almost forgot."

Joe pulled a tissue-wrapped package from his inside suit pocket. He held it out on the palm of his hand. "Happy birthday."

I was already reaching for it with the automatic response most people make when an object's offered. At his words, though, I hesitated. The package tipped from his hand and missed mine, hitting the ground, where I bent to pick it up with a hasty apology.

"You didn't have to get me something." I blushed. Hard. "I hope it didn't break."

"I think it's okay. Open it."

I did. It was a small hand-dipped candle from a local boutique. A pale purple, it smelled distinctively of lavender.

"How did you know?" I asked, lifting the candle and sniffing it.

"You told me." Joe sounded surprised, as if my question made no sense. "You said it was your favorite scent."

"I did?" I wrapped the candle back in the tissue and held it close to me. "Really? It is, actually."

Joe smiled. "I thought you did. Anyway. Happy birthday, Sadie."

"Thank you." I reached into my bag and pulled out the gift I'd decided not to give him, and gave it to him anyway. It was a book, the latest hardcover thriller from a well-known author. "Surprise. I hope you don't already have it."

He didn't. We beamed at each other until our smiles said too much and we had to look away. Joe took a few steps back before turning and heading off down the path. I stared after him, the faint scent of lavender surrounding me.

* * *

Much is said about brilliance. Less attention is paid to those who live next to it. Spouses, children, assistants…if anyone thinks of us at all, it's generally to remark upon how lucky we are to bask in the light of genius.

In the first years of our life together, I basked in Adam's brilliance. At parties, I was proud to introduce myself as Adam Danning's wife, to accept compliments on his behalf. I was often asked if I, too, was a poet.

"No," Adam always said proudly. "My Sadie is a doctor."

Not once did anyone seem surprised I wasn't also a literary whiz, but I always enjoyed that moment of expectation in their eyes while they waited to see if I was. I never wished for the sort of creative brilliance Adam had, nor envied it of him. There wasn't room in our house for another Adam. We'd have been like Tweedledee and Tweedledum, colander helmets and all, prepared to battle.

Sylvia Plath gassed herself. Ernest Hemingway shot off his face. Richard Brautigan apparently grew tired of trout fishing and also took the way of the gun.

Does madness bring creativity? Or does creativity cause madness? Can an artist create without the ups so high and the downs so low? As a psychologist, I felt I should know the answers. I should be able to understand my brilliant, talented husband. Yet, I didn't.

The mood swings baffled me. When I needed to work, I went to my desk. I read. I studied. I accomplished my goals steadfastly, each in a row so tidy I could literally check them off on a list.

Adam disappeared into his office for hours and hours to emerge with bleary eyes, cursing and moaning, saying he was unable to write. He sometimes wept and threw dishes against the wall, only to laugh himself hoarse an hour later at inane television programs. My lack of comprehension about his creative impulses infuriated him.

We clashed. We fought. We made brilliant, creative, genius love that sometimes left us both weeping.

I knew him, but I didn't understand him.

I learned to ignore his moods as unrelated to me or anything I'd done, and to leave him alone when he was mopish. I read his poems when they were published, as they all were, to increasing popularity and acclaim. I went with him to parties where sycophants fawned on him and fed us champagne and caviar, where placards with his face and the cover of his books stared at us from across the room.

I loved Adam and he loved me, and we made a life that was full of ups and downs—but it worked. I studied. He created. He pulled me along and I was not his anchor, for Adam wouldn't be anchored. I was, instead, his ballast. Something to keep him from bouncing quite so high or diving quite so low.

His first book tour didn't land him on *Oprah* or *The Tonight Show*. His publisher booked him at colleges and bookstores where he appeared in his leather jacket and earring and read his poems to rapt audiences of suburban housewives and English majors. There was talk of his being considered as Pennsylvania's next Poet Laureate, a possibility that might have been pulled from the thin air of his publisher's hopefulness but had Adam floating on that high for weeks.

Then he hit a tree and woke up in a hospital bed, and everything was gone. If he'd written anything since then, I didn't know about it. I was afraid to suggest it. Writing to Adam had been as necessary as breathing or eating or fucking. He couldn't do any of those things on his own any longer. Maybe he couldn't write, either. Writing had been Adam's addiction. His high. There was no mistaking the fact he suffered from its lack, but he wouldn't talk to me about it.

Much like the shoemaker's children who went barefoot, the husband of the psychologist went without therapy. Adam was adamant he didn't need it, wouldn't have it.

"If I didn't need it before, when I was half out of my fucking head, I don't need it now," he said. "I'm a quadriplegic, Sadie, not crazy."

I didn't bother to explain that I don't deal with "crazy" people, and neither do my colleagues. Adam had made up his mind. His accident hadn't made him any less stubborn.

So we focused on the chair, the hourly medical care, the minutiae of evacuating his bladder and bowels and caring for a body that could no longer protect itself even from its own weight. We labored under the pretense that nothing had changed when everything had, and I understood him, but I no longer knew him.

Adam had always been brighter. Stronger. I'd been content to circle him the way the earth revolves around the sun, dependent on him to lead me.

What happens when the weaker becomes the stronger? When my independence became a choice no longer, but a necessity if we were both going to survive? The places we'd built for ourselves no longer fit. Like poor Honey, we were trapped in the past, stuck developmentally, locked into habits that had served us in the past but weren't allowing us to grow.

Once, it had been enough to be what Adam wanted. Now, I tried to be what he needed. The two didn't seem to be the same. The night I got the call that Adam had been taken to the hospital, my first fear had been that I'd lost him. Four years later, I'd somehow lost myself, instead.

I'd never know the woman I'd have been if I hadn't met Adam. Until I met Joe, I hadn't wondered.

Who was I now?

Chapter 08

May

This month, my name is Amy, and I've come in from out of town to be my college roommate's maid of honor. The unwritten code of weddings says either the bridesmaid's dress or the best man will be ugly enough to make you wish you were blind. Bonnie's promised me something cute to wear and cuter to stand beside in the photos. I've been in enough weddings by now to doubt that will happen, but when I see the best man I'm prepared to forgive her for the dress.

He's an attorney. His teeth are straight and white and he wears his tux as easily as if it were a sweat suit. He's just that cool.

"What did I tell you?" Bonnie whispers from the back of the church where we're waiting for the wedding rehearsal to begin.

"He's cute." I crane my neck a little to catch a better glimpse of him. "What's his name?"

"Joe Wilder." The name suits him.

The rehearsal is a disaster, but Father Peck assures us that bodes well for tomorrow. The whole crowd of us head over to Angelina's Riverside, where Brian's parents have paid for a pretty extravagant rehearsal dinner. I manage to sit next to Joe.

He apologizes for bumping me. "I'm a lefty. Sorry."

We switch seats. Now he's on the end, and I don't have to share him with the other bridesmaid who'd been sitting on his other side. She's not happy about that, but I don't really care, since I am the maid of honor, not her. Let her glom onto her own groomsman. The best man is mine.

"Nervous about tomorrow?"

"Oh, no. This is my fifth wedding this year."

When I tell this to Joe, he laughs and sips water from his glass. I like the way the corners of his eyes crinkle when he smiles. "This is my first one."

"Oh, a wedding virgin." I lean a bit closer.

"Be gentle with me." He leans closer, too. "Since it's my first time and all."

We laugh. We eat. And later, after dinner is over, we go to the bar and drink. A bit after that, we dance.

He's an excellent dancer and holds me just close enough to lead me without making it seem like he's coming on to me. I think he *is* coming on to me, but I appreciate his subtlety.

The wedding code says all hook ups need to wait at least until the reception. It's only common courtesy to the bride and groom. I was at a wedding once where the best man and maid of honor hooked up at the rehearsal dinner, then with different members of the wedding party at the reception. They ended up throwing cake in each other's faces and ruining the wedding pictures.

So I'm just about to regretfully tell him I have to get back to my hotel when he beats me to the punch and says he's got to get going. He's meeting the other groomsmen to take Brian out for some drinks. He's already late.

"At a strip club, maybe?"

Joe's got the grin of a little boy caught with his hand in the cookie jar. "Maybe."

"But Brian told Bonnie he wasn't going to do that."

Joe acts like he let the cat out of the bag. "Oops. Are you going to tell her?"

Bonnie swore there was no way she was going out drinking and carousing the night before she got married—not when she'd have a hundred people taking her picture the next day. We'd had our bachelorette shindig a month ago. We had, in fact, gone to see a male dance revue. I didn't personally see what the big deal was about Brian going out to see a little bit of tit and ass before he got married. I mean, if you can't trust your man, you shouldn't be marrying him.

"I guess not."

"Want to come along?" His grin got broader, as if we were sharing a dirty secret.

"Oh, right. The guys would so like that."

"I'll tell them you're there to make sure I keep Brian in line."

"Then they'll really hate me!" I shake my head, but laughing. "Brian won't want me there, Joe. I'll ruin the fun."

"Bet you won't. You don't look like that sort of girl. Besides, you know Brian, right?"

"Since college."

"So, don't you want to send him off to be married in grand style?"

This was a slippery slope, but it was either go back to my empty hotel room or go with Joe, and suddenly, all the wedding rules didn't seem to matter.

"Do you really want me to come?"

He nodded and pulled me close for a dip. When he pulled me up, his breath gusted along my ear and made me shiver.

"Yes. I do want you to come."

Fuck the rules. A nun wouldn't have been able to resist him. I sure as hell couldn't.

In the parking lot of the Sahara, which looked like any other bar from the outside except for the big sign in the window that said alcohol prohibited, Joe's cell phone rang.

"Wilder."

I giggled at the way he answered his phone. Joe smiled at me. I leaned forward to look through the front window at the building while he talked.

"What? No way. Really? Damn. You're sure?"

That didn't sound good. I looked over at him. He held up a finger, mouthing "one minute."

I waited. Men talk so differently than women. Short, sharp sentences without the frills and furbelows we add to every conversation, no matter what it's about. Joe listened, he spoke, once in a while he nodded. Finally, he closed his phone and looked at me.

"Bonnie found out about Brian's plans so now he's not coming."

"Oh…too bad." I hadn't realized how excited I'd been by the thought of going to see the strippers until just now. "Well, he's got to keep her happy, I guess."

Joe made a flicking gesture with his hand. "He's whipped."

I felt bound to defend my friend, though I didn't disagree. "They're getting married."

Joe's smile is like a sliver of sunshine. "Yeah. Lucky bastard."

"You think so?" I'm at the age where most of my friends have been steadily taking the leap into the marital abyss. "I'm not so sure I'm ready to get married."

"Everyone says that," Joe answers. "Until they meet the right person."

My heart skips a little, but I remind myself he's not talking about me. We just met. Even though weddings can make people all starry-eyed, it's not necessarily a good indication that it will last.

"So, what do we do now?" I ask.

Joe looks toward the Sahara. The door opens and music and light spill out, along with a crowd of pretty rowdy guys who head for a truck a few spaces over. They look like they're drinking something out of a paper bag. They all look pretty drunk, already.

"Why don't they serve alcohol?" I point to the sign.

"Pennsylvania law." I hadn't forgotten Joe's a lawyer. "Any place that serves alcohol can't have full nudity."

I blink. "You mean…the girls in there are totally naked?"

He smiles. "Yep."

I blink again. "Wow. I thought they'd have a G-string on or something."

"No. Not a stitch. Want to go in?"

Somehow, being part of a big group of carousing boys watching girls in pasties and thongs dance seemed way different than Joe and I going in to see totally bare-assed women shake their stuff.

"Yeah, sure." I sound more confident than I feel.

Joe reaches for my hand. "Don't worry. I'll protect you."

I laugh at that, feeling silly. "All right, c'mon."

My stomach's jumping nervously when we go inside. I'm not sure what I'm expecting, but it's not this. The inside of the Sahara looks something like a cross between a cheap hotel lobby and a frat house basement. Several small stages, complete with poles, scatter the area. Worn couches provide seating. There's art on the wall, of the cheesy pin-up variety. I see girls dressed in typical stripper outfits circulating with money sticking out of their garters. Some of them stop to talk to the men sitting all around, and every so often, one of them will get up and go toward a back room with one.

Joe has to pay a cover charge for himself, but not for me. The man behind the counter doesn't even seem surprised to see me. Maybe they get more girls in there than I'd thought.

At any rate, I'm a lot less nervous as Joe takes my hand and leads me toward a love seat near the front of the room. It's right in front of the main stage, the one with three poles and a set of gymnasts' rings.

"Hi, hon," says the first girl to come up to us. Closer inspection reveals she's not a girl. She's got to be older than me. She's thin but has stretch marks on her thighs, and I'm pretty sure she's wearing a wig. Suddenly, I feel a lot better about myself.

"Hi," Joe says. "How're you?"

"Oh, can't complain, hon, can't complain. Either of you want a lap dance?"

She looks at me when she asks, and I freeze, unable to answer. Do I want a lap dance? And if I do, do I want one from a stripper who looks as though she'd be making a grocery list in her head while she does it?

"Maybe later," Joe says easily. "We just got here."

"Fair enough, hon." She winks, and her smile shows several prominent gaps. "We got three girls starting in about two minutes, so you just enjoy, okay?"

She wanders to the next table where I hear her asking the same questions. Joe turns to me.

"I'm sorry, I should have asked you if you wanted one. Did you?"

"Uh...no...no thanks."

He laughs and leans in to whisper in my ear. "Later, maybe."

I think it'll be a cold day in hell before I pay for a lap dance from a woman, but it would be rude to say so. The next moment, I jump at the blast of loud music that blares from the speakers. Joe takes my hand again, his thumb passing back and forth over the back of it and making me shiver.

Okay, so watching *Showgirls* has in no way prepared me

for what's going on in the Sahara. Some raunchy hip-hop tune that's all about oral sex has these three girls writhing and wriggling. They don't seem to have any sort of real routine or anything, they just twirl around on the poles and strip out of their already scanty outfits. And, yeah, they get down to bare skin, all the way.

I watch as one girl gets on her back, crotch pointed toward the edge of the stage, and does a trick with her vagina that makes it look like some sort of underwater creature. I'm repulsed and fascinated. I look around at the men in the room, who are all staring at this woman's cunt like it holds the secrets of the universe, until I turn to look at Joe and see he's staring at me.

"Wow," is all I manage to mutter.

He smiles and turns his gaze to the stage, where the girls are finishing up and heading into the audience to collect their dollars.

A few more take their place on stage and the routines begin all over again. I spot two of the girls heading our way and I'm determined not to look like an asshole, even though they're both naked and their tits are about to poke me in the eye.

"Thanks, hon," says one to Joe when he slips a bill into the garter on her thigh. "You let me know if you want a lap dance, okay?"

After about fifteen minutes, I've become numb to the sight of undulating cunts and flopping tits. Joe and I are getting a lot of attention. I'm not sure if it's because he is, hands down, the hottest guy in the room, or because he's with me and therefore seems less creepy than the guys who are there alone. At any rate, I'm warming up enough that I'm able to put a few dollars into garters myself, and to laugh a little at the women who flirt like it's a job, not a pleasure.

They all ask if we want lap dances. Joe's so good at declining, he makes it sound like he'd like to have a lap dance from each and every one of them. After an hour, I notice they're talking about him. I know this because I know women, I know the way we gather and lean our heads together for discussion. The strippers are plotting something.

A new girl comes out on stage. She's about my age. My height. Hell, she's even got the same color hair, though hers looks like it came from a bottle. She's wearing a skin-tight sheath dress that makes it impossible for her to use the pole until she takes it off, and she's dancing to a slow, silky bump'n'grind instead of some loud song with dirty lyrics. It would be incorrect to say she's subtle, but compared to the other dancers, she was.

She's prettier than some there, but not the prettiest. She doesn't have the best body, either. Still, something about her catches my attention.

Joe's, too.

Together, we watch this girl shimmy out of her clothes. Then, it strikes me. This girl dances as if she's enjoying herself. She smiles and makes eye contact with the men in the audience. She dances like she's seducing each and every one of us with her eyes, which are a bright, liquid blue.

When she's done and goes throughout the audience collecting her cash, I hold my breath, waiting for her to disappear into the back room with one of those ogling men. Surely, she will. Certainly, someone will want to pay for her to dance privately.

"Thanks, sugar," she says to Joe when he tucks some money into her garter. She turns to me. "How about a lap dance?"

"Yes," I hear myself say. I feel Joe's eyes on me, but I'm too busy looking into the girl's to pay attention to him.

"Well," she says, her voice like smooth, hot caramel. "Let's go, then."

She takes me by the hand and motions to Joe. "C'mon, darlin', you, too."

Laughing, he gets up, too, and takes her hand. She leads us to the back room, which is painted like midnight and lit by black lights that turns our smiles and the whites of our eyes fluorescent.

"Three songs," she says. "What do you like to listen to, sweetie?"

She's asking me, her attention focused on me, her hand still holding mine. I've never held a woman's hand before. Not like this, fingers linked, palm to palm. I hope suddenly my hand isn't sweating.

"Whatever you like." I feel like I'm speaking through a mouthful of cotton. Heat sweeps up and down my body in waves that make me shiver. She nods and lets go of my hand to move toward a small window set into the wall I hadn't noticed earlier.

I look at Joe. He smiles and holds out his hand to me. I take it. He pulls me close enough to whisper in my ear.

"Good choice."

I shiver again at the feeling of his breath in my ear. I don't even have the benefit of alcohol to blame this on. What the hell am I doing? But I have no time to back out now, because she's sauntering back to us.

"My name's Cherry," she says.

"I bet it is." Joe's grin is a crescent of white in the darkness.

She laughs. "As far as you're concerned it is."

"Fair enough."

"Have a seat," she tells us and points to the twin chairs set out in the middle of the floor. We do, facing each other. There's just enough room between us for her to walk without bumping our knees.

Cherry smiles. "You two a couple?"

"No." Joe shakes his head.

"First date?"

I laugh, nervous. "Sort of. We're in a wedding together, tomorrow."

Cherry has a slow, smooth giggle that's like bubbles in champagne. "Nice."

Then the music comes on. "No Ordinary Love" by Sade, a song I've always liked. It's slow and sexy, and she begins to dance just the way she did on stage. As if she's seducing us both.

Joe, I think, is probably used to women coming on to him, but I'm not. I sit stiffly in my chair as Cherry moves her body over and around us. She sits on Joe's lap, facing me, and slides her body up and down him while her eyes hold mine. Turning, she makes the same move on me.

A lapful of warm, slightly sweaty woman is such a shock to me I make a small sound. Her hair, which smells of strawberries, is tickling my face and tumbling every which way over her shoulders, and I have time to wish mine would do that when she turns around and rubs herself all along my front.

I'm reminded of the way a cat will butt its head against your palm to make you pet it. Cherry is turning, rubbing, writhing, moving back and forth from me to Joe and back again. I don't know where to put my hands. If anyone else was touching me this way, I'd be touching back...but somehow I get the idea we're not supposed to touch her.

Cherry parts my thighs and slides between them to press her body along mine. The chair has a high, straight back, and I've no place to retreat. Her mouth ends up by my ear and she blows into it, lightly. I quiver. She laughs and pulls away, looking into my eyes again, before turning around to do the same to Joe.

When she's working on him, I can clearly understand the term "heart-shaped ass," because she's got one. She's got one knee on Joe's thigh, her hands on his shoulders. She's tipped forward and up, so I can see the fluff of her pubic hair and catch a glimpse of her pussy. Unlike the blatant display out front, this is tantalizing, just a peek as she rocks her pelvis.

Cherry knows what most men seem to ignore. That sometimes, mystery is sexier. Then again, maybe having a vagina has made me immune to the allure of close-up views.

Three songs is about ten minutes, but after the first one

is over I couldn't tell you what comes next. Each is slow and smooth. It's the longest ten minutes of my life.

And the most expensive, as when the last song is over, Cherry stands up straight, flicks her hair over her shoulders, and says sweetly, "A hundred even, sweetie, though I won't say no to more."

I can't move off my chair yet, still glued there by the experience. I hope this place takes credit cards, and I can kiss lunch out goodbye for a month or two, but it's totally been worth it. I don't have to worry, as it turns out. Joe stands and hands Cherry a few bills from his wallet, then a few more.

"Hey, thanks! You come see me any time, you hear?" She's got a pretty smile. She winks. "See you out there."

It is, I realize, watching her walk away, just a job. She's very, very good at it, but it's just a job for her the way a job is to everyone else. I'm not sure if that disappoints or relieves me, since I'm still reeling from the realization that I'm hornier than I've ever been in my life.

"You ready to get out of here?"

Joe's hand cradles my elbow and he helps me up. I want to look down and see if he's got a hard-on, but I don't dare. My nipples are hard, and I can feel slick wetness between my legs.

"Yes." My voice is hoarse and I have to clear my throat to say again, "Yes, I'm ready."

I expect to regain control by the time we get to Joe's car, but I don't. My hands are definitely sweating. He opens the door for me, but before I get in, I turn to him.

We fall on each other like we're starving. His tongue

moves over my jaw and his hands cover my breasts, rubbing my nipples just lightly enough to make me moan. He does have an erection. I can feel it against me. The car door jams against my back and without saying anything we both turn and twist so he can get inside on the passenger seat. A second later I'm on his lap and the door slams shut. I've got one hand braced on the dashboard while the other pulls down my panties and lifts my skirt. I hear the clash of metal as he undoes his zipper. I lift up, waiting. He's taking longer than I expect and I look over my shoulder to see him fumbling out a small silver packet from the car console.

I would take the time to think about what sort of guy keeps condoms so handy, but I'm just glad he does. The moment after that he pulls on my hips, positioning himself under me. Then he fills me with a grunt and I let out a low cry.

We're parked in shadows but that doesn't mean we can't be seen. I don't care. Joe pumps into me, hard and fast, and his hand reaches around my front to stroke my clit. I'm surprised by this consideration, but as grateful for it as I am for his caution. It doesn't take much to get me off. His fingertip rolls my clit in time to his thrusts, and I come with a cry I bite back.

My fingers grip the dash so hard I dimple the padding. Joe pushes into me a couple more times and comes with a grunt. The whole act's taken maybe three minutes.

He relaxes back against the seat, his hands on my hips pulling me back a little. He's still pretty hard inside me, and I relax for a moment, too, trying not to think too much about what has just happened.

He moves beneath me after a bit and hands me a box of tissues, which I use as I disengage from his penis. It's close quarters now, and we bump a lot, but he makes it all very matter of fact and easy, so I don't feel too embarrassed.

He must do this a lot, I think. That does embarrass me, but not as much as I thought it might. I mean…it was pretty spectacular sex, and it's not like I wasn't hoping to hook up with him anyway.

Somehow we manage to get ourselves covered up and in our right seats. The car reeks of sex, but I can't roll down the window until he starts the engine. Joe sits behind the wheel for a few seconds, as if he's gathering strength or something. He turns to me and grins.

"Did you have fun?"

I don't know if he means inside or out here, but the answer is the same, anyway.

"Yes," I tell him. "I sure did."

"Good," says Joe as he starts the car. "I'm glad."

That was the first time I heard what Joe does for a living, and his last name. I found these two details more intimate than the description of the car sex or the way it felt to have a stripper writhing on his lap.

"So what happened at the wedding?" It was the only thing I could think of to ask. I was still trying to process what I thought about this latest story, and how Joe always manages to find the women who will do things such as fuck in cars on the first date. Or who will get lap dances from strippers, for that matter.

"It was fine. Every time I looked at her, she started to

giggle. We held it in pretty much during the ceremony but at the reception she got toasted and couldn't stop laughing."

"So…did you go home with her that night, too?"

"Nah."

"No? Why not?"

Joe smiled and shrugged. "Been there, done that?"

This answer annoyed me. "You know, for someone who claims he's not a slut, you sure don't prove it."

"Sadie," Joe said patiently. "She lives in another state. It was a wedding hook up, that's all. Happens all the time."

"To you," I said, grouchy. "Not everyone in weddings hooks up."

"What, I should've gotten her e mail address? Promised to keep in touch? She didn't even pretend that's what she wanted."

He sounded smug about it, so I glared. "You could've resisted the urge to fuck her in your car."

"But why?" He seemed honestly curious. "Sadie, she wanted to do it. Nobody got hurt. I was careful. I'm always careful. What's the big deal?"

The big deal was jealousy, and I wasn't sure if it was envy at his constant ability to seek pleasure and find it, or the more insidious jealousy that dozens of women were getting to feel Joe's cock inside them, and I never would.

"You say you want to settle down. Find someone. But you just keep fucking your way through woman after woman. That's the big deal. I think you're full of shit."

We'd gone more than a year without an argument and now we were having the same one twice. What that meant about our relationship did not hide its face from me, that fighting can be as intimate an act as fucking.

"And I think you're being a judgmental bitch," said Joe.

My jaw dropped before I could gain enough control to close my mouth with an audible snap. He leaned against the back of the bench, arms outstretched along it, and gave me a smug smirk. I twitched away from him, though he hadn't touched me. We stared at each other, and I wasn't stupid enough not to notice the tension between us wasn't entirely borne of anger.

"I don't hurt any of them, Sadie."

I sniffed. "So you say. All I ever hear is your side of it."

"Would it be better if I pretended I intended something I don't? If I took them out on lots and lots of dates, got their hopes up? Would that make me a better person?" Joe's pose seemed affected, as if he was trying too hard to look casual.

"How do you ever expect to find someone if you never give them more than one night? If you 'been there, done that' to everyone?"

He ran a hand through his hair and squinted at me. "Maybe I'm looking for something special."

"Well," I said stiffly. "How do you think you're going to find it if you keep hopping in and out of beds all over Harrisburg?"

"It was in a car," he pointed out, but I was less than amused.

"The point is, Joe, you say you want something but you show no intentions of making lifestyle changes to support it."

I don't even use a tone that prim and stuck-up with my patients. I've certainly never used it with Joe. It was too late to call it back.

He sat up straight. "You make it sound like I fuck every woman I meet."

"Don't you?" I know he doesn't. That would be impossible, really, to have sex with every woman. I was being facetious.

Joe didn't fall for it. He just leaned forward a bit more, his eyes dark and his mouth curved downward. "No, Sadie. I don't."

He meant me. I knew it. He knew I did. But we said nothing more about it, just turned back to our sandwiches and drinks and finished our lunch as though the entire conversation hadn't even occurred.

I'm usually undeniably refreshed when I come home from work on the first Friday of every month. This Friday was an exception. I'd stopped to pick up some take-out. The argument with Joe had me craving something I could enjoy.

"Hello, handsome," I purred as I pushed open the door with my hip.

Adam was already in bed, watching TV. He barely looked at me as I came in. I looked to see what had him so enthralled.

"*Baywatch?* Should I be worried about you?" I teased as I set up the table with our dinner.

Adam didn't laugh. "Why? Because I enjoy looking at jiggle television?"

Okay. Tonight was not a night for teasing. I moved to the bed to kiss his forehead, and he made a disgruntled noise and tried to pull away.

"I'm watching this."

"Fine. I brought take-out from Passage to India. I thought we'd eat and then watch a movie?"

"Since when do you like Indian food?"

Joe had introduced me to it, bringing with him to lunch the delicious curries and breads I'd discovered I adored. I kept that information to myself as I opened containers and ladled food onto plates. "Since…a long time?"

"I thought you didn't like spicy food."

"You do," I pointed out. "And tastes change. C'mon, I got your favorite. Stop with the third degree and let's eat."

He looked over at the table and his expression softened. "Aw, thanks, baby. That was nice."

I kissed his cheek and this time, he didn't protest. "I thought it would be a nice date."

Adam snorted. "Some date."

"Hey," I said softly, making sure he was looking into my eyes. "It's the best kind. We don't have to dress up for it or anything."

"You're dressed up."

I looked down at my clothes. "Not really. Just for work."

He shook his head, faintly. "You're wearing your silk shirt. Which means you've got on your Victoria's Secret bra, which means the matching panties. And the garter-belt. Am I right?"

I looked down at my clothes again, then up to his eyes. "You're good."

His smile curved on only one side. "And you're wearing perfume."

He turned his face to sniff my neck, where I had, indeed layered my skin with perfume that morning. I couldn't even smell it any longer.

"The expensive stuff," he murmured. "Your special occasion scent."

Heat flushed me, burning in my cheeks and the tips of my ears. I laughed lightly and pulled away, turning to the table so I didn't have to show my guilty face.

"What's the special occasion, Sadie?"

"Do you want chicken or lamb?" I fiddled with the containers while I got my expression under control and turned back to him with a smile.

"Sadie?"

The hardest lies to detect are the ones surrounded by truth. In school, we'd been paired up and prompted to lie to random answers to a set list of questions. It became a challenge to see if we could fool each other. What was most interesting was not what some of us chose to lie about, but about what some of us chose to tell the truth.

"I felt like dressing up. That's all."

I felt his eyes on me as I pulled the wheeled table over to his bed and began cutting up his food.

"Well, you look beautiful."

I put down the knife and fork and looked into his face. Love rushed up inside me so strong I thought I might cry from it. I cupped his cheek, one of the few places I could touch him and have him feel it.

"Thank you, honey."

"You always do, Sadie." He smiled and kissed my palm. "But always especially on the first Friday of the month."

Neither of us spoke for a moment. The food was getting cold, but I didn't care. I kept my eyes on his, and this time, there was no need to lie.

"I love you, Adam. Only you."

After another long moment, he nodded. "I know you do."

I leaned in to kiss him. "I heard Dennis leaving. We don't even have to lock the door."

I wiggled my eyebrows suggestively, hoping to make him laugh. He smiled, but it was a faint shadow of his usual grin.

"I'm starving. And pretty tired."

Concerned, I pressed my hand to his forehead. "Do you feel all right?"

He gave an irritated sigh and jerked his head away. "I feel fine. I'm hungry and tired, I said. I thought we were going to eat and watch a movie."

"Yes, but—" But I thought maybe we could fool around didn't seem quite the thing to say. In our past, Adam had sometimes worn me out with his constant desire, with his need for me. Back then the food would have been left to get cold while we satisfied our other hunger first.

But this was now, not then, and my ego wasn't so solid that his rejection wouldn't wound me.

"Right," I amended. "Food. And then a movie."

"Why don't you go change, first," Adam said, his voice cold. "Maybe take a shower, too. Your perfume's giving me a headache. I'll finish watching *Baywatch*."

I wished he'd come out and accuse me. I could defend myself against accusations but could do nothing against his silent conviction of my infidelity. If he'd asked me, I could have told him the truth, all of it.

He didn't ask, and so I didn't tell.

Chapter 09

June

*T*his month, my name is Sassy. It's really Sarah, but Sassy suits me just as well. I have hair in multiple shades of blue and green and a penchant for making devil horns with my fingers. I favor striped stockings worn with vintage Converse sneakers and short skirts held together with safety pins, and I've a lot of piercings you can see and some you can't.

I've known Joe for about six months. I'm the computer tech who comes in to service the system his practice uses. I tease him about having to clear his cache of porn and he jokes back about having to wear sunglasses to guard against the atrocities of my fashion.

I like Joe a lot, and I'm pretty sure he likes me. He's a good-looking dude, a real smart suit, but he's got a great sense of humor, too. A rare thing, I tell him, compared to his co-workers. Once in a while he saves a doughnut for me from the box in the lunchroom. I sometimes pick him up a bagel with cream cheese and lox from the deli downtown.

It's a good working relationship, but that's all it is until the day I come across him sitting at his desk staring at his monitor with a scowl so fierce it's as if he's trying to burn a hole in it with his eyes.

"It's a virus, it's nothing personal," I tell him as I set up the scan and prepare to clean his hard drive. "Half the practice got it."

It's going to set him back a day's work, he complains, and I reassure him I'll have him up and running in no time at all.

"If you can do that," Joe says, "I'll buy you dinner tonight."

It's not like we've never flirted before. I mean, I flirt with most everyone. It doesn't really mean anything. But this time…well, this time I'm tempted to put on a little extra Sassy charm for Joe. It's very clear to me, as it's been for months, Joe's in terrible need of someone to take care of him. I don't mean in just a sexual sense, though I'm sure he's got his share of offers. No, I mean Joe needs someone to ask him how his day was when he comes home, someone to draw him a bath once in a while, cook him soup. Joe needs some petting, something I'm pretty good at, but of course I can't offer it to him just out of the blue. I tell myself it's because he seems so down about the computer, and he's seemed bummed the past couple times I've been in, but the flat-out reality is—Joe's beautiful. He's got features that line up just right, so pretty. It makes me want to sketch them.

He's surprised when I tell him that later over dinner. It only took me fifteen minutes to get his computer working again, and he made good on his word.

"I didn't know you were an artist."

"I'm not, really. Art's something I do for fun. It's not my career."

"You don't have to make a living at it to be considered an artist." Joe leans across the table, gaze intent upon me.

I feel the weight of his gaze all over me, covering me like a blanket. I might be out of my league, here. There's flirting, which we've been doing for about six months. And then, there's flirting with intent, which until tonight neither of us bothered with.

"So," I ask him over dessert, a very good cheesecake we share, not because I'm the sort of girl to moan about my waistline, but because we both ate so much we can only stuff in half a piece each. "When you're not wasting company time downloading Internet porn, what do you like to do?"

He's got coffee. I've got tea. He stirs sugar and cream into his cup. I watch the dark liquid turn light as his spoon makes swirls. At first I think he's not going to answer me, but then he does.

"I like to read."

"Don't sound so ashamed," I say, teasing. "You do mean other than Internet porn, right?"

He laughs. Joe's got a great laugh to go with his smile. The real smile, which he doesn't use as often as the smarmy one.

"Yeah, besides Internet porn."

We launch into a discussion of literature, lofty and base. I admit a passion for ridiculous science-fiction. Joe prefers mysteries and thrillers, he says because he likes the challenge of figuring out whodunit before the end of the book.

Dinner's over and they're giving us significant looks that say they want to clear our table, so Joe and I finish our drinks and the cheesecake and head out into the night. It's later than I expected it to be, but conversation with him was so easy and nice it made the evening fly by.

On the drive home, the car is filled with tension he does nothing to alleviate and I analyze. Do I want to fuck Joe?

My gut answer is an unequivocal yes. I mean, I like sex. I like Joe. I don't have a boyfriend and if he's got a girl-friend, that's not really my problem since he's never mentioned her and he doesn't keep her photo on his desk at work.

So yes, sure, I want to. I'm not worried it will cause awkwardness at work, either, because I'm pretty sure we'd both take it for what it is. I'm not looking for a boyfriend, even a real cutie like Joe. He's too much suit for me, with my slightly vagabond lifestyle and eclectic taste in clothes.

When he pulls up in front of my house, he seems surprised. I live in neighborhood that used to be bad but has since become trendy and therefore, overpriced. I laugh at his expression and get out of the car. Gavin, the kid from two houses down, waves to me with the hand not holding onto his girlfriend. I wave back.

"The previous owner went to live with her son. It was in pretty bad shape. I've been refinishing it myself. I'll sell it at a profit in a year or two."

Inside, I get a rush of warmth at the appreciation he shows of my efforts. I show him the floors I stripped, sanded and varnished by hand, the walls I plastered and painted, the kitchen I'm slowly refitting with antique and retro appliances. I don't have much furniture and the decor is plainer than he must have expected, based on what he sees of my personality.

"Most people live beige lives," I explain in the bare living room, where paint cans and brushes still scatter the tarp-covered floor. "I want to sell this place to a nice, upwardly mobile yuppie couple, if they still exist."

Joe's laugh is rueful and self-effacing, and it makes me suddenly like him even more than I already did. "They do."

He's loosened his tie and his hair is a bit tousled. His cheeks hold a hint of color in that tawny skin and his eyes are bright, maybe from the wine I'd given him in my kitchen.

"I don't live in most of the house. But upstairs, in my bedroom…"

Our eyes meet. I'm going to take him upstairs and let him take off my clothes. I'm going to give him what pleasure I can and assume he'll offer some to me. I know this, and I'm pretty sure he does, too, but for one moment we stand as if frozen and look into each other's eyes.

"I'd like to see it." He lifts the wine and sips. Gives me that grin, the one I'm used to, the one that says he's flirting. Funny how Joe's regular flirting smile isn't any different than the one he uses for flirting with intent.

Maybe I only think mine is, so I test it out. I sweep my gaze up and down his body, taking in every inch, before I look back into his eyes. I slide my tongue slightly along my lower lip, give him the lift of chin, the tilt of head, that says I'm dead serious.

"Then c'mon upstairs." I'm challenging him, a little.

Heat flares between us. My flirting does have subtle layers after all. I crook my finger and he steps closer. He puts the glass on the newel post. I take his hand and link our fingers together, and then I take him upstairs.

I pause before I open the door. I turn to Joe and we stare at each other. He's smiling. I am, too.

"Sassy." Joe strokes the length of my hair, twining blue and green and violet.

"Joe," I answer with a little wiggle of my eyebrows.

"Maybe I should go."

My hand's on the knob behind me, and I'm turning it. My other hand is still in his. I'm not letting him go. I push open the door and back inside the room, pulling him with me.

"Do you want to go?"

"No."

"So then don't." Now we're all the way inside and he seems about to say something but instead he just looks around.

This room rocks. Deep blue walls and ceiling, matching deep blue carpet. There are small specks of luminescent paint in the shape of constellations on the walls and ceiling. My bed's a stack of mattresses on the floor, covered with dark blue blankets. I have a plain wooden dresser painted to match the walls. It's like walking into the universe.

"Wow." He turns as far as he can in a circle while being tethered by my hand. He looks at me. "You *are* an artist."

His compliment touches me. "Thanks."

He pulls me closer. I'm shorter than I seem and have to tilt my head way back to look into his face. His hands fit nicely on my hips, the curves of which I'm not shy about. I reach up to tug at his tie, loosening it further. I slip it from the loop of his collar and unbutton the next button of his shirt.

Joe puts his hand over mine. "Sassy, wait…"

I put my other hand over his and look up. "Shh. It's okay. This will be fun, I promise."

I'd always had the idea Joe was a bit of a player. I mean, a guy like that, no girlfriend, means he's on the market for a reason. Usually it's commitment issues, looking for the next great thing, can't seem to settle down. Whatever. I've seen my share. His hesitation makes me think maybe I misjudged him, and a thought crosses my mind.

"You're not gay, are you?"

His face goes so shocked it makes me laugh. "No! Why? Do I act like I'm gay?"

"No." I undo the next button. "But you'd have to be gay to turn me down."

He laughs. "I'm not gay."

By this time I've got half his buttons undone and his chest is yummy. I quickly finish with the rest and fold open the material to get a better glimpse.

"Joe, sweetie, listen. I don't know what kind of girls you're used to, but let me take a guess, okay?"

"Okay." The ease of his answer tells me he's sure I'll guess wrong.

"You like women. You're not as picky as a guy like you could be, and that's not bad. It's a good quality." I trace my finger down the ridge of his sternum and then around each of his nipples, which tighten quite nicely. Sweet. "But you're looking for something in particular, which is why you keep looking, am I right?"

His gaze has been focused on my finger's path, but he looks at me. "Yes."

I pull his shirt from his waistband slowly and let my palms skate up his skin to his shoulders to slide his shirt off. His skin prickles into gooseflesh, though the room's more than warm enough. I smile. My touch is making him shiver, and that's very flattering.

"You're not a player. I was wrong about that." I lean forward to nuzzle against his skin. He smells clean. Too many guys like to bathe in their aftershave.

"I'm not?" He puts his hands into my hair and gathers it at the base of my neck. It's my turn to shiver.

I lick his skin and smile again when a small hiss slides out of him.

"No. A player is someone who sets out to fuck his way through women without giving regard to their feelings. A player gets off on getting what he wants and then leaving. A player gets off on the escape. But you, Joe, you..." My hands go to his belt buckle. Below it his cock is already half-hard, and I slide a hand down to cup him through his pants. "You want to be caught. Don't you."

He pulls my hair to tilt my head back, and it's my turn to hiss because his touch is a little rougher than I'm expecting. He looks angry. I'm not scared. I know I'm right. I stroke his cock through his pants and we stare each other down until his fingers loosen.

"It's not that simple, Sarah."

"It never is."

I unbuckle his belt and reach my hand inside. I find his hot length and ease it from the confines of his briefs. I like the way he feels like this, all heat and hardness, a small, tight throbbing.

Joe's cock is thick enough to curve my fingers and hard enough that I've got it out of his pants—it makes me think of steel. Moving my hand up and down just a little while keeping a firm grip moves his skin, just a little, up and down. From what I can see so far, he's got a pretty dick.

His head's tipped back a bit, his eyes closed. I could hate him for his gorgeous lashes. They make small flickering shadows against his cheeks.

His lips have parted. I let my hand move a little more, sliding along his length instead of just gripping it. I twist my wrist as my palm goes up and over the head of his cock, and he makes a low noise.

It's a sexy noise, and my body reacts at once. It's been quite a while since I went to bed with anyone, not from lack of opportunity, mind you. Let's face it, any girl can get laid if she wants it bad enough and doesn't have her standards set too high.

No, I've just been busy and my standards are rather high. Joe's the first man I've invited inside my house for months, and the first I've taken upstairs in longer than that. This, along with the rare glimpse of the man inside the designer suits, makes me feel quite tender toward him.

I want to make Joe smile, a real smile, not the charming

one he uses so well. I want, even if it's just for tonight, to make him happy. Give him a little bit of what he wants.

He murmurs my name and I let my stroking slow. A slight flush has crept across his cheeks and down his throat, a sight I find unbearably sexy. He opens his eyes and looks down at me, and I sense a hesitation.

I bring his hand to my breast, urging his thumb to pass across my nipple and the ring through it. It stiffens under the thin fabric of my shirt. I want him to be certain this is what I want, too, that he's turning me on. Because he is. This is.

Together we back toward my bed. He stops at the edge to push his pants and briefs down and step out of them. He toes off his socks while I pull my shirt over my head and unhook my bra. The air still feels as warm in here as it did before, but I shiver like he did when I touched him as he covers my breasts with his hands. My nipples are tight, hard pegs against his palms and I can't wait to feel his mouth on them. And between my legs. Something tells me Joe isn't the sort of guy to shy away from going down, and the thought excites me so much my thighs contract in spasms of anticipatory pleasure.

We're naked in a few minutes, and a slow smile tilts his lips.

"Smug appreciation," I tell him. "I'll take it."

I put a hand on my hip and cock it, thrusting my breasts forward in a parody of seduction.

His laugh sounds surprised. "What?"

"Your smile. Smug appreciation. You're a man of many smiles, Joe. I've seen smarmy charming, sincere humor and reluctant wistfulness. Now I've seen smug appreciation."

His thumbs brush against my nipples as he ponders this. I think it bothers him, a little, but he doesn't deny any of it. Instead, he takes his hands away to look over my body again, and this time, there's no smugness in the appreciation at all.

"How's that one?" he asks, and we both laugh.

"Very nice."

"You're very nice." His hands move back to my body, sliding up and down and around to cup my ass.

"Don't sound so surprised," I tell him, pinching his nipple lightly. "I might not be the sort of girl you're used to—"

He stops me by pulling me close to his body, skin on skin. "And I'm your type of guy?"

This closeness, the pressure of his erection against my bare belly, makes my voice hoarse. "Not really. No."

"Too clean cut? Not enough ink?"

He traces the line of the tattoo I have on my belly, an intricate Celtic knot surrounding a Star of David.

"You got it." That's not really true, but to talk about the real reasons Joe isn't my type while he's licking my throat is a bit of fragrant bullshit. What we both want is to fuck and have it be good and unemotionally tangled. It doesn't really matter that we're not each other's "types."

He pushes me gently back on the bed and looms over me on hands and knees. His mouth now has moved lower, to sweep along my breasts and finally, oh, fuck! To take a nipple between his lips.

"Funny, I thought I'm any woman's type," he murmurs, licking and sucking at my nipples while I mewl in pleasure.

"Is that your problem?" I ask when he takes a brief break from my tits to concentrate on my throat again. "They all think you're their type?"

His body covers mine, but he's good enough to keep from crushing me with his weight. His mouth pauses in its exploration of the curves and hollows of my throat. His hand, stroking my hip, stops.

"Yes," he says.

His face is buried against me and I can't read his eyes, but I don't have to. This feels like an honest answer, probably more honest because he doesn't have to look at me when he says it. I run my fingers through his hair. It's soft, but short, and if he uses product in it, it's not much.

"Poor Joe," I whisper. "They all want you but none of them know you."

This raises his head and he stares, mouth slightly open and glistening with the saliva he's been painting on my skin with his tongue. He blinks rapidly a few times. We're glued together at the gut, his dick rubbing the softness of my belly.

I take his cheeks in my hands and hold him still to stare into his eyes. "Why don't any of them know you?"

He shakes his head and pulls away a little, but not hard enough to take his face from my hands. I wait until he looks at me again, and I tell him something that seems pretty straightforward to me but appears to take him by surprise.

"Sweetie, it's all everyone's looking for. Someone to know them."

His body tenses, like he wants to flee, and expecting him to get up, I let him go. After a moment he lays down on top of me again and presses his mouth to the beat of my pulse. We stay like that for some silent moments until I realize our breathing has timed itself to each other. In. Out. His skin has humped into gooseflesh, thousands of tiny bumps that scratch my fingertips as I stroke my hands down his back over and over.

His arms have gone around me as best they can in our position. We're hugging each other. I wrap my legs around his waist and hook my ankles together to embrace him as completely as I can.

He's not saying anything, but his cock's still hard and his heart is thump-thumping against mine.

"How many women?" I whisper in his ear, my breath caressing him.

"A lot. Too many. Not enough."

This makes sense to me and I feel sorry for him again. I might be alone, but I'm never lonely. I want someone to know me, someday, but I'm not desperate yet for that someone to find me. Joe seems to think it will never come.

"When's the last time someone took care of you?"

Mute, he shakes his head against me. His fingers splay against me, and we grip each other tighter. I can count the number of bumps in his spine, though he's anything but frail.

"Roll over," I whisper into his hair.

He does, onto his back. I turn off the lamp to make this easier for him, and it takes a moment for my eyes to adjust to the darkness. By the time they do, the stars have begun to glow against the ceiling. There's a little bit of light from the window, enough to outline him in silhouette, but nothing else.

I crouch over Joe's body with my knees on either side of his hips and my hands on the bed next to his ears. I can sense his body, the heat of his cock, but I'm not touching it. I let my hair hang down over both of us and move so it trails along his skin.

He sighs. The bed shifts as he moves, arching a little. I fasten my mouth on the line of his jaw, orienting myself. His skin tastes good. Smallish bristles scrape my lips and I bare my teeth to press them on his skin. I nibble him and dart out the tip of my tongue to flick along the places my teeth have touched.

He's touching me any place his hands can reach, mostly my hips and ass and thighs. He hasn't yet slipped between my legs to stroke me there, but that's okay. There's time enough for that. I don't intend to rush.

I move down his throat to the hard bump of his collarbone. I bite and lick and suck his skin until he cries out. I shush him and soothe the hurt with kisses. His cock throbs harder against my belly. He likes that. I make note.

My hair trails over his face and arms as I move down his chest. I lose myself in nuzzling into the patch of hair there, which smells like him but more. When I find the small button of his nipple and take it between my teeth, his entire body jerks.

I laugh against him. "Sorry."

His voice is hoarse. "Jesus, Sassy."

"Should I be more gentle with you?" But I know the answer to that. With every bite his prick's gotten harder, his breathing a little harsher. He lifts his hips against me whenever my lips part and my teeth scrape his skin. I do that now, before he can answer, and whatever he intended to say is lost in a garbled sigh.

I think Joe's fucked a lot of women, maybe even made love to a few of them. But from the way he's reacting to this it doesn't seem he's had many do the same for him. Which is a shame, because he's got a body that begs to be made love to, all smooth muscles and perfect alignment. Some women, I think, scoffing, don't know what the fuck to do with a beautiful man.

I don't mind the darkness, even if it does make me a little clumsy. Half the fun is having his dick end up in my eye instead of down my throat the first time. I make up for it by kissing his cock very sweetly on the tip, once I've got a handle on where, exactly, it is.

It bobs against my mouth. I grip the base and stroke upward, a feather touch. I kiss it again, small tender kisses on the most sensitive part. I stroke it a few more times while I let my breath kiss him, and I wait until his hand snakes down to tangle in my hair and his hips thrust upward before I open my mouth and ease him inside.

He moans when I do, though mine's muffled. I keep my grip firm just below the head and concentrate on sucking lightly until he stops thrusting. I admire his control and open my mouth wider, relaxing my throat to take him down the back of it.

Sucking cock is an art. Like playing the piano or painting, it takes practice. Enthusiasm. Skill. I like sucking cock for an appreciative man, the sort who'll let me do what I want to do instead of trying to control it all.

I make love to him that way until my jaw begins to ache.

By that time he's moaning a lot, and I'm wet enough to feel it without having to touch myself. My clit tingles and I squeeze my thighs together and let them go repeatedly, a little trick that can get me off if I do it just right.

I stroke his cock and move between his legs to lap at his balls. I find the sweet spot at the base of his testicles and press him with my tongue and fingers until his thighs tense beneath me and his groans take on a certain quality I recognize.

I ease off, moving back up to suck a little at the tip of his cock. I crawl up his body, kissing along his chest and shoulders until the notch of my cunt aligns with his cock. When his prick strokes my clit, I shudder. I rub myself back and forth along him like that a few times, then lean up to grab a condom from the nightstand drawer. I lift up enough to put it on him.

He's gone quiet. I have a hand on his bicep to support myself, and the muscles there are trembling. Slowly, slowly, I maneuver myself onto his erection, shifting and rocking my hips to get the perfect fit. It's been so long since I've had a man inside me I wanted to savor every second. That, and though I'm wet and the condom lubricated, Joe's big enough to stretch me. When the tip of him nudges my cervix, I take a deep breath, but that's it, he's all the way inside me. My thighs grip his hips. I put my hands over his nipples and tweak them lightly.

He surges inside me. I wait until he settles and lean forward, changing the angle just enough so he can push inside me a fraction more. Then I move. Slowly, because I think he needs it that way.

We rock together like a boat on a lake. Gentle, back and forth waves with every so often a bigger one to tip it and make you remember just how deep the water is, and that you can't swim.

We fuck that way for a long time. He lets me control it. If he gets too frantic, I stop. I bite his throat, his shoulder, a nipple, and lick the spot after. I rub my clit against his belly with every thrust. It's an intermittent, tantalizing pressure that sends me into oblivion.

I come for a very long time, and it's wonderful. Joe, bless him, waits until I've finished before he picks up the pace and thrusts inside me ever faster until at last he's done, too.

My body falls forward. He puts his arms around me. My face fits perfectly into the curve of his shoulder. My hair's gone all over the place, tickling, but I'm too sated to push it into a semblance of order.

The moment he softens and begins to slip out could be awkward, but it's not. I reach to my drawer and grab out a clean washcloth, kept there for this very purpose, and I get us both cleaned up and the dispose of the rubber in the garbage as easily as defragging a hard drive. I settle down next to him, a leg thrown over his, and pull up the covers over both of us. It's a bit chilly in here.

We're not saying anything, but neither is he getting up and leaving. I don't want him to feel he has to go, but I don't want him to feel he has to stay, either. So I wait a few more minutes in silence before I kiss his shoulder and lift myself on an elbow to look at him.

I can see only the outline of his face as he turns to me.

Cheeks, nose, chin, the hollows of his eyes. He could be smiling, he could be glaring, but somehow I imagine he's only looking.

"What is it?"

"Why don't you have a boyfriend?"

"That's a million dollar question." I touch his chin with my fingertip. "I don't want one right now, I guess. I'm not looking for one, anyway. I mean, I guess I wouldn't turn one down if life threw him in my lap, you know? But I'm not trolling."

"You're not like most of the women I know, then."

"Honey, if I had a nickel for every time someone told me that, I'd be able to retire."

We laugh, gently, and I tuck myself against him again. I stroke my hand down his chest, over and over, petting him just the way I thought he needed it earlier today at the office.

If he were a cat, I think Joe would be purring. He's gone all loose and warm and his voice sounds drowsy when he answers me.

"I mean, most of the women I meet want a boyfriend. They might say they don't. But they all do."

"Well, sure they do. Most people, if you ask them, want someone. Nobody likes to be alone."

"They see a suit and a car and a job."

I wonder if he'd regret saying these things when the sun is up. If he'd have said them across the dinner table instead of in post-coital splendor. But he's said them, and I appreciate his honesty.

"And you see tits and ass and hair."

Beneath me, his body stiffens but relaxes almost instantly. "Yeah. I guess I do."

"You could meet a nice girl...in church..." I venture, smiling.

Joe snorts. "I don't go to church."

"How come?" I'm curious, always, about what makes people tick. "Are you Jewish? Joe!"

I get up on my elbow again, dramatically. "Omigod, if you're a nice Jewish boy, my dreams have come true! Marry me and have babies!"

He laughs and his hand comes up to stroke down my hair again. "I'm not Jewish."

"Well, damn," I tell him. "Too bad. I thought all your problems were solved."

He's too nice a guy to tell me there's no way in Gehenna he'd actually marry a girl like me, but then I'm too nice to say the same about him. We laugh together, and it's nice. He yawns and I glance at the clock. It's late. I don't have to be up early in the morning, but he probably does.

"Tell you what, bunny," I say. "Stay here tonight and get some sleep, and in the morning I'll make sure you're up and out the door in plenty of time to run home and get ready for work. I'll even make you eggs."

"You will?" His head turns on the pillow and his eyes catch a hint of silver from the faint moonlight.

"Sure." I stroke his chest again, to assure him. "Turn over."

He hesitates, but does, and I spoon him from behind. My belly fits just right against the curve of his ass. I put my arm over his chest and find his hand, which I hold against us both. At first, he's almost vibrating with tension but in a few minutes I feel his muscles relaxing, one by one by one until he's breathing deep and I know he's asleep.

I hated Sassy. I wanted to rip out every single blue hair from her head. I hid it by pretending great interest in my sandwich.

"So, did she make you eggs?" I took a bite of sawdust and washed it down with bile.

"No. I woke up before she did and left." Joe wasn't eating yet. He leaned back against the bench and stretched out his legs.

I try not to be smug and satisfied with that answer. "So…are you going to see her again?"

He looked at me. "I see her almost every week."

I'd like to pretend this fact doesn't make my gut twist. "So it's going well for you."

"She comes into work, that's all, Sadie. I haven't gone out with her again."

"Why not?" I put down my sandwich and concentrated on the soda, sucking so hard the straw rattled the ice in the cup.

"Because she's not my type, and she's not looking for a boyfriend, anyway."

I knew this; he said as much in the telling of the tale. Still, he'd spent the night with Sarah, which he never did. And I couldn't get the vision of her holding him out of my head.

"I like her," Joe said, after a few moments.

"There's nothing wrong with liking her," I answered crisply. "She sounds very likeable."

From the corner of my eye I see him looking at me intently. "What do you see, Sadie? When you look at me? Am I just a suit and a car and a job?"

I watched the second hand on my watch spin around the dial twice before I answered. "No."

"Look at me, Sadie."

I did.

"What do *you* see?"

I gave my head a small, purposeful shake and looked away. "I should be getting back. I have an appointment in half an hour."

Joe has a very nice laugh, a deep and hearty chuckle that's like listening to the ocean. The noise he made just then aspired to become laughter but didn't quite make it.

"See you next month."

I nodded, still not looking at him. He didn't get off the bench. His gaze burdened me.

I am always watching Joe walk away from me. Today I was the first to my feet and turning my back. I left him sitting on the bench, and though I wanted to, I didn't turn back to look at him when I went.

Chapter 10

I had a robe, a locker key and a pair of rubber sandals. The other women in the locker room seemed to have come in pairs or trios, even quartets, and they squawked and nattered like birds gathered around a handful of scattered grain. The open area ringed with lockers reverberated with the rise and fall of feminine chatter, in the midst of which I stood alone.

Katie had given me the gift certificate to Daffodil's Day Spa for Christmas, but I'd been putting off using it. Since I couldn't take the time on the weekend or in the evening, I'd finally broken down and scheduled the appointment during the week. Now I was feeling guilty about taking time away from my patients to succumb to the allure of being pampered.

The cheerful attendant who'd checked me in invited me to use the sauna, hot tub and steam rooms while I waited for my massage. The sunken hot tub was big enough to seat ten women. The bubbling water was a perfect complement to the rise and fall of giggling and confidences, of the complaints about husbands and children.

Nobody looked at me oddly when I came in by myself, but I still felt out of place as I hung my robe on a handy hook and slid into a spot next to a broad, red-faced woman wearing a skirted bathing suit in a bold leopard print.

"Hey, hon," she said at once. "Can you move over? I'm saving that spot for my sister. She's in the steam room."

I acquiesced, of course, automatically, even though there was plenty of room in the hot tub and her sister was nowhere in sight. The woman turned back to her companion on the other side and dove back into her loud, blatant conversation about her husband's outrageous sexual demands.

"He watches those late night cable movies," she declared like she was at home discussing this over coffee instead of in a public place in front of half a dozen strangers. "Then he gets all these…ideas!"

Her friend, a nip/tucked blonde with crimson nails, sighed dramatically. "My husband wants to touch me all the time! He wants to hold my hand, or sleep next to me, and I'm just like, get off me!"

I couldn't listen to this. It wasn't that they sounded malicious. On the contrary, both sounded pretty fond of their husbands, content in the fact their men still loved and desired them enough to demand their attentions. They hadn't dropped into the bitter tone of women who profess to love their husbands but genuinely loathe them.

Even so, I already felt awkward and out of place being

by myself when everyone else was with friends. Sitting here listening to them bitch and moan, no matter how good-naturedly, was like repeatedly hitting myself on the head with a frying pan. Pointless and painful.

The conversation didn't even pause when I got up and went into the empty steam room. Here, at least, I could be alone without feeling like a social misfit. The tiles were warm and the air thick with steam that writhed around me like the embrace of a phantom. I settled onto the bench and breathed deeply, letting the heat and moisture embrace me. Unlike the locker room and hot tub, the steam room cosseted me with its silence. Somnolent. Lugubrious. Stygian.

I made myself laugh a little, thinking of the very best and most flowery words to describe this small room. Thus, I was cheered a bit by the time they called me for my appointment.

My masseuse introduced herself as Marta, and she stepped out of the room while I got comfortable under the sheet. Comfortable wasn't exactly what I felt. The staff recommended nudity for massage, and when was the last time I'd been naked in front of a stranger?

She rapped quietly on the door and came in at my murmured assent that I was, indeed ready. She asked me a few questions and dimmed the lights. Soft music burbled from hidden speakers. She positioned herself behind my head.

"You tell me if you need more or less."

I promised I would and tensed with the waiting for her touch. The music shifted and changed. Marta's strong, nimble fingers cupped the back of my neck and worked tension spots at the base of my skull. I wanted to ask her how she knew what I needed, how she know how and where to touch me, to ease aches I hadn't even noticed, but fortunately for my dignity, such silly questions were rendered impossible by my mouth's refusal to form words. I floated in that dim room, with music and the scents of lavender and rosemary to cradle me while she worked.

After a few moments she left my neck and moved to my side, exposing my arm but tucking the sheet around my body to maintain my modesty. Her hands moved along my bicep, then my forearm, working muscles I abused with daily typing and writing of my notes, but to which I rarely paid notice. I let out a small groan when she hit a particularly tender spot on the underside of my wrist. Her fingers pressed and kneaded and worked their way down toward my hand where she tugged each of my fingers. My hand in hers, my fingers closed and opened involuntarily as she massaged my palm and the back of my hand. She closed both hands over mine, holding it between them for a second or two before massaging between each of my fingers.

Emotion rushed into my throat with the force and bitterness of acid. When was the last time someone had held my hand this way, with such tenderness and care? When was the last time anyone had held my hand at all?

I forced myself to swallow against the knot lodged in my throat, but could do nothing about the sting of tears behind my closed eyelids. Marta moved to my other arm and worked it with the same tender force she'd used on the first. By the time she got to my right hand, her palm against mine as she manipulated my fingers, I couldn't even pretend not to be weeping. Tears made silent, burning trails down my cheeks, puddled in my ears and leaked down the side of my neck.

"I'm going to ask you to roll over now." She squeezed my hand between both of hers, then patted my shoulder.

Grateful for the chance to hide my face and gain control, I rolled quickly onto my stomach and nestled my face into the doughnut-shaped cushion at the head of the table. The smooth, crinkling paper covering pressed coolness to my heated face, against my eyes, so I didn't even have to close them in order to blind myself. It blocked out everything, cocooning me.

Nobody touched me anymore. A handshake or the kind of casual hug that kept inches between upper bodies and didn't even come close to lower body contact were not enough for me. I missed Adam's all encompassing hugs, his legs and thighs and pelvis pressed against me. I missed being engulfed by him.

Dealing with someone else's tears is never a comfortable business, not even when you're expecting them. I tried to keep them silent, to keep my shoulders from tensing with sobs I couldn't bear to release. Marta had to know I was crying, but said nothing, only kept up her work.

I wept in silence, without sobs, without effort. I heard the snap of the cap opening, the liquid slush of oil poured into her hands, and felt them once more my skin. My knotted muscles unraveled, and so did I.

Marta placed her palm flat on my back, between my shoulder blades. "I'm finished. I'll get you a cup of water. I'll be back in a minute."

She discreetly left a bunch of tissues next to me. I waited for the door to close before I sat, clutching the sheet around my breasts with hands still slick from oil. I wiped my face and pulled on the spa's robe, recovering a bit by the time she returned with a paper cup of tepid water I didn't really want to drink.

"I'm sorry," I said, feeling like a puppy who'd piddled on the rug.

"You don't have to be sorry. Massage releases endorphins and can be an intensely emotional experience." She squeezed my shoulder kindly. "Have a good rest of your day, okay?"

I nodded, feeling less of a fool than I thought I would.

I stepped into my quiet house without announcing my presence. I moved with muscles still loose and soft, feeling something like a dancer in the way I set each foot heel to toe along the hardwood floor and the sweep of my hands as I unbuttoned my coat and hung it up, as I settled my briefcase onto the hook. I paused, listening to the noises of a house not expecting my presence.

The soft tick of the grandfather clock in the living room melded with the low mutter of daytime television from the kitchen, and the steady sound of a knife on a cutting board. I put my hand to the newel post, my foot to the stair and drank in the peace of my home with eyes closed and slow, deep breaths.

"Dr. Danning?"

I opened my eyes at once. "Hi, Mrs. Lapp."

"You're home early." She looked concerned. "Are you sick?"

"No. I had an outside appointment today and decided to come home early, that's all."

She still looked concerned. I figured the evidence of my afternoon's distress was stamped all over my face. Wiping her hands on a dishtowel, she nodded, looking unconvinced but perhaps not certain of what wasn't convincing her.

"All right," she said. "Do you want me to go, then?"

"If you'd like to, that would be fine."

She nodded. "I'll call Samuel. We've got the grandkids for a few days while Emma and her husband are on a trip."

"Then of course you should go home," I told her. "Go spend time with them!"

She beamed, her gaze still sweeping me up and down. "I'll be back tomorrow."

She bustled away and I went upstairs. The quiet up here was more pervasive. Dennis would be sleeping, most likely, since he usually didn't get up until around 5:00 p.m. Adam was probably working.

I moved on quiet feet to his door and pushed it open a little. "Adam?"

He wasn't working. He was in bed, his computer on but open to a blank document. He'd turned his face toward the window, where early afternoon sunshine moved in shadows cast by the tree outside.

I'd seen him thousands of times this way, his long, lean body covered with sheets and blankets to keep him warm because he could no longer regulate his temperature effectively on his own.

"Hey," I said quietly, little more than a whisper.

He turned to look at me. Once, his eyes or the curve of his mouth would have told me what he was thinking. He'd have reached for me, murmuring my name, and taken me to bed where he might have undressed me slowly or barely bothered at all, and we'd have made love for hours.

"What are you doing home?" he said, instead, his voice hoarse with a touch of a cold.

"I used the gift certificate Katie gave me today." I moved toward the bed to sit beside him. I reached to smooth his hair off his forehead. It was getting too long again. "You need a trim, Cap'n."

"How was it?" His eyes moved over me, and I wondered what he saw.

"Very relaxing." I stroked my fingers through his hair. It felt different, now. He'd always worn it long, like silk against my fingers. They'd had to shave his head in the hospital to put him into traction, and it had grown back thicker, but coarse. "Let me cut this for you."

"It's fine, Sadie."

I pushed my fingers through his hair again, letting it caress the back of my hand. "It's too long. It's getting in your eyes."

He gave a long-suffering sigh. "All right."

I leaned to kiss his cheek, pausing to breathe him in, my husband. "I'll get the scissors."

In the bathroom, my reflection confronted me. My hair had come loose from its clip and feathered around my cheeks in tousled waves. My eyes were red and my cheeks flushed, my clothes in disarray. I'd ignored the complimentary showers and lotions at the spa, unable to face being there any longer than necessary, and left without doing more than dressing and grabbing my jacket. I looked like I'd just rolled out of bed. No wonder Mrs. Lapp had looked at me with such consternation. Now I knew what Adam had seen when he looked at me. I wondered what he thought, or if he believed me.

I grabbed the comb and the barber scissors and went back to him. I adjusted the bed to full sitting position and fastened a towel around his neck. I finger-combed his hair so it fell over his eyes the way it used to, making him a rogue.

"Cut it short," he said suddenly. "Really short."

I hesitated. "How short is really short?"

Adam smiled. "Just short of shaved."

I raised my eyebrows. "Are you sure? I thought you liked your hair."

"Each man kills the thing he loves, Sadie."

His tone gave no hint as to his mood, teasing or serious, and I again ran my fingers through his hair. I knew the reference to Oscar Wilde's poem, but I didn't know what it meant for him to say it now.

"Are you sure?"

I'd often been in envy of Adam's eloquence. His use of language to express emotion in a way many people never managed. Now, I waited for his answer, my gaze on his, wishing just once for words to not escape me.

"Cut my hair."

"Adam—"

He gave a minute shake of his head, his mouth thinning. I stopped. I picked up the comb and the scissors, but couldn't force myself to begin.

Adam was not a beautiful man. His features were too bold and asymmetrical for beauty, his eyes deep-set and nose crooked from an old break. But his hair was beautiful, the color of autumn, all deep browns and bits of red, and rare, gleaming strands of gold.

"Cut it," he said.

And so I did.

There was no point in trimming it snip by snip. Like ripping off a bandage, the only way to do this was to do it all at once. The first chunk fell onto the towel on his front, bright against the plain white cloth. Another cut and another, his hair uneven and butchered but getting shorter as he'd wanted.

It was difficult to manage the back with his head resting on the pillow, but I managed. Cut by cut, my scissors flashed, revealing to me the shape of his head and sweetness of his ears, the uneven pattern of his hairline, the vulnerability of the nape of his neck.

It took far too few minutes to finish. I ran my hand over the remaining bristles. The cut made him look younger. Bared. I brushed the stray hairs away and tidied the towel, setting it aside to clean later.

"Do I look like a prisoner?"

I leaned in to take his face in my hands. "You look gorgeous."

He closed his eyes, his mouth going tight and thin again. I kissed his mouth, a brush of lip on lip. "You look beautiful to me, Adam. Like you always do."

His lips parted and the kiss got deeper. He breathed out, and I drew him inside my body. I needed to make him a part of me.

He opened his eyes. Still holding his face, I stroked his cheeks with my thumbs. "I love you, Adam."

"A thousand poets could write for a thousand years," he whispered, "and none of them would ever be able to describe how I feel about you."

I toed off my shoes and pulled down the blankets and got into bed beside him. There wasn't much room for me there, in his bed, but I made it work. I tucked myself up against him and pulled the blankets up around us. I put my hand on his chest and felt the steady thump of his heart, the rise and fall of his breath.

"I hate letting you down," he whispered and broke my heart.

"You've never let me down." I held him closer, but there was no comfort in my embrace for him. "Not ever, Adam."

I waited for his words, but he lay silent. "Talk to me."

"What do you want me to say?"

"Whatever you have to," I said. "Whatever you want to. Just...talk to me, Adam. The way you used to."

His eyes were still closed. "I'm tired, Sadie."

I held him closer for a moment, and then, though I wasn't even close to being ready to let him go, I did. I got up and rearranged the blankets, tucking them around him firmly. I brushed a few more stray hairs away from his face and neck, adjusted the bed, arranged his computer for him. I gathered the towel covered with his hair.

"I'll let you take a nap." I didn't have words like Adam did but nor did I have the talent of keeping my emotions out of my voice. At least not with him. "Do you need anything before I go?"

"I need everything."

I had to lean in to hear what he'd said, and even then I couldn't be certain I'd heard him right. "Adam?"

Eyes still closed, he was hidden from me. He gave another small shake of his head. I waited, hoping, but he didn't open his eyes or say more. I reached to touch him, but in the end, only smoothed the blankets over his leg, a caress he didn't even know.

His voice caught me at the door.

"Thank you for cutting my hair."

"You're welcome," I said, and waited, hoping for more but getting nothing.

It took me an hour to capture from the towel every strand of hair I'd cut. I put them in a small cardboard box and tucked it away in the bottom of my drawer where I didn't have to see it to know it was there.

From my office window, I could see the Susquehanna River. The ice had melted months ago, but the water kept its gray-green winter shade. Across the wide, flat expanse I saw City Island, its colors also muted. It was starting to bustle with summertime activity on the batting range, the baseball field, the small train that circled the island.

It wasn't the view that captivated me and kept me from hearing the knock on my door. I was making lists. Things to plan and do, errands I needed to run in preparation for my upcoming houseguests, groceries I needed to buy, bills I needed to pay. I should have been writing them down, these details of my life, but for the moment I was content to sit and stare out the window, watching the bustle of downtown Harrisburg's lunch hour. The weather had brought out the suits and dog-walkers in droves. I envied them.

"Dr. Danning?"

Embarrassed, I spun in my chair to face the doorway. "Elle! Oh, goodness, is it time already? I'm so sorry, come in."

"I knocked," she said hesitantly. "I guess you didn't hear me."

"I was wool-gathering." I shook my head. "Spring fever, I guess."

Nodding, she sat. I offered a couch for those patients who felt they could speak better on their backs, but Elle had never used it until today. She perched on the edge like she was expecting to sit upon a whoopee cushion, or a pin. Like she expected to up and fly away at any second.

"Iced tea? I have some lemonade, or soda," I offered. "The weather's too warm for something hot."

She shook her head again, sharply, her dark braid swinging. Her fingers twisted and turned in her lap like restless kittens. I said nothing, watching. She looked up at me, and I'd never seen such a look from her before.

"Elle?" I asked gently. "What's wrong?"

"Nothing's wrong," she said. "I mean, wrong implies something bad, or incorrect."

"True."

She squirmed a bit, cutting her gaze from me. Her cheeks had flushed. She crossed and recrossed her legs. When she looked at me again, her smile was tentatively exuberant.

"Do you have something to tell me?" I asked, smiling myself.

She nodded. "Yes, Dr. Danning. I do."

Slowly, she held up her hand. A diamond sparkled on her finger, its beauty not from its brightness or the simplicity of its cut, but in what it meant for her to be wearing it.

"He asked me to marry him," she whispered, as if she was afraid to speak out loud. "And…I said…yes."

There's a time for doctorly distance and a time for genuine congratulations, and this was definitely time for that. I let out a small whoop and came around the desk to shake her hand.

"Congratulations! That's marvelous news!"

Smiling, her hand clutching mine, she burst into tears. I had the tissues ready and sat next to her, patting her shoulder while she had a small fit of hysterics I found utterly reassuring in their sincerity.

"I'm sorry," she said when the tears had tapered away. "I'm sorry, I just…I should be happy…I am happy! But I can't seem to stop crying!"

She blew her nose loudly, took a few deep, shuddering breaths and burst into more tears. I handed her tissue after tissue and held her hand, saying nothing. There wasn't much to say I hadn't said dozens of times already.

I didn't have a brutal childhood. Not even an unhappy one. I had a good relationship with my parents and sister, I'd been popular in school, had met and married the man of my dreams. I didn't have "issues" with my life. I'd been blessed. I'd had self-esteem to spare.

I'd become a psychologist to help people not as fortunate as myself. It had been inconceivable to me that people could destroy each other, over and over again. I had thought back then I could make a difference with my advice, that I could offer comfort. That I could erase damage.

Watching someone I'd come to respect a great deal suffer this way, I felt helpless and futile and worthless. Elle had worked hard with me, never resisting anything I suggested, even when facing her demons was more difficult than running away. She had made great changes in her life, and I wasn't too modest not to take credit for helping her do it. She'd wept and wailed before. She'd screamed and raged, and sat in stoic silence. Until today, I'd never seen her break down so utterly and completely lose the sense of self-composure that had been a point of pride for her as long as I'd known her.

She sobbed into her hands as though her heart was breaking, and I had nothing to do for her but sit beside her and rub her back and hand her tissues.

She gripped my hand so tightly my fingers went numb. Her tears wet my fingers like hot splashes of acid. Her body shook, each sob sounding as harsh as broken glass.

"It's all right to be afraid," I said at last.

She nodded and wiped her face, the tears tapering off into a series of small, hitching sobs that eventually became a soft sigh. She let go of my hand and wiped her face with another handful of tissues. She pushed a strand of hair behind her ear and stared at her hands again.

"I've been counting again."

I patted her shoulder and got up to pour us both glasses of lemonade from the pitcher in the small fridge. She drank hers in a gulp and I poured more, then took my glass and sat next to her.

"And that upsets you."

"Of course it does," she said. "But it helps me, too."

Elle counted things—tiles, leaves, window panes, whatever was on hand—when she felt stressed.

"So long as you understand your reasons for doing it," I said, "It's a way of self-soothing. That's all. You're not drinking or anything like that, are you?"

She shook her head. "No. No, but I'm wearing Dan out, poor guy."

She laughed, after a moment, and her laughter was good to hear. "He says he doesn't mind, but…three times a day is a lot for any guy. You know?"

I'd known once, but it had been a long, long time since I'd had to worry about that. "I bet he doesn't mind."

She laughed again and finished the second glass of lemonade and put the glass down. She wiped her eyes once more and pressed her fingertips to her swollen eyes.

"He says he doesn't care what it takes to get me to walk down that aisle. If I have to wear him down to a nub, he'll do it."

I moved back behind my desk, now that she'd gotten a bit more control of herself. "But you're still afraid. Of what?"

Two of the things that made her such a great patient were her willingness to embrace discussion and the sense of self-awareness that made her emotional problems so poignant. Elle knew exactly what had caused her issues and what she needed to do to overcome them—she struggled with feeling inadequate in her ability to do it, not with not understanding what she needed to do.

"That marrying him will ruin what we have. That I won't be able to do the domestic thing."

"You live together now."

She laughed. "Yes. To my mother's chagrin."

"But your mother likes Dan, doesn't she?"

"She wants me to be married," Elle said, pointing a finger to the ceiling. "She accepts Dan because it's pretty obvious he's the one I'm with and she'd rather see me nicely settled into wedded bliss than be single."

We'd spent a lot of hours discussing Elle's mother. We could probably have spent twice as many more and never reached the bottom of that barrel. They tell us in school not to project our patient's lives onto our own but I could never help but be grateful for my relationship with my mom whenever Elle talked about hers.

"I'm afraid," she continued, "that I said yes to Dan because I'm still trying to please my mother. And not because I really want to be married to him."

"Hmmm," I said, agreeing she had a point. "Struggling with your desire to please your mother is something you've worked on for a while. Do you think you haven't made progress?"

"Do you think I have?" She deftly turned that one

around on me, but shot me a grin that told me her hysterics were over.

"Yes." I hesitated. "I'm very pleased with the progress you've made, Elle. You've come a long way."

"Farther than you ever thought I would?" She asked, rather sagely, I thought.

"I think you've come farther than you ever thought you would."

She nodded slowly. "Yes. I think so, too."

"This will be a good thing for you," I told her, thinking she needed affirmation.

Again, she nodded, the wad of tissues crumpled in her hand. "My heart says so. But my head…" She shook her head and gave me a watery smile. "My head's filled up with all the reasons it won't work. And I keep running the figures, over and over, but I can't seem to come up with an answer."

"You can't distill life down into a set of calculations. I wish we could. It would make things so much easier, wouldn't it?"

"Hell, yeah," she said, and laughed again.

We looked at each other across my desk. Every doctor-patient relationship has to end at some point. Either the healing is done, or it never will be.

"I'd like you to come," Elle said. "I'd like you to be there."

"I'd be happy to come," I told her.

Her smile was like the sun through a prism, all scattered pieces of brightness, but I could tell it was genuine. I returned it. She wiped her eyes again and it was time for her to go.

To really go, and we both knew it.

She stood and offered me her hand. "Thank you, Dr. Danning."

I shook the hand she offered me. "Good luck, Elle."

She nodded again and lifted her chin.

"Take care," she said, a statement that could have been trite but wasn't.

"You, too."

There was distance between us again, the way it had been when she'd first started coming to me. A necessary distance. I watched her leave and wished there was a way to know for sure she'd be all right.

But the problem was, there never is a way to know.

Chapter 11

July

This month, my name is Priscilla, and I'm an investment banker. I wear my blond hair in a tight French twist.
I wear pearl earrings in the tiny, perfect lobes of my ears.
Everything about me is flawless, slim, put-together. I'm not
beautiful, but nobody ever notices.

My friend Tandy's party is sedate and leisurely. Conversation buzzes about stocks, bonds, the theater, books.
The background music is something classical with strings
and piano, and I don't bother pretending I care what it is.
I've got wine in my hand, but nothing to eat although the
table's laden with plates of fancy food.

"But if you compare the Utopian future of Huxley's
Brave New World and the Dystopian future of Orwell's
1984," the man beside me says earnestly, "don't you have
to agree that neither one is a viable scenario when you take
into consideration the current financial and moral
climate?"

Save me, I mouth to the man inching past me toward the buffet. He's a couple inches taller than I am, and I'm wearing my tall shoes. He's blond, too, with light eyes of which I can't tell the exact color. Like attracts like, and it's evident even from the first that we're a nicely matched set.

"The point is," the new man says easily, "both are fiction, Benson. Fiction. Means made up. Get it? And both of those novels reflect the society the author was living in at the time, so of course their ideas of what the future will be like are way different than what we can extrapolate now."

I'm impressed. He's fast, this one. He reaches around behind me to snag a couple biscuit-wrapped frankfurters, putting a casual hand on my forearm to keep from bumping into me as he does. Benson's eyes lock onto the hand on my arm and he steps up the argument.

Do men really still think it's about the conquest?

Apparently Benson does, because he leans in closer, sandwiching me effectively between the two of them. "I know it's fiction, Wilder. I'm not a moron."

Wilder, who hasn't moved away from me although he could, laughs. "Of course you're not."

Benson seems to think Wilder's mocking him, because he scowls. "Look, man, I'm just saying that today's society doesn't leave room for a Utopian future, but nobody expects Big Brother, either."

Beside me, his shoulder brushing mine with every movement, Wilder pops a frankfurter into his mouth. "Frankly, Benson, if I'm going to read futuristic fiction, give me some about Pleasurebots and unlimited sex."

Benson looks aghast, his gaze going immediately to my face as though to check for my reaction. While the comment has taken me rather aback, it's exciting, too, to hear something so blatant. Besides, Benson is boring me. Wilder…is not.

"What about you?" Wilder turns to me, an easy smile spreading across a mouth made for it. "What do you like to read?"

I don't read fiction, usually, and when I tell them both so, Benson looks scandalized. Well, I'm pleased, because whatever he was looking for in me must have included a passionate interest in reading novels. He backs up a step, giving up the pursuit but with a disdainful glance toward Wilder as if to say Benson wasn't beaten—he was voluntarily dropping the pursuit.

I'm not sad to see him go. Benson was becoming overbearing. Wilder, on the other hand—

"Priscilla Eddings." I hold out manicured fingers for him to squeeze.

"Joe Wilder." His hand holds mine for just a second longer than necessary for a social greeting.

I don't mind. I also don't mind he's still standing so close I can smell him, a cologne I can't place. I can also see that his eyes are not gray, as I'd thought, but a greenish-blue.

No matter. We still look good together, both tall, slim, well-dressed and coiffed. We're even wearing complimentary colors, his suit dark charcoal and mine pale dove.

"So, Joe Wilder," I say. "What do you do when you're not rescuing women from overexuberant discussions of literature?"

"Save people from overexuberant discussions about alimony and child support."

"You're a divorce attorney?" I flick my gaze over his body again, taking a second look at the suit, which, yes, is more expensive than I'd first thought. I like that. He's not ostentatious.

"Mediator, actually. In divorce and family affairs."

Even more interesting. Attorneys can be self-absorbed pricks. Mediators tend to focus more on other people, and they still make the same amount of money.

Not that I need a man who makes money since I make my own, and quite a bit of it. But it's better to be with one's own sort. Slumming gets tiresome after awhile.

I have a feeling there's no slumming with Joe. In fact, the more he says, the more convinced I become that Joe is exactly the sort of man I'm looking for. I put on a wide smile and lean in, just a little.

"I'm going to get a drink…"

"Let me. What can I get you?" He looks toward the bar, then back at me, his eyebrow raised in expectation.

It's the perfect answer. "White wine, please."

He nods and heads toward the bar where Tandy's husband Bill is pouring drinks. I watch his walk. I like it.

"I see you've met our Joe." Tandy is a dear friend, but she tries too hard to be stylish. You either are, or you're not. You can buy clothes, but you can't buy style.

I watch Joe chat with Bill. "What makes him 'your' Joe?"

Tandy also tends to simper. "Oh, you know. Just that he's our best single, worthwhile male friend."

The key word being worthwhile, as it seemed likely Benson was single, too. "I'll keep that in mind."

"Ta, sweets," says Tandy and returns to her role as hostess.

Tandy might lack style, but she clearly doesn't lack taste. When Joe comes back with the drinks, I've decided I'm going to spend the rest of the night talking to him.

Which I do.

I'm used to getting what I want, in business and in pleasure. In this, too, Joe and I appear to be well-matched. Our conversation is carefully worded, a game we both know how to play. I speak. He listens. He talks and I weigh what he says against what he means and find little difference between them. I respect that. I'm used to men wanting me but being either too intimidated to tell me so, or else being so arrogant they're certain they can woo me into acquiescence.

There's no wooing to be done with me. I know what I like and what I want, and I'm not really interested in pretense. I don't go to bed with men who don't hold an interest for me long-term, who don't meet my minimum standards.

Sex is as much an act of business as it is of pleasure. I'm not interested in the mess and complications of passion. I like my sex to be as neat and tidy as my appearance. Not without strings or emotion, of course, I'm not an entirely cold fish.

"Benson is giving us the evil eye." Joe leans in to whisper in my ear.

His breath is hot, and I turn to look across the room where Benson is, indeed, watching us. I dismiss the other man with a sniff and turn my gaze to Joe. He's smiling as he sips from a glass of very good whiskey.

"Let him look," I say.

Joe lifts his glass to me. "Absolutely."

We negotiate with glances and casual touches. Joe moves into my personal space, and I allow him. The rest of the room goes away as I focus on him. It pleases me to see he isn't looking over my shoulder to scope out other possibilities. His responses to what I have to say are pertinent and interested.

He's got good stories to tell, but he doesn't overwhelm me with solely talking. He listens, too. The night moves on and the party gets a little raucous. Alcohol loosens inhibitions, makes people friendlier or more combative. Tomorrow morning a lot of the men and women here are going to wake with throbbing heads and regret the alliances they've made and broken as a result of too much wine.

Benson appears to have moved on. Joe and I can hear his impassioned speech from across the room, where he's cornered a stunned-looking brunette who works for my bank. The couple next to us are about to start tongue-kissing at any moment, both of them giddy and flushed, their glasses empty. I move closer to Joe to get away from them, since they've obviously lost all sense of propriety.

"Another?" Joe points to my empty glass, but I shake my head.

He's going to ask if he can see me home, and I'm going to let him. "I should be going."

"Do you have a coat?" he says right away. "Let me get it for you."

This time when I watch him walk away, I smile. Oh, there's time for it to sour, for him to muck up our unobtrusive negotiations by behaving like so many men do with overeager hands and mouths. I'll be sad if that's the case, because Joe's not only good-looking and charming, he's smart, too. He gets it.

He brings my Burberry trench coat and helps me on with it with a compliment. He's got one almost the same, and this satisfies me, too.

Because I only live three blocks from Tandy's house, I walked to the party. Standing on Tandy's front porch with the night air cool but not uncomfortable, it would be easy for Joe to say good-night and leave me. I know he's not going to.

"May I walk you home, Priscilla?"

Neither of us pretend he's offering only to be polite. The negotiations have stepped up a bit. I can't deny the small flutter I feel in the pit of my stomach. It's the same sensation when a particularly good investment comes through, or I finagle a deal that nobody else has managed.

It's sweet anticipation and it makes me smile.

"I'd be delighted."

The brick sidewalk is uneven and though I can walk miles in these heels, I don't mind taking the arm Joe offers. He charms me further on the walk to my house with stories of his childhood menagerie of constantly escaping pets. I share details about my last vacation. These are not intimate stories, but they take us one step along the path we both seem interested in taking.

At my door, I pull out my keys but don't fumble with the lock to give him an excuse to help me, therefore initiating an invitation inside. We stare at each other, both with pleasant smiles. Now's the time he'll either sink or swim, and though I'm hoping he'll swim I've had it all go south at my door more times than not.

"Good night, Joe."

We're standing close enough that the hems of our coats brush with the slightest shift of our legs. I hold my keys in my left hand, and I glance at the lock before looking back up at him. I tilt my head the barest inch to meet his eyes.

"Good night, Priscilla."

Joe's voice is warm and friendly. Both of us pause and the air between us thickens again with anticipation. I wait, wondering if I've read him wrong after all, and he'll turn out to be one more just like all the others.

"I had a great time tonight."

I smile. "I did, too."

I wait. He smiles. The hems of our coats kiss, but we do not.

Joe holds out his hand for me to shake, which I do, and in that moment there is no question in my mind that I'll be seeing him again.

I sat in silence. Stunned. I hadn't even touched my salad, though my stomach had been grumbling since this morning. Now it churned.

Joe sat up straight on the bench, staring directly ahead. A woman jogged by, the cords of her headphones dangling from beneath her baseball cap. She turned her head to look at him as she passed, a gesture that seemed so automatic as to be unconscious. Joe didn't seem to notice.

After another few minutes in which the only sounds

between us were the rush of traffic and the occasional barking of dogs, Joe turned his head toward me with a motion stiff and precise, almost robotic.

"Ask me, Sadie."

I shook my head.

"Ask me why I didn't fuck her."

I couldn't look away from his face. *If he smiles*, I thought, *I'll walk away and never come back.*

"Don't you want to know?"

I didn't want to know. He'd broken the rules, unspoken but understood. If there was no story to tell, I had nothing to listen to. And we had no reason to meet.

"I've seen her three times since then." His voice wasn't defiant, nor smug, only matter-of-fact. "I'm seeing her again tonight."

I swallowed my response like it was a spider, bitter and sick-making. When I said nothing, Joe straightened his body on the bench again. A soft breeze lifted the end of his tie. He crossed long legs, his trousers pulling up to show dark, patterned socks. The intimacy of seeing the bump of his anklebone was too much, and I had to look away.

"Why didn't you fuck her, Joe?"

He looked at me again. "Because she's different."

His description of her appearance, their conversation, the way she smelled, all had told me this woman was not the same as the dozen others he'd shared with me. He'd spoken of others with more admiration. More lust. Even some with more enthusiasm.

But until today, he'd never admitted to dating any of them.

"Don't you want to know why she's different?"

I shook my head. "No, Joe. I don't."

He looked away from the emptiness of the path in front of us. I gave a tiny shrug, a little raise of brow and tilt of lip. He ran his fingers through his hair and scrubbed at his eyes, made a disgruntled groan and got up.

A young mother holding a child by the hand crossed the path in front of us. The boy toddled with determination, almost falling once but deftly caught by his mother. Joe and I both watched them until they rounded the corner and disappeared.

"Have a good time tonight."

I sounded so sincere I almost convinced myself I meant it. I wasn't so sure I convinced Joe, but he didn't say anything. He just nodded and walked away.

"He looks like you." I studied the tiny, wrinkled face of the infant in Katie's arms.

Katie, face drawn with exhaustion, smiled. "Gee, thanks. You're saying I look like a bald old man?"

"Of course not. But he has your nose." I touched the sleeping fuzzy head. "When are Mom and Dad coming back?"

"Evan had to go in to work for a few hours, so they'll bring Lily in from pre-school. About an hour."

"I should go, then. Let you get some rest."

"Sadie—"

I looked up from my examination of my new nephew. "Hmm?"

"Do you want to hold him? I have to pee."

"Sure. Of course."

We made the trade. Katie got out of bed gingerly and disappeared into the bathroom. I stared down at my armful of infant.

James Trevor Harris had ten perfect little fingers and toes, and a rosebud mouth, pursed now, perhaps in dreams of milk. He had perfect golden lashes shut over sweet, smooth cheeks. He had perfect little brows, furrowed a bit in the effort of existence outside the womb. Everything about him was perfection.

He startled when my tear dropped onto his small face, but didn't wake. I wiped it away before it could slide down his forehead to his cheek. His skin felt like rose petals. He took a deep, shuddering breath, and I held mine in anticipation of a wail that didn't come.

"You don't have to leave before Mom and Dad get here," Katie said quietly. She got into bed with a wince and a groan. "You know they're going to want to see you."

"I know." I didn't want to be there, though, to watch them fussing over Katie. Simple and selfish, but true.

Katie gave a weary laugh. "Sure. Abandon me to the smothering. Thanks a lot."

"You'll live. Maybe they'll focus on James." I returned her son to her arms. "He's beautiful."

Katie smiled, lost in contemplation of her son. "He is."

"Congratulations."

She looked up. "You sure you have to go?"

"I do, actually, I have to—"

"Get back to Adam. I know." She nodded. "Okay."

I hugged them both, mother and son, and slipped away.

* * *

"Everything looks good, but we'll need to keep an eye on that pressure sore starting on his left buttock." The visiting nurse was new and borderline manic. She smiled so fiercely it looked like she was baring her teeth instead of grinning, and I thought, she must be new to this.

"I'm over here." Adam's didn't waste his efforts trying to sound falsely genial.

The nurse turned to look at him. He gave her a harder version of the grin I fell in love with. It was like watching a puppet with my husband's face. The same expressions but slightly off.

"Beg your pardon?" She had to be new, unless she was just one of those irritating caregivers who should know better but insist on thinking spinal cord injury means brain damage.

"I'm over here. You can address me." He was in his chair, as he preferred to be when the homecare assistants came. It was because it made him feel more in control of what was going on.

The nurse turned to him. "I'm sorry, Mr. Danning. As I was saying to your wife, everything looks good, but we'll have to—"

"I did hear you," Adam said, impatient. "The first time."

I said nothing. I was there to observe and make note of this one small piece of the immeasurable amount of care he needed on a daily basis. I was there because it was my job as his wife to know what was going on with his health, even though the nurse's breezy, tossed-aside commentary only served to make me more anxious than ever.

She seemed chastened. "I'm sorry."

Adam was entirely out of sorts, and she didn't know him well enough to realize when it was a good time to leave him alone. She blathered on for another few minutes about matters so basic I didn't blame him for being insulted she felt she had to instruct him upon them.

"My accident was more than four years ago," he told her, voice dripping with sarcasm when she explained for the second time how it was important for him to drain his bladder every four to six hours. "I know all about how to piss through a tube."

"Well, all righty then," I broke my silence to say in a bright tone I could see set his teeth on edge. "Thanks so much, Mrs. Carter, but I think I can take it from here."

Bless her do-gooding heart, she still didn't get it. She kept chirping as merrily and irritatingly as a parakeet about bowel programs and intermittent catheters as I escorted her down the stairs and out the front door. I bid her goodbye on the front porch and shut the door against her unfailingly cheerful advice.

I didn't mean to be rude, but she'd put Adam into a bad mood. A brilliant mind trapped in a body that doesn't work the way it should leads to inventive cruelty. He couldn't hit out with his fists, so he lashed out with his tongue, instead.

I heard him cursing before I entered the room. I was almost a coward and didn't go in, but Dennis wouldn't be on duty for another few hours, and I had no choice. Adam needed me, much to his disgust and my despair.

As if he heard me outside the door, he stopped muttering, and I went inside. He had his face turned away, toward the window. Bars of late afternoon sunlight striped his cheeks.

"Don't have her back again," he said.

"All right. I'll make sure."

"I'm not a fucking idiot."

"I know that." I was never sure what to do for him when he was like that. In the past. I'd have left him alone to work it out, but I couldn't leave him alone now. Even if I left the room, he'd be calling me back in a few minutes to help him with something. Sometimes, maliciously.

"Do you want some lunch?"

He grunted an answer that I took to be yes.

"Anything in particular?"

Another grunt. I didn't push. I made sure the intercom was working and clipped the monitor to my pocket before going downstairs to fix him some food.

Marriages fail all the time from lesser disruptions than the unexpected disability of a spouse. It takes work and compromise to keep even an untested marriage strong, and ours was anything but untested.

When Adam had his accident I was working part-time as a junior counselor at a college health center until I could get my license. The money was bad but the hours made it possible for me to spend most of my time at the hospital. Adam had woken from his coma and taken the news of his injury without even blinking. He'd taken on recovery like a man shot from a cannon in flames. He'd been determined to heal, to function. Despite all advice to the contrary, I'm sure he was determined to walk.

As time passed and Adam began his hours of physical

therapy, I was able to spend more time away from the hospital. The few hours I spent at home became a refuge, a haven away from the stink of antiseptic and human waste. A quiet place where I could weep or scream as loud as I wanted, where I didn't have to keep on the brave face. I broke down at home, or spent hours looking through our photo albums, or simply made myself a meal that didn't taste of the hospital. I guarded those precious few hours jealously, as the key to my maintaining sanity.

We had insurance and we qualified for grants, but we were two years away from the settlement from the company whose faulty ski bindings had caused Adam's accident. We had enough to pay for a few hours of care a day while I was at work or school, but the bulk of his care fell to me. In the hospital I'd been his voice when he didn't have the strength to speak. The blanket to shield him from the cold. I was his nurse, his maid, his advocate, his door and his window. Now, I was the wall against which he could throw his fury and frustration and the hands he used to smash it.

I thought I was ready for him to come home. It was all we'd spoken of from the time he could talk again. Of how it would be when he could be home again. Of how it would work, what we'd do, how it would be so much better when he could be in his own environment again. When we could again maintain the happy bubble of exclusivity we'd enjoyed for so many years. When we could have our privacy back.

The doctors assured us that though our lives were forever changed, they didn't have to be ruined. Adam had an excellent outlook. There was no reason why he couldn't, when he'd healed, work. Make love. Be a person again instead of a patient.

I cried when I moved myself out of the bedroom I'd refinished and loved so much. I wept when the work crew began reconstructing the bathroom, when I had to sleep alone in our bed staring at an unfamiliar ceiling.

I didn't weep when Adam came home. I was Superwife. He needed everything done for him. It was a job, a duty—a role—and I did it without complaint.

We'd never experienced what Katie called "baby blur," the state of mind caused by lack of sleep from being woken every night. Adam was not an infant, but he needed as much, if not more, care. He had to be rolled every two hours to prevent bedsores. Our budget didn't allow for the special bed that inflated or deflated, or for overnight care. It was up to me to set the alarm and take care of him. Night after night, until I no longer knew quite whether I was awake or dreaming, I woke and stumbled to his side to make sure he was taken care of. Every muscle ached, but I dared not complain because at least I could feel the pain. Adam couldn't feel anything.

Adam needed constant attention. He could do nothing for himself; not until after the settlement were we able to afford the mouth and voice operated equipment that gave him the independence he had now. No sooner did I sit to eat, to read, to go to the bathroom, when he paged me via the monitor.

For two years, we'd struggled together, the extent of his injuries making anything else but struggle impossible. But we'd done it, worked hard, and he'd made such progress it was difficult to believe he wouldn't really get up and walk again, someday. When the settlement came from the ski boot company and we could hire Mrs. Lapp and Dennis to take some of the burden off me, when I could return to work and when we could afford the adaptive equipment that allowed Adam to explore his independence again, I thought our lives would improve even more. Yet that was when he started to change. Surrounded by machines and gadgets that could let him read and watch television, operate a wheelchair and answer the phone, Adam began to withdraw. The more he could do, the more apparent it became there was so much he couldn't do. That was when the anger began.

Four years later, I'd gained more empathy for my patients than I ever could have before. I understood the need for oblivion so great it drove people to drink and drugs. I understood affairs. How the simple need for touch could obliterate rationale, how the desire for passion could override everything else.

I didn't want to know this.

"Sonofafuckingbitch," Adam said when I brought in the tray of Mrs. Lapps's good vegetable soup. "I'm hungry, Sadie. I don't want that."

I didn't let him rile me. "That's what I made. If you're still hungry after you're done I'll make you something else."

"I don't want goddamn soup!"

"Then you should have told me what you did want when I asked." I kept my voice even, calm.

"You know I don't like soup," he gritted out.

I paused in laying out the napkin and spoon. "Since when?"

"Jesus, Sadie." Adam's tone dripped with sarcasm. "Since fucking forever."

He wasn't being truthful. He was trying to bait me into argument. I steadfastly refused to look at him as I stirred the soup to cool it and settled into the chair, ready to feed him.

"I don't want it."

"Adam," I said. "You have to eat something, and this is what I made."

"Fuck you, Sadie. Shove the fucking soup up your god-damned ass!"

My hand stopped halfway to his mouth. "That's uncalled for."

His eyes gleamed. "Why? Because I'm not allowed to be pissy, is that it?"

"Of course not!" I put the spoon down. My shaking hand made it clatter on the tray before I let go of it.

"Because I should be the happy crip, right? Look at how brave? I'm not disabled, I'm differently abled, right?"

His words were as sharp as glass, dripping poison. His mouth twisted with their bitterness. High color rose in pallid cheeks as his head jerked in the only range of motion he had.

I had to fist my hands in my lap to keep them still. My stomach churned and my throat got tight.

"Say something, Sadie!"

I shook my head, mouth clamped shut, doing my best to refuse to rise to his challenge.

Adam sneered. "What, you can't shout back at me? You're going to let me talk to you like that? Just sit there and take it, because why? Because you don't want to upset the crip?"

"Stop it, Adam!" I got up and made to take the tray away.

"Fuck you, Sadie! It's true, isn't it? Fuck you and fuck your soup and fuck that nurse!"

I lifted the bowl before I knew it. It shattered against the wall and left a stain. The spoon landed on the carpet and bounced, reflecting a stray bar of sunlight.

"Fuck you!" I shouted so loud it hurt my throat. "You can fucking starve for all I care, you bastard!"

"Yeah, you'd love that, wouldn't you? Let me starve to death? Then you wouldn't have to worry about any of this anymore, right? No more taking care of me–"

"You shut up!" I screamed it into his face, kissing distance. "Shut your goddamn mouth, Adam, and quit being such an asshole!"

His eyes, those blue eyes, blazed. "Quit being such a fucking cunt and tell me the truth!"

"I don't know what you're talking about." My voice was cold as I bent to begin cleaning up the soup. Giving him my back was about the worst insult I could give, since he was powerless to do anything to make me face him.

Adam launched into a tirade of insults so inventive and vile I would have admired his creativity if that venom hadn't been directed at me. He hit me in every place he knew would hurt, pushed every button I had, played upon every insecurity I had ever shared and many he only guessed at. He dissolved me into weeping, on my hands and knees at the base of his chair, and even though I knew he did it out of hatred for his situation, it felt too much like he did it because he hated me.

"Admit it," Adam said finally, his voice cracked from screaming. "You wish I'd died."

I got to my feet. Again, I got in his face, giving him the aggression he was giving me. He couldn't shrink away. I think he wouldn't have, even if he could.

"Yes," I told him. "Sometimes I wish you had."

We stared at each other for what felt like a very long time.

"So do I," Adam said.

I didn't know what to do with him when he cried, except to hold him as best as I could. To stroke his hair, to shush, to kiss his mouth that tasted now of tears. I could hold him, but he couldn't hold me back. There was no one to hold me when I cried, nobody to tell me it was going to be all right. There could be no room for selfishness in this marriage any longer. No room for anything but struggle.

"I'm sorry," Adam said, over and over, and I told him, over and over, it was all right.

I didn't know what to give him except my compassion, and it didn't seem I'd ever have enough.

Chapter 12

August

$\mathcal{T}$his month, my name is Priscilla again. Joe and I have been seeing each other regularly, once or twice a week. We've gone to the movies, to dinner, to a concert. Today we are going to the Pennsylvania Renaissance Faire at Joe's suggestion. I've agreed because I understand that if you want to have what you want most of the time, there are other times you have to give someone else what they want.

We're greeted at the front gate by a man in a kilt and a huge sword strapped to his back. In a Scottish accent, he asks my name, calls me "Lady Priscilla" and kisses the back of my hand. I give Joe a sideways glance to see his reaction to this blatant flirtation, but he's grinning and doesn't seem at all upset some other man just licked my hand.

A woman in a low-cut peasant blouse, a corset pushing her breasts into eye-catching mounds of flesh, tucks a flower into Joe's shirt pocket. She's flirting with him, asking his name and offering him her "services." Another, this one a redhead with a laundry basket, sidles up to him and introduces herself as the "cleanest wench in the shire." A third, a brunette, joins the other two and together they flaunt and tease Joe until he's laughing. But he's not backing away. He looks as though he's enjoying the attention from three buxom young women, and while I suppose I can't blame him, I'm annoyed he's not paying more attention to me.

Trumpets blare and announce Queen Elizabeth, whose arrival apparently sends all these people into paroxysms of ecstasy. They abandon us in favor of throwing themselves prostrate on the ground in front of Her Majesty's procession.

Joe's grinning, arms crossed over his chest. I've got sunglasses on but Joe's squinting. If he's not careful, he's going to get crow's feet. Well. Men can get away with that, can't they?

The queen is throwing candy or something to the children in the crowd, and the actors are all trailing behind her, hooting and hollering. The washer wenches are moving through the crowd and accosting other people. I don't want them to come back here.

Joe's not paying attention to me, so I reach up and slip my hand into the curve of his elbow and tug lightly until he uncrosses his arms. Then I take his hand, linking our fingers. He seems hesitant but only for the briefest moment, and I can't help the triumphant smile when he keeps my hand in his.

This is our tenth date. I intend there to be many more. In fact, before today is over, I intend to convince Joe we need to become a couple.

"Want to head inside?" Joe turns to me and points at the gate, through which most of the crowd has passed. "Grab something to eat?"

I nod, giving him what he wants so I'll be sure to get what I want, later. And I want him. Joe's been nothing but a gentleman so far. I appreciate that. But it's time to step it up. Men want sex, they all do, and even though Joe hasn't exactly been pressuring me, it's time.

He leads me through the gate. Inside, the fair has made an attempt to look like a renaissance village with shops, paths, games, booths. It's hard to tell at first glance which people are actors and which are patrons, since many of the guests have dressed in costume and speak with accents. Some wear elaborately designed gowns and others have cobbled together outfits from what looks like thrift store purchases. It's creative, but sloppy. In my capri-length jeans and cute white tank top, I'm glad I didn't attempt to dress up "in the spirit." I'm even happier Joe didn't, either.

"What are you hungry for?" Joe's still got my hand and he turns, looking expectant.

I study the main street, where vendors hawk their "Steak on a Stake" and assorted other carnival type food. Nothing looks low fat or low carb, and I can't help wrinkling my nose. "I'm not hungry right now."

"Okay." Joe nods. He's looking around like a kid at the circus, but he's still holding my hand. Sweat slicks our palms because the sun's so hot, but I'm not about to let go.

We find a stand selling smoked turkey legs, which look nauseating. Joe eats one. I consent to nibbling on a grilled chicken sandwich without the bun. Joe wants to try haggis, whatever that is, and I won't have any. He eats the whole plate.

The sun's making freckles come out on his nose and cheeks. "You should be wearing sunscreen. Or a hat."

He wipes a hand across his face, then looks at the booth a few yards away. "C'mon."

This stand sells hats. Not respectable hats. Hats with feathers and lace and bows, big floppy creations and conical princess caps with long scarves fluttering from the tips. Joe picks up a shapeless velvet monstrosity with a long ostrich feather and puts it on his head.

"How do I look?"

"It doesn't go with your outfit."

Joe laughs and tries on another. There's a large mirror along the shop's back wall, and he mugs at his reflection. He pulls me closer, grabs up one of the pink princess hats and snaps the elastic under my chin before I can stop him.

"What do you think?" He strikes a pose, looking at our mirror faces.

"I look ridiculous." I reach to pull off the hat, but Joe stops me. He pulls me closer, one step, then two.

"You look beautiful."

He's smiling and staring at me. I think he's going to kiss me, but I can't ignore the way the elastic on this hat is cutting into my skin and the feather on his is fluttering dangerously close to poking me in the eye. I don't lean in to let his mouth have its way with me.

Joe looks back into the mirror, then takes off the hat and hangs it up. "No good?"

Relieved, I remove the princess hat, hoping with an inner cringe that the last person who'd tried it on wasn't some lice-ridden child. Joe puts it back on the rack. I fix my hair in the mirror and turn to see him looking at me.

"What?"

"Nothing."

This time, I let him pull me into his arms and kiss me. Though it's brief enough not to be inappropriate, I enjoy every second. His hand lingers on my waist when we're done.

He touches me a lot today. We hold hands. He puts his arm around my shoulder, around my waist, rests his hand on my knee while we sit to watch one of the many, many shows.

This isn't such a bad day, though I'm getting bored and Joe shows no signs of losing interest. I convince him to grab us some drinks and sit in the shade on a long bench in front of huge cement pit filled with water. While we're there, one of the women from this morning comes over and begins to wash some clothes in the water. The other two join her momentarily, squabbling over something, and the three begin hollering something about a show. Since we're already sitting there we stay to watch.

It's clever and interactive, a condensed retelling of Antony and Cleopatra that involves a lot of silly jokes. I'm laughing a bit when the redhead comes into the audience and plucks Joe to take part in the show. He goes readily enough, leaving me behind, and though I know it's just a show, I cross my arms, annoyed.

The redhead's sitting on the wall of the pit behind Joe, her arms and legs wrapped around him and telling him he needs to come up with a "good pick-up line."

Without missing a beat, Joe looks at her and says, "If I said you had a beautiful body would you hold it against me?"

It's groan-worthy, but he earns a high five from the wench and the show goes on. I think the one who picked him is enjoying it a little too much. Acting is one thing, but she spends too much time touching him. I don't like it one bit. By the time the show is done, I've decided I'm ready to go home.

Joe, however, lingers after the end of the show to laugh and talk to the three wenches, who are lounging without shame in the water of the pit. The redhead takes a swig of water from her mug and demonstrates her spitting technique, pretending to be a fountain. The others laugh and tell jokes, encouraging Joe and the other few people still gathered around to talk to them.

I wait for a minute before joining him. There's no mistaking the possessiveness in the way I take his hand. Joe might not notice, but the redhead does. She backs off, and I have to concede that it's quite likely she wasn't flirting with serious intent but only as part of the show. Even so, Joe's here with me, and I don't mean for him to forget it.

We spend the rest of the day there, then stop for dinner at a quaint inn before going home. Joe chats about the day. He bought me a metal rose scented with perfume. The sun's turned his nose and cheeks pink, and the gold's been heightened in his hair.

He holds my hand the whole way home except when he has to shift gears. I invite him inside and offer iced tea. In my kitchen he backs me up against the counter, his hands on my waist, and I let him kiss me harder than he's ever done before.

Our mouths open. I taste sugar and lemon from the tea. His tongue is cold but warms quickly. He's a good kisser. When he puts a hand behind my neck to tilt my head back, I break the kiss to take a breath.

Joe's mouth hovers over mine. He presses his body all along mine. He smells like summer. His belt buckle is cold on my belly where my tank top has ridden up a little.

He's waiting for something. Permission, perhaps. I give it by opening my mouth beneath his. This kiss is deeper. The hand on my waist slides around to cup my rear, to press us together harder. My hand goes to his bicep, where the muscles bunch and tighten. He's deceptively strong despite seeming so slim, and my breath catches a little in my throat.

Joe nibbles at my lips and then moves to my jaw, tipping my head back with a nudge of his mouth. The skin of my throat is sensitive and I shiver when he grazes his teeth along it. My nipples tighten. I squeeze his bicep, my fingers gripping.

How far will he push this? How far does he think he'll get? He's kissing me without haste, nuzzling and nipping, and suddenly I feel more like an entrée than a woman.

I push him back a little bit. "Joe. Stop."

He pauses, and for a moment I think he's not going to stop. That he'll just keep kissing me, maybe start rubbing me, too. For an instant there's a look in his eyes that says he's a man used to getting what he wants, and he's tired of waiting for it.

Then he backs off without a word. He doesn't move away, our bodies are still touching, but he's put distance between us. The hand behind my neck slides to my shoulder.

I put my hands up to his shoulders. "I like you, Joe."

"I like you, too."

I'm not afraid to ask for what I want. I've never been afraid. So when I rub my fingers along his collarbone, I'm already certain there's not going to be any surprises in this discussion.

"Then I think we should talk about what's going on with us."

Joe nods, and I'm sure he's been expecting something like this. You don't go out with someone ten times, after all, unless you expect to talk about what's going on. Both his hands go back to my waist, holding me loosely.

"Okay."

I lay out what I want and expect from him. It's negotiation, as it's been all along, and at the end of it, we've both determined where this is going and what we both will gain from the merger. If I have a few more requests and expectations, it's because I have high standards. There's no point in continuing something if both parties aren't on the same page.

Another kiss seals this round of bargaining, and I'm feeling generous.

"Come upstairs with me," I tell him as I take his hand, and that's what we do.

I waited, but the story was done. Joe bit into his sandwich, chewing rapidly and washing down the food with a gulp of his drink. I peeled open the wrapper on my granola bar. We ate in silence.

Shade from the tree overhead dappled his face. His summer freckles had indeed come out. Sunshine was good to Joe. Today he wore a lightweight suit, the jacket off, tie loose, sleeves rolled up to expose the golden hair furring his forearms.

"It all sounds very…" I paused, not sure what to say. Professional seemed wrong. Stilted? Contractual?

Joe looked at me with a small smile. "Surprising?"

"That, too."

He shrugged and wiped his mouth with a napkin. "Priscilla is a woman who knows what she wants and isn't afraid of asking for it. Precisely."

That had been clear from the story.

I worked for the words, aware my conflicted feelings were affecting what I wanted to say. "And what about you?"

I found many facets of Joe's personality charming, but perhaps the most appealing was his self-awareness. He never dissembled. He didn't try pretending he didn't understand my inadequately phrased question.

"We're a matched set." Joe squinted up to the tree above us, where sunshine slanted through the branches. Then he looked at me. "A pair of prancing ponies. We'll look good pulling the same carriage."

"But is that what you want?"

Oh, how I wanted him to say no. How I wanted him to admit Priscilla didn't please him. That what they had done upstairs had left him dissatisfied.

"To quote the Rolling Stones," Joe said, "You can't always get what you want."

"But is she what you need?" I gulped back the suddenly desperate tone of my voice and slammed shut my mouth.

Joe folded his paper napkin in half, then half again. Then once more, making a small, thick square he clenched. When he opened his hand, the paper slowly, slowly opened like a stop-motion flower unfurling, and I couldn't look away from it.

"I think so, Sadie."

No. No, no, no, I wanted to say, but didn't. Instead, I steadied my voice with a long sip of tepid water. Everything has to end. The good and the bad. Especially the ugly.

"You don't think I can do it, do you," he asked without accusing.

I looked over at him. "That's not my place to say."

Joe laughed. "I think it might be, Sadie. You know more about my sex life than anyone ever has. You know more about my life than anyone ever has."

"If you're asking me to make judgment—"

"I'm asking you to tell me if you think I can do this."

"That's not up to me to say, Joe!"

We'd turned to face each other. We weren't even close to touching, but there wasn't enough space between us. Joe waited, patient, while I thought on how to answer.

There wasn't a question of me not answering. We'd come too far for that. The question was how much truth I'd give him.

"No," I said finally. "I don't think you can do this."

He nodded, as if he was expecting that answer. He sat forward on the bench, his elbows on his knees. He looked at his hands, clasped together, then back at me.

"I think you're wrong."

He got up. He tightened up his tie and put his jacket back on. With greedy self-indulgence, I drank in every detail of him, certain this would be the last time I'd see him.

"I hope you're right, Joe."

He looked at me so long and hard it burned. "Well. We'll find out next month, won't we?"

"Tell me a story."

Adam stretched out on the bed, an arm behind his head. I wanted to lick the smooth stripe of skin exposed between the hem of his shirt and his belt. I settled for running a finger along it. At my touch he promptly rolled onto his back, his shirt riding up higher, giving me his skin.

"Another one? Sadie, I've told you all of them."

"You can't possibly have." I spread my fingers flat on his firm belly and rubbed in slow circles.

Adam's sigh sounded annoyed, but I knew he was faking. He loved telling me stories as much as I loved hearing them. He shifted as I stroked his stomach and tugged his shirt higher, over his chest and then his head to bare him to me.

"Fine. Once upon a time, there were three bears…"

"No!" I protested, laughing, my hands on his belt buckle. "Adam, no!"

"Why not? You don't think bears are sexy?"

I slipped the leather from the buckle and eased his zipper down. His cock pulsed under my palm as I slipped a hand inside his jeans. I worked my fingers around the tight denim, shoving it down his thighs.

"I'm not into bestiality."

"You assume she's going to fuck the bears." He said this archly as he lifted his hips to allow me to undress him.

"Isn't she?"

"You'll have to wait and see, won't you?"

But I never heard the end of the story, because I bent to take him in my mouth and we let other matters distract us.

Memory is a funny thing, sometimes slippery, but that day had secured a firm place in my mind. It was the last time we'd made love before Adam's accident. If I'd known it was going to be the last time he'd ever hold me, I'd have paid better attention.

But I hadn't, complacent in the belief we'd go on as we always had, that we were untouchable.

I thought of that day a lot in the days following Joe's last story. Adam had always told me stories, weaving classic fairy tales with erotic poetry and urban legends. I would tease him with my mouth and hands while he described towers of glass, or he'd trace the words upon my clit with his tongue until I came just as the prince arrived to rescue his fair maiden. Sometimes Adam was the king and I the fairy queen, others he the faithful beast and I the beauty who transformed him. He could fuck me as thoroughly with his voice as he could with his cock, all of it tied up in one passionate package.

Now he didn't fuck me and he barely talked to me. He no longer told me stories. And now, neither would Joe.

There was nothing to be done. I had no claim on Joe, could not expect what we were doing to continue indefinitely. All things end, and this had needed to end, should have ended, a long time ago. It should not, in fact, have ever started, but it had and now I wondered what I would do without it.

I didn't want to see Adam when I got home, but there was no real choice in that, either. I had to stop in, make sure he was all right, give him the attention he didn't seem to want and refused to be grateful for.

Our fight had left a tension in the air that couldn't be ignored. In the past we'd have fucked our way through it. Now all we could do was wait until it passed.

Dennis noticed, of course. He knew when to put on the Stooges and get Adam laughing in a way I simply didn't any longer have the wherewithal to do. Mrs. Lapp noticed, too, fussing with cakes and pies neither of us wanted to eat. I waited until she went home, then scraped the desserts untouched into the garbage, covering the evidence with newspapers so she wouldn't notice.

I paused outside Adam's door. I heard the soft murmur of the television. I put a smile on my face that felt more like a grimace and pushed open the door to his room.

"Hey, baby, c'mere." Adam sounded as contrite as he always had after a fight.

I sat on the edge of his bed. "Hey."

"I'm sorry, baby. I was an asshole."

My smile became a little more sincere. "Yes. You were."

"Well, I'm sorry."

I ran my hand over the bristles of his hair. "I'm sorry you were an asshole, too."

"Hey!"

We both laughed. I kissed his cheek. He didn't smell like Adam any more.

"It's just that sometimes, I get so pissed off…."

He was quiet. I said nothing, hoping that maybe, for once, he'd stop pretending he was okay. Then I could, too. That we could both forget the roles that had so long bound us.

I waited a bit longer, but he didn't continue. I stroked his cheek. "Adam, it's natural for you to be angry."

His jaw tightened under my fingers, and he cut his gaze away. Steely. Stoic in a way he'd never used to be.

"I don't want to talk about it."

"I want to talk about it—"

He whipped his head around. "I said I don't want to talk about it! Jesus! Don't push me!"

I pulled my hand away. I so desperately didn't want to fight with him again. I took a few breaths but the tears from before threatened to slide down my cheeks again.

"Don't you do it," he warned me. "Don't you fucking start."

It was so unfair, that I shouldn't be allowed to cry. I understood. I knew why he didn't want to see it, but it was so damned unfair, just the same.

"I liked it better when you used to throw dishes!"

"In case you hadn't noticed," he said, voice thick with the sarcasm I loathed, "I can't throw anything."

"You never used to never hold anything back. You used to let yourself be angry. Or sad. Or delirious with joy, Adam, you used to let yourself be overcome—"

"And you used to hate it!" His shout was hoarse and I couldn't stop myself from fussing with his blankets. His face clenched. "Stop it, just fucking stop it, okay? Dennis can do that."

"I want to make sure—"

"I said stop it."

I stopped. We stared at each other. Glared, really, and I waited for him to let fly with the blistering invectives that would reduce me to tears.

He reined it in. I was torn between relief and despair. I crossed my hands under my arms, tight against my stomach. They were cold.

"I didn't hate the way you were." The words slipped out before they could stop them. "I miss it. I miss you, Adam."

It was the wrong thing to say. He turned his face from me again. I walked around the side of the bed to force him to see me.

"I think it would be better for you to talk about it with me. I think we need to talk…I need to talk about this. About us. About this. You never tell me stories anymore." I gestured at the bed, the wheelchair.

"What are you, three years old?"

I refused to let his words sting. "You never talk to me about what you're feeling anymore."

"I don't want to talk." The emphasis he put on the last word made it sound dirty. "You can put shit on a Kaiser roll and call it a sandwich, Sadie, but it's still shit."

"Well, it's shit I think we need to talk about!"

"Stop fucking trying to analyze me!" He tried to shout but it came out more like a wheeze.

"I'm not your analyst. I'm your wife."

"Then be my fucking wife," he snapped. "And quit trying to get inside my head. I've got nothing to share with you. This is my thing, Sadie. Mine. Not yours. Quit trying to make it all about you. I'm so fucking tired of you trying to make this about you."

It wasn't the nastiest thing he'd ever said to me, but it was the cruelest. It hurt worse than being called a cunt, or stupid. I recoiled as physically as if he'd slapped me.

He turned his head again, expression stony. I thought I'd cry, but my own face felt like it had been carved from marble. I blinked, hard, but my eyes stayed dry.

I left the room and bumped into Dennis in the hallway. He put out a hand to pat my shoulder. We shared a look. I was in his arms before I could stop myself, my face pressed against his chest while I cried in silence. Dennis patted my back, his big strong arms like pillars around me.

Adam shouted for him. The next second the intercom buzzed, and I pulled myself from Dennis' comforting embrace though I was far from finished needing it. Dennis wasn't there for me.

He looked concerned, though, and I forced a smile. "Go on. He needs you."

Dennis chucked my chin. "This happens, Sadie...."

"I know." I swiped my tears. "I know. I'm okay. Go ahead."

He nodded again and patted my shoulder before disappearing into Adam's room. I thought I might cry some more, but I took a page from Adam's book and forced myself to stoic calm.

September

I was twenty minutes later than usual on the first Friday of the month. I'd told myself I wouldn't go, but I left my office fluffing my hair and applying my lipstick in the shiny reflection of the elevator doors on the way down. I held my brown lunch bag crumpled in my hand like a prize, and my heels click-clicked on the pavement as I headed for the spot on the bench I thought of as ours. September afternoons were still warm enough to sit outside, but today was a little overcast, the breeze cool enough to make a sweater necessary.

There was no way for me to pretend my heart didn't leap when I came around the corner to the small, hidden spot that held our bench. He was there. He wore a suit I recognized, the tie I'd complimented, and his eyes caught mine. I could have used a hand to catch me, because in the next moment my shoe slid on a stray piece of gravel and I ingloriously stumbled.

Joe was there, but he wasn't alone.

I knew at once who she was. The blond hair in the twist and the pearl earrings gave it away, as did the cool way she turned her head to view my graceless approach.

Joe did not stand. He did not smile. His hand snaked along the back of the bench to rest upon the sleek, padded shoulder of his companion, and she inched closer with a look down at the bench as though she wanted to scold it for being dirty.

"Are you all right?" His voice was neutral. It stung more than if he'd been cold. "Watch your step."

"They really should clear these paths more often," said Priscilla, and fucking hell, even her voice was poised and perfect. "You could have turned your ankle."

"I'm sorry," I heard myself say as though from very far away. "I didn't realize this bench was occupied."

Priscilla glanced at the side of her not nestled against Joe. "We could move over…"

"No, that's fine." I shook my head. "I'll find another one."

"Are you sure?" Joe asked. I watched his finger trace the back of Priscilla's neck. "There's room for one more."

We both looked at him, and if our faces wore similar expressions it was because we both were feeling the same thing.

"No. Thank you." I shook my head and put my foot back to the path leading away from them. "Enjoy your lunch."

Bastard. Motherfucking bastard. Asshole. The invectives filled my head as I stalked away. Behind me, I heard him murmur. The soft trill of Priscilla's laughter made me want to vomit.

Behind the wheel of my car I gave in to disgusted tears I hid behind my hands. They didn't relieve any of my tension. They only made it worse, and I stopped them with the heels of my hands pressed to my eyes so hard I saw flashes of color. I wouldn't allow myself the luxury of wallowing in grief I had no right to feel.

The face in my rearview mirror didn't look like me at first, until I blinked a few times and wiped my face with a handful of crumpled tissues that came apart in my hand. Picking off the tiny pieces of shredded paper gave my fingers something to do while my mind caught up. By the time I'd cleaned off my skirt and shoved the tissues into a plastic grocery bag I kept for trash, I regained enough calm to be able to drive.

I've never been one to reapply my makeup, but I sorely needed it today. I spent another ten minutes retracing the line of my lips with color, coating my cheeks with powder. I had no mascara or liner to undo the damage my tears had wrought, but it was the best I could do.

My sobs had felt like thorns in my throat. And that's what it was, with Joe, wasn't it? All briars. No roses. Lesson learned, the painful way.

Chapter
13

I couldn't pretend to hide my relief when Adam told me his mother and sister wouldn't be visiting, after all.

"Did they say they'd make it another time?" I settled my tote bag, filled with reading material, some work and the scarf I'd been knitting for a million years, onto the recliner.

"No."

I didn't look at him as I arranged the small table next to my chair and refolded the afghan. Friday night rituals I didn't have to think about, so used were my hands to performing them. I picked at a small hole in the arm of the recliner, where something had snagged the material. I'd have to repair it before it got bigger.

"I'm going to get a needle and thread," I said, turning, but Adam's gaze stopped me.

"Sadie." The way he said my name was the iceberg that sunk my heart. "I told them not to come."

The knitting needles in my hand clattered as my fingers squeezed, and I put the mess of yarn aside. "Did you? Why?"

"Because I don't think I can deal with them right now."

I'd been relieved more than was kind to learn they weren't coming. Hearing Adam had been the one to decide it made me feel marginally better, but not much. I moved to his side and stroked my fingers through his hair. His skin was warmer than I liked, and I shifted the sheets off his body to help it cool.

He was silent while I fussed. Again, his gaze snared me tighter than if he'd been able to reach out and grab me. I laid my hands flat on the crisp white sheet and ran the edge of it through my fingers, back and forth. This would have annoyed him had he been able to feel it; it annoyed him watching the repetitive motion of my arms, and I stopped abruptly.

His eyes looked me over, up and down, peeling away my layers and leaving me naked in front of him. "I'm sorry, Sadie."

"You have nothing to be sorry about." I said this firmly, allowing no argument. "This is what it is. We'll work things out, Adam, like we always have—"

"No." He bit out the word.

I leaned in, unwilling to give up. "Yes."

In the past, if I'd won any arguments it was because Adam had relented, not because I'd been better able to plead my case or because I'd been the one throwing the bigger fit. When we fought, it was spectacular and sometimes messy, but Adam was the sound and fury and I simply waited quietly until he'd finished.

Not this time.

"I am not giving up on you." I shook my head to emphasize my point. "No matter how much of an asshole you are."

I'd hoped to get a smile from him, but his gaze just went darker.

"I'm not playing around, Sadie. This—all this—"

"All this what?" My fingers crumpled the sheet. "Our marriage? Our life? What, Adam?"

It felt good to push at him. He glared and made a rude noise. I glared, too.

"Yeah, all of it."

I wasn't about to let him stop there. "What about it?"

I'd never seen him without words. Either he had them to spare or he doled them out as rewards, but he always had them. I felt triumphant and destroyed at the same time, watching him struggle.

"I think…I want a divorce."

I reacted as if I'd stepped on a rake, recoiling. "What?"

"I want a divorce." It seemed saying it the first time had been difficult, but the second was a piece of cake.

"Absolutely not!" I put my hands on my hips to keep from making fists. "Go to hell! Fuck you!"

"That's the problem, isn't it?" he shouted, voice hoarse as if it tore his throat. "I can't fuck you! Not now, not ever! Not for the rest of my fucking life!"

I said nothing in the face of this truth. Heat had flared between us. My breath came faster, driven by my fury.

"You can," I muttered finally. "You just won't, you selfish prick."

Adam blinked. His mouth thinned, grim, straight, like he meant to force back his retort. In the next moment, though, he let it all out.

"I want to put you up against a wall and fuck you until

you scream, Sadie. How ridiculous is that?" He looked down at his immobile body, then back up at me. "I can't even take care of myself, much less you."

"I know." I kept my voice hard, though I wanted to soften. "And it sucks. A lot."

His voice cracked. "I thought I'd always be able to take care of you, Sadie. That you'd always need me more than I needed you. And now, you go out every day and live a life I have no part of, and I...I don't know how you can not need me, anymore."

I kissed him, then, no longer angry. "I still need you."

He shook his head a tiny bit. "No—"

I stopped his movement with another kiss. "Yes, Adam. I still need you."

"But I can't—"

I shushed him. "You can."

We looked into each other's eyes. I let my fingers stroke down the sides of his neck, where he could feel my touch, and he sighed. I slipped a hand inside the collar of his pajama shirt to trace the ridge of his collarbone. Adam's mouth parted and I kissed him, waiting for his tongue to delve into my mouth before stroking it with my own.

"I love you," I whispered against his lips. "That hasn't changed."

My fingers shook as I pulled down the covers and unbuttoned his shirt, folding it open to reveal his chest. I'd seen his body plenty of times, assisted with showers and changed his clothes. I knew the changes in it. They no longer frightened me as they had the first time I'd seen him, unconscious, rubbed raw and bleeding in places that now bore faint white scars.

I traced the line of the largest, where a tree branch had gouged him from just above his right nipple and around his side to the jut of his hipbone. I bent to kiss the small, puckered star of scar tissue at the top, and when I did, Adam groaned. I slid my lips down along the line, pressing gentle kisses to his flesh.

It had been years since I'd kissed him anywhere but the mouth, neck or hand. We'd never spoken about his feelings about his body, or why in our sporadic lovemaking we both chose to focus on what I could do to myself rather than what I could do to him.

My hands stroked his skin as I moved my mouth upward again to find his mouth. I kissed him softly as I rubbed his chest and sides. I slid my hand into the elastic waist of his pajama bottoms. The brush of his pubic curls against my fingers made me gasp a little, my knees weak with longing.

"Will you touch yourself?" Adam whispered, voice thick.

I shook my head. "I want to touch you."

His eyes fluttered closed, but when he opened them, the lust in his gaze seared me. We kissed again, mouths open and hungry, while my hands roamed every place I could reach.

I rediscovered his body, its curves and lines. It wasn't the same as it had been before, but what ever is? And if I had to struggle a bit to ease down his pants to reveal the rest of him to me, well, a prize is always sweeter for having to work for it.

Adam laughed when I told him that in a voice slightly out of breath from having to move his body in order to pull down the pants. "You're optimistic."

"Shut up," I ordered from the foot of the bed, where I was lifting his feet to take off the pants.

He lifted his head to look down at me. I imagined myself framed between his thighs as I moved up the bed, my own clothes already shed before I crawled. I rubbed his legs, thinner than they'd ever been. I kissed his knees and brushed my cheek against his thighs, then crouched between his legs and reached for the bed controls to lift him higher.

"I want you to be able to watch this."

"Sadie—" He sounded alarmed.

I looked up. "I want to do this."

And oh, how I did. Though much about him had changed, Adam's cock remained the same. When I reached to stroke him, he turned his head away and closed his eyes, mouth turning down like my touch hurt him.

I murmured his name. I bent to brush my lips along his pubic hair, the soft flesh of his lower belly, his thighs. I kissed his penis at the base and let my mouth whisper along it while I slid a hand beneath to cup his testicles.

There was much I couldn't do for him, but there was also much I could. I could lick him. I could stroke him. I could kiss him all over and let my hair trail over his body the way he'd once loved.

I heard him say my name, and when I looked up, saw tears gleaming. He licked his mouth. Beneath my hand, his penis stayed soft and still.

It didn't matter. Naked, I eased my body along his, skin to skin in a way we hadn't been since before the accident. I stretched out beside him, my thigh over his, my cunt snugged up tight against him. I licked his shoulder at a place I knew he could feel, and Adam groaned.

"I miss touching you," I told him. "I miss you holding me, yes, but I miss touching you just as much. And you never seem to want to let me."

His breathing was hoarse. I thought he might not answer. "You touch me all the time. Every day. You feed me, you dress me, you wipe my ass. Your hands are always all over me, Sadie, and I can never feel them."

I caressed his collarbone and the tops of his shoulders. "I know."

"No," Adam said through gritted teeth. "You don't."

With conscious effort, I timed the in and out of my breath to his, so our chests rose and fell in tandem. I kissed his shoulder and kept my lips there, feeling the warmth of his skin. My hair had tangled beneath my cheek and I lifted my head to smooth it.

Adam looked at my face. "If you had a lover, I wouldn't blame you."

Shame shot heat through my entire body. "I don't have a lover."

I caught a glimpse of the old Adam, the man who'd have called out any man who dared look at me with lustful intent. Just a glimpse, but it lifted my heart. I leaned in to kiss him.

"Good. Because I can't exactly beat the shit out of him, can I?"

I shook my head, putting aside thoughts of Joe. "You don't need to worry about that."

Adam tipped his head a bit, seeking my mouth, which I gave him. "Get on top of me."

The edge in his voice sent a thrill through me. I sat, running my hand down his body, over his stomach. "You want me to…"

"Straddle me. Sit on my cock."

Desire flooded me at his words, the words of the Adam I knew before, who'd never hesitated to tell me what he wanted. I got up, put my leg over his abdomen, his penis nestled between my thighs.

"Kiss me," he demanded, and I bent to do that, too.

Adam took command of the kiss, caressing my tongue with his until I gasped. I was timid, fearful of leaning too much of my weight on him, but his growl convinced me to lean closer and open for his kisses.

"Stop thinking." He came after my mouth again, and though his hands remained at his sides, I felt them on me, one on the back of my neck to hold me to him. "Kiss me."

We kissed for a long time, the way we had that first time in his apartment. With the bed upright I could straddle Adam's lap, my knees clamped tight to his sides, my pussy rubbing against the bulge of his cock and his belly. He kissed me fiercely. Hungrily. He was in charge, and I let him take control.

"Rub yourself against me," he ordered. "Are your nipples hard?"

"Yes…"

"Let me suck them."

I lifted my breasts to his mouth, one and then the other, and he lapped and suckled them until I cried out and shuddered on the verge of climax. His mouth slowed, tongue slipping out to stroke my tight flesh before his lips closed once more over my nipple. I arched into his mouth, lost in the ecstasy of being touched this way. He paused, teasing me. Pleasure built with anticipation and I moaned. Then, slowly, he sucked a little harder, a little harder, until I could no longer keep still.

"That's it," he said against my skin. "Come all over me, Sadie."

Rubbing my clit against him had brought me even closer to the edge. At his words, and the following stroke of his tongue along my breasts, I came.

I didn't breathe while eternity revolved around me. My entire body clenched, released, my cunt contracting in spasms of pleasure so intense it was almost pain. Sex noises are never pretty, but I didn't care. I couldn't have held back the moans shuddering out of me if I'd tried.

"Come for me, Sadie."

Adam's voice cracked and broke, and I opened my eyes to look into his as I tumbled over the edge. It was more intimate than anything we'd ever shared, looking into his eyes at climax. There was nothing he did not see in me then, and nothing I wanted to hide.

He grinned after a moment and slid his tongue along his lips. "Next time, I'm going to taste you."

The breath I'd forgotten to take rushed back into my lungs. "Let me recover from this, first. Okay?"

"Wimp."

I kissed him slow and tender. "I love you."

"Love you, too."

I hugged him, my head nestled into his shoulder, feeling boneless and satisfied. When he yawned, though, I knew I had to move. Reluctantly, I did, making sure to touch and stroke him wherever I could reach as I did.

"Quit fondling me, you brazen hussy."

We laughed. His cheeks flushed, and his eyes sparkled in a way I hadn't seen from him in far too long. Love for him rushed over me in a force so strong I would have staggered had I not been holding on to the edge of the bed. Now was not a time for tears, and I held them back.

Adam was effusive as I brought warm washcloths to wipe him clean and rearranged his pajamas. He talked about his lectures and students, about his plans for next year…about taking a vacation.

"Really?" I paused in buttoning his shirt. "You want to go on a trip?"

He nodded. "Think we can manage it? Someplace with a beach? I could look online for disability-friendly resorts."

I'd never been the one to deny Adam the right to leave the house. He'd always chosen not to go anywhere, claiming even going downstairs to the garden outside was too much of a hassle. For him to express interest in taking a much grander trip so surprised me I didn't know what to say.

"No? Yes?" His eyes followed me as tucked in all his

limbs and smoothed the covers over him. "You hate the idea? What?"

"I think it's a fine idea."

He enthused further, talking rapidly, words tumbling one over the other while I listened and put on my nightgown. He talked while I brushed my teeth and tied up my hair, while I folded out the recliner and settled into it with my blanket and pillow, while I set the alarm to wake me so I could turn him.

"It'll be work for you, Sadie, I know it," he said finally. "But maybe we can take Dennis with us. So you can get a break. Go to a spa, sit on the beach. It could really work."

"It could really work," I agreed, content to listen to his enthusiasm.

"I've done my best to drive you away, Sadie," he said suddenly. "But you've never left me."

"No. I don't want to leave you." I smoothed a hand over his hair, letting it tickle my fingers. "I'm not going to leave you, Adam."

He paused for a moment, his expression serious. "Things are going to be different from now on, Sadie. I promise you."

I got up to kiss him again. "Lots of things will be different."

And for a while, they were.

Adam was noticeably cheerier. Flirtier, too. He even started talking about looking into erectile aids, a prospect that intrigued and concerned me, since drugs could always have side effects.

"Just think," he said with a wink one night as I lay beside him. "A four-hour hard-on."

"I wouldn't need four hours," I said with a roll of my eyes. "Jesus, Adam."

He wasn't deterred. "If I can get hard, Sadie, then…there's a chance…"

I propped myself up on my elbow to look him. "Yes?"

"We could have a baby."

Stunned, I sat. "Do you want a baby?"

"Don't you?"

I didn't know how to answer that. I didn't know if I did or didn't…but the fact he'd brought it up meant things had changed, indeed. I could only shrug in response.

"Lots of quads have been able to have children," Adam told me. "It's just something to consider, that's all."

A child. A son, perhaps, with Adam's wicked grin. Maybe a daughter with a sense of practicality. A baby? Years of responsibility, of diapers and vomit. Of sweet baby hugs and childish kisses.

A part of Adam I could keep forever.

"Hey, hey," he said, alarmed. "Don't cry, Sadie-me-love, don't cry!"

I wiped my tears at his command. "Do you really think we could?"

"Sadie," Adam said in a voice that left no doubt. "I really think we could."

That night was the first since the accident that he licked me to orgasm. After, sated, the room filled with the scent of sex, he whispered poetry into my hair and we spoke of the future as something bright with possibility.

* * *

I did not intend, on the first Friday of October, to return to the bench. Joe had made his intentions clear by bringing Priscilla to our place, and the new start with Adam had left me not needing Joe's stories.

When I kissed Adam goodbye that morning, he'd tilted his head to sniff my neck, giving me a look I wasn't sure how to interpret.

"Have a good day," he told me.

I meant to. With sunshine and warm but not blistering weather, it was a good day to eat lunch outside. I didn't have to go to that bench. There were plenty of places to enjoy, some along the riverfront, where I could enjoy the early October sunshine.

I had the best intentions, but as I shrugged into my light cardigan and grabbed up my lunch box, my feet refused to take me in any direction but toward the park where I'd spent my first Friday for the past two years.

All things must end, I told myself. Resolution.

I didn't mean to meet Joe again.

But in the end, I did.

Chapter 14

October

This month, my name is Kitten. That's not my real name, but nobody here needs to know my real name. Besides, I am a kitten. A pussy, ready to be petted. That's all anyone needs to know.

The man tells me to call him Joe, and that might be his real name, or not. I don't really care. Joe is clean and has all his teeth, and he's got a wallet full of cash that means I'll follow him wherever he wants to go. It's enough to make me his for the night, a prospect I don't mind. A bird in the hand, and all.

Joe seems to like my headband with its little kitten ears. He reaches up to flick them with his finger, then strokes my sleek, black hair. It's a wig, but a really good one. Most guys don't know the difference. Most of them don't bother to pay attention to anything above my shoulders, anyway.

Not this guy. He's staring at my face like he wants to memorize it. This would creep me out, maybe, except he looks so sincere doing it. Like maybe he's trying to figure me out or something.

"What?" I ask, self-conscious suddenly.

"You're very pretty."

"Thank you." I run a finger down his chest to end at his belt buckle.

"Do you have some friends who'd be interested in talking about books?"

We don't take money for sex, you understand, since that would be illegal. Men pay me for companionship. Anything beyond that is at the agreement of two consenting adults. If it so happens that we both consent to get naked and fuck like rabbits in a club where dozens of other couples are doing the same thing, well…all I can say is, I'm not paid for sex. I'm paid for companionship.

"I think so." I give him a wink. I've got my highest heels on and can look him almost in the eye. "Want me to introduce you to her?"

He nods. I take him by the hand and lead him through the club, where music is pounding from upstairs and the black-painted walls make me feel as though I'm in outer space, sometimes. Barbie's slouched in one of the love seats along the back wall, deep in conversation with Candy. By the waving hands, I can tell they're discussing the latest episode of the prison drama show they're both hooked on. They both look up when I come over with Joe.

"This is Joe," I tell them. "He likes books."

I like working with Barbie because she's got a smoking hot little body. Blond and blue-eyed, she looks like a fashion doll and likes to dress in a lot of frills and bows.

We make a nice pair, me with my sleek china-doll wig and black leather catsuit. Candy, on the other hand, likes the slutty schoolgirl look, which makes me roll my eyes.

"Hello, ladies," Joe says.

"Hello, Joe," Barbie purrs, crossing her legs so her short pink skirt rides up on tanned, tight thighs. "What do you know?"

That's a lame joke, but he laughs anyway. A real laugh, too, not some forced chuckle. I like this Joe, who is making my job so much easier. Sometimes guys are so nervous or excited they ruin all the fun.

"What kind of books do you like, Joe?" Candy's pigtails bounce as she sits up straight. Her head's right at crotch level, and don't think she doesn't know it.

Joe must know it, too, because he tilts his hips a little in her direction. Subtle body language, but something you learn to pick out. Okay, so he's into the slutty school-girl look. Barbie and I share a glance. She's my best friend here, and we can read each other like…well, like the books Joe says he wants to discuss.

"Let me guess." My fingers link through his, our palms moist and warm against one another. "Romance novels?"

Joe smiles.

"Stroke books," Candy says with an unsubtle parting of her thighs. Some girls, I swear, just don't know how to work it right.

"No," says Barbie, sounding serious. She stands. She's even taller than I am, and she can look him right in the eye. "Joe likes…mysteries."

"That's right," Joe says, not sounding at all surprised.

Barbie moves closer. I know very well how those luscious, soft tits feel, so when she brushes them against Joe's chest I'm not surprised that his fingers grip down on mine. Barbie puts her hands on his shoulder and leans in to whisper into his ear, the one closest to me, so I know what she's saying.

"What do you say we go someplace more private, and you can tell me all about your favorites?"

Joe's head turns to murmur into Barbie's ear. "I say that sounds like a good idea."

"Good." She steps back and we share a smile. I like working with Barbie. A lot. "Kitten's talked to you about the arrangements?"

He hasn't asked for pricing for more than one girl, so we'll have to work that out, but I don't get the feeling he's going to balk.

"We've talked," I say.

Joe's thumb strokes the back of my hand. "I'd like the three of you."

Barbie raises an eyebrow, and we share another look. Two girls is a pretty common thing, and we've worked out a good routine. Adding Candy to the mix will shake things up a bit, but if that's what Joe wants, I guess that's what he'll get.

Candy stands and throws me and Barbie a triumphant look. I don't bother reacting. I'd never pick Candy on purpose, and she knows it. Neither would Barbie. But we're professionals, so we'll work with her if that's what Joe wants. She doesn't have to act like she's just won some sort of bonus prize.

I take Joe upstairs, past the dance floor where people are bumping and grinding. Then up another set of stairs to the private floor. Gene gives us a nod from his chair on the landing.

"Ladies," he says, and unlocks the door for us. "Sir."

Joe says hello. They don't, usually. Most men ignore Gene, as if pretending he's not there makes this somehow something other than what it is. Like maybe they just got lucky downstairs instead of the truth, that they've got to pay a girl to agree to become a consenting adult with them.

The room at the end of the hall is my favorite, because it's a little bigger and has the biggest bed. It's also got a chair and a couch, which makes it more interesting. Once inside, Candy makes a beeline for the CD player and puts in something jazzy and smooth. I'm actually impressed by her choice.

Barbie closes the door behind us, then tells Joe exactly what the hourly fee is for "conversation," and that if he'd like to pay in advance that would be all right with all of us.

Joe has no problem with paying in advance. The wad of money in his wallet is truly impressive, and Barbie and I share another glance. He pauses in thumbing out a handful of twenties and looks us over, including Candy. Then he separates another couple hundred from the bundle and hands the whole pile to Barbie, who counts it all and then puts it in the lockbox on the dresser where it will stay until Joe leaves. I've only once had a man try and stiff me, but the lockbox makes it impossible even if he tried.

Barbie reaches up and loosens his tie. "So. What shall we talk about?"

It might be a surprise to know that they do, indeed, talk about books, at least for a while. Barbie likes to read, too. She unbuttons his shirt while I slip off his jacket and hang it up. Candy hangs back, watching, one of the problems with having more than three in a group. There's only so much room and so many places for hands.

Barbie's telling Joe about some novel she read as we strip off his shirt, and she pauses to make a little "woof." I love that about her, the way she enjoys her work.

I make a noise of my own when I run my hands over his back. Satin smooth, with two of the cutest fucking dimples just above his ass, one on either side of his spine. I want to lick them. Let's face it, most men who pay me for my time aren't hot, they hardly ever smell this good, and sometimes it takes a lot of effort to get into this.

Somehow, I doubt it's going to be a problem with Joe.

Barbie and I share a glance over his shoulder. She undoes his belt, but before she can go for the zip, he stops her.

"I'd like it if you and Kitten discussed books for a little while."

I hear a smile in his voice, and Barbie's grin tells me she finds him as charming as I do.

"While you watch, I presume?"

"If that would be all right."

She doesn't need to tell him that whatever he wants is all right, since he's the guy whose money's in the lockbox. Joe knows how this is played. But he's making it fun for us, too, and that makes it easier to get into it.

Barbie holds out her hand to me. "Sure thing. I like talking about books with Kitten."

We kiss in front of him. Barbie's mouth is soft and wet. She tastes a little like cherry, from her lip gloss. She runs her tongue over my lips, tickling, and my nipples get hard right away. We put our arms around each other, stroking, and I grab two handfuls of her soft, curved ass. I love the way it feels covered in satin and lace. Barbie's not wearing a thong, so I trace the edge of her panties with my fingertips, caressing the underside of her bum until she shivers.

We kiss some more, putting on a show for him, but it's frankly not hard to get into it. When I turn my head to let Barbie suck my neck, I see him sitting. Candy's between his legs, her ass peeking out from under her short, plaid skirt. She is wearing a thong. She's got Joe's cock in her mouth. Her head moves up and down, fast, until he puts his fingers in her hair and tells her to slow down.

Barbie turns my face back to hers and kisses me again. Her tongue strokes mine as her hands slide up my sides and cup my tits. I'm not as big as she is, and she manages to fill her hands with my flesh. She kneads and squeezes, just hard enough to get me gasping, because she knows that's the way I like it.

Barbie might look soft and sweet like pink cotton candy, but she's nowhere near innocent. She unzips my cat suit as she backs me toward the bed and lays me down. Cool air hits my skin, and I shiver a little as her hands pull off my clothes and leave me bare. The comforter is soft beneath me. She pushes me back, spreads my knees and climbs between them.

I tense in anticipation, lifting my hips a little, but Barbie's not ready to give me what Joe wants to see. She strokes my thighs with her fingernails, scratching just hard enough to make me moan.

"You like that?" Her voice is throaty and pleased.

"Yes, baby, I like that." Guys don't just like to watch. They like to listen, too.

"Good. You want me to lick that sweet pussy?"

"Oh, yes," I purr, lifting my cunt up to prove I'm telling the truth. "Lick me."

Barbie slides her hands under my ass and settles between my legs. I close my eyes, waiting, and a moment later I'm rewarded by the flat of her tongue on my clit. It feels good. I let out a groan and pump my hips. Barbie licks me with slow, smooth strokes, keeping the sort of steady pace only another woman truly understands.

I turn to look at Joe. Candy's still between his legs, though she appears to have found a pace he likes better. He pets her hair every so often, almost absentmindedly.

Maybe he'll want to fuck us, and maybe he won't, but for now I lay back and enjoy Barbie eating my cunt. She's an expert, using her tongue and lips and fingers in ways guaranteed to make me writhe and moan. I do, loudly, giving in to the urge to make noise as my pleasure grows.

"Don't let her come." Joe's command makes Barbie pause.

I let out a little whimper of protest. My nipples are diamond-hard, my pussy slick with Barbie's saliva and my own juices. She's got three fingers up my snatch and her thumb against my asshole, and one or two more flutters of her tongue would have had me going over.

Still, he's the one in charge and though I shudder when Barbie pulls her fingers out of me, I don't come. She leans down to kiss me again. I taste myself on her mouth, underlaid with the faint remaining taste of cherry.

When I look over at Joe, I see Candy's sitting up. Her hand moves along his cock, offering me a tempting glimpse of skin as she jacks him. Her shirt's askew and her hair's a mess, but she's looking up at him adoringly. It could be an act, but if it is, she's perfected it.

"Come here." Joe points to Barbie. When she obeys, he takes the hand she'd had up my cunt, and he sucks her fingers, one by one.

The sight hits me like a two-by-four to the back of the head. It's seriously the hottest thing I've ever seen a guy do, paying for my company or not. Barbie seems to like it, too, because her breath eases out of her with a little groan I recognize as real.

Joe leans forward with her fingers still in his mouth and Candy's hand still jacking his prick. He puts his hand between Barbie's legs. I can see his arm moving as he rubs her. She spreads her legs and puts a hand on his shoulder for support. Her skirt rides up, and Candy gives it some help, pushing the tight fabric higher until Barbie's cute pink panties show.

Nothing about Joe is fast. His hand moves, up, down, against Barbie. When I see her thighs shake a little my cunt clenches. He's turning her on. We can pretend a lot of things, but some of our body's reactions can never be faked. I've felt that little quiver in the sweetness of her groin enough times to know when someone's getting her off.

From her place on the floor, Candy leans over to kiss Barbie's leg. Candy's got her fingers down the front of her thong, her other hand still moving on Joe's dick. They're quite a picture over there, the three of them. Once again, where does the fourth person go?

I can't see Joe's face, but I can watch his hand stroke, stroke, stroke between Barbie's legs. She's leaning harder on his shoulder now, her head tipped forward so her blond hair hangs down. Her hips are moving. Candy's mouth is tracing patterns on Barbie's thigh, her hand moving faster on her cunt. I've got my hand clenched between my thighs, but I'm not rubbing myself. I'm gripping my fist with my thigh muscles, timing each clutch and release to the quickening beat of my heart. I can't come this way, but fuck, do I want to.

Joe lets Barbie's fingers slide out of his mouth. "Take off your panties."

To Candy, he says, "You, too."

So far, I'm the only one naked. I sit on the edge of the bed, watching. Candy stands and shucks off her thong while Barbie shimmies out of her panties.

"Kiss her."

Joe sits back in his chair, watching, as Candy and Barbie turn to each other. Candy's too eager and wants to force the kiss. Barbie has more patience than I would. She waits until Candy's calmed a little bit, then kisses her sensually. Open mouths, probing tongues. Roaming hands. Joe seems to be enjoying it. When he sees me looking, he crooks a finger. He pushes off his pants and socks while I walk over to him, so by the time I get there, he's naked.

He's got a nice cock. I measure it with my eyes. Length and girth, very nice. I can't tell much more, because of the condom Candy was smart enough to put on him. The fluff of hair around the base is thick and darker than the hair on his head and body, but looks well-groomed.

I take the hand he holds out to me. He pulls me gently onto his lap, where I sit perched on one knee. My pussy must be wet against his leg, and I wonder if that excites him, to know that Barbie got me so aroused.

"Put your hand on my cock, Kitten." He says my name like it amuses him. Hell, it amuses me, too. I do as he says, feeling his heat through the latex. His cock pulses a bit in my fingers.

Together, we watch Barbie and Candy kissing. Joe's hand moves around in front of me. He circles my clit with the tip of his finger. I'm already set on fire from Barbie's excellent cunt-eating, so Joe's touch makes me push my pussy into his hand.

"Sit still."

It's hard to do that when he keeps rubbing my button. "Slower," he says when my hand starts moving faster on his erection.

"Candy, I think I'd like to see you lick Barbie's pussy."

The three of us let out a little gasp/sigh/moan at that. I'll say one thing for Joe, he knows how to orchestrate this. I've been with guys who barely know what to do with one girl, much less three. Or guys who get so turned on watching us go at it, they shoot their loads right away. Or even guys who get pissed off when they feel they're not getting enough attention.

Not Joe, though. He's stroking my clit so nicely I'm jittering on the edge of coming, and his cock shows no sign of getting soft or shooting off. Candy's on her knees in front of Barbie, spreading her pussy and lapping away at it with more enthusiasm than skill, but like I said, Barbie's got more patience than I. She tilts her hips against Candy's mouth, cooing encouragement. One hand goes to Candy's head, guiding her, while the other twists and twirls her nipples to tight little peaks just begging to be sucked.

"Are you going to come?" Joe's words startle me a little and I have to swallow hard before I can answer.

"I...I think so."

He stops and puts his hand flat over my pussy, pressing my clit with the heel of his hand. "Do you usually come with your gentlemen?"

I laugh at that, more at his use of the term *gentlemen* than anything else. The motion of my laughter rocks me against his hand, and I give a little gasp. "Sometimes."

"If they pay you enough?"

Candy's still going to town, but Barbie turns her head to look over at us.

"That helps."

"Tell me," Joe says. "Have I paid you enough?"

Barbie answers before I can. "Yeah, Joe. I think so."

She looks at me, and I look at her. We share a smile. I love working with Barbie. I wish it were me lapping her sweet honey instead of Candy, who doesn't really like girls all that much. Joe presses my cunt and I shift on his knee.

"Get on the bed. Candy, on your back. Barbie and Kitten, on your hands and knees."

We manage to arrange this somewhat awkward position with a minimum of giggling and shifting. When we're done, Candy's spread on her back while Barbie and I, our asses in the air and our feet hanging over the bed's edge, are half-straddling her, facing her pussy. We give each other a look. This is definitely something I've never done before, but I can't wait to see what he tells us to do next.

My cunt feels soft and open. Slick. My clit's a hard, tight bump, aching to be touched. I wait. I have a feeling this is going to be good.

Candy's breath caresses my pussy and thighs. I consider hers. She's shaved her pubic hair into a heart. Cute. I might not like Candy as much as I like Barbie, but I'll admit she's been good to work with tonight.

Joe's hand weighs on my lower back. I look at Barbie, who's grinning widely. If I turn my head a tiny bit more, I can see that Joe's between us, his hand just above her ass, too.

I turn my neck harder to look at his face. He's looking at us like he's solving a mystery in one of the books he's paying us to discuss. His smile doesn't quite reach his eyes, and for a second a shiver of unease goes through me. He doesn't exactly look like a man who's getting his rocks off, even though his jutting prick makes no mystery of his arousal.

I've only been in a situation that went bad once, and when it did, it went really bad. Blood and hospital stay bad. Later, I found out the guy who assaulted me had made a habit of it. He'd killed the girl after me. He'd looked a little bit like Joe does now.

I tense, and he looks at me. His hands smoothes over my ass. I must look scared because he shakes his head the tiniest bit. His palm strokes my skin like he's soothing what I've become, a skittish Kitten.

"Shhh," he whispers.

Barbie knows what happened to me. She's turning to look at him, too, and I see her face go dark. Barbie can kick a fucker's ass, if she has to. But Joe shushes her, too, and we're both staring at each other. My heart's beating hard. Sweat cools, and I shiver.

Candy shifts likes she's bored. The motion breaks the spell. Joe's hands are moving over my skin, and Barbie's.

"Lick each other," he says.

Two mouths dip into Candy's heart-shaved pussy. Barbie and I take turns licking her, kissing in between. Tongues twist like snakes, in each other's mouths and in her cunt. She goes back and forth between the two of us, fluttering and lapping at us.

Barbie grunts beside me, then sighs. She tips her ass higher. Joe's fucking her. His hand grips her hip, while the fingers of his other hand slip into me from behind. I've got a tongue on my clit and her fingers up my cunt. I rock with it, licking and sucking Candy from above. I take a break to nibble and kiss her belly and thighs while Barbie puts her expertise to work. Pretty soon, Candy's hips are lifting. Her pussy's open and wet. Her clit's a pretty shade of pink, peeking out from the tiny tuft of pubes at the base of the heart. I flick it with my tongue and she cries out. I can see it move as her orgasm starts. I love watching women come. I love the way their bodies move, all trembling and shuddering. If I had my fingers inside her, I'd feel her cunt bearing down on them with each spasm. I feel it start to echo inside my own pussy just as Joe fills me with his cock.

It takes more room than his fingers had, and I make almost the identical sound that Barbie did when he pushed inside her. Shit, it feels good. He fucks me slowly, then faster.

Candy's flailing all over the place and Barbie and I are pinning her down. She's making these little high-pitched squeals, and selfishly, I wish she'd finish coming so she can get back to licking me.

I'm close. Every stroke of Joe's cock inside me urges me toward the edge of an orgasm I know is going to blow my fucking mind. It's a rare thing, one I'm tempted to believe isn't even really true but the product of some male-oriented fantasy of pleasing three women at once, except there's no denying the push and pull of my cunt and ass as my body prepares to explode.

It's the noise he makes that sends me over at last. He grunts once, low in his throat and thrusts so deep I shout. Climax tears me apart so far and so hard I can't believe I'll ever do anything but come forever.

His thrusts ease as I shake and quake. He pulls another, smaller orgasm out of me by changing the angle just enough to rub my G-spot. Candy makes a muffled noise of surprise. I try to breathe and can't.

When he pulls out, I collapse alongside Candy. We both watch while Joe moves back to Barbie and fucks her so hard she lets out a hoarse, fierce shout. I'm not sure she came until her eyes open and she looks dazed, like she can't believe it really happened, either.

Joe finishes a moment after that. He's got a good come-face. Not too twisted or ridiculous, but then again, I'm looking at it through the haze of post-orgasmic bliss. He pauses, panting, only briefly, before he pulls out and Barbie joins me and Candy in a pile on the bed.

"Ladies," Joe says from the doorway. How did he get dressed so fast? "It's been a pleasure."

Then he's gone, and none of us quite know what to say. Things like this happen in porno movies all the time, but I never believed it would happen to me. Maybe, I think, still dazed, it hasn't. Maybe it's all just a story.

A book.

A mystery.

I was off the bench before I realized it, taking two steps away from him. What did I say? That I didn't believe him? That I couldn't?

He gave me a look as though challenging me to deny his story, but I couldn't say anything. If I chose not to believe this, would I have to admit the others had been lies, too? If I accepted this one as truth, what did that mean?

I knew much about Joe, but in the end, I couldn't be sure I knew anything about him at all. When I spoke, I couldn't keep the triumph out of my voice no matter how much I wished I didn't feel it.

"Do you want me to say I told you so?"

A tiny smile tipped the corners of his mouth. "Do you want to say it?"

"No." I gave him an honest answer. I'd come here today to end this on my terms, not Joe's.

Pride is a nasty creature, but I had no illusions it was anything else that had brought me back to that bench. Joe had broken the rules by taking Priscilla to our place. He'd mingled real life with the fantasy one we'd been sharing. I didn't pretend to know his reasons for it, but I wasn't about to let him be the one to finish it. Not like that.

"No?" He cocked his head, his smile growing wider. "You're sure?"

"Is that what you want?" Confident in my superiority, I couldn't help sounding smug. "To say I knew you couldn't do it? I knew you'd never make it last?"

Joe studied me. Despite the smile, his expression was unreadable. For the first time since he'd sat, I noticed he was wearing the tie he knew I liked.

"Fine," I said coldly. "I told you so, Joe. I knew you'd never be able to make it last. I knew you'd never be able to be faithful. But that doesn't matter anymore, because this is over. It's done. I'm not coming back here anymore."

He nodded throughout my mini-rant, which only annoyed me.

"No more stories," I finished, almost sneering. My throat had gone tight with tears I swallowed. There was too much emotion here, things I didn't want to face. Guilt not the least, but other, far more tangled threads of desire and affection I wanted to make go away.

"No more stories," Joe said.

His calm reaction stole some of my thunder. I brushed hair from my face and straightened, unwillingly grateful that he was allowing me to have my say and letting me have what I wanted. To be the one finishing it.

"Good luck, Joe."

"Thanks, Sadie." He stood, facing me. "I'll need it."

I felt the question on my face but it didn't escape my lips.

Joe, however, seemed to understand me without my needing to speak. He put his hands in his pockets in a gesture I was shamed to find so familiar.

I'd sounded smug. He looked triumphant. He leaned in close, lowering his voice as though he meant to tell me a secret, one more serious and titillating than any of the others. I knew before he said a word that he wasn't going to let me be the one to finish this, after all. I wanted to slap him, angry at him but furious with myself for giving him the chance to end this, whatever it had been, on his terms. Yet all I could do was listen while he made that true.

"I asked her to marry me, Sadie. And she said yes."

What had been lies? What had been truth? And in the end, did it matter?

In Joe's stories he'd played the parts of prince and villain with equal skill...but I'd never been one of his stories. Would I become one? A secret story, kept to himself? Or had he already told Priscilla about our lunches and the stories shared? I guessed I'd never know.

There were no more chapters to this novel; Joe had written "The End" and there was no point in hoping for an epilogue. The story was over.

Chapter 15

November

I didn't know what to do with myself the first Friday in November. None of my clothes fit, my hair refused to curl, my mascara clumped. The air had the bite of snow and I couldn't find my gloves. My car smelled like onions. The universe was conspiring against me, the holiday atmosphere in my office suffocating, my body rebelling and demanding to be fed on a day I didn't want to go to lunch.

I went out anyway. There are some things not even will-power can control, and my hunger was making me nauseous and grouchy. I avoided the atrium and the park. That entire side of town, in fact. I went to the mall, meaning to grab a quick bite at a small sandwich café and maybe treat myself to retail therapy. Adam had banned Christmas from our house years ago, saying he hated the pomp and circumstance of celebrating a holiday he didn't believe, but I had family and colleagues who still expected gifts.

The mall was crowded, not unexpectedly. I gave up the idea of trying to shop after buying only one gift, a picture frame for my mother. Jostled and bustled, I finally got in line at the café, placed my order, took my latte and looked for a place to sit. Spotting a table near the back, I headed for it. I wasn't quite fast enough. A pair of lunching ladies had apparently decided not to frequent their usual hoity-toity habitats and were slumming in the sandwich shop. They got to the table first, their cloud of perfume heady and expensive. I wanted to sneeze but didn't even have the chance to do that before I was bumped from behind by someone pushing out of his seat. My bag hit the ground.

Someone bent to pick it up before I had a chance. Our hands touched. He let the bag go as I stood, clutching it.

"I hope it didn't break," said the man at the table.

"I think it's fine."

His smile was crooked, but friendly. He pointed to the empty seat across from him. "This seat's empty, if you don't mind sharing."

I looked around, but there was no other place. I sat. "Thanks."

We stared at each other for a few moments, strangers at a table. I sipped my latte self-consciously, uncertain what to say. My new companion seemed in no mood to break the silence, either. His broad, pleasant smile urged me to return it.

"I'm Greg, by the way." He held out his hand, which I shook.

"Sadie."

"It's nice to meet you, Sadie." His fingers squeezed mine briefly. His hand was very warm. In the next moment, so was my face.

I was saved at that moment by the arrival of the sandwich I'd ordered, and a scant minute later, Greg's salad and soup. Around us the chatter of conversation rose and fell. It seemed rude not to talk to him, so I did.

It didn't matter what we said. The weather was nice; yes, it was a shame about that fire downtown; of course the city needed new taxes like a cow needed a tennis racket. Greg carried the conversation without effort, leading me from topic to topic. The area became more and more crowded, necessitating us to move our chairs closer and closer. By the time we'd finished our lunches, we were sitting almost thigh to thigh.

He didn't touch me on purpose. It was clearly the fault of the man behind us, who laughed loudly and shook his chair, causing Greg's leg to rub mine. Just as it was the fault of the café employee squeezing by us for making Greg have to lean forward with his hand on my shoulder to keep from being bonked on the head by a tray. The napkin holder, too, conspired against us, for refusing to give up a napkin without Greg's manly help.

Sitting next to Greg was like licking a battery. Shocking, sizzling and stupid. Each slight caress, every nonchalant stroke, echoed in the tightness of my nipples and the friction between my thighs. We danced, and if I fumbled the steps from lack of practice, Greg was a skilled enough partner to make up for it. I hadn't thought it would be so easy to be seduced.

I didn't want this. I craved it. I couldn't. I would.
I didn't.

If he'd been Joe, we'd have ended up going to a hotel room, or at least back to his car. But…he wasn't Joe, this wasn't a story. It was real life, and when lunch was over, so was the flirtation. When the crowds cleared and there could be no excuse to linger, Greg stood. I did, too. His gaze fell on the band on my finger. I looked at his hand, which wore a similar ring.

"It was nice meeting you, Sadie."

"You, too. Thanks for letting me share your table."

He had a nice smile, but the heat between us, if there had been any beyond my imagination, had faded. "Anytime."

I hadn't done anything wrong, even less than in the hours I'd spent listening to Joe tell his tales of sexual excess. Yet I felt twice as bad as I'd ever felt about that, and it took me some hard thinking to figure out why. It came down to something simple. It wasn't the stories but Joe himself I'd come to depend upon. Substituting a random, unexpected flirtation wasn't harmless, not when it meant I was trying to replace something I'd come to care about very much with something pretending to be as important.

The parking garage wasn't the best place for contemplation, but with one hand on my car and the other holding my bag, I closed my eyes and let myself think about what I'd been avoiding all day. It was the first Friday of November and I hadn't seen Joe. I might not ever see him again. The rest of my life would have no Joe in it. I'd lost something precious, and no matter how much things with Adam were changing, I missed what I'd had no right to have.

"Dr. Danning?"

I opened my eyes, turning, embarrassed at having been caught in such a socially awkward state. "Elle, hi!"

If Elle had seen my close-eyed contemplation, she didn't show it. "How are you?"

"Busy," I said with a small laugh designed to hide the shakiness of my voice. I stood up straight and offered my hand to Elle's companion. "Hello, I'm Sadie Danning."

"This is my mother." Elle took a deep breath. "We've been shopping."

"Have you?" I smiled. "That sounds nice."

Mrs. Kavanagh snorted. "Nice? If you like trudging around store after store and buying nothing, yes. Very nice."

Elle's smile didn't waver. "My mother thinks I need to update my wardrobe."

Comparing the two of them, I couldn't agree. Elle's mother might have been dressed in pieces of obvious expense and classic style, but Elle wore her simple black skirt and pale blue cardigan with far more class. I gave Elle's arm a quick squeeze.

"That's a pretty sweater," I told her. Yes, to make her mother grit her teeth.

Elle beamed. "Dan bought it for me."

Again, Mrs. Kavanagh snorted. Elle gave her mother a narrow, sideways glance, which the older woman saw. "What?"

"My mother," said Elle with a serenity that could only have come from long practice, "thinks Dan's tastes sucks."

"Language, Ella! Mother Mary!"

Elle's sweet smile remained unchanged as she shrugged innocently. I had to bite back a smile of my own. The heat in my cheeks started to fade.

"Did Ella call you doctor?" Mrs. Kavanagh, perhaps sensing she couldn't niggle her daughter any further on the subject of clothes, piped up. "What kind of doctor are you?"

Before I could answer, Elle reached to touch my upper arm. "She was my shoulder."

I've been called many things in my life, but that was one of the nicest. The affection in her voice made my throat thick. "Thank you, Elle."

She nodded. Her mother looked confused, a state of mind in which I doubted she'd often found herself. She turned to her daughter with a frown.

"What's that supposed to mean?"

I wasn't about to tell Mrs. Kavanagh the role I'd played in her daughter's life if Elle didn't want me to. Consequently, for a minute neither of us spoke. This didn't sit well with Mrs. Kavanagh, who really needed a house dropped on her.

"Ella?"

"Dr. Danning was my doctor."

Silence while Mrs. Kavanagh assessed this. "Your…?"

"My shrink, Mother." Elle sounded exasperated and amused.

The curl of Mrs. Kavanagh's lip should have offended me, as should the looking over she gave me. I'd never been more aware of my shoes needing a polish or my stockings having snags as under Elle's mother's eagle eye. She sniffed.

"Well." She put more meaning into that single word than if she'd recited a soliloquy.

"My mother doesn't approve of psychologists," Elle said. I don't think I was mistaken about her glee.

"I'll try not to let that bother me," I said. Elle and I laughed. Her mother, predictably, did not.

"I'll be waiting for you in the China Orchid," Mrs. Kavanagh said, "if you want to…talk."

Talk or kick puppies, perhaps? She made both actions sound as horrible. Elle sighed and waited until her mother had gone out of earshot before she spoke.

"Sorry about that. But I guess now you see what I mean."

"I never doubted you were telling me the truth," I said. "How are things?"

She laughed behind her hand, the sound echoing in the garage. "Much better, if you can believe it. With the wedding to plan she's got caterers to give hell to. She leaves me alone. Sort of."

"Yes, that's in a couple weeks. You must be excited."

Elle raised a brow. "That's one way to put it. I'd have said sick to my stomach and ready to pull out my hair, but sure. Excited works."

We laughed again. Her smile softened. She touched my arm again, a gesture of some significance, since she was not the touchy-feely sort.

"I miss our talks, Dr. Danning."

"Do you think you need to see me again?" The question came out sounding professional.

She shook her head. "No. Not in that way. I'm doing

really well, actually. Just that…it was nice to have someone to talk to. It's nice to have someone you can tell your secrets to, you know? Without being afraid? I knew I could always tell you anything, and you'd give me advice but you wouldn't judge me or get angry with me. It was nice to have a shoulder to cry on."

I nodded, touched. "I'm glad I was able to help."

She chewed her lower lip, looking awkward. "It's important to have someone like that? Don't you think?"

"I do." I studied her.

"I mean, I talk to Dan. He listens. To everything. I think he might wish I didn't talk so much, actually. It's been…interesting. But he listens."

"That's good." I meant it, even as once again I found myself in the unenviable position of envying her.

"So, anyway. I should get back to my mother. I'll see you next week?"

"Of course. I'm looking forward to it."

She laughed with genuine humor. "I'm glad someone is!"

"Oh, Elle," I told her. "You don't mean that, do you?"

She shook her head after a pause. "No. I guess I don't. Tell me something, Dr. Danning. It's worth it, isn't it? Getting married?"

If we'd been in my office with a desk between us, my answer might have been different. Standing in the parking garage, with her no longer my client, my reply was more forthright. "I used to think so."

She made a small noise, as if she understood my answer so completely it needed no comment. I nodded, a wind-up doll with rusted gears. She stepped back and gave a little wave, walking backward a few steps before turning and disappearing around the corner. I couldn't move at first, when she'd gone, but after a moment I managed to unlock my door and slide behind the wheel, where I sat for a very long time.

I wished I had someone to talk to.

It was difficult to mourn losing something I wasn't supposed to have. I might have spent more time quietly missing the stories I'd never hear again, but I frankly had no time. Adam up was happier than Adam down, but twice as exhausting. He stopped sleeping as much as he'd been, preferring to stay up late chatting. Instead of spending most of his time in bed, he insisted on getting into his chair. He wanted to go places, do things he'd been refusing to do for years.

"But I don't want to see that movie," I protested, halfheartedly. I sprawled on the recliner, watching Adam looking up film showings on the Internet. His hair was growing back, but he was still pale. He looked frailer in the chair than he did in bed. "Why don't we just go out to dinner? Or better yet, stay home?"

He spun around to face me. "I thought you'd want to go to the movies!"

"Well…" I tried to think of an answer that didn't sound lame. "I'm tired, Adam. I've worked all week. I was sort of hoping to take it easy."

"I've worked all week, too, Sadie."

Adam never wheedled. He never pleaded his case. He

didn't even try to make me want what he wanted. He just tried to get me to agree to give him what he wanted.

"I don't like serial killer movies." I took off my shoes and stood to strip out of my nylons with a breath of relief.

"We could see something else."

"Tomorrow?" I tossed my shed stockings into the laundry basket. "We can go to a Saturday matinee."

"Fine." He spun the chair again and ordered his computer to close the browser.

I sighed. "Honey, I think it's great you want to go out and do things. But I'm tired. Okay? I get up at 4:00 a.m. every day—"

"Forget it." I didn't need to see his face to know he was frowning.

"How about I order some Chinese and we watch those episodes of *Monty Python* we have on DVD?"

I could see the shrug he meant to make, though it was the barest lift of shoulder. I sighed. Now he was pissed.

"You bitched because I didn't want to do anything, now you bitch when I do."

That stung. "I'm not bitching! We'll go tomorrow, it's not a big deal!"

"I said fine."

In the past I'd have tried to placate him, or allowed him to goad me into an argument. This time, I simply left the room. I went to my own room, picked up a book I'd been trying to read for months and snuggled into my easy chair to finish it.

It took him fifteen minutes to shout for me. I put the book aside and answered his call. He was muttering curses.

"Your fucking shoes, Sadie!"

I'd left my shoes on the floor and he'd rolled over one. Now it lodged against the wheel, preventing him from moving. All he needed to do was back up and go around it, which I explained as I moved the offending items and cleared his path.

"I'm sorry, though," I added. "I know to be more careful."

Adam launched into a diatribe. I got up and left the room. This time, I was ten pages from the end of the book before he called for me again. I made him wait until I was done before I went back in.

"Damn it, Sadie! Don't walk away from me!" Again, he started being derisive.

Again, I walked away.

I listened to him ranting for half an hour before I came back in with two bowls of ice cream and the *Monty Python* DVDs. Adam looked sullen. I set the ice cream on the table and fussed with the television.

"What if I needed you?"

I turned to him. "You do need me for a lot of things. But I don't need to take shit from you. I love you, Adam, and I want to be here for you, but you've got to stop hating me for it."

"I don't hate you," he said, but in a low voice.

"Don't you?" I asked calmly. I don't think I'd have asked before, but somehow everything that had happened with Joe made me feel like there was no point in pretense any more.

"No." The way he cut his gaze from mine told me something different.

It still stung. Even though I understood it, even though

I knew if the situation were reversed I'd probably have spent a great deal of time hating him, too, it still stabbed me.

"I don't hate you," Adam repeated. "But sometimes…"

I waited. The ice cream melted. The TV annoyed me with its blather until I turned it off. "Sometimes?"

"Sometimes I can't stand you."

I sat, still and small, made insignificant by a truth I couldn't even blame him for sharing. It wasn't fair, but it was honest. I'd asked him to tell me, and he did.

"I can't stand the way you fuss over me, or how you wait outside the door before you come in. I know what you're doing out there, Sadie. I know how you have to force yourself to smile. I can't stand the way you make excuses for me to people."

"I do that because—"

"I know why you do it. And fuck 'em. You don't need to make excuses for me, okay? I don't want you to make me better for anyone. You get it? And I can't stand that I'm your excuse for not having a life."

"Don't say that. I don't think that." I blinked, expecting tears, but my eyes were dry.

Adam gave me a long, hard stare. "Nobody's going to fault you for getting out once in awhile."

"I never said they would."

"All you do is work and come home and take care of me. You never go out with friends anymore. What are you afraid of? That they'll think you're a shitty wife if you leave me to go out?"

I shouldn't have been surprised he turned the tables on

me. He'd always been good at it. "I'm afraid *you'll* think I'm a shitty wife if I go out."

His mouth twisted. "You don't get it."

"No. I guess I don't."

We stared at each other. His gaze flickered, unreadable. I'd wanted him to speak. Now I wished for silence.

"When you're around me, all I can think about is all the things I'm not, anymore," Adam said. "All the things I used to do."

"Things have changed, yes, but—"

"It's easy for you to say that when you're not the one in the chair!"

Adam's shout struck me into silence. He was right. I could make no judgment about his feelings. I wasn't in his place.

"See? You say you want to hear it. But you don't."

I spread my hands, unable to answer. Adam made a disgusted sound.

"Now you know why I've kept my mouth shut. You don't want to hear what I have to say. You don't want to know how I really feel. You want to fuck? Okay, fine. You want to go places? Fine, I'll do that, too. But when you tell me you want me to talk, I know you're lying."

"I want things to be the way they used to!" I cried.

"Well, they can't."

"Then I want us to try and make them work they way they are, now." I reached to touch him and he turned his face. "Adam. Why can't we make this work?"

"Sometimes," he said after a second that lasted a million years, "things get broken. And they can't be fixed."

"Is that us? Are we broken?"

"You tell me."

"It's not my fault I can't follow you anymore," I whispered.

"If I wasn't in this chair, would you have left me by now?" He did a slow, deliberate spin.

I sighed. "If you weren't in that chair, would you be such an asshole?"

He glared. I shrugged. He moved away from me, and I didn't follow.

"Do you love me, Adam?"

He shook his head the barest amount. "I don't know."

It would've been easier if he'd said no.

"Well," I said, getting up, "let me know when you've figured it out."

Then I left him alone until he needed me again, but we didn't speak.

"I'm going to start handing out autographed pictures," Adam said as I closed the door to the van. "Charge 'em five bucks each. What do you think?"

I looked over to the line of people outside the new Mexican restaurant. No matter how many times we're told as children it's not polite to stare, few of us remember it in adulthood. A good many of them were watching as I made sure Adam was secure in his chair and walked with him toward the small ramp up to the sidewalk.

"They're not trying to be rude." I waited until he'd successfully traversed the bumpy patch of concrete before walking by his side. "Besides. It's been forever since we had dinner out, together. Let's enjoy it."

Once our marriage had been precious. Now it had become fragile, too. Our argument the night before had been swept beneath the carpet, ignored by both of us out of self-preservation. We were both too brittle for truth at the moment.

"You must be Danning, party of two?" The smiling hostess had very pretty eyes that skated serenely over Adam and rested on me. "You have a reservation."

Of course she knew who we were. I'd called to make certain the restaurant had adequate facilities to handle Adam's chair. Before I could answer, Adam spoke up.

"How'd you guess?"

The hostess looked startled that he'd spoken to her. "Oh, I…well, I…"

Adam had always been a flirt. I don't think the girl waiting to seat us knew quite what to do. By the time we got to our table, though, she was laughing and blushing. He'd thoroughly charmed her. She left us with several backward glances. I saw her talking with one of the waitresses, pointing.

"Well," I told him. "You certainly made an impression."

"Don't I always?"

A flash of a long-familiar grin made my heart ache. "Yes, Adam. You do."

"What looks good?" He indicated the menu with a lift of his chin. "I'm in the mood for something spicy."

We looked over the menu and ordered drinks. The waitress looked surprised when Adam ordered a Corona. She looked to me for confirmation, which I could see annoyed him even though he should have been used to it.

"Don't worry, sweetheart, I won't drink and drive."

Flustered, she scribbled our orders and fled the table. I gave Adam a look. He gave me one, too.

"What?"

"Do you have to be so belligerent?"

He frowned. "Hey, listen, I'm not a kid. If I want a drink, I should be able to have one."

"It's not fair of you to expect everyone in the world to understand, Adam."

He made a disgusted noise. "Ask me if I give a rat's ass about everyone in the world."

"Do you give a rat's ass about anyone else?" The words popped out before I could stop them.

The waitress brought our drinks and we ordered our food. She asked Adam what he wanted this time, not speaking to him through me. I waited until she'd gone before saying, "See?"

"Of course I care," Adam snapped. "What are you trying to say?"

"I'm trying to say," I said quietly, "that you hold everyone around you up to very high standards of expectation, and I think you do it so you have the right to be disappointed."

He said nothing. I pushed the lime to the bottom of his bottle and held it up for him. Beer through a straw had once been a college trick to avoid foam and get intoxicated faster. Now it was simply an easier way for him to drink.

"Why would I want to be disappointed?" Adam asked when he'd finished sipping.

"I don't know. Because then you can be angry at that instead of the fact you're in a chair? You tell me."

It had been a long time since we'd discussed philosophy and punk rock, way back when we'd had hours of life and the desire to live it together. Nothing then had been too weighty a topic. I'd been happy to listen to him then, and I was happy to listen, now.

"It's what people see. The chair. Are you saying I shouldn't expect them to get their heads out of their asses?"

I shook my head. "No. But you could be kinder about their failures."

He snorted. "Beer."

I held it up and he drank. "I guess I don't have your patience, Sadie."

"No. Really? I'd never have guessed."

We smiled at that, a moment of connection I hadn't felt in a really long time. Our food came and we ate it, and if people stared and pitied us because I had to cut and feed him his food, Adam and I ignored them. We talked, the way we used to, about nothing serious. It was far from the easy way we'd once been but better than the way we'd become.

Getting out of the restaurant proved to be slightly harder than getting in had been. The crowd had grown, filling every table and spilling into the aisles. We had to say a lot of "excuse me" and "can you scoot in" but Adam, perhaps taking my words to heart, maintained a cheerfully polite air about it all even when people stared or whispered as we passed. I walked behind him to make sure I could help if he got caught up on anything, my gaze on his wheels.

In a bigger city, running into someone I knew would have been coincidence, but in Harrisburg it was merely inevitable. I expected to see an acquaintance in the restaurant. I didn't expect a sleek French twist and pearl earrings.

"Pardon me," Priscilla said as she shifted her chair so Adam could get by, but I wasn't looking at Priscilla.

Of course, I was looking at Joe.

"Thanks," Adam told her as he passed.

I stopped, frozen for what seemed forever while Joe and I stared. I was the first to look away. I put my hands on the back of Adam's chair, though he didn't like that. I thought, perhaps, I could push him faster, harder, though that was silly since he operated the chair and no amount of shoving from me was going to get him through a space too narrow.

"Sadie, hold on," Adam said, irritated. "Wait a minute, someone's got to move or something."

People were staring even more at the small commotion we were causing, but Adam stayed calm. I was the one who felt frantic and stressed, my hands shaking and cheeks hot. I wanted to move, but hemmed in by Adam in front and diners on either side, I couldn't.

"Here." Joe stood, moving with easy grace, and tapped the oblivious man at the next table on the shoulder. "Can you move, please?"

He arranged the chairs and cleared the way in no more than half a minute, and he did it without making it seem awkward or a big deal. He even bent to pick up a napkin that had fallen, no barrier to Adam's chair but a considerate gesture anyway. Then he stood back, out of the way, to allow us to pass.

"Thanks, man," Adam said.

"No problem." I heard Joe's smile though I was steadfastly not looking at his face. "Have a nice night."

"Joe, darling," said Priscilla from behind me. "Sit down."

I gave her a glance. She was smiling, too, pleasantly, with her perfect red lips and perfect white teeth. Her perfect hair and face and life. I nodded, quickly, then followed Adam out of the restaurant.

At home I was quiet as I helped Adam get ready for bed. We went through the routine, so familiar now we didn't need to think about it. My fingers fumbled on the controls of the lift I used to get him from the chair into bed and for one heart-stopping instant I thought he was going to fall.

"Easy," Adam said. A few minutes later, when he was settled and changed into pajamas, he added, "Are you all right?"

"No." I started to cry, and this time, he didn't tell me to stop.

I cried for a very long time, sobbed myself to sickness, and wished desperately for a hand to hold mine. Adam couldn't give me that. Not ever. But I laid my face down against his shoulder and wept, and he whispered to me, offering the comfort of his words. They had to be enough.

"How did we get here?" Adam's breath ruffled my hair. "I thought we'd always love each other. Was it just the accident, Sadie? Or would this have happened, anyway?"

"I don't know." With my eyes closed and the softness of flannel beneath my cheek, the words were easier. "I don't know anything anymore, Adam."

"I used to know everything for both of us," he said. I felt the brush of his mouth against my temple. "Back then. I wish I still did."

I lifted my head to look into his face. "I don't. Things change. They have to change in order to grow. We're not the same people we were when we met."

"No? Who are you, now?"

I think he meant to be smart, but I told him the truth anyway. "I don't know, Adam. I'm trying to figure it all out."

"You're Sadie Danning. You're my wife."

Silence hung between us for a moment. "There's more to me than just being your wife."

"I know that."

"I think...I need to know it, too."

He sighed, heavy. "So what happens now? Do we keep trying?"

"Do you have a better idea?"

Much had changed, but Adam's smile was the same as it had always been. "Not a damn one."

I got up, meaning to go to the bathroom and wash my swollen eyes, but he stopped me.

"Sadie. I do love you. I still do."

"I love you, too."

A red ribbon, a poem. Our love, mad, bad and dangerous to know. Once it had been enough to build our lives around. Now I wasn't so sure, and both of us knew it.

We were broken, brittle and fragile. The question was, were we still precious to each other? Or, instead of everything falling into place, had it fallen into pieces?

"*You* sure you'll be all right?" I tugged anxiously at the sleeves of my suit and ran my hands over my hair.

I caught sight of Adam's reflection in the mirror. He was rolling his eyes but stopped when I turned, though it was obvious I'd caught him. I put my hands on my hips.

"What's that look for?"

"I'll be fine."

I crossed to his chair and did a swift check, tucking and smoothing, until he made a disgusted noise. "I'd feel better if Dennis—"

"Dennis had these plans for months, Sadie. Besides, I'm sure the person the agency sends will be fine. You'll only gone a few hours."

He was right, but even his calm, slightly annoyed tone didn't make me feel better. "But—"

"Sadie," Adam snapped, really annoyed now. "You leave me every day for longer than you'll be gone today."

"Yes. I know. You're right." I shrugged. "I can't help it, okay? I worry."

He sighed. "Yeah. I know you do. But I'll be fine. Really. Shouldn't you get going?"

I looked at the clock. "The guy from the agency's not here yet."

He was late. I'd scheduled him to arrive an hour before I needed to leave so I'd have plenty of time to instruct him and make sure everything was going to be fine. Having Dennis and Mrs. Lapp had spoiled me, and I was unquestionably nervous about leaving Adam with a stranger.

Despite being late, the attendant who showed up set my mind at ease. He was dressed professionally, gave my hand a firm shake and looked me in the eye as he introduced himself as Randy. He was young, maybe in his early 20's, but he knew his way around the equipment with enough skill to make me feel much better about leaving Adam with him.

"Have a good time, Mrs. Danning," Randy said.

"I know I told the agency I'd be home at five, but I think it'll be closer to two. You have my number—"

"He's got the goddamned number, Sadie!"

Randy and Adam exchanged the looks of men who understood how frustrating women can be. I knew when to shut up. I kissed Adam's cheek and left. I only had to stop myself from going back inside three times before I managed to get to my car. I fought myself back from calling to check up on them for twenty whole minutes.

"If you call here again I'm going to hang up on you," Adam warned. "Go. Have a nice time. I'll see you when you get home."

And then he did hang up on me, the bastard, before I could say another word.

* * *

"If there's one thing I have to give my mother credit for," Elle told me, "it's that she makes things happen."

Moments before she'd been surrounded by the satellites that circle every bride before she walks down the aisle, and it wasn't difficult to see from the way she clutched the bouquet of wildflowers that she needed a few minutes to herself. I was proud of her, though, as she calmly told her mother and Marcy, the matron of honor, that she was going to take a few minutes to talk to me in private. Now we stood in a small back hallway overlooking the parking lot.

"My mother," she said after another moment, "lives for this sort of thing. Honestly, if not for her we'd still be picking out invitations."

This wasn't the place for analysis, even if she'd still been my patient. Even so, the response came automatically. "How do you feel about that?"

Elle's smile sometimes looks as though it's not quite sure it has the right to be on her face. "I'm getting married."

She wore a simple, tailored suit in cream and hadn't yet put on the veil that would cover her face for the traditional Jewish ceremony, but there was no mistaking the fact she was a bride.

"You sure are."

She laughed, sounding a bit shaky. "Thank you for being here."

I squeezed her shoulder. "I told you I would be."

She drew in a breath and let it out. "I think I need a drink."

"You can do this," I told her, and I meant it.

"Yes," she said, straightening her shoulders and looking toward the entrance to the sanctuary, where her mother paced. "I know."

The ceremony was brief but lovely. I felt a bit out of place among the friends and family gathered to share Elle and Dan's joy, but I didn't regret being there. There are few enough occasions in this life when we are allowed to feel as though we have truly made a difference in someone's life, and joy is something that should always be celebrated.

"Wither thou goest, I will go. Where thou lodgest, I will lodge. Thy people shall be my people, and thy God, my God."

I wasn't the only one wiping tears when Elle Kavanagh said those words to Dan Stewart and became his wife. Her mother wept with less theatricality than I expected, and Dan's eyes gleamed suspiciously bright, but Elle's face had been transformed by a smile that sat on her mouth knowing it had every right to be there.

As much as I knew the invitation had been sincere, I felt it inappropriate to attend the reception. I paid my respects in the receiving line, instead. I did watch from my car, though, as Elle and her new husband posed for photographs on the synagogue steps. They looked happy together, and I was happy for her.

"Don't hang up on me," I said to Adam as soon as he answered the phone.

"How was the wedding?"

"Beautiful. How are you?"

"Also beautiful."

I cradled the phone against my shoulder as I dug in my purse for my wallet. "Listen. About what you said earlier…"

"Yeah?" He sounded distracted, and I could too well imagine the look on his face.

"I thought I'd give Katie a call. See if she wants to grab a cup of coffee."

"Sure, sure." I imagined his impatient expression. It sounded like I'd interrupted him.

"What are you doing?"

"Working on something," he said, voice clearing a bit as he managed to focus on me. "You're going out with Katie? Good, good."

Working on something meant writing. A sudden smile lifted my voice. "What are you working on?"

"Something," he said stolidly, which meant it was definitely writing.

I didn't push, but hearing that Adam was writing again made me feel like doing a cartwheel. Or maybe just jumping up and down. "So yeah, I thought I'd give Katie a call."

"Have fun."

"You're okay?" I asked. "You're sure?"

This time his hesitation sounded less like distraction. "Yeah. Fine."

"How's Randy?"

That was it, I'd pushed him too far.

"He's fine! Damn it, Sadie, what part of 'I'm working' don't you get?"

I couldn't even be offended. "Sorry. Can you tell him I'll be home at five, just like I'd originally said?"

"Yeah. See you."

"I love you," I said, but to the buzz of the dial tone. He'd hung up on me.

"Ass," I said, but fondly, then dialed Katie's number.

"You can't even begin to imagine how much I needed this." Katie toasted me with her latte. "I mean, I love my kids, but I'm going crazy being home all day with them. Evan's great, but he just doesn't get it, you know? You just never know how much you can possibly love someone until you've had to clean up their poop. Man, that's love."

Something must have shown in my face, because she looked stricken. "Oh, sweetie, I'm sorry. That was—"

"No. It was fine. You're right." I laughed, not wanting her to feel bad. "You're absolutely right."

Katie looked embarrassed. "I shouldn't be complaining. I mean…my two rugmonkeys are nothing compared to what you have to deal with."

I meant to wave off her comments, but she spoke again.

"You know, Sadie, if you want to talk about it—"

And I was undone.

I did want to talk about it. I told her how it felt to have to stick a piece of rubber tubing up your husband's penis to allow him to pee, of how it felt to cut up his food and feed it to him, piece by tiny piece, and being terrified the entire time of what would happen if he choked on it. What it was like to lie awake listening for the sounds of the caregiver shifting him so I could be sure he wouldn't lay too long in one position. Of the ache in my arms and legs and back from operating the lift that got him in and out of the chair. I told her about Joe and about Greg and how those stories had kept me going through long months without physical affection.

I told her how it felt to be proud of Adam for getting up every day when I would have given up long ago. How much I admired his strength, even when he faltered. How I wished I could do more for him. And I told her how much I loved him, even now, when everything was crumbling away.

I thought maybe it was too much, because when I finally ran out of breath, Katie got up from the table without a word. I thought she meant to leave me, and I wouldn't have blamed her. I'd just unloaded four years of grief in half an hour.

She didn't leave. She went to the counter and brought back two of the biggest chocolate cupcakes I'd ever seen. She put them in front of us and handed me a fork.

"The icing's made of Godiva," she said. "And if ever a woman needed an overdose of premium chocolate, it's you."

A good sister is one who won't be embarrassed when you burst into tears in public. A better one will hand you tissues until you stop. The best is the one who will go get you another latte to go with the ginormous chocolate orgy she's already laid in front of you.

"Why didn't you tell me any of this before?" she demanded, stabbing her fork at me. "God, Sadie, you must have been going out of your mind."

"It's not that easy to talk about." I licked icing that had come straight from heaven. "And you had Evan and Lily to deal with, and then you were pregnant again and having James…you didn't need to listen to my grief."

She made a face. "I'm pissed at you."

"You are?" I paused with my fork halfway to my mouth.

"For thinking I wouldn't have listened."

"You'd have listened," I told her, "but it wouldn't have been fair of me to make you."

She looked like she wanted to protest, but then nodded. "You're right. I wouldn't have been able to listen well enough. I'm sorry. I suck."

Our sisterhood fit like a pair of faded jeans. I'd missed Katie.

"I didn't want you to think I don't love him," I admitted. "And when he stopped wanting to go out it felt…"

"Disloyal." She nodded, as though she understood.

"Yes. Disloyal."

"Nobody would blame you for having a life."

"That's what Adam said, too." I thought of the one support group meeting I'd attended. The wives had taken turns praising each other's sacrifices and trying to outdo each other's martyrdoms. Scowling, Katie stabbed her cupcake when I told her about it.

"It's just like those holier-than-thou mothers in my playgroup. God, you'd think I was committing a mortal sin by hiring a sitter for my kids so I can get my hair cut."

"It's not like I didn't understand them," I said. "I mean, from a professional point of view, I could see how focusing on the tiny details is the only way some people can deal with trauma. Understanding them only made it harder, though. Because I know I shouldn't feel guilty for being angry sometimes, or bitter."

"Knowing something is beans," Katie declared. "Besides, I don't have a problem with anyone who thinks devoting their entire life to the happiness and comfort of someone else, be it a husband or a child, is what makes them a good person. My problem is when they act like anyone who doesn't spend hours scrapbooking every freaking detail of their kid's first tooth is not only a bad person, but a shitty mother, too!"

We stared at each other for a moment, then burst into laughter.

"God, that felt good to say," she told me.

"I'm sorry it's been so long, Kates."

"Me, too. Don't let it happen again, or I'll have to kick your ass. Or steal your cupcake."

I made a show of guarding it. "I'd like to see you try."

Chocolate, caffeine and girl-bonding left me languid with relaxation. I gobbled the feeling as greedily as I'd done the cupcake.

"Don't tell the mommy police, but I'm thinking of going back to work. From home, at first, until the kids are older. A few mortgages here and there. I ran into Priscilla from the old bank a week ago, and she told me they're looking for someone part-time."

I blinked and found my coffee suddenly very interesting. "Oh, really?"

"Yep. Oh, and you'll get a kick out of this. Remember how we used to mock those people who used those wedding invitations with the pictures of little kids on them? The ones that say 'I'm marrying my best friend' or something like that?"

I remembered.

"Well, Priscilla's getting married and she showed me her invitations. And guess which ones she's using."

Chocolate lurched to my throat, but I couldn't tell if it was from bitter satisfaction or morbid fascination. "Today, I marry my friend?"

Katie crowed, clapping her hands. "Right on, sister. Ugliest invitations I'd ever seen. Ever. I mean, c'mon, the woman's in her thirties, for God's sakes."

"When's she getting married?"

"In June, apparently. But she's like the checklist queen, so..." Katie shrugged. "I think she's got everything planned out to the millisecond. Her poor fiancé, I bet she's got him jumping through hoops."

"He probably doesn't care."

"Well," said Katie, "A guy who agrees to use wedding invitations with little kids on them sure as hell can't be very good in bed, I'll tell you that."

To this, I said nothing, and the conversation switched gears again. In my car, where once I'd sobbed against the steering wheel because of him, now I gave in to laughter that was no less hysterical. Every time I thought I was done, I'd picture those invitations again and burst again, until at last I was wrung dry.

At home, Adam was absorbed in his computer, which didn't concern me. The fact that that I found Randy snoring downstairs in front of the television, however, did. I shook him awake and dismissed him with a brusqueness that seemed to offend him, but he was lucky I didn't kick him in the ass on the way out the door.

"Don't think I'm not going to call the agency tomorrow and complain, either." I pounded Adam's pillows in preparation for helping him into bed. "I didn't even ask him to stay to help me do the transfer, that's how angry I was."

"Sadie-me-love," Adam said quietly. "Did you have fun with Katie?"

I turned from my molestation of his bedding. "I did. Yes. A lot, actually. It felt really good."

"Good." He closed the open documents and then maneuvered his chair away from the computer. "I'm glad. Don't let him ruin that."

"Adam, he was supposed to be watching you, not dreaming!"

"I was fine," he said. "I told him to leave me alone."

"That doesn't matter." I took off my jacket and laid it over the back of the recliner, then unbuttoned my blouse. "Did he at least take care of you if you needed something?"

He didn't answer me at first. When I looked up, he'd gone pale, his eyes squinted tight like he was in pain.

"Adam?"

He opened his eyes and gave me a smile I failed to believe. "Got a headache, that's all. Eye strain, maybe."

Alarmed, I started checking him over. His face was clammy, his forehead damp with sweat. When I put a hand inside the front of his shirt, his chest was dry and hot.

"Adam, talk to me."

I opened his shirt and ran my hands over him, checking as best I could for signs of an irritation. I bent to run my hands up and down his legs, straightening them. I checked his feet at once for an ingrown toenail, anything that could be causing his body trauma.

"When's the last time he cathed you?" I looked up and fear tried to steal my voice. I forced it aside. "Adam. Look at me."

His head was drooping, eyelids fluttering. His body trembled slightly all over. He didn't respond.

Fuck fear. Terror crashed over me and tried to pin me to the floor. I ran for the bathroom, where I wet a cloth with cold water and brought it back to place on the back of his neck. He was gasping a little.

Autonomic Dysreflexia. It happens as a result of distress, even something as simple as not emptying the bladder often enough. If not treated immediately, it can be fatal.

"How long have you had the headache?"

The headache's caused by a spike in blood pressure. The body's protection mechanisms are amazing.

And he might be having a stroke.

I put aside my terror as though I'd shoved away an annoying dog nipping at my shins. I knew how to take care of this. I could take care of it. I would. I would do this…

I did not think. I acted. I yanked open the drawer storing the catheter supplies, spilling out plastic packages all over the floor. My fingers skidded on the slick packets as I tried to open his pants with one hand and grab up the catheter in the other.

I had to stop and center my actions before I continued. It was only a second, but every second counted. I opened his pants. I tore open the sterile package, yanking out the coil of thin, flexible tubing, which promptly slipped from my fingers onto the floor. I couldn't stop to untangle it. I grabbed another package, ripped it open and pulled out the catheter.

"Just a minute, Adam. Adam, stay with me, baby, please."

I said his name, over and over, explaining every step. I took him in my hand, ready to insert the tube that would drain his bladder and stop his body's stress reaction. No bowl to catch the urine, nothing but a towel slung over the arm of the chair.

No time to find a bowl, no time to care if I spilled or made a mess. Time to steady my fingers, but only then because they had to be steady in order to do what was needed.

"Stay with me," I murmured, over and over while I worked. "Gonna take care of this, Adam, just stay with me. Damn you, don't you dare pass out on me!"

I made a messy job of the catheter, bringing blood. The moment I slid it in, the tube filled with dark yellow urine, too much of it. It flooded over my hands. Wetness dropped on me from above, and I thought he must be crying.

It wasn't sweat or tears but saliva, a long, silver string of it I slapped away as I got to my feet. I pushed his head back, looking into his eyes. I didn't know what to do. Panic gnawed me.

"Don't you leave me!" I shouted. "Damn you, Adam, not now! Don't do this now!"

Adam blinked in slow motion, each open and close of his eyes taking too many seconds. I grabbed the phone and punched in 911. The voice on the other end asked me the state of my emergency, and I could not answer, struck dumb by panic.

"Please state the nature of your emergency."

Adam opened his eyes. He saw me, I know he did. I want to think he smiled at me.

"I need an ambulance! My husband's a quadriplegic and he's—" I could not say it, but I didn't have to.

"We'll have someone there right away."

And I'm sure they did, though I couldn't tell you how long it took them. Hours or minutes, in the end, it didn't matter.

Forever is how long it takes to search for the reason your husband is dying in front of your eyes and being unable to find it.

I don't know why our society seems to think grief is something to be shared when everybody really prefers to view it from afar. The people in my life sat beside me at the service and hugged me seemingly at random, though my stiff inability to hug them in return seemed to put them off. They brought me casseroles and sent cards and flowers, or made donations to the Christopher Reeve Foundation. They left messages on the answering machine telling me to call them if I needed anything, oblivious to the fact I could barely manage to figure out which shoe went on which foot, much less focus on dialing a phone number and asking for what I needed.

In the days and weeks after Adam's accident I'd yearned for this sort of support, but I guess illness and injury are terrifying in a way death is not. Perhaps people don't fear catching death the way they do a broken spine. At any rate, when all I wanted to do was sit in silence to mourn, I found myself at the mercy of friends and family who, bless their hearts, meant well.

My mother meant well when she said, "See? I knew you'd be strong." My father meant well when he said, "It's better this way."

They praised my strength, so I was strong. They complimented my composure, so I was composed. They spoke in whispers they thought I wouldn't hear about how "good" I looked, and how "well" I was taking it, so I was good and took it well. Everyone made a point of being "with" me, yet I was always alone.

Adam's mother meant well when she moved in and took it upon herself to fire Mrs. Lapp and Dennis. Maybe she thought I genuinely didn't need them any longer, and she was doing me a favor. More likely, their presence made her as uncomfortable as they always had, a constant reminder just how much care Adam had needed.

She rearranged my kitchen cabinets, brought in my mail and answered my telephone. She helped a lot while doing nothing, buzzing around me like a fly I didn't have the energy to swat. Maybe like everyone else, she was waiting for me to tell her what I needed.

Katie didn't wait. She came the week after the funeral, ignored my mother-in-law's unsubtle protests that she "meant" to get to it, and washed, dried, folded and put away three weeks worth of clothes and bedding. She also mopped my floor, cut and stored my plethora of casseroles into single servings complete with dated labels, and sorted my mail into neat piles with post-it notes on the bills that had to be paid at once.

Then, most gloriously of all, she left.

It was the greatest thing anyone had ever done for me,

though at the time I could do no more than nod my thanks. She understood.

"I'll call you," she said, and wonder of wonders, she did. Not just once, but every few days. She called to ask me what I needed.

For three weeks I listened to Adam's mother sob at night when I couldn't shed a single tear. I said nothing while she ingratiated herself into our house as if by entwining herself with me she could bring him back. I greeted her over the breakfast table and listened to her mourn, her grief solid and all-encompassing and selfish. It left no room for mine. I let her stay not out of compassion, but of the inability to ask her to leave.

Until the Baby Jesus did me in.

I came downstairs from a night of restless sleep, groggy and wanting only the palliation of coffee to get me started. Stubbing my toe on the manger scene sent the cradle and its holy contents skidding across my kitchen floor. The camels protested by breaking. I gave my commentary in a serious of one and two syllable words, mostly ending with "ing."

Someone had vomited Christmas all over my house. Long unused decorations scattered most empty surfaces. Elves might have been the likely culprit, but for the fact they didn't exist, and I knew at once it was my mother-in-law's hand. Rearranging my cabinets and peeking at my credit card bills was one thing; this was an invasion of an even more personal sort. I found her in his bedroom, sorting a pile of clothes from his dresser.

"I needed to keep busy," was her explanation.

"I'd rather you didn't touch Adam's things. I'm going to take care of them."

"But, Sadie," Mrs. Danning said, slightly aghast. "I'm his mother!"

I'm not proud to say I lost it. My temper, my patience. Quite possibly, my mind. People often speak in anger and later claim they didn't mean what they'd said, but I meant every word. It wasn't the first fight we'd ever had, but it was probably the worst. She wanted to be in the house where her son had lived. I wanted her out of the place where he'd died.

I won, in the end, though victory was bitter. It gave me no satisfaction to tell her I would be the one to decide what would be done with Adam's possessions, or that she wasn't welcome to comment on my choices. She was grieving, too, and if I could barely comprehend what it was like for me to have lost my husband, I couldn't come close to imagining how she felt at losing her son.

"But we need each other!" she cried.

"I'm sorry," I told her. "But I can't be what you need right now."

She drew herself up. "Well, if you don't want me here—"

"I don't need you here," was the kindest answer I was able to give her.

When the door shut behind her, I waited, at last, to weep.

And yet, I found no tears. Where had they gone? I knew myself not incapable of crying, for I'd wept when they put him in the ambulance and later, at the hospital when he didn't wake from the stroke that killed him. Yet, surrounded by people who were judging my grief like it was some measure of my love, I'd been stony-faced and dry-eyed. Three weeks since Adam's death, and I slept, ate dressed and bathed, spoken and been spoken to...but I had not cried.

I tried, standing with one hand against the front door for support. I let out a sigh, long and slow, giving myself permission to let go. It was like anticipating a sneeze, or perversely, an orgasm. I could feel the sorrow lodged in my gut and the tears waiting in the backs of my eyes, but neither would come out. I imagined tugging it, like a hook caught in a fish's throat. Yes, it would rip me apart when I pulled it free, but at least it would be gone.

I waited for a long time, and there was nothing but the pain of wanting something I couldn't seem to find.

My world had many different colors. All of them were gray. Depression is insidious and masks itself as fatigue, aches and pains, general malaise. It would have been easy to let myself fade into the gray. To stay in bed when I knew I should get up, to wear the same clothes instead of choosing fresh. I could have allowed my grief to consume me.

I don't pat myself on the back and brag about how wonderfully I pulled through. If anything, my refusal to give in to sorrow was as much a mistake as wallowing in it would have been. Maybe if I'd allowed myself a few weeks of wallowing I'd have been better off, but the problem with looking back when you should be walking ahead is that you usually end up walking into something that hurts.

So I got out of bed. I showered. I dressed. I ate sensible meals, when I thought of it, and oatmeal or toast when I didn't. I saw my patients, who, if they noticed my consideration of their problems had become considerably less warm and fuzzy, they didn't complain.

Day by day the need to weep leached away until I wondered how I could ever have thought tears would make me feel better. Week by week I set about recovering my life, getting back to the business of working and paying bills. I expected the holidays to be hard, but all I felt was relief. No tree. No decorations, not even the ones Adam's mother had tried to put out. I didn't have to cook a meal and I could accept my parents' invitation without worrying what to do about Adam. I was a guest all season long, dining out on the premise of my sorrow.

It was marvelous.

There were some eyes that cut away, uncomfortable in the presence of my loss, but for the first time in four years, I was able to talk about Adam, and I did. With my parents. Katie and her husband. With once-a-year acquaintances at the holiday parties and dinners. It felt as though people were able to pity me without feeling awkward about it. Adam had died. They could relate to that. They could offer their condolences, pat my shoulder, nod sympathetically in understanding when I spoke of him. Death was somehow less embarrassing than disability.

Death is also only briefly fascinating to anyone not right next to it. Eventually, the parties ceased, the calls and cards stopped coming. The world moved on with everyone else in it, leaving me behind.

Dennis invited me to dinner one night, and I went. He took me to a little place I'd driven past a dozen times but never been to. The food was good, the conversation better. It was good to sit and talk about Adam without the burden of supporting someone else's sadness. Dennis was smart enough to listen more than he spoke.

"I miss him," Dennis told me after dinner, in the parking lot. "He could beat my butt at chess like nobody else."

"He was so glad to have you to play with. I could never learn."

"I feel guilty," Dennis said suddenly. "Maybe if I'd been there—"

"I don't blame you, Dennis."

He wiped his eyes, and I tasted bitterness that he could find tears while I had none.

"He was a good man."

"Yes," I said. "He was."

"I just feel so guilty."

"I feel guilty, too," I told him. "But not because I think I could have done something different or because I left him that day or anything else."

Dennis's earring gleamed in the parking lot lamp as he tilted his head. "No? That's good, though, Sadie, because those things weren't your fault."

"And it wasn't your fault you were on a trip and we had to leave him with someone who fucked up, either, Dennis."

The strength in my voice seemed to surprise him. He nodded, his features rearranging in relief. "Yeah. I know. But still—"

"I know."

"At least he's not in any pain," Dennis said. I'd heard the platitude a dozen times, if not more. "He's free."

So was I, but I couldn't say that to Dennis even though he might have understood. He hugged me, a big, broad man who'd been part of my life for years and now no longer was. He meant it as a comfort, and it was, but more for him than me. Then we parted, Dennis unburdened and I with a bigger weight than before.

Seeing Mrs. Lapp again was easier, because she merely enfolded me into her smothering embrace and rocked me back and forth for a few minutes. Then she clucked over my eating habits, bragged about her grandchildren and showed me photos of the trip she'd taken the week before.

"Samuel and I are going to New York City next week," she told me. "We're going to see a Broadway show!"

I smiled at that. "Samuel's agreeing to this?"

"He's never been to the city," she said. "We're taking a bus trip with our church group."

I'd met Samuel Lapp many times when he came to retrieve his wife from my kitchen. He was pleasant but silent, and wore faded bib overalls and a plaid shirt on every occasion I'd ever seen him. I couldn't quite picture him watching a Broadway musical.

"Sounds like a lot of fun," I told her.

I'd actually wanted to ask her if she'd consider coming

back to work for me. Cleaning my own house and cooking my own dinner didn't hold any new appeal for me. Hearing her rhapsodize over her upcoming plans, I knew I couldn't do it.

"I'm busier now than I ever was when I worked," she said, pushing a slice of homemade shoo-fly pie toward me across her broad kitchen table. "I've been waiting for years to retire. I'd have done it a long time ago, but…"

She looked up, her eyes kind and a bit embarrassed. I poked my pie so I wouldn't have to look at her. "I appreciate everything you did for us, Mrs. Lapp."

She tutted. "It was plenty good, most of the time, even when he was grexy."

I smiled at her use of the Pennsylvania Dutch slang. "He could be very grexy. And now you can go to New York with Samuel. Or any other place you want."

She nodded. "Well, Dr. D, forgive me for saying so, but…so can you."

I wanted to answer that, but I took a bite of pie, instead. The conversation turned to television, the weather and sundry other safe topics. I ate three pieces of Mrs. Lapp's pie and left with a sick stomach.

"You call me if you want to talk," she said from the doorway as she waved goodbye.

I promised I would, but we both knew I wouldn't.

Katie didn't stop calling to find out what I needed. Just like when we were kids and she knew when to bring me the second half of her grape popsicle, my sister knew how to comfort me. Her gifts now were expensive wine and chocolate and an armful of chick flicks, but they were as welcome and sweet as her grubby, half-eaten popsicles had once been.

She settled on my couch with a loud, indulgent sigh and kicked off her shoes. She'd cut her hair and wore makeup, and though she wore track pants and a t-shirt, they were stylish. She didn't look as tired, either.

"You've lost weight," I said.

"Damn straight!" Katie grinned. "Now that I've gone back to work part-time I can afford to pay for the gym. So when Lily's at preschool, I take James and get a workout in. Then I work while they're both napping."

I kicked off my own shoes. My sweatpants were far less stylish than my sister's but that was nothing new. What was new was that I didn't compare myself to her and feel dowdy.

"I'm glad you could come over. I've been wanting to watch *Moulin Rouge* for a while." I leaned forward to sift through the movie choices.

"Yeah…"

I looked up at Katie's hesitant reply. "What? We could watch something else."

She shook her head, her expression one I didn't know how to read. "No, that's fine."

I sat back. "Well?"

She bit her bottom lip, then let out the giggle she must have been trying to keep inside. "It's Mom, that's all."

"What about her?" I wanted to be worried but Katie's laughter meant there wasn't a problem.

"She…told me I had to come over."

This made very little sense to me. "What do you mean by that?"

Katie snorted another stream of giggles. "She told me I had to come over and spend time with you. That she was...worried about you."

For a moment I sat, silent. Then I started giggling, too. "No way!"

"Yes!" Katie guffawed. "She absolutely did!"

We laughed for a few minutes, until I shook my head. "Wonder of wonders."

"So, I told Evan I had no choice, I needed to be there for my big sis, or my mom would have my hide."

"And he couldn't complain about that, huh?"

"Evan going against Mom? He knows better. And look at this." She held up her cell phone with a laugh. "Turning it off. Evan's going to have to just learn to deal with the poop explosions on his own."

"That sounds scary." I poured wine and opened the gold box of candy.

"It's good for daddies to learn how to take care of their babies," my sister said. "Especially when they think they can't. Besides, Lily's a big help."

I laughed, imagining my niece's "help." "Poor Evan."

"He'll be fine." Katie sipped wine slowly, an expression of bliss on her face. "I haven't had wine in...years. My god, I'm so glad to have my boobs back. I love my children, Sadie, but holy hell, I'm going to be glad to have some of my life back again."

I thought I was laughing, but it was the sound of my wineglass shattering on the tile floor. Then I knelt among the shards, my fingers reaching without care toward the glittering sharpness.

"I'm glad to have my life back, too," I said, each word a fishbone in my throat. "I'm glad, Katie. I know I shouldn't be glad, but I am."

Many times I had helped her when she'd fallen, but now it was Katie's turn to pull me away from the mess. She cleaned the cut on my finger and wrapped it in a bandage the way I'd done so many times to skinned knees and elbows, and she handed me tissues for the tears that boiled out of me at long last.

"You're such a mom," I managed to tell her when my sobs had tapered into hitching sniffles.

We made it back to the sofa in the den, and Katie tucked her feet up underneath her. "Yeah, funny, huh? Who'd have thought?"

We shared a smile. She handed me the box of chocolate. "Eat that."

"Great. Just what I need to feel better about myself. Fat thighs."

She reached to pluck out one for herself. "Fuck fat thighs, bitch, and eat the chocolate."

There was no denying the power of chocolate, especially not this premium sort that melted on my tongue. "It's like…a little piece of heaven in my mouth."

Katie made devil horns with her fingers. "You said it."

Devil horns and chocolate. There were some things nobody understood about me better than my little sister. Not even Adam known some of those small pieces of me.

"I miss him, Katie."

"I know you do. I miss him, too, Sades." She licked chocolate from her fingers and gave me a serious look. "Nobody expects you not to miss him."

"I went to the grocery store after work, and I didn't have to call home, first. I didn't have to make sure anyone was at home to take care of him. I didn't have to wonder if he was all right, or if I'd get home and find out something had happened…or get home and have an argument because I'd been gone too long. And I sleep, Katie." I swallowed more tears. "I sleep all night long. Every night. And I don't have to wake up, not once."

Her hand was the rope thrown into the sorrow trying to drown me, and I clutched it.

"None of that means you didn't love him, Sadie."

It didn't feel true, though I wanted it to be. "He could be such an asshole! And I knew it was because he was depressed and upset, but he was so fucking mean sometimes! It was like he wasn't even the same man I'd married. It was like he woke up from that coma with a different person inside his head."

"And none of that means you didn't love him, either," my sister said. "Because you're right, he could be an asshole. But he could be an asshole even before the accident."

From anyone else I'd have self-righteously protected my husband's memory, but I couldn't do that with my sister. "Yeah. I know. But he could also be the best man in the world, when he wanted."

"It's not your fault that he stopped wanting." Katie squeezed my hand.

I nodded, more tears seeping from my eyes. "I never got the chance to fix it. I never got the chance to find out if we could."

"Yeah." She pushed more chocolate on me. "I know."

And I knew she did. I didn't need my sister to tell me the truth, but it wasn't until her words became the mirror reflecting what I already knew that I believed it.

"Wanting to be able to go to the bathroom by myself and fit into a regular bra doesn't mean I don't love my children with every breath I have," Katie said. "And wanting to take your life off hold doesn't mean you didn't love Adam."

"How'd you get to be so good at giving advice?" I asked her.

My sister smiled. "I learned it from my big sister."

Then we both cried.

Grief goes away like a cold sore, painful even as it fades, and sometimes leaves a scar to remind you always where it had been. Missing Adam didn't mean I loved him any more than not missing him meant I did not. Time would mend and mesh my emotions and all I had to do was let it happen.

I made an attempt at moving on. I joined the gym. I cancelled my subscription to the DVD rental service and joined a book discussion group. I filled my time with all the things I'd denied myself for so many years.

They didn't all bring me joy. In fact, I soon dreaded going to the gym more than I'd regretted being unable to workout. Reading and discussing books took more effort than watching movies. Still, for the most part I allowed myself to enjoy my new life and not let guilt weigh me down.

I could fill my life with activities but I couldn't fill myself. Something was missing. Something left undone. The feeling of something lacking insinuated itself in the back of my mind like a hole in a snagged stocking, bit by insidious bit.

I thought it was Adam's room, which I'd left unchanged since his death. I thought maybe I needed to get rid of those final reminders of his life after the accident so I could focus on remembering better things. I stood in the hall, my hand on the knob, and it took me only a moment to understand my problem wasn't this door I'd kept closed.

It was the door I'd left open.

Chapter 18

February

I knew he'd be there. There was no reason he shouldn't, other than perhaps the same long habit that had drawn me back. Like toads returning in the spring to the pond where they'd hatched, Joe and I both made our way to the bench.

Someone had changed the plants in the atrium. The hanging potted ferns had been replaced with spider plants. The spiky, dangling clusters made a different sort of shadow. I couldn't decide if I liked it.

I'd dressed carefully for the occasion in colors that flattered, shoes that made me feel tall. My lipstick was a shade that always gave me confidence, but as I sat and waited, I wasn't sure if I needed it or not.

The moment I saw him, I no longer had a question. I wasn't sure what I'd feel upon seeing Joe again. I'd imagined anger, or disappointment. Maybe a surge of recalcitrant lust. I hadn't expected relief.

It washed over me with an almost physical force when he sat next to me. The breath I tried to take stabbed my throat and my hands twisted into knots in my lap. It was like losing someone in a crowd in a strange place, that heart-skipping moment of fear before your eyes at last capture the sight of the familiar face among those of strangers, and you realize you are no longer lost.

"It's good to see you, Sadie."

I nodded and squinted up toward the sun shining through the glass. The ferns had made shade. The spider plants did not, and I decided I didn't like them, after all.

"I figured you weren't going to come back."

"My husband had a stroke," I said quietly, looking toward him at last. "He died."

I thought I'd grown used to saying it. Making it real with words. It had been easier to say than "My husband is paralyzed from the neck down." Easier to say and easier for people to offer condolences for a dead spouse than one who's disabled.

The words sounded as if I'd said them easily, but the ground blurred and I put a hand to my face to cover my eyes. I felt his hand on my shoulder. We moved closer without moving at all.

It was the first time he'd ever touched me.

I whispered, but had no fear he wouldn't hear me. "Do you have a story for me, Joe? Because I really need one."

This month, my name is still Priscilla and I wear a diamond on my finger that tells the world I'm engaged.

It's big enough to draw comment from strangers. I love it.

Today, I'm meeting my fiancé for lunch with one of the seven caterers I'm considering hiring for the reception. She's going to let us sample all the menu items I've checked off as possibilities, including the cake. We have the choice of strawberry shortcake and chocolate layer cake, both gourmet. No grocery store wedding cake for me, thank you. After all, a woman only gets married once, if she does it right the first time.

"Darling!" There he is. My Joe. He turns and I tut-tut at the way he's standing with his hands in his pockets. "Baby, you're doing it again."

He takes them out at once with that apologetic smile I find so charming. "Sorry."

"You're too handsome to look so sloppy." I'm wearing flats today and must stand on my toes to kiss his cheek. He smells very clean. "I'm going to get you some cologne."

He slips his hands over my hips, pulling me closer and looking down into my face. "You don't like the way I smell?"

"You smell fine. But I like cologne, that's all." I kiss his cheek again and push away. "Come on. We don't want to be late."

"Of course not. Heaven help us if we break out of our schedule."

I stop to give him a narrow-eyed look. Is he mocking me? With Joe, sometimes, I'm not quite sure. Most of the time we seem to be on the same page, but every once in a while he comes up with something ridiculous.

"It's rude to keep someone waiting." I don't mean to sound curt, just firm. He should know by now how I feel about that. It's not like we haven't discussed it at length.

He reaches out to snag my wrist and pull me back toward him. I don't want to kiss him, but he bends me with such grace I end up doing it, anyway. He tastes like mint.

He sounds sincere. "I'm sorry. I know you hate being late."

I smile when he says that, and kiss him with a little more enthusiasm. I take his hand. "Come on, Joe."

Inside, the caterer treats us to samples of tiny sandwiches, cubes of cheese, spirals of meat and lettuce. She's got a little of everything, all on those fancy toothpicks with the plastic fringes. Joe plucks bite after bite, chewing and swallowing, and I know he can't possibly be savoring the differences between the teriyaki chicken and the barbecue. His eyes look as glazed as the honey ham.

The caterer gives him a look, then me a sympathetic glance. "As I was saying, Miss Eddings, the entire hors d'oeuvres platter would serve 300 guests—"

"Three hundred!" That's caught his attention, and he turns, mouth open. "What…Cilla, I thought—"

I hate it when he calls me that. "Joe, darling, that list I gave you was already pared down to the absolute minimum."

For a moment, I think he's going to argue with me, right in front of the caterer, who has the discretion to look down. She's seen her share of connubial spats, I'm sure, but I'll be damned if I give her fodder for the gossip circles. I sit up straight and fix him with a look meant to temper the discussion, and it works. He shrugs. I return to discussing the prices of petit fours and canapés.

It's not my fault Joe's guest list consisted of his family and three or four friends. I know a lot of people. I have business associates, family, friends, people who aren't friends but will have to be invited anyway because they think they're friends. My life is as layered as the cake we sampled today, and this wedding is important to me. I tell the caterer I'll call her by the end of the week.

At my house, Joe takes off his jacket and his tie and stretches out on the couch to watch TV while I make us dinner. It's simple again, whole wheat pasta in a light tomato sauce and a green salad, but it conforms to my rigid diet. I refuse to look like an overstuffed chair in my wedding dress. Joe complains sometimes, but since he's not the one cooking, I say he's hardly got the right. Tonight he says nothing, just eats what's put in front of him.

He's a good listener, better than any man I've ever dated. I pause in the middle of an anecdote about my day when I catch him staring at me. "What?"

When he gets up and comes around the table to kiss me, I can't help the thump-thump of my heart. He tastes like oil and garlic, which means I do, too. I pull away a little. "Joe…"

His hand slides along the back of my neck, under my hair. He tips my head back to meet his mouth. His tongue strokes mine as his hand holds me in place, so I can't move away. I sigh and give up. Give in to him.

His other hand drifts down to caress my breast. My nipple gets hard and I want to squirm, but I don't. He always makes me feel this way, like I can't stay still. As though he's touching me all over, even when he's only kissing me.

"Come upstairs."

It's not a plea. It's not a request. It's not quite a command, either, but I get up, anyway.

He's kissing me on the way up the stairs. He unbuttons my blouse, my skirt, pushes open my door and takes me to the bed to finish undressing me. In my bra and panties I give in to his kisses and the stroking of his hands along my body. I allow him to unhook my bra and slide it off, baring my breasts to his gaze. The sight of my bare skin seems to capture his attention more than the caterer's samples did, but I'm not surprised. I work hard to keep my body in shape.

His mouth drifts lower. He sucks my nipples, one at a time until I arch upward a little. He knows just how to touch me. What I like. What I don't.

His hand drifts over my thighs and belly, where it circles briefly in my navel. He puts his palm flat on my skin, taut and firm from hours of crunches. I tense a little bit, expecting him to move lower, down between my legs.

His kisses have slowed. After one more, he stops and pulls away to look into my eyes. I usually like the way Joe looks at me. He's usually smiling.

Now he stares and his hand comes up to smooth a strand of hair from my face. He bends to hover his mouth over mine, and hot breath caresses my face. I still smell garlic, but I ignore it. My lips part, waiting for his kiss, which doesn't come.

"Kiss me," I say.

When he does, it's on my jaw, then my throat and neck, where he nips me lightly. I make a little noise of protest and say his name in a scolding manner, but the truth is that little nip has tightened my nipples. I feel like I want to shift my hips and press upward against his hand, or push his fingers down between my legs to touch me there. So that's what I do, impatient.

He obliges without a word. His fingers turn and twist, stroking along the lacy front of my panties. It took us several sessions of lovemaking before Joe learned to touch me the right way, the way I like it, but now he knows it's like I've got a secret sex button between my legs only he knows how to push.

He's on one elbow looking down at his hand on my crotch. At this angle I see the faint crow's feet in the corners of his eyes and the way his nose has the tiniest bit of a bump at the tip. Small lines bracket his mouth, and I wonder why he's frowning. I wonder why he looks older than he did when I met him.

"Yes, just like that." My voice has gone husky. I spread my legs. "Take off my panties, baby."

Obligingly, he hooks a finger into the lace and tugs them over my thighs. He follows the journey of my panties onto the floor and stands. Then he puts a hand on each of my ankles. When he touches me this way, I'm always surprised at how large his hands are. He can circle my ankles completely. He slides them upward, over my calves, until my body breaks the bracelets of his fingers. He shifts his hands to smooth over my knees, teasing the underside. Then to my thighs. He puts a knee on the bed to get closer to me.

I shiver at his light, teasing touch. "C'mon, baby. Take off your clothes."

Joe looks up from his place at my feet, his hands still on my legs. He nods slightly and moves to take off his tie. As he unbuttons his shirt, I put an arm behind my head to watch him get naked for me. His skin is faintly golden, the hairs on his chest like burnished copper, and I admire the tufts around his nipples and under his arms. The thatch around his penis, revealed as he removes his trousers, is neatly trimmed.

"I'm so pleased you take care of yourself." I lick my lips in appreciation. "So many men couldn't care less about taking the time."

Joe pauses on one leg in the process of removing his socks. He's got the form of a statue, all lean lines, though I suspect he must be sneaking cupcakes on the side. His abs are still pretty tight, but his sides are bumpier than they were a few months ago. I'll have to step up our workouts.

He finishes taking off his socks and crawls up on the bed over me. "How many men?"

I like his warmth and the way his body fits with mine. Not too tall, not too short. His penis is a hard, hot branch against my thigh. I'd really rather have it inside me, and I shift with impatience.

"How many men, Priscilla?"

He's repeated the question I assumed was rhetorical. "Most of them, I guess."

I push him off a little so we can roll on our sides, facing one another. His erection rubs my belly. I want it lower.

"Most of them in the world? Or most of the ones you know?"

"Both. Why are you being so…combative?"

"I'm not being combative. I'm just asking. I don't think it's out of line to ask, is it?"

He's talking when I want him to be making love to me, and it's my turn to frown. "Exactly what are you asking?"

"How many men have you been with?"

I'm not sure that's any of Joe's business. It doesn't impact our relationship in any way. I don't even keep in touch with former lovers, and I tell him just that.

"Priscilla." Joe's voice is slow and deep, a little amused. "Tell me how many men you've been with. I want to know."

"Enough to know you're the one I want to be with for the rest of my life."

That is a very good answer, but it doesn't seem to satisfy him. His hand goes between my legs, right where I want it, but even though I move against his hand, he doesn't stroke me. I give a frustrated sigh.

"Why do you want to know?"

"Curiosity."

"Killed the cat." I'm not even ashamed of using such an old cliché.

"I'm not a cat."

"Ten," I say, finally, through gritted teeth. "All right?"

His hand moves, then, like he's rewarding me. "Yeah."

He pushes my shoulder so I roll onto my back. His fingertip circles my clitoris. I'm not appeased, but I don't stop him. I've gone tense, though, and it won't be easy to make me come.

"You've dated more than ten men." He kisses the slope of my breasts.

"Well, yes."

"But you've only gone to bed with ten?"

Joe's mouth covers my nipple, sucking gently. His fingertip strokes down to dip inside me before coming back up to slide over the bead of my clit. I can feel myself getting slick. I wish sex wasn't so messy.

"Priscilla?"

"Yes!"

He says nothing for the next minute while he concentrates on licking his way down my torso. I spread my legs a bit wider in anticipation. Though I'm not a fan of fellatio, I fully support Joe's appreciation of cunnilingus.

"Did they all get you off?"

The noise from my throat can't be misconstrued as pleasure. "Stop it."

"I want to know." He licks my ribs, each one, with soft, light flickers of his tongue. "Did they do this to you?"

His quick glance toward the place his hand works tells me what he means.

"Yes."

"And you liked it."

"When they did it the way I liked it, yes."

"Like this."

He demonstrates by pinching my clit between his thumb and finger. My startled gasp trails off into a moan. This is not something I taught him to know about me, that little pinch. It's something Joe does all on his own.

"No…yes…"

He goes back to making small, tight circles. His mouth leaves wet imprints on my skin. When he blows on them, a chill skitters up and down my spine. I open my mouth wider, breath deeper.

"Did they put their mouths on you? Like this?"

His mouth replaces his finger. I don't answer, not at first, because that exquisite first moment when his tongue laps my clit is always too intense to allow for speech. Instead, I sigh and moan and raise my rear a little to press against him.

Joe's tongue is soft. Hot. Wet. He flicks it along my folds and clit before settling into a slow, steady pattern of laps and licks.

He's still talking.

"Did they make you come this way?" Every word presses his mouth and lips and tongue against me, but the words aren't muffled. I can hear every one.

"…sometimes…"

"Only sometimes?"

When his tongue presses hard against me, I jerk. "Yes!"

"Or only some men?"

"That, too." My voice is thick.

Joe's hands slide beneath my butt and lift me closer to his mouth, but he pauses again in licking. "Were they the ones who took care of themselves? Or not?"

"If they don't take care of themselves," I answer, annoyed, "I don't go to bed with them! Why are you talking so much?"

"Oh, I forgot. No talking during sex."

"I never said that." I get up on my elbow to glare at him. "I said no conversation during sex. I can't concentrate. Talking is fine. How do you expect to know what I want if I don't tell you?"

Joe says nothing, just dips back to my clit while he looks up at me. I don't like looking at this, seeing him down there, but for some reason tonight I can't look away. He closes his eyes and makes love to my vagina with his mouth. Seeing him flick my clit at the same time I feel it is a jolt for which I'm unprepared.

"Make that noise again," he murmurs.

I shake my head, meaning to say I can't just do it on command, but his tongue flicks against me again. I make that noise. He smiles against me. I can't look away.

He opens his eyes. "Did any of them make you sound like that?"

"No." It's true. Joe's the first.

He takes his time, now, even when I'm desperate enough to writhe. Pleasure steals my thoughts and leaves me blind, nothing but a puddle of bliss under his fingers and mouth. For the first time since we met, he doesn't give me what I want. He makes me wait for it. Draws it out. Makes me beg.

"Oh, please, Joe!"

I come a bare second after he slides inside me. Filled, stretched, I burst into ecstasy as he thrusts. When he fastens his mouth on my throat and sucks, biting, I come again. I'm startled by this second orgasm, unexpected, and my fingers rake his back.

Joe hisses and pumps faster. His head fits into the curve of my shoulder, but I want to see his face when he comes. I push his chest so he'll lift onto his hands, and he does.

"Open your eyes, baby. Look at me." I urge him, but he doesn't.

He finishes with a grunt, biting his lower lip. Sweat drips from his forehead onto my chest, and I wipe it away. I'm already thinking about the shower.

He rolls onto his back, limp and loose, eyes still closed. He yawns. I nudge him.

"Move so I can shower."

He cracks open an eye. "In a minute."

"Not in a minute, Joe. Now."

He doesn't move. What on earth is wrong with him lately? Everything about him is an effort. I sit up, frowning.

"What's wrong with you?"

"Nothing." Another yawn.

I poke him, harder. "Don't fall asleep like that."

"I'm not going to fall asleep."

I roll my eyes. "Well, fine! So get up, then!"

He sits and yawns again. I scoot past him, meaning to head for the bathroom, but he snares my wrist. I stop to look at him.

Naked this way, the sheets tangled and damp, the scent of sex still lingering, I feel the urge to lean in and kiss him. So I do. He takes it, his eyes closing. They stay closed for a minute after I pull away.

"Are you upset?" I ask him tenderly. "About the men? Is it too many?"

He looks at me. "Do you think it's too many?"

"No. Do I wish I hadn't slept with most of them? Yes, but only because it was a waste of time."

"Then it's not too many."

I lean to kiss him again. I feel flirty with Joe in a way I haven't with anyone else. "You're not intimidated?"

"No."

I'd meant to tease him, but he didn't seem to find it as lighthearted as I did. "You are upset. I knew it. That's why I didn't want to say. Men don't like it when a woman has more experience than they do."

He laughs, though I'm not sure why. "Depends on the man, Priscilla."

"Well, don't you worry, Mr. Wilder," I tell him. "I'll teach you everything you need to know."

"Oh, I don't doubt that."

"What's that supposed to mean?" If I weren't so sated and languid, I'd be far more annoyed.

"Nothing."

I give him a narrow look and sit up against the headboard, arms crossed over my chest. "You're being vague."

He sighs heavily. "God forbid I'm vague, Priscilla."

"I don't like your tone."

With a low snort, Joe gets out of bed and pads toward the bathroom. I hear water running in the sink. I'm not pleased he walked away from me. I get up and follow him. He's brushing his teeth, and I see he's left the cap off the toothpaste. Again.

"What is your problem?" I demand. "Are you jealous?"

Another snort from him turns my mouth down. I put my hands on my hips. He slides his toothbrush back into the holder and wipes his mouth with the back of his hand. He turns to me.

"No, Priscilla. I'm not."

"I'm not sure what's going on with you, Joe."

"Nothing's going on with me."

I study him, making note of his posture. "Are you leaving?"

"Yeah. Got to be up early tomorrow."

"I thought you were going to stay." There's no harm in being sweet to him.

"I can't."

Except when he refuses to let me.

Cross, I scowl. "Well, fine, but don't forget we have dinner with my parents tomorrow night and the meeting with Father Harris on Friday."

"I won't forget."

"Good. Let's not fight, baby, it makes me upset." I stand on tiptoe to kiss his mouth.

Joe turns his head.

I'm caught flat-footed, and my mouth skips along his jaw before it lands on his cheek. I pull away.

"Kiss me."

He does nothing.

"Joe!"

He sighs heavily again, but he doesn't move.

"Look, Joe," I say. "I'm sorry you've got a burr in your briefs, but you don't have to be so immature about this."

Joe says nothing. He leans against the sink, arms crossed, and I am so irritated I have to stomp. The tile floor is cold and hurts my toes.

"Don't you ignore me!"

"What's my favorite color?"

"What?" I'm at a loss for words, a situation in which I rarely find myself.

"What color," Joe says slowly, patiently, "is my favorite?"

My hands fist on my hips. "Why?"

"Your favorite color is beige. You like vanilla ice cream with chocolate syrup, but you hate walnuts in your brownies, when you eat brownies, which is almost never. You wear a size seven shoe. Your middle name is Anne."

"And?"

"What's my middle name?"

I gape, catching sight of my reflection, which reminds me that it's not a flattering expression. My jaw shuts with a snap. I don't know Joe's middle name. He never told me he had one. There isn't one on the invitations.

"It's Philip."

I do not like where this conversation is going. "Fine. Is this about the invitations? Because if you wanted your middle name on them, you should have said something before."

"No, Priscilla. It's not about the invitations. I could not possibly care less about the invitations. Or the food. Or the music."

"I knew it!" I cry. "I knew you didn't care!"

Joe scrubs his eyes with the tips of his fingers. He's not looking at me when he says, "I care about the things that are important."

There is a long silence I break with a sniff and an icy reply. "If you are saying I don't care about things that are important, then maybe you should just go!"

I meant it as a threat, but Joe seems to take it as a gift. Still silent, he doesn't need to speak because his face says it all. Stunned, I can't say anything either as he pushes past me. I find my voice when I see he's already dressed.

"How can you expect me to know these things if you never told me?"

No answer.

"If you walk out that door, don't think you can come back!"

He pauses in the doorway, but doesn't turn around.

"You'll be sorry!"

My threats are coming fast and wild, but how dare he? How dare he leave me? Even if I'm the one telling him to go?

"You just…get out!" I scream.

And he does.

"You can say I told you so," Joe said as soon as he'd finished.

"No. I don't want to say that."

We sat in companionable silence. I didn't ask him how long ago the story had taken place. It didn't seem to matter.

"Why didn't you ever tell her?"

"She was happy with me the way things were. She didn't seem to need to know those things."

"But…you knew them about her. Did she tell you? Or did you just pay closer attention?"

He sighed. "It doesn't matter, now."

"Will you tell me something?"

He looked into my eyes. "Sadie. I think you know I'll tell you just about anything."

We both laughed, and oh, it was so good to feel that my grief didn't need to be all I had. "Did you want her to not know?"

"Are you asking me if I wanted to fail?"

"Yes." Our hands were close together on the bench, not touching, but close. "Did you?"

"I didn't think so at the time."

"Someday, Joe, you're going to run out of stories."

He laughed, shaking his head, and got to his feet. "I don't think so. See you next month?"

I shook my head. "I don't know. Maybe not."

Joe put his hands in his pockets and rocked on the balls of his feet before answering. "I hope I do, Sadie. I really do."

I looked up at him. He smiled. As always, I did, too. "Thanks."

He nodded and silence that wasn't quite sure what it wanted to be fell between us. Then he took a step back. I got up. We faced each other, no bench separating us. Nothing but air and uncertainty.

"Thank you," I said.

Joe leaned closer, just a hair. "You're welcome."

We left at the same time but in different directions. Yet when I made to cross the street, Joe stood on the corner. We laughed, self-conscious, before parting again, and I tried not think about how different paths had led us to the same place.

Chapter 19

March

A dark and rainy Saturday night seemed perfect for a long, hot shower, new pajamas and a pot of Earl Grey tea to go along with a new release by my favorite author. I was in the kitchen pouring boiling water over the loose tea, secure in its strainer ball, when the doorbell rang. I stopped, startled, my eyes going automatically to the clock. It was just past eleven.

And I was alone.

For the first time since Adam's death, having the house to myself seemed a disadvantage. I set the kettle back on the burner and listened, body tense. I'd half-convinced myself I'd imagined it when it rang again. I crept down the hall. Through the curtained windows on either side of the front door I saw the faint black shape of my visitor.

I snagged the poker from the fireplace and held it close to my side as I unlocked the door and eased it open. Outside, rain lashed the trees on the street. Faint blue-white lightning lit the sky above the rooftops, followed shortly after by the far-off rumble of thunder. The street-lights silhouetted my guest from behind, keeping his face in darkness, but I knew who it was at once.

"Joe?"

I stepped back, and he came forward. Rain slicked his hair over his forehead and dripped off his nose. His clothes hung, sodden, the white shirt made sheer. He carried a bottle of whiskey. He made a puddle on my rug and gave no greeting, no word of explanation, made no noise but the slightly raspy hiss of his breath.

I was already reaching for him when he put his arm around my waist and pulled me against him. The rain was cold. He was hot, burning beneath the wetness, his skin a furnace burning with such fury I expected to see steam. The whiskey bottle was hard between my shoulder blades.

I drank the taste of smoke and whiskey from his mouth. He didn't smell as good as he always did, but better, the tang of musk beneath the scent of soap and water not even the rain could wash away. He kicked the door shut behind him without leaving my mouth.

We made it to the stairs in three steps, but got no farther. The ridge of the step bit into my back as he pressed me down. He swallowed my gasp, sipped my breath and stole my air, then gave it back to me with his next exhale. He was wet and cold and hot, and so was I, shivering under his touch. The bottle slipped to the steps beside me, the solid thunk of glass on wood an exclamation mark we both ignored.

"Sadie, Sadie, Sadie..."

I tasted my name on his tongue. Joe's hands were everywhere. They cupped my breasts, my sides, reached down to slide the hem of my nightgown up over my thighs. His hand slid against my bare skin without preamble. I needed none.

There were buttons on the front of the nightgown from the high neck to the hem, but it was easier for him to push it up than to open it. The fabric, damp from the kiss of his clothes, bunched up around my neck and caught under my ass. Joe bent his head to my breasts, and I arched in anticipation. He didn't disappoint me. He kissed my breasts as he cupped them together. His breath skated hot over skin his clothes had made moist. He licked and sucked my nipples, each one, until I cried out.

I didn't have to move, not to shift, not to ready myself for him in any way. Joe did it all. He left my breasts, his hands already parting my thighs, and not even the steps biting into the back of my neck and back kept me from arching my entire body when he put his face between my legs.

I thought of nothing, but everything. He parted my curls with his thumbs and found the sweetness of my clit with his tongue. It was not as I'd imagined it would be.

It was better.

Pleasure surged inside me when Joe traced my body's curves and lines with his mouth. I felt lips, tongue, a hint of teeth that made me gasp and lift toward him. It wasn't soft or tender, not even graceful, the way he went down on me. It didn't matter.

Thunder rumbled outside, closer. His mouth left ecstasy

like lightning in its path. My body tensed, electric, humming with it.

I looked down. He looked up. He licked his mouth. Swallowed. He got up, and I was sure he meant to leave. It was in his eyes, that knowing he should go.

He stayed. He leaned in with a hand on the stair behind my head. The other went between my legs, his palm pressed to my flesh. He kissed me, and I tasted myself mingled with his flavor.

His eyes had specks of gold around the pupils, which had gone large and dark. Each eyebrow seemed perfectly groomed, each hair like a golden wire. Faint freckles dotted his nose, invisible at a distance but deliciously plain at this close range.

He slanted his mouth to capture mine again and kissed me slowly as his hand moved on me. I drew a breath and held it.

We didn't move. Locked in his gaze with the taste of myself mingled with him on my lips, I let out the breath I held. Slowly, slowly, and slowly, too, I drew in another. My chest rose with it. My body shifted. Joe pressed the heel of his hand on me.

That was all it took. Pleasure came over me. We were looking into each other's eyes when I came, and neither one of us looked away.

The world shifted back into focus around me. The storm outside, the awkward folding of our limbs, the whiskey bottle as it got nudged from its place and fell down the final step to the floor, where at least it didn't break. I'd opened the door less than ten minutes before.

"Sadie." Joe's whisper brushed my face as he put his forehead to mine. "Don't make me leave."

He wasn't as drunk as I'd first thought. Maybe not even drunk at all, despite the half-empty bottle. He slipped a hand between my body and the steps, easing my discomfort. When I stood on the step above him, I could look him in the eyes.

His tie, already askew, came off with barely a tug. The tack at his collar gave me a moment's fight, but was soon undone, as were the rest of his buttons. His jacket made a wet noise as it hit the floor, but we were kissing, so neither of us looked to see where it had fallen.

Stepping back, I led him up the stairs and left a trail of clothes in our path. We didn't bother with the buttons on my nightgown. I pulled it over my head. By the time we got to my bedroom, I was naked and Joe wore only a pair of damp boxer briefs.

I'd never imagined hesitation from him, but he held back when I led him to my bed. I pulled. He stepped closer. Goosebumps pebbled his skin, and his fingers linked in mine were cold.

If I'd had any doubts about what I was doing, they disappeared with his reluctance.

"Joe," I whispered, reaching to stroke his arm, also grown cold. "Come to bed with me. It's all right."

Still, he hesitated.

"Your favorite color is blue," I said. "You hate tomatoes and love cucumbers. You drink whiskey but hardly ever get drunk. You smell like soap and water. I know you, Joe. It's all right. Come to bed with me."

I'd suffered months of guilt for wanting to go to bed with Joe, but at the moment I let go of shame. I needed him. I thought he needed me. Right and wrong, good and bad, the lines are blurred when it comes to matters of the heart. Anyone who has never felt that has no right to judge, and anyone who ever has won't have to.

I took his face in my hands and kissed him, once for the good. Once for the bad. Then I took his hand and pulled him with me to my bed, where I laid him down amidst the softness and warmth of flannel sheets and a down comforter. Under the blankets, I took off his briefs and tossed them out. Then I aligned my body with his until we'd warmed each other enough to stop from shivering.

In the darkness of the cave I'd made, nothing could touch us. I learned the lines of his body, all the places I thought I already knew and all the ones I didn't. My fingers traced his collarbone and slope of his shoulders, broader than they appeared. His chest and the smooth, crisp curling hair around his nipples tickled my face. He groaned when I tasted him. His heart thumped faster under the pucker of his nipple. Lower, lines of tight muscle gave my fingers places to play. The jut of his hipbone gave my mouth a spot to land before I discovered the bulge and curve of thigh and knee. His cock fit the curve of my fingers with perfect precision. I felt faint at the noise he made when I stroked him, head to base. He pushed into my hand when I tested the weight of his testicles in my palm. He was warm, alive, this part of him no longer secret or imagination. It was truth. He was real.

We spoke in murmurs and sighs. His fingers threaded in my hair, but he didn't try to direct my exploration of his body. The shivering stopped, though occasional trembling replaced it.

I took him in my mouth, my tongue eager for his taste. Joe gripped my shoulders, his hips lifting. His cock nudged the back of my throat, and I took him down it for one brief moment before we both moved again. Up and down, slow, soft sucking, and rapid strokes of my tongue. I was a woman starved. For touch, for pleasure, for the taste and touch and scent of a man, but even then, it was not just a man I did my best to please. It was Joe. All along, right or wrong, it was Joe.

At last, gasping, I had to throw off the blankets. Moonlight painted Joe's face, turning his golden countenance to silver. Cool air washed over us, and I drank it interspersed with his kisses.

As though I'd given him permission, he put his hands on me, pulled me on top of him. Connected at mouth, chest, hip, cunt and cock, our feet tangled, hands exploring, I was no longer sure where I ended and he began. Sweat sealed us. Saliva glistened on his throat where I kissed him. He found the soft, tender spot at the curve of my neck and sucked gently, bringing blood to the surface and a moan to my throat.

He rolled us, covering me. I arched and writhed, hungry for him, but though he moved against me with increasing urgency, Joe didn't push inside me. I reached between us to touch him, and he buried his head in my shoulder with a low cry.

I whispered his name. "I want you."

"I want you, Sadie…but…"

He was bare in my fist. Of course. Not even in the stories had Joe ever been incautious. I knew why. I kissed him, pumping his cock in my fingers and he grew even harder.

"Wait." He rasped the word. "Sadie, wait."

I waited. Hearts thumped in time while our breath became a perfect give and take. He moved a little against me.

"Give me a second," he said. "Just…don't move."

"You mean, don't do this?" I closed my fingers, stroking.

Joe jerked, groaning. "Ah, Sadie—"

I pulled him down against me, his cock on my belly. I traced the line of his ear with my tongue. I put my hands on his tight, firm ass and I urged him to move against me.

His hips pumped forward. Sweat slicked our bodies and let his cock slide without sticking on my skin. I pulled him toward me again and hooked my ankles around the backs of his calves.

"I want to be inside you so bad."

"I want that, too."

Sex is rarely elegant. It's bodies slapping, and mess, and the awkwardness of placing hands and limbs where they need to go without pinching, of poking only places meant for poking. It's getting your partner off on your stomach because you haven't got a condom. It's making the best of what you have into something pretty damn good.

He moved against me. Though I ached for him to fill

me, and this was not the way I'd ever imagined it to be, I couldn't stop myself from twitching in reaction when he thrust harder. Faster. When he moaned my name. When his teeth found my shoulder, I cried out. He bit into me. I felt his cock jerk on my belly, felt heat and liquid warmth. I smelled the sweet tangy musk of his come, and I tipped over the edge into my own startled orgasm.

We lay glued together for a few minutes while our breathing slowed. Joe moved off me just a bit, one leg still thrown over mine. His hand cupped my hip.

I tried disbelieving what had just happened, but it didn't work. Not with the scent of fucking all around us and the stickiness of him still coating my skin. His fingers drifted idly up and down my side. I tensed, expecting it to tickle, but Joe's touch soothed, instead.

I turned my head. He looked up at me. When he smiled, I smiled.

"I'm going to use the bathroom," I said after a moment. That was something that didn't happen in stories. Dealing with the aftermath.

He nodded and moved away to let me up. I didn't bother with the lights as I ran the hot water and wet a cloth to wash my skin. I splashed my face, too, and rinsed my mouth, using the extra time to search for the disbelief that still hadn't arrived.

I stopped in the arch between my bedroom and the sitting room. Even in the darkness I could tell the bed was empty. I heard the noise of footsteps on the stairs. Then the sound of the front door opening and closing.

My bed smelled of Joe when I got into it. The blankets

and the pillow were no replacement for arms around me, but I figured I'd manage. I couldn't be surprised, after all.

The front door opened and closed again, and there came the sound of footsteps on the stairs. Joe slid into bed behind me, cold enough to make me yelp as he buried his nose between my shoulder blades. He put his arms around me, pulling me against him. In his hand, against my belly on the place I'd urged him to come, was a small, flat package.

"Always prepared," he said, voice muffled against my skin.

Laughing naked is a curious experience. I started, and he joined a moment later. We rocked the bed with it, and it left us breathless, not unlike the sex of a short time before.

I turned toward him and reached to touch his face. He kissed me. I felt the promise of that foil packet against my back, and the thought of what it meant skipped my heart so fast it almost hurt.

First, we talked.

Memory can refuse to let you forget what you'd like to and run away with what you want to remember. It's an unreliable bitch, or your best friend. Sometimes, it's both at once.

I remember every word we spoke, every sigh and glance we shared. The whisper of his skin on my sheets. The way he smelled. Tasted. I clung to each detail as if it were one of his stories, certain it would become one told to someone else.

Not to me.

Laughter became sighs when he kissed me again, when he slid down my body to worship me with his mouth. Without urgency he licked me, and my body responded. I opened for him, neither of us worrying how long it took. The night was a hundred years long and we spent every second of it discovering how to please each other.

The pressure of his kiss amplified the flutter of my clit when I came again. I cried his name, and he eased off, then crawled up my body to kiss my mouth. I gathered my breath. His cock had grown again, heat on my thigh.

"I want to be inside you, Sadie."

"I want that, too."

This time prepared, he did just that. Joe put himself inside me, where he fit like he'd been made to fill me. It had been so long for me—it was like starting over again.

He made love to me for a long time. I got lost, a little, in the sensation, but he brought me back with a murmured word or a touch. Even though the moonlight had faded and darkness cloaked us, I had no trouble remembering whom I was with. Joe anchored me to him with his murmured words, his touch, the way he turned our bodies every so often to make sure he wasn't hurting me.

We shifted onto our sides, spooning. He pushed inside me from behind, harder and deeper than before. He touched me, too, his fingertip circling on my clit. We rocked that way for a long time, pausing occasionally while he stroked me to the edge of climax and backed off. I floated in pleasure, anchored by his words and hands. By his cock. He fucked harder, his breath getting ragged.

"Oh, God, Sadie. I want to come inside you so bad…."

Lovers' talk is inelegant, but it worked for me. I'd lost track of how many times I'd climaxed by then; after the first two my body had simply hummed with constant, unending pleasure without diminishing. I pushed against him, our bodies arching and shifting so he could plunge inside me deeper still. Faster, we fucked, and harder. The small pain as he hit my cervix only made the pleasure more intense. His hand closed over my cunt from the front, no longer targeting my clit.

I came and didn't stop long enough to count the spasms. Joe thrust faster. The wet sound of my ass slapping his stomach became incredibly erotic as I imagined the slickness of my cunt coating his erection, of how hot and wet I was for him. Of how it must feel to be buried inside me, how my body caressed his cock and held it. My body embraced him, each thrust pulling another groan from me, groans he answered with whispered commentary about how much he loved this.

Fucking me. How good I tasted, how soft I felt, how delicious I smelled. Joe spoke the story of us as he fucked me, and I lost myself not only in the delights of our bodies but in the tale he spun so well.

He moaned my name when he finished, thrusting so hard inside me it thumped the headboard against the wall. Muscles in his stomach leaped against my ass. The hand cupped between my legs moved, his fingers finding my clit again and pinching it gently up and down.

I couldn't even make a sound, so breathless with pleasure had he left me. My final orgasm didn't wash over me in waves. It reared up and slapped me hard enough to make me see stars. It left me shaking and light-headed.

Then his arms were around me, our bodies still linked even though he was softening inside me. His face nuzzled into the softness at the nape of my neck and he held me tight and tighter.

I caught my breath, blinking into darkness. I couldn't move, boneless in the aftermath of such glorious sex. I was aware of the tangled sheets around us and the dampness beneath, but I couldn't make myself move.

I waited for Joe to let go of me, but I fell asleep before he did.

I woke to sunlight and Joe still tangled up with me. His deep breathing said he wasn't yet awake, and I was careful not to disturb him as I extricated myself and hobbled to the bathroom.

Had I run a marathon? My body felt like it. Stepping under the steaming water, I winced as I rinsed myself and discovered a myriad of stings. I was raw and bruised, aching.

I waited for the guilt to hit me when I looked at my reflection while brushing my teeth. I waited for it while I threw on a robe and slippers and pulled my wet hair into a knot on the top of my head. By the time I headed downstairs to make some breakfast, I was ready to tell guilt to go fuck itself, when and if it ever bothered to show.

The smell of pancakes must have drawn him out of bed, because Joe appeared as I was setting the table. He'd showered and wrapped a towel around his waist. In the bright morning sunlight he was every bit as beautiful as I'd known he'd be.

He came up behind me to kiss the back of my neck. His hands slid into the gap of my robe and found my breasts. I let him touch me, my nipples getting tight under his touch, but after a moment he stopped and pulled away.

"This smells good."

"Sit down. Help yourself."

I'd made coffee, too, and poured us both mugs to sip while we ate. He made appreciative noises about the pancakes, but put his fork down after a few bites.

We looked at each other.

"Last night," he said quietly. "Are you sorry about it?"

"No. Are you?"

He shook his head. "No."

I sipped my coffee, watching him. He had spent the night. He had kissed my mouth. But none of that meant anything, in the end. Did it?

"Do you want me to leave?" he asked suddenly, leaning forward.

"Do you want to go?"

After a moment in which he wouldn't look at me, he shook his head.

"Joe," I said gently, and waited until he gave me his gaze before I finished. "I think it might be better if you did."

His mouth tightened.

"I'm not ready for this to be anything more than what it was."

"What was it, Sadie?" He sounded angry, but he looked…sad.

I didn't have an answer for him, at least not one I came up with fast enough to suit. Joe crossed his arms and frowned.

"What should I do?" he asked. "Pretend it didn't happen?"

"Maybe that would be best."

"For who?"

"For both of us."

He got up. The towel slipped lower, revealing a bit of hair I had to turn my eyes from. He scowled, looking fierce.

"For you, maybe."

"Fine." It took effort to keep my voice calm. "Yes. For me. It would be best for me if you left."

He came around the table like he meant to reach for me. I didn't realize until he did how I'd react. I pushed my chair back so abruptly it screeched along the linoleum like someone stepping on a cat. He withdrew. We squared off.

"Why?" he asked finally, gesturing between us.

"Because my husband just died, Joe, and I'm not in a good place to start anything new!"

His scowl deepened, lines bracketing his mouth. "This isn't new."

I took my plate to the garbage to scrape it clean and put it in the dishwasher. I felt him behind me, but he didn't touch me this time.

"I'm sorry, Joe."

"You're not really asking me to go."

I kept my back to him as I went to the sink to wash the mixing bowl and griddle. "This is absurd."

"Why?" From behind me, his tone had gone deep. "Why is it absurd?"

"Because it is!"

"That's not an answer!"

I turned. "I don't have a better one, okay?"

We faced each other across the small expanse of my kitchen. In all the months of imagining, I'd never imagined him here. Joe wasn't a part of this life, this reality. At least, he hadn't been meant to be. Things were different now.

It terrified me.

"You can't possibly think we're ever going to be together." When his only answer was a solemn look, I babbled on. "Because that's just messed up, Joe. That's really messed up. There are so many things wrong with that scenario, I can't even begin to list them."

"Try me."

I shook my head, vehement. "No. No, I don't want—"

"Sadie." Joe put his arms around me from behind again. His chin fit just right into the curve of my shoulder. His breath was warm on my face. "I know you better than you think I do."

I wanted to push him away, but he didn't seem to want to go. I wished he were dressed. It seemed unfair to have this conversation with him when he had only the protection of a towel and I wore a robe, in such an intimate reminder of the night before.

"I'm sorry, Joe. I can't do this with you. Not now."

"Because of your husband?"

I turned in his embrace to meet his eyes. "No. Because of me."

He let me go and stepped back. "Last night," he said finally, with the dignity of man whose back is straight only because it hurt less than slouching. "You said you wanted this. Whatever it is."

"How many stories have you told me?" My voice was hoarse.

"That doesn't matter."

"It does."

He frowned. "It shouldn't."

"I wish it didn't," I said. "But it does. For years I've listened to your stories. Now, here I am, inside one. Right where I wanted to be all along. And I'm not sure what to do."

Joe sighed and put the heel of his hand to one eye, as if his head hurt. Then he took it away to give me his full gaze. "You are not just another story to me."

I drew in a soft, hitching breath. "I wish I could believe that."

"But you can't."

We stared at each other. I wanted to touch him, to let him touch me, but it was suddenly all too much. Without the safety of knowing I couldn't have him, I wasn't sure how to want Joe, anymore.

"I'm sorry."

"I don't want you to be sorry. Shit. Be anything but sorry." His hands opened and closed into fists at his sides. "What if we started over?"

I wasn't sure what to say. He kept talking, filling in the silence so I didn't have to. "What if we started at the beginning?"

I didn't know what to do with my hands, so I gripped the edges of the sink and watched the foam dissipate, giving me a glimpse of dirty water beneath. I took small, shallow breaths that didn't give me enough air.

I didn't turn, though he moved so close behind me I felt the warmth of his body. "I need time," I whispered. "To make sure I know who I am. How can you say you know me when I don't even know myself?"

"I wasn't the only one telling stories, Sadie. For two years I've seen you once a month, every month. I am not the only one who told stories. I just used more words, that's all."

I faced him. He stopped an inch away from touching my face. After a moment, he put his hand on my shoulder, and the weight of it was as familiar as a favorite story heard for the first time after years untold. For a while, two minutes or ten, the only sound in the kitchen was our breathing.

"Why do you think I kept coming back?" he asked. "Why do you think I kept telling you, month after month, everything about me that nobody else seemed to see?"

I looked into his eyes. "I can't be your answer, Joe. I can't be the one who saves you from yourself. I don't have what you're looking for. I'm sorry, but I'm not ready to be your redemption."

He took his hand away, and nodded once, slowly. He took step by careful step away from me until once again there was a universe between us. The lifted burden of his hand upon my shoulder left me not lighter, but heavier under the weight of that distance.

I washed every dish and pan under water so hot it turned my hands to crimson gloves at the ends of my wrists, but I didn't notice the sting. I hadn't had time even to finish when I heard a step in the doorway. I didn't turn.

"From the first time you laughed with me, all those months, and all those stories," Joe said quietly. "They were all you, to me. All of them were you."

I waited too long to turn, because when I did at last, he'd already gone.

Taking my life off hold didn't want to be easy, but I no longer refused to let it happen. I cherished my memories, the good and the bad, and didn't discriminate between them. There were days I loved Adam with every breath I took and days I hated him for leaving me. For being unwilling to try. For making it impossible for me to remember there had been good times. For failing to stay the knight in untarnished armor he'd been to me.

Grief didn't fall away all at once. Like paint chipping, it flaked off to reveal the original surface beneath. I had to strip myself down to that surface before I could think about refinishing. Spring brought flowers and sunshine. I worked in my garden and planted flowers Adam had loved…but I also planted ones I adored and he hadn't liked.

There were days I forgot Adam was gone until I passed the still-closed door to his room. Days when my heart ached for him so fiercely I could do little but miss him. And then, there were days when I went to bed and dreamed of the scent of lavender and the taste of whiskey and rain.

I spent my time reconnecting with friends and family. Building my practice. I took my time in mourning that soon felt less like grief and more like growth.

Long ago, I'd been happy to be what Adam wanted. What he needed. I didn't regret it, even now. I'd loved him with everything I had, but it was time to figure out what was left now that he was gone.

I thought I'd cry when I began to dismantle Adam's room. There were charities that distributed used equipment, and it pleased me to know someone would benefit from the items we'd so carefully chosen to make Adam's life easier. His chair, the bed, the adaptive devices, I packed them all up without even blinking and put them in the truck that came for them. His clothes went into boxes for the thrift store. His books I delivered to friends who'd appreciate them. Piece by piece, day by day, I took apart the room that had been his self-made prison, until all that remained were the bare floors and green-painted walls and the memories of how once we'd made love and laughed there.

Powering up Adam's computer felt like holding his hand again. This was where he'd worked. Where he'd written. I'd joked to him that he'd have married that computer, if he could, and he'd never denied it. I meant to erase this last piece of him without even looking. Peeking into Adam's files felt like a betrayal of the greatest magnitude, worse even than my months of listening to Joe's stories had been. The box of wires and circuits was as much a part of my husband as the color of his eyes or his smile.

I didn't need any of the data on the hard drive. I kept my own computer with all our financial data. Adam's lectures were all saved on disk and the software was easily reloaded from the originals. Since I intended to donate the computer to a local preschool, I wanted to make sure everything else was wiped clean.

In the end, I couldn't erase what was all I had left. I grabbed a handful of blank CD's and began backing up his data. The class lectures and notes I deleted, along with the folders full of e-mail. His correspondence didn't concern me. Nor did I bother transferring the websites he'd bookmarked or the copies of his online orders.

When I came to his personal documents, however, I stopped. I stare at the computer for a full, long minute before I could open the folder he'd titled "Sadie."

He'd always craved feedback, reading me ten or twenty versions of his poems, the only differences between them the placement of a comma or choice of a word. When he no longer talked about his writing, I'd thought he stopped. But in that, as I'd been in so many other places, I was wrong.

Two quick clicks of the mouse took me to a place inside Adam's head he'd refused to allow me for a long time. Here he'd typed, meticulously and with what must have been agonizing slowness, dozens of poems he'd never shared.

He wrote about his anger. Frustration. He wrote about the joy and satisfaction of being able to write, and of his despair when the words wouldn't come. He'd filled document after document with his careful phrases, the small spare haiku and long, rambling free-form poetry he'd once mocked as cheating.

He wrote about how he loved me.

He wrote about how he hated me.

It was the most honesty I'd had from him since his accident, and he'd hidden it from me. Angry, I dragged it all to the trash. I hovered the mouse over the delete button, but at the last minute, I undid what I'd done and returned my husband's words to the file he'd named after me. I burned them to a disk, which I labeled carefully and put away in the box where I stored special things like the clippings of his hair.

Those were Adam's thoughts and dreams. Himself and me, painted in pictures of words. They were his perceptions and images, and whether or not they were true made little matter, now. They were Adam's pictures. Adam's stories.

Not mine.

It was time to stop being what Adam had needed me to be, or what he thought I was. Time to stop trying to be the wife I thought I had to be and become the woman I wanted to be, instead.

Epilogue

August

I'm a psychologist, and I love my work. I like to run and read, I like peppermint-stick ice cream and scary movies, and my favorite color is red. I love the smell of lavender. These are not things I have just discovered, though some of them were hidden from me, for a time.

I've stopped being surprised by my face in the mirror. I know the shape of that face, the color of those eyes, the fall of hair. Now my reflection shows someone I recognize, even if I'm still learning who she is.

Today the wooden bench cradles my back as I lean. The flowers along the path in front of me nod yellow petals in a breeze that stills smells like summer.

There was much I needed to figure out before I could decide if this bench was a place I needed to be. It's taken me a while. I'm still uncertain what this means, but I'm sure of my desire to find out.

I have no place to go and nothing to do but sit and wait,

and the waiting is pleasant enough that I don't mind. Mothers pushing strollers and people walking dogs hurry past. Squirrels chase each other around the trees, while birds peck for bugs in the grass.

Then, he is there, covered in sunshine. He wears it like a suit of gold, shining. He sits beside me carefully, and the bench shivers at the new weight.

There is, perhaps, much to be said, but neither of us says it. Time and circumstance have made us new to each other. I look at him, but he's looking at his hands, linked in his lap.

At last he looks up at me with one eye squinted shut against the brightness. He straightens and turns. He holds out his hand, and I take it, waiting, breathless.

"Hi." His fingers close around mine. "My name's Joe Wilder."

"Hello, Joe," I say, and add with utter confidence. "I'm Sadie."

Our fingers squeeze together. "It's nice to meet you, Sadie."

There are many things I don't know, but quite a few I do. I know you can't be lost if you know where you are. I know that life is full of precious and fragile things, and not all of them are pretty. I know that the sun follows the moon and makes days, one after another. Time passes. The world turns, and we turn with it, and though we can never go back to the beginning, sometimes, we can start again.

"It's nice to meet you, too, Joe."

I'm uncertain of how the story will end, but sitting in the sunlight with Joe's hand in mine, I have no doubts about how it begins. There is only one truth of which I feel confident, one thing I know that nothing else can change.

This month, my name is Sadie.

A One-Year Anniversary has never been this hot...

Celebrate the first anniversary of SPICE by indulging in the sexiest, most scintillating stories destined to ignite your senses!

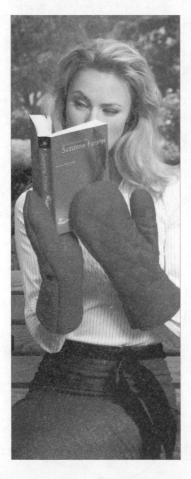

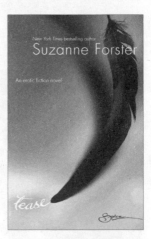

Megan Hart

Megan began writing short fantasy, horror and science fiction before graduating to novel-length romances. She's published in almost every genre of romance fiction, including historical, contemporary, suspense, comedy, futuristic, fantasy and, perhaps most notably, erotica. She also writes nonerotic fantasy and science fiction, as well as continuing to dabble occasionally in horror. Her first three books for Harlequin Books' Spice line will be released in 2007.

Megan's goal is to continue writing spicy, thrilling stories with a twist. Her dream is to have a movie made of every one of her novels, starring herself as the heroine and Keanu Reeves as the hero. Megan lives in the deep, dark woods of Pennsylvania with her husband and two monsters…er…children. Learn more about her by visiting www.meganhart.com.

Spice